The Grandissimes

The Grandissimes

A STORY OF CREOLE LIFE

by George W. Cable

FOREWORD BY SUZANNE JONES

Brown Thrasher Books
THE UNIVERSITY OF GEORGIA PRESS
ATHENS AND LONDON

Foreword by Suzanne Jones
© 1988 by the University of Georgia Press
Athens, Georgia 30602
All rights reserved
The paper in this book meets the guidelines for permanence and du-
rability of the Committee on Production Guidelines for Book Longevity of
the Council on Library Resources.

Printed in the United States of America

92   91   90   89   88   5   4   3   2   1

Library of Congress Cataloging in Publication Data

Cable, George Washington, 1844–1925.
    The Grandissimes : a story of Creole life / by George W. Cable;
foreword by Suzanne Jones.
        p.   cm.
    "Brown thrasher books."
    Bibliography: p.
    ISBN 0-8203-1020-4 (pbk. : alk. paper)
    1. New Orleans (La.)—History—Fiction.   I. Title.
PS1244.G63G68 1988
813'.4—dc 19   88-4876
                                                                         CIP

British Library Cataloging in Publication Data available

The Grandissimes was first published in November 1879 by *Scribner's
Monthly.*

Foreword

Although George Washington Cable had written local color sketches of New Orleans and collected them under the title *Old Creole Days,* he had no plans to begin a novel until the New Orleans *Bulletin* refused to print a second letter from him advocating the integration of the public schools in New Orleans.[1] The *Bulletin* editor had reluctantly printed one letter from Cable but had added an editorial repudiation of equal length. Determined to voice his opinion, Cable turned to fiction: "It was impossible that a novel written by me then should escape being a study in the fierce struggle going on around me, regarded in the light of past history—those beginnings—which had so differentiated Louisiana civilization from the American scheme of public society."[2]

For Cable the conflict of cultures in New Orleans typified the South's historical predicament in the United States. Although a product of American capitalism and democracy, the South depended on slavery and agriculture for its economic life and on a system of racial hierarchy, social conformity, and personal honor

1. Elmo Howell, "George Washington Cable's Creoles: Art and Reform in *The Grandissimes,*" in *Critical Essays on George W. Cable,* ed. Arlin Turner (Boston: G.K. Hall and Co., 1980), 225.
2. Edmund Wilson, "Citizen of the Union," in *Critical Essays on George W. Cable,* 150.

for its cultural identity. Writing *The Grandissimes* for *Scribner's Monthly* in 1879, Cable tried to reconcile this contradictory heritage in his novel's characterization and plot. He introduced the northern democrat, Joseph Frowenfeld, to the Creole values of tradition, family unity, and communal ritual, and the southern aristocrat, Honoré Grandissime, to the American ethos of democracy, equality, practicality, and individualism. Cable used *The Grandissimes* not only to examine the problems of reconstruction but to challenge his readers' own assumptions. To this end, he deliberately confused his audience with masked balls, mistaken identities, and unexplained behavior, trying to break readers—both northern and southern—of customary modes of thinking.

Eager to present the complex social conflicts of reconstruction from the safer perspective of an earlier era, Cable combined the conventions of the novel of manners and the historical romance. Cable found that such a combination of genres best embodied his belief that the past affects the present because of the ongoing influence of tradition.

The shape of *The Grandissimes* bears the influence of Sir Walter Scott, one of Cable's favorite novelists. Cable has fictional characters participate in historical events, such as the Louisiana Purchase, and interact with historical figures who orchestrated the transition from French to American rule. Honoré Grandissime is similar to Scott's "middling hero," a character whose personal conflicts reflect the cultural conflicts of his era. Honoré's problems are those of Creole society: the validity of Grandissime land grants, feuds with other aristocratic families, and the relationship with his mulatto half-brother, Honoré Grandissime f.m.c. (free man of color). Like Scott, Cable used the conflicts of an earlier time to reflect those of his own day. For Cable viewed the struggle in the 1870s between New Orleans natives and northern reconstructionists and between blacks and whites as essentially a continuation of the same struggle that had begun in 1803 after Jefferson purchased Louisiana from Napoleon. Although New Orleans had to some extent made a political and economic transition, it had never made the social and cultural transition from a Creole society based on caste and privilege to an American society based on equality and democracy. In the novel Agricola Fusilier embodies the Creole disapproval of the territorial cession. He believes that Yankee occupation is only temporary, and he defends slavery and extols Creole customs. In not siding with this character, Cable departs from southern romantic novelists of his day, who created nostalgic and tragic myths of futile gallantry and genteel chivalry.

The Grandissimes, however, certainly has all the trappings of southern romance novels—plantation homes and rebellious slaves, murder and miscegenation, voodoo rituals and masked balls, passionate loves and vengeful duels—but these romantic conventions were New Orleans realities, and Cable grounds them in the social problems of his day. Aware that such events might appear exotic and romantic to outsiders, Cable perhaps used them as bait to entice readers whom he hoped to enlighten. His method of narration so resembles Dr. Charlie Keene's storytelling within the novel that Cable surely viewed it as a paradigm of his own relationship with his readers:

> To Frowenfeld—as it would have been to any one, except a Creole or the most thoroughly Creolized American—his [Dr. Keene's] narrative, when it was done, was little more than a thick mist of strange names, places, and events; yet there shone a light of romance upon it that filled it with color and populated it with phantoms. Frowenfeld's interest rose—was allured into this mist-and there was left befogged. As a physician, Doctor Keen thus accomplished his end—the mental diversion of his late patient,—for in the midst of the mist Frowenfeld encountered and grappled a problem of human life in Creole type.

Like Charlie, Cable developed a realistic novel of manners beneath the facade of historical romance.

Cable used the conventions of the novel of manners to explore the reasons reconstruction had not been effective in either era. Cable's other main character, Joseph Frowenfeld, is like the protagonist in a novel of manners, who, because he is an outsider, must learn the power of local myths and manners. In several scenes, Cable uses the contrast in manners between Joseph and the Creoles as a silent means of momentous communication. The quadroons, Palmyra and Honoré f.m.c., both learn from Joseph's manners that he accepts them as equals. However, such unorthodox behavior alarms the Creoles because they take it to be a sign not only of Joseph's respect for black people but of his contempt for white values. Sylvester Grandissime's public announcement of Joseph's politeness to quadroons becomes a call to arms—to protect the values and structure of the community and to defend the honor of the whites, who hold these beliefs. When Cable uses manners to reveal unspoken meanings and beliefs, he implements a principle that he subscribed to but sometimes had difficulty following, that a novel must "teach without telling."[3] It is through such scenes that Cable succeeds in showing why the reconstruction of southern society was so difficult.

Cable combined in his own person the perspectives of his two protagonists. Although Cable was born in New Orleans, his father's ancestors were from Germany, and his mother's, from New England. Cable's loving descriptions of the "delicious" New Orleans climate and the delightful Creole ladies combine with his biting social criticisms of the city's moral weaknesses to mark him in some ways as both insider and outsider to the society. As a reformer Cable was more interested in change than continuity, but he found that he had to study the society's manners—the instruments of continuity—to answer the questions that plagued him: Why was the clash between opposing civilizations so violent? Why was the logical transition from a lower form of social organization to a more civilized one so slow to materialize? Why were the southern attitudes so entrenched? "Slowly and painfully guessing out the riddle of the Southern question"[4] became a challenge to Cable. He found that his study of New Orleans and United States history and his observation of Creole manners for his column in the New Orleans *Picayune* not only provided him with the answers to his questions but shaped his literary career as well.[5]

Like Joseph Frowenfeld, Cable searched for logic and consistency[6] in southern conventions and thus found it difficult to understand why the South sought to perpetuate a social structure that was as Joseph says, "defective, dangerous, erected on views of human relations which the world is abandoning as false." A study of how manners function in society gave Cable a paradoxical answer: while tradition works to unify and solidify a society, it can also work to rigidify it, thereby making change difficult. In *The Grandissimes* Cable explores several reasons why the strength of inherited manners and conventions can inhibit reform: they fix social roles, they rigidify thought, they impede communication between cultures, and they reduce the possibility of independent behavior. When

3. Arlin Turner, *George Washington Cable, A Biography* (Baton Rouge: Louisiana State University Press, 1966), 93.
4. George Washington Cable, *The Negro Question*, ed. Arlin Turner (New York: Doubleday, 1958), 14.
5. Turner, 90.
6. Turner, 74.

people act without thinking, the possibility for intellectual and moral honesty is lessened.[7]

Convention structures a society by assigning roles to its members, thereby establishing their identity, defining their conduct, and determining their fate. Cable's irony emphasizes the absurdities of the Creole society's prescribed roles. For example, although the intelligent slave, Bras-Coupé, could have helped his inept white master, Don José, through some lean years on the plantation, his inferior status prohibits his giving advice. The quadroon Palmyra, who has more mental acumen, more conversational adroitness, and more strength of will than her former mistress, Aurora, must hide her talents behind cunning and manipulation because of her color. Even Aurora, a white woman, is confined in her role. Because ladies do not work in Creole society, this widowed and penniless woman and her daughter Clotilde must struggle with "how to get a living without making it." The love plots further underline the complications of the social roles: Palmyra is in love with Honoré Grandissime, whom she should not love because of her color; Aurora is in love with Honoré, whom she should not love because of her family.

The telling of the Creole myths and the Grandissime legends discourages change as much as the social roles do. As Joseph learns, Creole society keeps "the flimsy false bottoms in its social errors only by incessant reiteration." Cable uses storytelling throughout the novel to emphasize its power in southern society. For example, whenever Charlie Keene introduces new people to Joseph, Charlie tells him their family stories so that Joseph can better understand their behavior. One story repeatedly mentioned by blacks and whites alike is the story of Bras-Coupé's escape, recapture, and maiming, and of the vengeful curse that he placed on his master and his plantation. It is a double-edged story of white supremacy and black power, of white victimization of blacks, and black revenge. By placing the story at the center of the novel, Cable suggests the centrality of its meaning, not only for Creole society but for the South as well. Three men with very different social positions use the story to justify their actions. Loyal to the Grandissimes and a traditional way of life, Raoul tells the story to reaffirm his beliefs in white superiority and the

---

7. See Gary Lindberg's excellent book *Edith Wharton and the Novel of Manners* (Charlottesville: University Press of Virginia, 1975) for theory about the novel of manners as a genre.

necessity of slavery. Unhappy with his status as a mulatto but afraid to fight for equality, Honoré f.m.c. tells the story to justify his passivity. Torn by conflicting loyalties between his immediate family and a more inclusive human family, Honoré Grandissime tells the story to inspire himself to change his society. Because Cable's interest lies more in the story itself than in how it is told, and only tangentially in the assorted motivations his characters have for telling it, Cable tells the entire story only once. But it reverberates throughout the novel as victimized blacks revenge themselves on whites. Cable's use of storytelling foreshadows the more complex use Faulkner and other southern novelists made of this device.

If the ingrained habits of mind that come from cultural myths and social roles make the possibility of reforming a society from within difficult, the differences in habits of mind between people of different cultures make imposing reform from without almost impossible. As an American immigrant, Joseph brings an egalitarian perspective to the New Orleans social hierarchy. Joseph's actions are frequently misunderstood because they convey different meanings than he suspects. An example occurs when Aurora leaves her purse in the drugstore and Palmyra offers to return it. Joseph does not want Palmyra to take the purse because he is afraid she will be robbed while walking home in the dark. Charlie Keene thinks his hesitancy is due to prejudice—that because Palmyra is a quadroon, Joseph cannot trust her. Keene, of course, is projecting his own feelings on Joseph. For a while the Creoles misunderstand Joseph's gestures of equality toward quadroons and blacks because their provincial attitude leads them to assume that he shares their prejudiced beliefs. Even when the Creoles listen to what Joseph says, they do not always hear what he intends because they bring different expectations to the situation. Too often Joseph finds himself saying, "Citizen Fusilier, if you will but listen!" Cable suggests that the Creoles are listening but that to them the words and gestures have different connotations. When they finally understand Joseph's pleas for equality and human rights, they respond with hostility because his ideas threaten their way of life.

In writing *The Grandissimes* Cable was addressing two very different audiences: southerners, like the Grandissimes, who blindly followed tradition, and northerners, like Joseph Frowenfeld, who wanted to change tradition but failed to understand its power. Through the novel Cable hoped to show that the reconstruction of southern society would never occur if the South refused to use its "conscience" to examine its traditions and the North continued using "force" to try to change these traditions: "I wrote as near to truth and justice as I know how upon questions that I saw must be settled by calm debate and cannot be settled by force or silence; questions that will have to be settled by the Southern white man in his own conscience before ever the North and the South can settle it between them. This was part of my politics and as a citizen I wrote."[8] The two protagonists in the novel, Honoré Grandissime and Joseph Frowenfeld, represent the two audiences Cable hoped to influence. The lessons each character learns about the other's culture are the lessons Cable hoped to impart to his two audiences.

Cable expected southern readers to identify with fellow southerner Honoré Grandissime, and in doing so to gain a new perspective on their society. Honoré comes to view New Orleans society more objectively because he studied in France between 1785 and 1795, during the French Revolution. There he replaced his patrician values with democratic ones. Later, back in New Orleans, he transcends his society's established roles and prescribed behavior. Cable hoped that southerners who read *The Grandissimes* would view their myths and manners more objectively. As Honoré explains to Joseph, the southerners' reluctance to integrate their society comes from a myopic point of view: "This people esteem this very same crime of caste the holiest and most precious of their virtues. Me-de'seh, it never occurs to us that in this matter we are interested, and therefore disqualified witnesses. We say we are not understood; that the jury (the civilized world) renders its decision without viewing the body; that we are judged from a distance. We forget that we ourselves are too *close* to see distinctly, and so continue a spectacle to civilization, sitting in a horrible darkness." To give southern readers a critical distance on their own society, Cable tries first to convince readers that traditions are conventions. Then he tries to make them question the logic of the manners that they have accepted as morals.

To prove that manners are social conventions and therefore subject to change as social values change, Cable shows that manners originate in societal need. Cable uses stories of social history to examine manners of different times and places. Cable positions the story of the Indian princess, Lufki-Humma, early in the novel to reinforce the view of traditions as social conventions rather than as

8. Cable, 14.

reflections of universal human nature. Cable points out that if Lufki-Humma had been born into her mother's tribe, which venerated women, rather that into her father's tribe, which venerated men, her social status would have been very different.

After this digression, Cable has Joseph question the Creole emphasis on blood and race. For southerners to begin to question their social code, Cable felt he needed to reveal the inconsistency and irrationality of their system. Cable uses mistaken identities to make his point. The confusion of identities at the masked ball, which opens the novel, focuses on the major absurdity of Creole society: if people concealed their names and covered their skin with masks and costumes, enemies would not only fail to see each other as enemies but would actually befriend each other as Aurora Nancanou and Honoré Grandissime do. Cable goes on to prove that if people in this society were in fact judged by their manners, as the Creoles purport to do, the quadroons would be ladies and gentlemen and the Grandissimes would be barbarians. Cable forces his readers to this conclusion by introducing them to Honoré f.m.c. without first revealing his lineage. Because of his light skin and impeccable manners, readers assume, as Joseph does, that this man is white. Throughout the novel Cable sets scenes this way: objectively giving the facts while withholding the subjective Creole interpretation. Cable hoped that southern readers presented with the facts would see not only the illogicality but the underlying inhumanity in their prejudice.

Southern reviews of *The Grandissimes* suggest that Cable's attempt to change the perspective of his southern readers failed. New Orleans newspapers praised the characterization of the Grandissime family members, the most prejudiced characters, and the characterization of Clotilde and Aurora Nancanou, the most sentimental and romanticized characters.[9] But the same reviewers doubted the authenticity of such characters as Honoré Grandissime with his liberal social views and Honoré f.m.c. with his perfect manners. Also, accustomed to seeing northerners portrayed as villainous carpetbaggers, southern readers were probably ill-prepared to accept Joseph as a hero come to rescue southerners from an antiquated social code. An anonymous southern pamphlet, *Critical Dialogue Between Aboo and Caboo on a New Book; or, A Grandissime Ascen-*

9. See reviews in *Critical Essays on George W. Cable* and an analysis of reviews in Louis D. Rubin, Jr., *George W. Cable* (New York: Pegasus, 1969).

sion, condemned Cable as writing "for the prejudiced and inimical North,"[10] hardly the only audience Cable had in mind.

Only northern readers, such as *Appleton's* reviewer, believed the novel to be realistic, the "picture of an epoch."[11] A reviewer for the *Atlantic Monthly* said that Cable "had a profound sense of the larger laws of history."[12] As an outsider to Creole society, Joseph has the point of view of northern readers who are unaccustomed to southern traditions. The advice Joseph's father gives him as they travel South is Cable's subtle but direct address to northern readers: "If the good people of this country could speak to us now, they might well ask us not to judge them or their land upon one or two hasty glances, or by the experiences of a few short days or weeks." But Joseph's father dies of the fever as soon as they reach New Orleans, and Joseph is left alone with his determination to reform Creole society. Joseph's zeal is grounded in moral ardor: a desire to dissolve a society teetering on fictions of racial inequality and to reconstruct it on facts. In such a society where a way of life is based on fictions, it would seem that reform would be simple—merely explode the fictions and establish the facts. Joseph tries just this tactic but in doing so is verbally and then physically attacked, treatment northern reconstructionists experienced.

An idealist, Joseph is blind to the complex realities around him. He cannot understand how Honoré's close family ties might make him reluctant to criticize their prejudice against blacks and their feuds with other families. Joseph says, "I can hardly believe you would neglect a duty either for family, property, or society." Thinking himself an advocate of truth, Joseph does not realize that when two cultures clash, there are least two "truths" clashing. Cable spells out the problem, "somehow, Frowenfeld's really excellent arguments seemed to give out more heat than light. They were merciless, their principles were not only lofty to dizziness, but precipitous, and their heights unoccupied, and—to the common sight — unattainable. In consequence, they provoked hostility and even resentment." To explain southern hostility and resentment, Cable gives Joseph Frowenfeld, and by extension northern readers, an inside view of Creole society. With Raoul as translator and Honoré as guide, Joseph learns the power of southern myths and manners.

Although Cable agrees with what Joseph says, he does not agree

10. Rubin, 97.
11. Rubin, 99.
12. "Review of *The Grandissimes*," in *Critical Essays on George W. Cable*, 13.

with his self-righteous method—a criticism Cable had of northern reconstructionists. Thus Cable uses Joseph Frowenfeld to voice his beliefs about the inequities in southern society, but he uses Honoré Grandissime to point out Joseph's and the North's naïveté in trying to reconstruct the South simply by passing laws. Advising Joseph to keep to the spirit of his values rather than the letter, Honoré warns, "you cannot afford to be entirely indifferent to the community in which you live." Joseph is so idealistic that he ignores the reality that his business cannot survive without Creole trade. The destruction of his shop painfully illustrates Honoré's lesson. Joseph learns that to succeed in the community he must compromise. Although he does not give up his beliefs, he involves the Creoles in his business and finds that those who work most closely with him eventually respect him and his values. Joseph, "who proposed to make no conscious compromise with any sort of evil," learns that only through compromise can he effect any good.

Because Cable thinks a society will better accept change from within, rather than that imposed from without,[13] he advocates Honoré Grandissime's tactics of compromise rather than Joseph's crusade of truth as a way of reforming southern society. Joseph's influence, though, causes Honoré to break the spell of silence and inactivity that he fell into when he returned from France. Using Honoré as an example, Cable shows that although the catalyst for change may come from an outsider who robs an insider of "his pleasant mental drowsiness," reform is best accomplished by an insider who has the trust of the community and who knows how to use the conventions of the society and the manners of its people. Thus when Honoré sells Grandissime land because of the title dispute, his relatives are upset, but they eventually accept his judgement: "Honoré knew; Honoré was informed; they had all authorized Honoré; and Honoré, though he might have his odd ways and notions, picked up during that unfortunate stay abroad, might safely be trusted to stand by the interests of his people." With the American governor as an accomplice, Honoré brings the Creoles into the new government after the Louisiana purchase. Knowing the extent of their pride, Honoré uses it to his advantage and manipulates them into accepting commissions. Ironically Cable had hoped to play the part of Honoré Grandissime in his home city, believing that the South "would read from a Southern man patiently what it would only re-

13. Rubin, 96.

sent from a Northerner."[14] But because Cable was not of an old Southern family, the southerners viewed him as the Creoles viewed Joseph Frowenfeld, an outsider with dangerous notions about equality and justice for blacks.[15] Eventually Cable left the South and joined his friend and fellow lecturer Mark Twain in Connecticut, determined to cut his children off from the South's "influence." Southern novelist Grace King reported Cable to say that he never felt "at home" until he came to New England.[16]

In *The Grandissimes* George Washington Cable solves the riddle of the southern question, concluding that "you have to overturn something stronger than government. . . . conventionality." However, Cable spends much time showing how manners rigidify a society and little time showing how conventions are changed. Either because Cable was optimistic about change or because his editors required him to be, *The Grandissimes* ends happily. But the novel itself seems evidence of the difficulty of reform. Cable realistically exposes the complex problems of the transition from a caste to a democratic society, only to solve them romantically through marrying members of feuding families, Honoré and Aurora, and conflicting regions, Joseph and Clotilde.

If the resolution of the cultural conflict is romantic, the lack of resolution of the racial conflict is realistic. Although Cable proves the equality of the races, he could not envision a way to integrate them, a problem disclosed by the novel's three endings: marriage for whites, exile for quadroons, and death for rebellious blacks. Although the novel's ending does not entirely break with nineteenth-century romantic conventions, the novel itself breaks with the traditions of the plantation novel that preceded it. Instead of looking with nostalgia on the old South and its way of life, Cable criticized the southern aristocratic tradition and its prejudice against blacks, thereby making *The Grandissimes* the first modern southern novel.

SUZANNE JONES

14. Cable, 14.
15. Daniel Aaron, "George Washington Cable," *Critical Essays on George W. Cable*, 234.

The Grandissimes

1 Masked Batteries

It was in the Théatre St. Philippe (they had laid a temporary floor over the parquette seats) in the city we now call New Orleans, in the month of September, and in the year 1803. Under the twinkle of numberless candles, and in a perfumed air thrilled with the wailing ecstasy of violins, the little Creole capital's proudest and best were offering up the first cool night of the languidly departing summer to the divine Terpsichore. For summer there, bear in mind, is a loitering gossip, that only begins to talk of leaving when September rises to go. It was like hustling her out, it is true, to give a select *bal masqué* at such a very early—such an amusingly early date; but it was fitting that something should be done for the sick and the destitute; and why not this? Everybody knows the Lord loveth a cheerful giver.

And so, to repeat, it was in the Théatre St. Philippe (the oldest, the first one), and, as may have been noticed, in the year in which the First Consul of France gave away Louisiana. Some might call it "sold." Old Agricola Fusilier in the rumbling pomp of his natural voice—for he had an hour ago forgotten that he was in mask and domino—called it "gave away." Not that he believed it had been done; for, look you, how could it be? The pretended treaty contained, for instance, no provision relative to the great family of Brahmin Mandarin Fusilier de Grandissime. It was evidently spurious.

Being bumped against, he moved a step or two aside, and was going on to denounce further the detestable rumor, when a masker—one of four who had just finished the contra-dance and were moving away in the column of promenaders—brought him smartly around with the salutation:

"*Comment to yé, Citoyen Agricola!*"

"H-you young kitten!" said the old man in a growling voice, and with the teased, half laugh of aged vanity as he bent a baffled scrutiny at the back-turned face of an ideal Indian Queen. It was not merely the *tutoiement* that struck him as saucy, but the further familiarity of using the slave dialect. His French was unprovincial.

"H-the cool rascal!" he added laughingly, and only half to himself; "get into the garb of your true sex, sir, h-and I will guess who you are!"

But the Queen, in the same feigned voice as before, retorted:

"*Ah! mo piti fils, to pas connais to zancestres?* Don't you know your ancestors, my little son!"

"H-the g-hods preserve us!" said Agricola, with a pompous laugh muffled under his mask, "the queen of the Tchopitoulas I proudly acknowledge, and my great-grandfather, Epaminondas Fusilier, lieutenant of dragoons under Bienville; but,"—he laid his hand upon his heart, and bowed to the other two figures, whose smaller stature betrayed the gentler sex—"pardon me, ladies, neither Monks nor *Filles à la Cassette* grow on our family tree."

The four maskers at once turned their glance upon the old man in the domino; but if any retort was intended it gave way as the violins burst into an agony of laughter. The floor was immediately filled with waltzers and the four figures disappeared.

"I wonder," murmured Agricola to himself, "if that Dragoon can possibly be Honoré Grandissime."

Wherever those four maskers went there were cries of delight: "Ho, ho, ho! see there! here! there! a group of first colonists! One of Iberville's Dragoons! don't you remember great-great-grandfather Fusilier's portrait—the gilded casque and heron plumes? And that one behind in the fawn-skin leggings and shirt of bird's skins is an Indian Queen. As sure as sure can be, they are intended for Epaminondas and his wife, Lufki-Humma!" All, of course, in Louisiana French.

"But why, then, does he not walk with her?"

"Why, because, Simplicity, both of them are men, while the little Monk on his arm is a lady, as you can see, and so is the masque that has the arm of the Indian Queen; look at their little hands."

In another part of the room the four were greeted with, "Ha, ha, ha! well, that is magnificent! But see that Huguenotte Girl on the Indian Queen's arm! Isn't that fine! Ha, ha! she carries a little trunk. She is a *Fille à la Cassette!*"

Two partners in a cotillion were speaking in an undertone, behind a fan.

"And you think you know who it is?" asked one.

"Know?" replied the other. "Do I know I have a head on my shoulders? If that Dragoon is not our cousin Honoré Grandissime—well——"

"Honoré in mask? he is too sober-sided to do such a thing."

"I tell you it is he! Listen. Yesterday I heard Doctor Charlie Keene begging him to go, and telling him there were two ladies, strangers, newly arrived in the city, who would be there, and whom he wished him to meet. Depend upon it the Dragoon is Honoré, Lufki-Humma is Charlie Keene, and the Monk and the Huguenotte are those two ladies."

But all this is an outside view; let us draw nearer and see what chance may discover to us behind those four masks.

An hour has passed by. The dance goes on; hearts are beating, wit is flashing, eyes encounter eyes with the leveled lances of their beams, merriment and joy and sudden bright surprises thrill the breast, voices are throwing off disguise, and beauty's coy ear is bending with a venturesome docility; here love is baffled, there deceived, yonder takes prisoners and here surrenders. The very air seems to breathe, to sigh, to laugh, while the musicians, with disheveled locks, streaming brows and furious bows, strike, draw, drive, scatter from the anguished violins a never-ending rout of screaming harmonies. But the Monk and the Huguenotte are not on the floor. They are sitting where they have been left by their two companions, in one of the boxes of the theater, looking out upon the unwearied whirl and flash of gauze and light and color.

"Oh, *chérie, chérie!*" murmured the little lady in the Monk's

3

disguise to her quieter companion, and speaking in the soft dialect of old Louisiana, "now you get a good idea of heaven!"

The *Fille à la Cassette* replied with a sudden turn of her masked face and a murmur of surprise and protest against this impiety. A low, merry laugh came out of the Monk's cowl, and the Huguenotte let her form sink a little in her chair with a gentle sigh.

"Ah, for shame, tired!" softly laughed the other; then suddenly, with her eyes fixed across the room, she seized her companion's hand and pressed it tightly. "Do you not see it?" she whispered eagerly, "just by the door—the casque with the heron feathers. Ah, Clotilde, I *cannot* believe he is one of those Grandissimes!"

"Well," replied the Huguenotte, "Doctor Keene says he is not."

Doctor Charlie Keene, speaking from under the disguise of the Indian Queen, had indeed so said; but the Recording Angel, whom we understand to be particular about those things, had immediately made a memorandum of it to the debit of Doctor Keene's account.

"If I had believed that it was he," continued the whisperer, "I would have turned about and left him in the midst of the contra-dance!"

Behind them sat unmasked a well-aged pair, "*bredouille*," as they used to say of the wall-flowers, with that look of blissful repose which marks the married and established Creole. The lady in monk's attire turned about in her chair and leaned back to laugh with these. The passing maskers looked that way, with a certain instinct that there was beauty under those two costumes. As they did so, they saw the *Fille à la Cassette* join in this over-shoulder conversation. A moment later, they saw the old gentleman protector and the *Fille à la Cassette* rising to the dance. And when presently the distant passers took a final backward glance, that same Lieutenant of Dragoons had returned and he and the little Monk were once more upon the floor, waiting for the music.

"But your late companion?" said the voice in the cowl.

"My Indian Queen?" asked the Creole Epaminondas.

"Say, rather, your Medicine-Man," archly replied the Monk.

"In these times," responded the Cavalier, "a medicine-man cannot dance long without professional interruption, even when he dances for a charitable object. He has been called to two relapsed patients." The music struck up; the speaker addressed himself to the dance; but the lady did not respond.

"Do dragoons ever moralize?" she asked.

"They do more," replied her partner; "sometimes, when beauty's enjoyment of the ball is drawing toward its twilight, they catch its pleasant melancholy, and confess; will the good father sit in the confessional?"

The pair turned slowly about and moved toward the box from which they had come, the lady remaining silent; but just as they were entering she half withdrew her arm from his, and, confronting him with a rich sparkle of the eyes within the immobile mask of the monk, said:

"Why should the conscience of one poor little monk carry all the frivolity of this ball? I have a right to dance, if I wish. I give you my word, Monsieur Dragoon, I dance only for the benefit of the sick and the destitute. It is you men—you dragoons and others who will not help them without a compensation in this sort of nonsense. Why should we shrive you when you ought to burn?"

"Then lead us to the altar," said the Dragoon.

"Pardon, sir," she retorted, her words entangled with a musical, open-hearted laugh, "I am not going in that direction." She cast her glance around the ball-room. "As you say, it is the twilight of the ball; I am looking for the evening star,—that is, my little Huguenotte."

"Then you are well mated."

"How?"

"For you are Aurora."

The lady gave a displeased start.

"Sir!"

"Pardon," said the Cavalier, "if by accident I have hit upon your real name——"

She laughed again—a laugh which was as exultantly joyous as it was high-bred.

"Ah, my name? Oh no, indeed!" (More work for the Recording Angel.)

She turned to her protectress.

"Madame, I know you think we should be going home."

The senior lady replied in amiable speech, but with sleepy eyes, and the Monk began to lift and unfold a wrapping. As the Cavalier drew it into his own possession, and, agreeably

5

to his gesture, the Monk and he sat down side by side, he said, in a low tone:

"One more laugh before we part."

"A monk cannot laugh for nothing."

"I will pay for it."

"But with nothing to laugh at?" The thought of laughing at nothing made her laugh a little on the spot.

"We will make something to laugh at," said the cavalier; "we will unmask to each other, and when we find each other first cousins, the laugh will come of itself."

"Ah! we will unmask?—no! I have no cousins. I am certain we are strangers."

"Then we will laugh to think that I paid for the disappointment."

Much more of this child-like badinage followed, and by and by they came around again to the same last statement. Another little laugh escaped from the cowl.

"You will pay? Let us see; how much will you give to the sick and destitute?"

"To see who it is I am laughing with, I will give whatever you ask."

"Two hundred and fifty dollars, cash, into the hands of the managers!"

"A bargain!"

The Monk laughed, and her chaperon opened her eyes and smiled apologetically. The Cavalier laughed, too, and said:

"Good! That was the laugh; now the unmasking."

"And you positively will give the money to the managers not later than to-morrow evening?"

"Not later. It shall be done without fail."

"Well, wait till I put on my wrappings; I must be ready to run."

This delightful nonsense was interrupted by the return of the *Fille à la Cassette* and her aged, but sprightly, escort, from a circuit of the floor. Madame again opened her eyes, and the four prepared to depart. The Dragoon helped the Monk to fortify herself against the outer air. She was ready before the others. There was a pause, a low laugh, a whispered "Now!" She looked upon an unmasked, noble countenance, lifted her own mask a little, and then a little more; and then shut it quickly down again upon a face whose beauty was more than

6

even those fascinating graces had promised which Honoré Grandissime had fitly named the Morning; but it was a face he had never seen before.

"Hush!" she said, "the enemies of religion are watching us; the Huguenotte saw me. Adieu"—and they were gone.

M. Honoré Grandissime turned on his heel and very soon left the ball.

"Now, sir," thought he to himself, "we'll return to our senses."

"Now I'll put my feathers on again," says the plucked bird.

2 The Fate of the Immigrant

It was just a fortnight after the ball, that one Joseph Frowenfeld opened his eyes upon Louisiana. He was an American by birth, rearing and sentiment, yet German enough through his parents, and the only son in a family consisting of father, mother, self, and two sisters, new-blown flowers of womanhood. It was an October dawn, when, long wearied of the ocean, and with bright anticipations of verdure, and fragrance, and tropical gorgeousness, this simple-hearted family awoke to find the bark that had borne them from their far northern home already entering upon the ascent of the Mississippi.

We may easily imagine the grave group, as they came up one by one from below, that morning of first disappointment, and stood (with a whirligig of jubilant mosquitoes spinning about each head) looking out across the waste, and seeing the sky and the marsh meet in the east, the north, and the west, and receiving with patient silence the father's suggestion that the hills would, no doubt, rise into view after a while.

"My children, we may turn this disappointment into a lesson; if the good people of this country could speak to us now, they might well ask us not to judge them or their land upon one or two hasty glances, or by the experiences of a few short days or weeks."

8

But no hills rose. However, by and by, they found solace in the appearance of distant forest, and in the afternoon they entered a land—but such a land! A land hung in mourning, darkened by gigantic cypresses, submerged; a land of reptiles, silence, shadow, decay.

"The captain told father, when we went to engage passage, that New Orleans was on high land," said the younger daughter, with a tremor in the voice, and ignoring the remonstrative touch of her sister.

"On high land?" said the captain, turning from the pilot; "well, so it is—higher than the swamp, but not higher than the river," and he checked a broadening smile.

But the Frowenfelds were not a family to complain. It was characteristic of them to recognize the bright as well as the solemn virtues, and to keep each other reminded of the duty of cheerfulness. A smile, starting from the quiet elder sister, went around the group, directed against the abstracted and somewhat rueful countenance of Joseph, whereat he turned with a better face, and said that what the Creator had pronounced very good they could hardly feel free to condemn. The old father was still more stout of heart.

"These mosquitoes, children, are thought by some to keep the air pure," he said.

"Better keep out of it after sunset," put in the captain.

After that day and night, the prospect grew less repellent. A gradually matured conviction that New Orleans would not be found standing on stilts in the quagmire, enabled the eye to become educated to a better appreciation of the solemn landscape. Nor was the landscape always solemn. There were long openings, now and then, to right and left, of emerald-green savannah, with the dazzling blue of the Gulf far beyond, waving a thousand white handed good-byes as the funereal swamps slowly shut out again the horizon. How sweet the soft breezes off the moist prairies! How weird, how very near, the crimson and green and black and yellow sunsets! How dream-like the land and the great, whispering river! The profound stillness and breadth reminded the old German, so he said, of that early time when the evenings and mornings were the first days of the half-built world. The barking of a dog in Fort Plaquemines seemed to come before its turn in the panorama of creation—before the earth was ready for the dog's master.

9

But he was assured that to live in those swamps was not entirely impossible to man—"if one may call a negro a man." Runaway slaves were not so rare in them as one—a lost hunter, for example—might wish. His informant was a new passenger, taken aboard at the fort. He spoke English.

"Yes, sir! Didn' I had to run from Bras Coupé in de haidge of de swamp be'ine de 'abitation of my cousin Honoré, one time? You can hask 'oo you like!" (A Creole always provides against incredulity.) At this point he digressed a moment: "You know my cousin, Honoré Grandissime, w'at give two hund' fifty dolla' to de 'ospill laz mont'? An' juz because my cousin Honoré give it, somebody helse give de semm. Fo' w'y don't he give his nemm?"

The reason (which this person did not know) was that the second donor was the first one over again, resolved that the little unknown Monk should not know whom she had baffled.

"Who was Bras Coupé?" the good German asked, in French.

The stranger sat upon the capstan, and, in the shadow of the cypress forest, where the vessel lay moored for a change of wind, told in a *patois* difficult, but not impossible, to understand, the story of a man who chose rather to be hunted like a wild beast among those awful labyrinths, than to be yoked and beaten like a tame one. Joseph, drawing near as the story was coming to a close, overheard the following English:

"Friend, if you dislike heated discussion, do not tell that to my son."

The nights were strangely beautiful. The immigrants almost consumed them on deck, the mother and daughters attending in silent delight while the father and son, facing south, rejoiced in learned recognition of stars and constellations hitherto known to them only on globes and charts.

"Yes, my dear son," said the father, in a moment of ecstatic admiration, "wherever man may go, around this globe—however uninviting his lateral surroundings may be, the heavens are ever over his head, and I am glad to find the stars your favorite objects of study."

So passed the time as the vessel, hour by hour, now slowly pushed by the wind against the turbid current, now warping along the fragrant precincts of orange or magnolia groves or fields of sugar-cane, or moored by night in the deep shade of mighty willow-jungles, patiently crept toward the end of their pilgrimage; and in the length of time which would at present be consumed in making the whole journey from their Northern home to their Southern goal, accomplished the distance of ninety-eight miles, and found themselves before the little, hybrid city of "Nouvelle Orleans." There was the cathedral, and standing beside it, like Sancho beside Don Quixote, the squat hall of the Cabildo with the calabozo in the rear. There were the forts, the military bakery, the hospitals, the plaza, the Almonaster stores, and the busy rue Toulouse; and, for the rest of the town, a pleasant confusion of green tree-tops, red and gray roofs, and glimpses of white or yellow wall, spreading back a few hundred yards behind the cathedral, and tapering into a single rank of gardened and belvedered villas, that studded either horn of the river's crescent with a style of home than which there is probably nothing in the world more maternally home-like.

"And now," said the "captain," bidding the immigrants good-by, "keep out of the sun and stay in after dark; you're not 'acclimated,' as they call it, you know, and the city is full of the fever."

Such were the Frowenfelds. Out of such a mold and into such a place came the young Américain, whom even Agricola Fusilier as we shall see, by and by thought worthy to be made an exception of, and honored with his recognition.

The family rented a two-story brick house in the rue Bienville, No. 17, it seems. The third day after, at daybreak, Joseph called his father to his bedside to say that he had had a chill, and was suffering such pains in his head and back that he would like to lie quiet until they passed off. The gentle father replied that it was undoubtedly best to do so and preserved an outward calm. He looked at his son's eyes; their pupils were contracted to tiny beads. He felt his pulse and his brow; there was no room for doubt; it was the dreaded scourge—the fever. We say, sometimes, of hearts that they sink like lead; it does not express the agony.

On the second day while the unsated fever was running through every vein and artery, like soldiery through the streets of a burning city, and far down in the caverns of the body the poison was ransacking every palpitating corner, the poor immigrant fell into a moment's sleep. But what of that? The enemy that moment had mounted to the brain. And then there happened to Joseph an experience rare to the sufferer by this disease, but not entirely unknown,—a delirium of mingled pleasures and distresses. He seemed to awake somewhere between heaven and earth reclining in a gorgeous barge, which was draped in curtains of interwoven silver and silk, cushioned with rich stuffs of every beautiful dye, and perfumed *ad nauseam* with orange-leaf tea. The crew was a single old negress, whose head was wound about with a blue Madras handkerchief, and who stood at the prow, and by a singular rotary motion, rowed the barge with a tea-spoon. He could not get his head out of the hot sun; and the barge went continually round and round with a heavy, throbbing motion, in the regular beat of which certain spirits of the air— one of whom appeared to be a beautiful girl and another a small, red-haired man,—confronted each other with the continual call and response:

"Keep the bedclothes on him and the room shut tight, keep the bedclothes on him and the room shut tight,"—"An' don' give 'im some watta, an' don' give 'im some watta."

During what lapse of time—whether moments or days—this lasted, Joseph could not then know; but at last these things faded away, and there came to him a positive knowledge that he was on a sick-bed, where unless something could be done for him he should be dead in an hour. Then a spoon touched his lips, and a taste of brandy and water went all through him; and when he fell into sweet slumber and awoke, and found the tea-spoon ready at his lips again, he had to lift a little the two hands lying before him on the coverlet to know that they were his— they were so wasted and yellow. He turned his eyes, and through the white gauze of the mosquito-bar saw, for an instant, a strange and beautiful young face; but the lids fell over his eyes, and when he raised them again the blue-turbaned black nurse was tucking the covering about his feet.

"Sister!"

No answer.

"Where is my mother?"

The negress shook her head.

He was too weak to speak again, but asked with his eyes so persistently, and so pleadingly, that by and by she gave him an audible answer. He tried hard to understand it, but could not, it being in these words:

"*Li pa' oulé vini 'ci—li pas capabe.*"

Thrice a day for three days more, came a little man with a

large head surrounded by short, red curls and with small freckles in a fine skin, and sat down by the bed with a word of good cheer and the air of a commander. At length they had something like an extended conversation.

"So you concluded not to die, eh? Yes, I'm the doctor—Doctor Keene. A young lady? What young lady? No, sir, there has been no young lady here. You're mistaken. Vagary of your fever. There has been no one here but this black girl and me. No, my dear fellow, your father and mother can't see you yet; you don't want them to catch the fever, do you? Good-bye. Do as your nurse tells you, and next week you may raise your head and shoulders a little; but if you don't mind her you'll have a back-set, and the devil himself wouldn't engage to cure you."

The patient had been sitting up a little at a time for several days, when at length the doctor came to pay a final call, "as a matter of form:" but, after a few pleasantries, he drew his chair up gravely, and, in a tender tone——need we say it? He had come to tell Joseph that his father, mother, sisters, all, were gone on a second—a longer—voyage, to shores where there could be no disappointments and no fevers, forever.

"And, Frowenfeld," he said, at the end of their long and painful talk, "if there is any blame attached to not letting you go with them, I think I can take part of it; but if you ever want a friend,—one who is courteous to strangers and ill-mannered only to those he likes,—you can call for Charlie Keene. I'll drop in to see you, anyhow, from time to time, till you get stronger. I have taken a heap of trouble to keep you alive, and if you should relapse now and give us the slip, it would be a deal of good physic wasted; so keep in the house."

The polite neighbors who lifted their cocked hats to Joseph as he spent a slow convalescence just within his open door, were not bound to know how or when he might have suffered. There were no "Howards" or "Y. M. C. A.'s" in those days; no "Peabody Reliefs." Even had the neighbors chosen to take cognizance of those bereavements, they were not so unusual as to fix upon him any extraordinary interest as an object of sight; and he was beginning most distressfully to realize that "great solitude" which the philosopher attributes to towns, when matters took a decided turn.

3 "And Who Is My Neighbor?"

We say matters took a turn; or, better, that Frowenfeld's interest in affairs received a new life. This had its beginning in Doctor Keene's making himself specially entertaining in an old-family-history way, with a view to keeping his patient within-doors for a safe period. He had conceived a great liking for Frowenfeld, and often, of an afternoon, would drift in to challenge him to a game of chess—a game, by the way, for which neither of them cared a farthing. The immigrant had learned its moves to gratify his father, and the doctor—the truth is, the doctor had never quite learned them; but he was one of those men who cannot easily consent to acknowledge a mere affection for one, least of all one of their own sex. It may safely be supposed, then, that the board often displayed an arrangement of pieces that would have bewildered Morphy himself.

"By the by, Frowenfeld," he said one evening, after the one preliminary move with which he invariably opened his game, "you haven't made the acquaintance of your pretty neighbors next door."

Frowenfeld knew of no specially pretty neighbors next door on either side—had noticed no ladies.

"Well, I will take you in to see them sometime." The doctor

14

laughed a little, rubbing his face and his thin, red curls with one hand, as he laughed.

The convalescent wondered what there could be to laugh at.

"Who are they?" he inquired.

"Their name is De Grapion—oh, De Grapion, says I! their name is Nancanou. They are, without exception, the finest women—the brightest, the best, and the bravest—that I know in New Orleans." The doctor resumed a cigar which lay against the edge of the chessboard, found it extinguished, and proceeded to relight it. "Best blood of the Province; good as the Grandissimes. Blood is a great thing here, in certain odd ways," he went on. "Very curious sometimes." He stooped to the floor, where his coat had fallen, and took his handkerchief from a breast-pocket. "At a grand mask ball about two months ago, where I had a bewilderingly fine time with those ladies, the proudest old turkey in the theater was an old fellow whose Indian blood shows in his very behavior, and yet—ha, ha! I saw that same old man, at a quadroon ball a few years ago, walk up to the handsomest, best dressed man in the house, a man with a skin whiter than his own,—a perfect gentleman as to looks and manners,—and without a word slap him in the face."

"You laugh?" asked Frowenfeld.

"Laugh? Why shouldn't I? The fellow had no business there. Those balls are not given to quadroon *males,* my friend. He was lucky to get out alive, and that was about all he did.

"They are right!" the doctor persisted, in response to Frowenfeld's puzzled look. "The people here have got to be particular. However, that is not what we were talking about. Quadroon balls are not to be mentioned in connection. Those ladies——" He addressed himself to the resuscitation of his cigar. "Singular people in this country," he resumed; but his cigar would not revive. He was a poor story-teller. To Frowenfeld—as it would have been to any one, except a Creole or the most thoroughly Creoleized Américain—his narrative, when it was done, was little more than a thick mist of strange names, places and events; yet there shone a light of romance upon it that filled it with color and populated it with phantoms. Frowenfeld's interest rose—was allured into this mist—and there was left befogged. As a physician, Doctor Keene thus accomplished his end,—the mental diversion of his late patient,—for in the midst of the mist Frowenfeld encountered and grappled a problem of human life in

Creole type, the possible correlations of whose quantities we shall presently find him revolving in a studious and sympathetic mind, as the poet of to-day ponders the

"Flower in the crannied wall."

The quantities in that problem were the ancestral—the maternal —roots of those two rival and hostile families whose descendants —some brave, others fair—we find unwittingly thrown together at the ball, and with whom we are shortly to have the honor of an unmasked acquaintance.

4 Family Trees

In the year 1673, and in the royal hovel of a Tchoupitoulas village not far removed from that "Buffalo's Grazing-ground," now better known as New Orleans, was born Lufki-Humma, otherwise Red Clay. The mother of Red Clay was a princess by birth as well as by marriage. For the father, with that devotion to his people's interests, presumably common to rulers, had ten moons before ventured northward into the territory of the proud and exclusive Natchez nation, and had so prevailed with—so outsmoked—their "Great Sun," as to find himself, as he finally knocked the ashes from his successful calumet, possessor of a wife whose pedigree included a long line of royal mothers,— fathers being of little account in Natchez heraldry, extending back beyond the Mexican origin of her nation, and disappearing only in the effulgence of her great original, the orb of day himself. As to Red Clay's paternal ancestry, we must content ourselves with the fact that the father was not only the diplomat we have already found him, but a chief of considerable eminence; that is to say, of seven feet stature.

It scarce need be said than when Lufki-Humma was born, the mother arose at once from her couch of skins, herself bore the infant to the neighboring bayou and bathed it—not for singularity, nor for independence, nor for vainglory, but only as one

17

of the heart curdling conventionalities which made up the experience of that most pitiful of holy things, an Indian mother.

Outside the lodge door sat and continued to sit, as she passed out, her master or husband. His interest in the trivialities of the moment may be summed up in this, that he was as fully prepared as some men are in more civilized times and places to hold his queen to strict account for the sex of her offspring. Girls for the Natchez, if they preferred them, but the chief of the Tchoupitoulas wanted a son. She returned from the water, came near, sank upon her knees, laid the infant at his feet, and lo! a daughter.

Then she fell forward heavily upon her face. It may have been muscular exhaustion, it may have been the mere wind of her hasty-tempered matrimonial master's stone hatchet as it whiffed by her skull; an inquest now would be too great an irony; but something blew out her "vile candle."

Among the squaws who came to offer the accustomed funeral howlings, and seize mementoes from the deceased lady's scant leavings, was one who had in her own palmetto hut an empty cradle scarcely cold, and therefore a necessity at her breast, if not a place in her heart, for the unfortunate Lufki-Humma; and thus it was that this little waif came to be tossed, a droll hypothesis of flesh, blood, nerve and brain, into the hands of wild nature with *carte blanche* as to the disposal of it. And now, since this was Agricola's most boasted ancestor—since it appears the darkness of her cheek had no effect to make him less white, or qualify his right to smite the fairest and most distant descendant of an African on the face, and since this proud station and right could not have sprung from the squalid surroundings of her birth, let us for a moment contemplate these crude materials.

As for the flesh, it was indeed only some of that "one flesh" of which we all are made; but the blood—to go into finer distinctions—the blood, as distinguished from the milk of her Alibamon foster-mother, was the blood of the royal caste of the great Toltec mother-race, which before it yielded its Mexican splendors to the conquering Aztec, throned the jeweled and goldladen Inca in the South, and sent the sacred fire of its temples into the North by the hand of the Natchez. For it is a short way of expressing the truth concerning Red Clay's tissues to say she had the blood of her mother and the nerve of her father, the nerve of the true North American Indian, and had it in its finest strength.

As to her infantine bones, they were such as needed not to fail of straightness in the limbs, compactness in the body, smallness in hands and feet, and exceeding symmetry and comeliness throughout. Possibly between the two sides of the occipital profile there may have been an Incæan tendency to inequality; but if by any good fortune her impressible little cranium should escape the cradle-straps, the shapeliness that nature loves would soon appear. And this very fortune befell her. Her father's detestation of an infant that had not consulted his wishes as to sex, prompted a verbal decree which, among other prohibitions, forbade her skull the distortions that ambitious and fashionable Indian mothers delighted to produce upon their offspring.

And as to her brain: what can we say? The casket in which Nature sealed that brain, and in which Nature's great step-sister Death, finally laid it away, has never fallen into the delighted fingers—and the remarkable fineness of its texture will never kindle admiration in the triumphant eyes—of those whose scientific hunger drives them to dig for *crania Americana;* nor yet will all their learned excavatings ever draw forth one of those pale souvenirs of mortality with walls of shapelier contour or more delicate fineness, or an interior of more admirable spaciousness, than the fair council-chamber under whose dome the mind of Lufki-Humma used, about two centuries ago, to sit in frequent conclave with high thoughts.

"I have these facts," it was Agricola Fusilier's habit to say, "by family tradition; but you know, sir, h-tradition is much more authentic than history!"

Listening Crane, the tribal medicine-man, one day stepped softly into the lodge of the giant chief, sat down opposite him on a mat of plaited rushes, accepted a lighted calumet, and, after the silence of a decent hour, broken at length by the warrior's intimation that "the ear of Raging Buffalo listened for the voice of his brother," said, in effect, that if that ear would turn toward the village play-ground, it would catch a murmur like the pleasing sound of bees among the blossoms of the catalpa, albeit the catalpa was now dropping her leaves, for it was the moon of turkeys. No, it was the repressed laughter of squaws, wallowing with their young ones about the village pole, wondering at the Natchez-Tchoupitoulas child, whose eye was the eye of the panther, and whose words were the words of an aged chief in council.

There was more added; we record only enough to indicate the direction of Listening Crane's aim. The eye of Raging Buffalo was opened to see a vision: the daughter of the Natchez sitting in majesty, clothed in many-colored robes of shining feathers crossed and recrossed with girdles of serpent-skins and of wampum, her feet in quilled and painted moccasins, her head under a glory of plumes, the carpet of buffalo-robes about her throne covered with the trophies of conquest, and the atmosphere of her lodge blue with the smoke of ambassadors' calumets; and this extravagant dream the capricious chief at once resolved should eventually become reality. "Let her be taken to the village temple," he said to his prime-minister, "and be fed by warriors on the flesh of wolves."

The Listening Crane was a patient man; he was the "man that waits" of the old French proverb; all things came to him. He had waited for an opportunity to change his brother's mind, and it had come. Again, he waited for him to die; and, like Methuselah and others, he died. He had heard of a race more powerful than the Natchez—a white race; he waited for them; and when the year 1682 saw a humble "black gown" dragging and splashing his way, with La Salle and Tonti, through the swamps of Louisiana, holding forth the crucifix and backed by French carbines and Mohican tomahawks, among the marvels of that wilderness was found this: a child of nine sitting, and— with some unostentatious aid from her medicine-man—ruling; queen of her tribe and high-priestess of their temple. Fortified by the acumen and self-collected ambition of Listening Crane, confirmed in her regal title by the white man's Manitou through the medium of the "black gown," and inheriting her father's fear-compelling frown, she ruled with majesty and wisdom, sometimes a decreer of bloody justice, sometimes an Amazonian counselor of warriors, and at all times—year after year, until she had reached the perfect womanhood of twenty-six—a virgin queen.

On the 11th of March, 1699, two overbold young Frenchmen of M. D'Iberville's little exploring party tossed guns on shoulder, and ventured away from their canoes on the bank of the Mississippi into the wilderness. Two men they were whom an explorer would have been justified in hoarding up, rather than

20

in letting out at such risks; a pair to lean on, noble and strong. They hunted, killed nothing, were overtaken by rain, then by night, hunger, alarm, despair.

And when they had lain down to die, and had only succeeded in falling asleep, the Diana of the Tchoupitoulas ranging the magnolia groves with bow and quiver, came upon them in all the poetry of their hope-forsaken strength and beauty, and fell sick of love. We say not whether with Zephyr Grandissime or Epaminondas Fusilier; that, for the time being, was her secret.

The two captives were made guests. Listening Crane rejoiced in them as representatives of the great gift-making race, and indulged himself in a dream of pipe-smoking, orations, treaties, presents and alliances, finding its climax in the marriage of his virgin queen to the king of France, and unvaryingly tending to the swiftly increasing aggrandizement of Listening Crane. They sat down to bear's meat, sagamite and beans. The queen sat down with them, clothed in her entire wardrobe: vest of swan's skin, with facings of purple and green from the neck of the mallard; petticoat of plaited hair, with embroideries of quills; leggings of fawn-skin; garters of wampum; black and green serpent-skin moccasins, that rested on pelts of tigar-cat and buffalo; armlets of gars' scales, necklaces of bears' claws and alligators' teeth, plaited tresses, plumes of raven and flamingo, wing of the ping curlew, and odors of bay and sassafras. Young men danced before them, blowing upon reeds, hooting, yelling, rattling beans in gourds and touching hands and feet. One day was like another, and the nights were made brilliant with flambeau dances and processions.

Some days later M. D'Iberville's canoe fleet, returning down the river found and took from the shore the two men, whom they had given up for dead, and with them, by her own request, the abdicating queen, who left behind her a crowd of weeping and howling squaws and warriors. Three canoes that put off in their wake, at a word from her, turned back; but one old man leaped into the water, swam after them a little way, and then unexpectedly sank. It was that cautious wader but inexperienced swimmer, the Listening Crane.

When the expedition reached Biloxi, there were two suitors for the hand of Agricola's great ancestress. Neither of them was Zephyr Grandissime. (Ah! the strong heads of those Grandissimes.)

They threw dice for her. Demosthenes De Grapion—he who, tradition says, first hoisted the flag of France over the little fort —seemed to think he ought to have a chance, and being accorded it, cast an astonishingly high number; but Epaminondas cast a number higher by one (which Demosthenes never could quite understand), and got a wife who had loved him from first sight.

Thus, while the pilgrim fathers of the Mississippi Delta with Gallic recklessness were taking wives and moot-wives from the ill specimens of three races, arose, with the church's benediction, the royal house of the Fusiliers in Louisiana. But the true, main Grandissime stock, on which the Fusiliers did early, ever, and yet do, love to marry, has kept itself lily-white ever since France has loved lilies—as to marriage, that is; as to less responsible entanglements, why, of course——

After a little, the disappointed Demosthenes, with due ecclesiastical sanction, also took a most excellent wife, from the first cargo of House of Correction girls. Her biography, too, is as short as Methuselah's, or shorter; she died. Zephyr Grandissime married, still later, a lady of rank, a widow without children, sent from France to Biloxi under a *lettre de cachet*. Demosthenes De Grapion, himself an only son, left but one son, who also left but one. Yet they were prone to early marriages.

So also were the Grandissimes, or, as the name is signed in all the old notarial papers, the Brahmin Mandarin de Grandissimes. That was one thing that kept their many-stranded family line so free from knots and kinks. Once the leisurely Zephyr gave them a start, generation followed generation with a rapidity that kept the competing De Grapions incessantly exasperated, and new-made Grandissime fathers continually throwing themselves into the fond arms and upon the proud necks of congratulatory grandsires. Verily it seemed as though their family tree was a fig-tree; you could not look for blossoms on it, but there, instead, was the fruit full of seed. And with all their speed they were for the most part fine of stature, strong of limb and fair of face. The old nobility of their stock, including particularly the unnamed blood of her of the *lettre de cachet*, showed forth in a gracefulness of carriage, that almost identified a De Grandissime wherever you saw him, and in a transparency of flesh and classic beauty of feature, that made their daughters extra-mar-

22

riageable in a land and day which was bearing a wide reproach for a male celibacy not of the pious sort.

In a flock of Grandissimes might always be seen a Fusilier or two; fierce-eyed, strong-beaked, dark, heavy-taloned birds, who, if they could not sing, were of rich plumage, and could talk and bite, and strike, and keep up a ruffled crest and a self-exalting bad humor. They early learned one favorite cry, with which they greeted all strangers, crying the louder the more the endeavor was made to appease them: "Invaders! Invaders!"

There was a real pathos in the contrast offered to this family line by that other which sprang up as slenderly as a stalk of wild oats from the loins of Demosthenes De Grapion. A lone son following a lone son, and he another—it was sad to contemplate, in that colonial beginning of days, three generations of good, Gallic blood tripping jocundly along in attenuated Indian file. It made it no less pathetic to see that they were brilliant, gallant, much-loved, early epauletted fellows, who did not let twenty-one catch them without wives sealed with the authentic wedding kiss, nor allow twenty-two to find them without an heir. But they had a sad aptness for dying young. It was altogether supposable that they would have spread out broadly in the land; but they were such inveterate duelists, such brave Indian-fighters, such adventurous swamp-rangers, and such lively free-livers, that, however numerously their half-kin may have been scattered about in an unacknowledged way, the avowed name of De Grapion had become less and less frequent in lists where leading citizens subscribed their signatures, and was not to be seen in the list of managers of the late ball.

It is not at all certain that so hot a blood would not have boiled away entirely before the night of the *bal masqué*, but for an event which led to the union of that blood with a stream equally clear and ruddy, but of a milder vintage. This event fell out some fifty-two years after that cast of the dice which made the princess Lufki-Humma the mother of all the Fusiliers and of none of the De Grapions. Clotilde, the Casket-Girl, the little maid who would not marry, was one of an heroic sort, worth— the De Grapions maintained—whole swampfuls of Indian queens. And yet the portrait of this great ancestress, which served as a pattern to one who, at the ball, personated the long-deceased heroine *en masque*, is hopelessly lost in some garret.

Those Creoles have such a shocking way of filing their family relics and records in rat-holes.

One fact alone remains to be stated: that the De Grapions, try to spurn it as they would, never could quite suppress a hard feeling in the face of the record, that from the two young men who, when lost in the horrors of Louisiana's swamps, had been esteemed as good as dead, and particularly from him who married at his leisure,—from Zephyr to Grandissime,—sprang there so many as the sands of the Mississippi innumerable.

5 A Maiden Who Will Not Marry

Midway between the times of Lufki-Humma and those of her proud descendant, Agricola Fusilier, fifty-two years lying on either side, were the days of Pierre Rigaut, the magnificent, the "Grand Marquis," the Governor, De Vaudreuil. He was the Solomon of Louisiana. For splendor, however, not for wisdom. Those were the gala days of license, extravagance and pomp. He made paper money to be as the leaves of the forest for multitude; it was nothing accounted of in the days of the Grand Marquis. For Louis Quinze was king.

Clotilde, orphan of a murdered Huguenot, was one of sixty, the last royal allotment to Louisiana, of imported wives. The king's agents had inveigled her away from France with fair stories: "They will give you a quiet home with some lady of the colony. Have to marry?—not unless it pleases you. The king himself pays your passage and gives you a casket of clothes. Think of that these times, fillette; and passage free, withal, to— the garden of Eden, as you may call it—what more, say you, can a poor girl want? Without doubt, too, like a model colonist, you will accept a good husband and have a great many beautiful children, who will say with pride, 'Me, I am no House-of-Correction-girl stock; my mother'—or 'grandmother,' as the case may be—'was a *fille à la cassette!*' "

The sixty were landed in New Orleans and given into the care of the Ursuline nuns; and, before many days had elapsed, fifty-nine soldiers of the king were well wived and ready to settle upon their riparian land-grants. The residuum in the nuns' hands was one stiff-necked little heretic, named, in part, Clotilde. They bore with her for sixty days, and then complained to the Grand Marquis. But the Grand Marquis, with all his pomp, was gracious and kind-hearted, and loved his ease almost as much as his marchioness loved money. He bade them try her another month. They did so, and then returned with her; she would neither marry nor pray to Mary.

Here is the way they talked in New Orleans in those days. If you care to understand why Louisiana has grown up so out of joint, note the tone of those who governed her in the middle of the last century:

"What, my child," the Grand Marquis said, "you a *fille à la cassette?* France, for shame! Come here by my side. Will you take a little advice from an old soldier? It is one word—submit. Whatever is inevitable, submit to it. If you want to live easy and sleep easy, do as other people do—submit. Consider submission in the present case; how easy, how comfortable, and how little it amounts to! A little hearing of mass, a little telling of beads, a little crossing of one's self—what is that? One need not believe in them. Don't shake your head. Take my example; look at me; all these things go in at this ear and out at this. Do king or clergy trouble me? Not at all. For how does the king in these matters of religion? I shall not even tell you, he is such a bad boy. Do you not know that all the *noblesse,* and all the *savants,* and especially all the archbishops and cardinals,—all, in a word, but such silly little chicks as yourself,—have found out that this religious business is a joke? Actually a joke, every whit; except, to be sure, this heresy phase; that is a joke they cannot take. Now, I wish you well, pretty child; so if you—eh? —truly, my pet, I fear we shall have to call you unreasonable. Stop; they can spare me here a moment; I will take you to the Marquise; she is in the next room. ⁂ Behold," said he, as he entered the presence of his marchioness, "the little maid who will not marry!"

The Marquise was as cold and hard-hearted as the Marquis was loose and kind; but we need not recount the slow tortures of the *fille à la cassette's* second verbal temptation. The colony

26

had to have soldiers, she was given to understand, and the soldiers must have wives. "Why, I am a soldier's wife, myself!" said the gorgeously attired lady, laying her hand upon the governor-general's epaulet. She explained, further, that he was rather soft-hearted, while she was a business woman; also that the royal commissary's rolls did not comprehend such a thing as a spinster, and—incidentally—that living by principle was rather out of fashion in the Province just then.

After she had offered much torment of this sort, a definite notion seemed to take her; she turned her lord by a touch of the elbow, and exchanged two or three business-like whispers with him at a window overlooking the Levee.

"Fillette," she said, returning, "you are going to live on the sea-coast. I am sending an aged lady there to gather the wax of the wild myrtle. This good soldier of mine buys it for our king at twelve livres the pound. Do you not know that women can make money? The place is not safe; but there are no safe places in Louisiana. There are no nuns to trouble you there; only a few Indians and soldiers. You and Madame will live together, quite to yourselves, and can pray as you like."

"And not marry a soldier," said the Grand Marquis.

"No," said the lady, "not if you can gather enough myrtle-berries to afford me a profit and you a living."

It was some thirty leagues or more eastward to the country of the Biloxis, a beautiful land of low, evergreen hills looking out across the pine-covered sand-keys of Mississippi Sound to the Gulf of Mexico. The northern shore of Biloxi Bay was rich in candleberry-myrtle. In Clotilde's day, though Biloxi was no longer the capital of the Mississippi Valley, the fort which D'Iberville had built in 1699, and the first timber of which is said to have been lifted by Zephyr Grandissime at one end and Epaminondas Fusilier at the other, was still there, making brave against the possible advent of corsairs, with a few old culverines and one wooden mortar.

And did the orphan, in despite of Indians and soldiers and wilderness settle down here and make a moderate fortune? Alas, she never gathered a berry! When she—with the aged lady, her appointed companion in exile, the young commandant of the fort, in whose pinnace they had come, and two or three French sailors and Canadians—stepped out upon the white sand of Biloxi beach, she was bound with invisible fetters hand and foot, by that Olympian rogue of a boy, who likes no better prey than a little maiden who thinks she will never marry.

The officer's name was De Grapion—Georges De Grapion. The Marquis gave him a choice grant of land on that part of the Mississippi river "coast" known as the Cannes Brulées.

"Of course you know where Cannes Brulées is, don't you?" asked Doctor Keene of Joseph Frowenfeld.

"Yes," said Joseph, with a twinge of reminiscence that recalled the study of Louisiana on paper with his father and sisters.

There Georges De Grapion settled, with the laudable determination to make a fresh start against the mortifyingly numerous Grandissimes.

"My father's policy was every way bad," he said to his spouse; "it is useless, and probably wrong, this trying to thin them out by duels; we will try another plan. Thank you," he added, as she handed his coat back to him, with the shoulder-straps cut off. In pursuance of the new plan, Madame De Grapion,—the precious little heroine!—before the myrtles offered another crop of berries, bore him a boy not much smaller (saith tradition) than herself.

Only one thing qualified the father's elation. On that very day Numa Grandissime (Brahmin-Mandarin de Grandissime), a mere child, received from Governor De Vaudreuil a cadet-ship.

"Never mind, Messieurs Grandissime, go on with your tricks; we shall see! Ha! we shall see!"

"We shall see what?" asked a remote relative of that family. "Will Monsieur be so good as to explain himself?"

Bang! bang!

Alas, Madame De Grapion!

It may be recorded that no affair of honor in Louisiana ever left a braver little widow. When Joseph and his doctor pretended to play chess together, but little more than a half-century had elapsed since the *fille à la cassette* stood before the Grand Marquis and refused to wed. Yet she had been long gone into the skies, leaving a worthy example behind her in twenty years of beautiful widowhood. Her son, the heir and resident of the plantation at Cannes Brulées, at the age of—they do say—

28

eighteen, had married a blithe and pretty lady of Franco-Spanish extraction, and, after a fair length of life divided between campaigning under the brilliant young Galvez and raising unremunerative indigo crops, had lately lain down to sleep, leaving only two descendants—females—how shall we describe them?—a Monk and a *Fille à la Cassette*. It was very hard to have to go leaving his family name snuffed out and certain Grandissime-ward grievances burning.

"There are so many Grandissimes," said the weary-eyed Frowenfeld, "I cannot distinguish between—I can scarcely count them."

"Well, now," said the doctor, "let me tell you, don't try. They can't do it themselves. Take them in the mass—as you would shrimps."

6 Lost Opportunities

The little doctor tipped his chair back against the wall, drew up his knees, and laughed whimperingly in his freckled hands.

"I had to do some prodigious lying at that ball. I didn't dare let the De Grapion ladies know they were in company with a Grandissime."

"I thought you said their name was Nancanou."

"Well, certainly—De Grapion-Nancanou. You see, that is one of their charms; one is a widow, the other is her daughter, and both as young and beautiful as Hebe. Ask Honoré Grandissime; he has seen the little widow; but then he don't know who she is. He will not ask me, and I will not tell him. Oh yes; it is about eighteen years now since old De Grapion—elegant, high-stepping old fellow—married her, then only sixteen years of age, to young Nancanou, an indigo-planter on the Fausse Rivière—the old bend, you know, behind Pointe Coupée. The young couple went there to live. I have been told they had one of the prettiest places in Louisiana. He was a man of cultivated tastes, educated in Paris, spoke English, was handsome (convivial, of course), and of perfectly pure blood. But there was one thing old De Grapion overlooked; he and his son-in-law were the last of their names. In Louisiana a man needs kinfolk. He ought to have married his daughter into a strong house. They say

30

that Numa Grandissime (Honoré's father) and he had patched up a peace between the two families that included even old Agricola, and that he could have married her to a Grandissime. However, he is supposed to have known what he was about.

"A matter of business called young Nancanou to New Orleans. He had no friends here; he was a Creole, but what part of his life had not been spent on his plantation he had passed in Europe. He could not leave his young girl of a wife alone in that exiled sort of plantation life, so he brought her and the child (a girl) down with him as far as to her father's place, left them there, and came on to the city alone.

"Now, what does the old man do but give him a letter of introduction to old Agricole Fusilier! (His name is Agricola, but we shorten it to Agricole.) It seems that old De Grapion and Agricole had had the indiscretion to scrape up a mutually complimentary correspondence. And to Agricole the young man went.

"They became intimate at once, drank together, danced with the quadroons together, and got into as much mischief in three days as I ever did in a fortnight. So affairs went on until by and by they were gambling together. One night they were at the Piety Club, playing hard, and the planter lost his last quarti. He became desperate, and did a thing I have known more than one planter to do: wrote his pledge for every arpent of his land and every slave on it, and staked that. Agricole refused to play. 'You shall play,' said Nancanou, and when the game was ended he said: 'Monsieur Agricola Fusilier, you cheated.' You see? Just as I have frequently been tempted to remark to my friend, Mr. Frowenfeld.

"But, Frowenfeld, you must know, withal the Creoles are such gamblers, they never cheat; they play absolutely fair. So Agricole had to challenge the planter. He could not be blamed for that; there was no choice—oh, now, Frowenfeld, keep quiet! I tell you there was no choice. And the fellow was no coward. He sent Agricole a clear title to the real estate and slaves,—lacking only the wife's signature,—accepted the challenge and fell dead at the first fire.

"Stop, now, and let me finish. Agricole sat down and wrote to the widow that he did not wish to deprive her of her home, and that if she would state in writing her belief that the stakes had been won fairly, he would give back the whole estate, slaves and all; but that if she would not, he should feel compelled to retain it in vindication of his honor. Now wasn't that drawing a fine point?" The doctor laughed according to his habit, with his face down in his hands. "You see, he wanted to stand before all creation—the Creator did not make so much difference—in the most exquisitely proper light; so he puts the laws of humanity under his feet, and anoints himself from head to foot with Creole punctilio."

"Did she sign the paper?" asked Joseph.

"She? Wait till you know her! No, indeed; she had the true scorn. She and her father sent down another and a better title. Creole-like, they managed to bestir themselves to that extent and there they stopped.

"And the airs with which they did it! They kept all their rage to themselves, and sent the polite word, that they were not acquainted with the merits of the case, that they were not disposed to make the long and arduous trip to the city and back, and that if M. Fusilier de Grandissime thought he could find any pleasure or profit in owning the place, he was welcome; that the widow of *his late friend* was not disposed to live on it, but would remain with her father at the paternal home at Cannes Brulées.

"Did you ever hear of a more perfect specimen of Creole pride? That is the way with all of them. Show me any Creole, or any number of Creoles, in any sort of contest, and right down at the foundation of it all, I will find you this same preposterous, apathetic, fantastic, suicidal pride. It is as lethargic and ferocious as an alligator. That is why the Creole almost always is (or thinks he is) on the defensive. See these De Grapions' haughty good manners to old Agricole; yet there wasn't a Grandissime in Louisiana who could have set foot on the De Grapion lands but at the risk of his life.

"But I will finish the story; and here is the really sad part. Not many months ago, old De Grapion—'old,' said I; they don't grow old; I call him old—a few months ago he died. He must have left everything smothered in debt; for, like his race, he had stuck to indigo because his father planted it, and it is a crop that has lost money steadily for years and years. His daughter and grand-daughter were left like babes in the wood; and, to crown their disasters, have now made the grave mistake of coming to the city, where they find they haven't a friend—not one, sir! They called me in to prescribe for a trivial indisposition, shortly after

32

their arrival; and I tell you, Frowenfeld, it made me shiver to see two such beautiful women in such a town as this without a male protector, and even"—the doctor lowered his voice—"without adequate support. The mother says they are perfectly comfortable; tells the old couple so who took them to the ball, and whose little girl is their embroidery scholar; but you cannot believe a Creole on that subject, and I don't believe her. Would you like to make their acquaintance?"

Frowenfeld hesitated, disliking to say no to his friend, and then shook his head.

"After a while—at least not now, sir, if you please."

The doctor made a gesture of disappointment.

"Um-hum," he said grumly—"the only man in New Orleans I would honor with an invitation!—but all right; I'll go alone."

He laughed a little at himself, and left Frowenfeld, if ever he should desire it, to make the acquaintance of his pretty neighbors as best he could.

7 Was It Honoré Grandissime?

A Creole gentleman, on horseback one morning with some practical object in view,—drainage, possibly,—had got what he sought,—the evidence of his own eyes on certain points,—and now moved quietly across some old fields toward the town, where more absorbing interests awaited him in the Rue Toulouse; for this Creole gentleman was a merchant, and because he would presently find himself among the appointments and restraints of the counting-room, he heartily gave himself up, for the moment, to the surrounding influences of nature.

It was late in November; but the air was mild and the grass and foliage green and dewy. Wild flowers bloomed plentifully and in all directions; the bushes were hung, and often covered, with vines of sprightly green, sprinkled thickly with smart-looking little worthless berries, whose sparkling complacency the combined contempt of man, beast and bird could not dim. The call of the field-lark came continually out of the grass, where now and then could be seen his yellow breast; the orchard oriole was executing his fantasias in every tree; a covey of partridges ran across the path close under the horse's feet, and stopped to look back almost within reach of the riding-whip; clouds of starlings, in their odd, irresolute way, rose from the high bulrushes and settled again, without discernible cause;

little wandering companies of sparrows undulated from hedge to hedge; a great rabbit-hawk sat alone in the top of a lofty pecan-tree; that petted rowdy, the mocking-bird, dropped down into the path to offer fight to the horse, and, failing in that, flew up again and drove a crow into ignominious retirement beyond the plain; from a place of flags and reeds a white crane shot up-ward, turned, and then, with the slow and stately beat peculiar to her wing, sped away until, against the tallest cypress of the distant forest, she became a tiny white speck on its black, and suddenly disappeared, like one flake of snow.

The scene was altogether such as to fill any hearty soul with impulses of genial friendliness and gentle candor; such a scene as will sometimes prepare a man of the world, upon the least direct incentive, to throw open the windows of his private thought with a freedom which the atmosphere of no counting-room or drawing-room tends to induce.

The young merchant—he was young—felt this. Moreover, the matter of business which had brought him out had responded to his inquiring eye with a somewhat golden radiance; and your true man of business—he who has reached that elevated pitch of serene, good-natured reserve which is of the high art of his calling—is never so generous with his pennyworths of thought as when newly in possession of some little secret worth many pounds.

By and by the behavior of the horse indicated the near presence of a stranger; and the next moment the rider drew rein under an immense live-oak where there was a bit of paling about some graves, and raised his hat.

"Good-morning, sir." But for the silent r's, his pronunciation was exact, yet evidently an acquired one. While he spoke his salutation in English, he was thinking French: "Without doubt, this rather oversized, bare headed, interrupted-looking conva-lescent who stands before me, wondering how I should know in what language to address him, is Joseph Frowenfeld, of whom Doctor Keene has had so much to say to me. A good face —unsophisticated, but intelligent, mettlesome and honest. He will make his mark; it will probably be a white one; I will sub-scribe to the adventure."

"You will excuse me, sir?" he asked after a pause, dismount-ing, and noticing, as he did so, that Frowenfeld's knees showed recent contact with the turf; "I have, myself, some interest in two of these graves, sir, as I suppose—you will pardon my freedom—you have in the other four."

He approached the old but newly whitened paling, which encircled the tree's trunk as well as the six graves about it. There was in his face and manner a sort of impersonal human kindness, well calculated to engage a diffident and sensitive stranger, standing in dread of gratuitous benevolence or pity.

"Yes, sir," said the convalescent, and ceased; but the other leaned against the palings in an attitude of attention, and he felt induced to add: "I have buried here my father, mother and two sisters,"—he had expected to continue in an unemotional tone; but a deep respiration usurped the place of speech. He stooped quickly to pick up his hat, and, as he rose again and looked into his listener's face, the respectful, unobtrusive sympathy there expressed went directly to his heart.

"Victims of the fever," said the Creole with great gravity. "How did that happen?"

As Frowenfeld, after a moment's hesitation, began to speak, the stranger let go the bridle of his horse and sat down upon the turf. Joseph appreciated the courtesy and sat down, too; and thus the ice was broken.

The immigrant told his story; he was young—often younger than his years—and his listener several years his senior; but the Creole, true to his blood, was able at any time to make himself as young as need be, and possessed the rare magic of drawing one's confidence without seeming to do more than merely pay attention. It followed that the story was told in full detail, including grateful acknowledgment of the goodness of an unknown friend, who had granted this burial-place on condition that he should not be sought out for the purpose of thanking him.

So a considerable time passed by, in which acquaintance grew with delightful rapidity.

"What will you do now?" asked the stranger, when a short silence had followed the conclusion of the story.

"I hardly know. I am taken somewhat by surprise. I have not chosen a definite course in life—as yet. I have been a general student, but have not prepared myself for any profession; I am not sure what I shall be."

A certain energy in the immigrant's face half redeemed this

36

child-like speech. Yet the Creole's lips, as he opened them to reply, betrayed amusement; so he hastened to say:

"I appreciate your position, Mr. Frowenfeld,—excuse me, I believe you said that was your father's name. And yet,"—the shadow of an amused smile lurked another instant about a corner of his mouth,—"if you would understand me kindly I would say, take care——"

What little blood the convalescent had rushed violently to his face, and the Creole added:

"I do not insinuate you would willingly be idle. I think I know what you want. You want to make up your mind *now* what you will *do,* and at your leisure what you will *be;* eh? To be, it seems to me," he said in summing up,—"that to be is not so necessary as to do, eh? or am I wrong?"

"No, sir," replied Joseph, still red, "I was feeling that just now. I will do the first thing that offers; I can dig."

The Creole shrugged and pouted.

"And be called a *dos brilée*—a 'burnt-back.' "

"But"——began the immigrant, with overmuch warmth.

The other interrupted him, shaking his head slowly, and smiling as he spoke.

"Mr. Frowenfeld, it is of no use to talk; you may hold in contempt the Creole scorn of toil—just as I do, myself, but in theory, my-de'-seh, not too much in practice. You cannot afford to be *entirely* different to the community in which you live; is that not so?"

"A friend of mine," said Frowenfeld, "has told me I must 'compromise.' "

"You must get acclimated," responded the Creole; "not in body only, that you have done; but in mind—in taste—in conversation—and in convictions too, yes, ha, ha! They all do it—all who come. They hold out a little while—a very little; then they open their stores on Sunday, they import cargoes of Africans, they bribe the officials, they smuggle goods, they have colored housekeepers. My-de'-seh, the water must expect to take the shape of the bucket; eh?"

"One need not be water!" said the immigrant.

"Ah!" said the Creole, with another amiable shrug, and a wave of his hand; "certainly you do not suppose that is my advice—that those things have my approval."

Must we repeat already that Frowenfeld was abnormally young?

"Why have they not your condemnation?" cried he with an earnestness that made the Creole's horse drop the grass from his teeth and wheel half around.

The answer came slowly and gently.

"Mr. Frowenfeld, my habit is to buy cheap and sell at a profit. My condemnation? My-de'-seh, there is no sa-a-ale for it! it spoils the sale of other goods, my-de'-seh. It is not to condemn that you want; you want to suc-*ceed*. Ha, ha, ha! you see I am a merchant, eh? My-de'-seh, can *you* afford not to succeed?"

The speaker had grown very much in earnest in the course of these few words, and as he asked the closing question, arose, arranged his horse's bridle and with his elbow in the saddle, leaned his handsome head on his equally beautiful hand. His whole appearance was a dazzling contradiction of the notion that a Creole is a person of mixed blood.

"I think I can!" replied the convalescent, with much spirit, rising with more haste than was good, and staggering a moment.

The horseman laughed outright.

"Your principle is the best, I cannot dispute that; but whether you can act it out—reformers do not make money, you know." He examined his saddle-girth and began to tighten it. "One can condemn—too cautiously—by a kind of—elevated cowardice (I have that fault); but one can only condemn too rashly; I remember when I did so. One of the occupants of those two graves you see yonder side by side—I think might have lived longer if I had not spoken so rashly for his rights. Did you ever hear of Bras-Coupé, Mr. Frowenfeld?"

"I have heard only the name."

"Ah! Mr. Frowenfeld, *there* was a bold man's chance to denounce wrong and oppression! Why, that negro's death changed the whole channel of my convictions."

The speaker had turned and thrown up his arm with frowning earnestness; he dropped it and smiled at himself.

"Do not mistake me for one of your new-fashioned Philadelphia '*negrophiles*'; I am a merchant, my-de'-seh, a good subject of His Catholic Majesty, a Creole of the Creoles, and so forth, and so forth. Come!"

He slapped the saddle.

To have seen and heard them a little later as they moved toward the city, the Creole walking before the horse, and Frowenfeld sitting in the saddle, you might have supposed them old acquaintances. Yet the immigrant was wondering who his companion might be. He had not introduced himself—seemed to think that even an immigrant might know his name without asking. Was it Honoré Grandissime? Joseph was tempted to guess so; but the initials inscribed on the silver-mounted pommel of the fine old Spanish saddle did not bear out that conjecture.

The stranger talked freely. The sun's rays seemed to set all the sweetness in him a-working, and his pleasant worldly wisdom foamed up and out like fermenting honey.

By and by the way led through a broad, grassy lane where the path turned alternately to right and left among some wild acacias. The Creole waved his hand toward one of them and said:

"Now, Mr. Frowenfeld, you see? one man walks where he sees another's track; that is what makes a path; but you want a man, instead of passing around this prickly bush, to lay hold of it with his naked hands and pull it up by the roots."

"But a man armed with the truth is far from being barehanded," replied the convalescent, and they went on, more and more interested at every step,—one in this very raw imported material for an excellent man, the other in so striking an exponent of a unique land and people.

They came at length to the crossing of two streets, and the Creole, pausing in his speech, laid his hand upon the bridle.

Frowenfeld dismounted.

"Do we part here?" asked the Creole. "Well, Mr. Frowenfeld, I hope to meet you soon again."

"Indeed, I thank you, sir," said Joseph, "and I hope we shall, although——"

The Creole paused with a foot in the stirrup and interrupted him with a playful gesture; then as the horse stirred, he mounted and drew in the rein.

"I know; you want to say you cannot accept my philosophy and I cannot appreciate yours; but I appreciate it more than you think, my-de'-seh."

The convalescent's smile showed much fatigue.

The Creole extended his hand; the immigrant seized it,

wished to ask his name, but did not; and the next moment he was gone.

The convalescent walked meditatively toward his quarters, with a faint feeling of having been found asleep on duty, and awakened by a passing stranger. It was an unpleasant feeling, and he caught himself more than once shaking his head. He stopped, at length, and looked back; but the Creole was long since out of sight. The mortified self-accuser little knew how very similar a feeling that vanished person was carrying away with him. He turned and resumed his walk, wondering who Monsieur might be, and a little impatient with himself that he had not asked.

"It is Honoré Grandissime; it must be he!" he said.

Yet see how soon he felt obliged to change his mind.

8 Signed—Honoré Grandissime

On the afternoon of the same day, having decided what he would "do." he started out in search of new quarters. He found nothing then, but next morning came upon a small, single-story building in the rue Royale,—corner of Conti,—which he thought would suit his plans. There were a door and show-window in the rue Royale, two doors in the intersecting street, and a small apartment in the rear which would answer for sleeping, eating, and studying purposes, and which connected with the front apartment by a door in the left-hand corner. This connection he would partially conceal by a prescription-desk. A counter would run lengthwise toward the rue Royale, along the wall opposite the side-doors. Such was the spot that soon became known as "Frowenfeld's Corner."

The notice "À Louer" directed him to inquire at numero —, rue Condé. Here he was ushered through the wicket of a *porte cochère* into a broad, paved corridor, and up a stair into a large, cool room, and into the presence of a man who seemed, in some respects, the most remarkable figure he had yet seen in this little city of strange people. A strong, clear, olive complexion; features that were faultless (unless a woman-like delicacy, that was yet not effeminate, was a fault); hair *en queue*, the hand-somer for its premature streakings of gray; a tall, well knit form, attired in cloth, linen and leather of the utmost fineness; manners Castilian, with a gravity almost oriental,—made him one of those rare masculine figures which, on the public promenade, men look back at and ladies inquire about.

Now, who might *this* be? The rent poster had given no name. Even the incurious Frowenfeld would fain guess a little. For a man to be just of this sort, it seemed plain that he must live in an isolated ease upon the unceasing droppings of coupons, rents, and like receivables. Such was the immigrant's first conjecture; and, as with slow, scant questions and answers they made their bargain, every new glance strengthened it; he was evidently a *rentier*. What, then, was his astonishment when Monsieur bent down and made himself Frowenfeld's landlord, by writing what the universal mind esteemed the synonym of enterprise and activity—the name of Honoré Grandissime. The landlord did not see, or ignored, his tenant's glance of surprise, and the tenant asked no questions.

We may add here an incident which seemed, when it took place, as unimportant as a single fact well could be.

The little sum that Frowenfeld had inherited from his father had been sadly depleted by the expenses of four funerals; yet he was still able to pay a month's rent in advance, to supply his shop with a scant stock of drugs, to purchase a celestial globe and some scientific apparatus, and to buy a dinner or two of sausages and crackers; but after this there was no necessity of hiding his purse.

His landlord early contracted a fondness for dropping in upon him, and conversing with him, as best the few and labored English phrases at his command would allow. Frowenfeld soon noticed that he never entered the shop unless its proprietor was alone, never sat down, and always, with the same perfection of dignity that characterized all his movements, departed immediately upon the arrival of any third person. One day, when the landlord was making one of these standing calls,—he always stood beside a high glass case, on the side of the shop opposite the counter,—he noticed in Joseph's hand a sprig of basil, and spoke of it.

"You ligue?"

The tenant did not understand.

"You—find—dad—nize?"

Frowenfeld replied that it had been left by the oversight of a customer, and expressed a liking for its odor.

"I sand you," said the landlord,—a speech whose meaning Frowenfeld was not sure of until the next morning, when a small, nearly naked, black boy, who could not speak a word of English, brought to the apothecary a luxuriant bunch of this basil, growing in a rough box.

9 Illustrating the Tractive Power of Basil

On the twenty-fourth day of December, 1803, at two o'clock, P.M., the thermometer standing at 79, hygrometer 17, barometer 29.880, sky partly clouded, wind west, light, the apothecary of the rue Royale, now something more than a month established in his calling, might have been seen standing behind his counter and beginning to show embarrassment in the presence of a lady, who, since he had got her prescription filled and had paid for it, ought in the conventional course of things to have hurried out, followed by the pathetically ugly black woman who tarried at the door as her attendant; for to be in an apothecary shop at all was unconventional. She was heavily veiled; but the sparkle of her eyes, which no multiplication of veils could quite extinguish, her symmetrical and well-fitted figure, just escaping smallness, her grace of movement, and a soft, joyous voice, had several days before led Frowenfeld to the confident conclusion that she was young and beautiful.

For this was now the third time she had come to buy; and, though the purchases were unaccountably trivial, the purchaser seemed not so. On the two previous occasions she had been accompanied by a slender girl, somewhat taller than she, veiled also, of graver movement, a bearing that seemed to Joseph almost too regal, and a discernible unwillingness to enter or tarry.

44

There seemed a certain family resemblance between her voice and that of the other, that proclaimed them—he incautiously assumed—sisters. This time, as we see, the smaller, and probably elder, came alone.

She still held in her hand the small silver which Frowenfeld had given her in change, and sighed after the laugh they had just enjoyed together over a slip in her English. A very grateful sip of sweet the laugh was to the all but friendless apothecary, and the embarrassment that rushed in after it may have arisen in part from a conscious casting about in his mind for something—anything—that might prolong her stay an instant. He opened his lips to speak; but she was quicker than he, and said, in a stealthy way that seemed oddly unnecessary:

"You 'ave some basilic?"

She accompanied her words with a little peeping movement, directing his attention, through the open door, to his box of basil, on the floor in the rear room.

Frowenfeld stepped back to it, cut half the bunch, and returned, with the bold intention of making her a present of it; but as he hastened back to the spot he had left, he was astonished to see the lady disappearing from his farthest front door, followed by her negress.

"Did she change her mind, or did she misunderstand me?" he asked himself; and, in the hope that she might return for the basil, he put it in water in his back room.

The day being, as the figures have already shown, an unusually mild one, even for a Louisiana December, and the finger of the clock drawing by and by toward the last hour of sunlight, some half dozen of Frowenfeld's townsmen had gathered, inside and out, some standing, some sitting, about his front door, and all discussing the popular topics of the day. For it might have been anticipated that, in a city where so very little English was spoken and no newspaper published except that beneficiary of eighty subscribers, the "Moniteur de la Louisiane," the apothecary shop in the rue Royale would be the rendezvous for a select company of English-speaking gentlemen, with a smart majority of physicians.

The Cession had become an accomplished fact. With due drum-beatings and act-reading, flag-raising, cannonading and galloping of aides-de-camp, Nouvelle Orleans had become New Orleans, and Louisiane was Louisiana. This afternoon, the first week of American jurisdiction was only something over half gone, and the main topic of public debate was still the Cession. Was it genuine? and, if so, would it stand?

"Mark my words," said one, "the British flag will be floating over this town within ninety days!" and he went on whittling the back of his chair.

From this main question, the conversation branched out to the subject of land titles. Would that great majority of Spanish titles derived from the concessions of post-commandants and others of minor authority, hold good?

"I suppose you know what —— thinks about it?"

"No."

"Well, he has quietly purchased the grant made by Carondelet to the Marquis of ——, thirty thousand acres, and now says the grant is two hundred *and* thirty thousand. That is one style of men Governor Claiborne is going to have on his hands. The town will presently be as full of them as my pocket is of tobacco crumbs,—every one of them with a Spanish grant as long as Clark's rope-walk, and made up since the rumor of the Cession."

"I hear that some of Honoré Grandissime's titles are likely to turn out bad,—some of the old Brahmin properties and some of the Mandarin lands."

"Fudge!" said Doctor Keene.

There was also the subject of rotation in office. Would this provisional governor-general himself be able to stand fast? Had not a man better temporize a while, and see what Ex-Governor-general Casa Calvo and Trudeau were going to do? Would not men who sacrificed old prejudices, braved the popular contumely, and came forward and gave in their allegiance to the President's appointee, have to take the chances of losing their official positions at last? Men like Camille Brahmin, for instance, or Charlie Mandarin: suppose Spain or France should get the province back, then where would they be?

"One of the things I pity most in this vain world," drawled Doctor Keene, "is a hive of patriots who don't know where to swarm."

The apothecary was drawn into the discussion—at least he thought he was. Inexperience is apt to think that Truth will be knocked down and murdered unless she comes to the rescue. Somehow, Frowenfeld's really excellent arguments seemed to give out more heat than light. They were merciless; their principles were not only lofty to dizziness, but precipitous, and their heights unoccupied, and—to the common sight—unattainable. In consequence, they provoked hostility and even resentment. With the kindest, the most honest, and even the most modest, intentions, he found himself—to his bewilderment and surprise —sniffed at by the ungenerous, frowned upon by the impatient, and smiled down by the good-natured in a manner that brought sudden blushes of exasperation to his face, and often made him ashamed to find himself going over these sham battles again in much savageness of spirit, when alone with his books; or, in moments of weakness, casting about for such unworthy weapons as irony and satire. In the present debate, he had just provoked a sneer that made his blood leap and his friends laugh, when Doctor Keene, suddenly rising and beckoning across the street, exclaimed:

"Oh! Agricole! Agricole! *venez ici;* we want you."

A murmur of vexed protest arose from two or three.

"He's coming," said the whittler, who had also beckoned.

"Good evening, Citizen Fusilier," said Doctor Keene. "Citizen Fusilier, allow me to present my friend, Professor Frowenfeld— yes, you are a professor—yes, you are. He is one of your sort, Citizen Fusilier, a man of thorough scientific education. I believe on my soul, sir, he knows nearly as much as you do!"

The person who confronted the apothecary was a large, heavily built, but well molded and vigorous man, of whom one might say that he was adorned with old age. His brow was dark, and furrowed partly by time and partly by a persistent ostentatious frown. His eyes were large, black, and bold, and the gray locks above them curled short and harsh like the front of a bull. His nose was fine and strong, and if there was any deficiency in mouth or chin, it was hidden by a beard that swept down over his broad breast like the beard of a prophet. In his dress, which was noticeably soiled, the fashions of three decades were hinted at; he seemed to have donned whatever he thought his friends would most have liked him to leave off.

"Professor," said the old man, extending something like the paw of a lion, and giving Frowenfeld plenty of time to become thoroughly awed, "this is a pleasure as magnificent as unexpected! A scientific man?—in Louisiana?" He looked around upon the doctors as upon a graduating class. "Professor, I am rejoiced!" He paused again, shaking the apothecary's hand with great ceremony. "I do assure you, sir, I dislike to relinquish your grasp. Do me the honor to allow me to become your friend! I congratulate my down-trodden country on the acquisition of such a citizen! I hope, sir,—at least I might have hoped, had not Louisiana just passed into the hands of the most clap-trap government in the universe, notwithstanding it pretends to be a republic,—I might have hoped that you had come among us to fasten the lie direct upon a late author, who writes of us that 'the air of this region is deadly to the Muses.' "

"He didn't say that?" asked one of the debaters, with pretended indignation.

"He did, sir, after eating our bread!"

"And sucking our sugar-cane, too, no doubt!" said the wag; but the old man took no notice.

Frowenfeld, naturally, was not anxious to reply, and was greatly relieved to be touched on the elbow by a child with a picayune in one hand and a tumbler in the other. He escaped behind the counter and gladly remained there.

"Citizen Fusilier," asked one of the gossips, "what has the new government to do with the health of the Muses?"

"It introduces the English tongue," said the old man scowling.

"Oh, well," replied the questioner, "the Creoles will soon learn the language."

"English is not a language, sir; it is a jargon! And when this young simpleton, Claiborne, attempts to cram it down the public windpipe in the courts, as I understand he intends, he will fail! Hah! sir, I know men in this city who would rather eat a dog than speak English! *I* speak it, but I also speak Choctaw."

"The new land titles will be in English."

"They will spurn his rotten titles. And if he attempts to invalidate their old ones, why, let him do it! Napoleon Buonaparte" (Italian pronunciation) "will make good every arpent within the next two years. *Think so?* I know it! *How?* H-I perceive it! H-I hope the yellow fever may spare you to witness it."

A sullen grunt from the circle showed the "citizen" that he had presumed too much upon the license commonly accorded his advanced age, and by way of a diversion he looked around for Frowenfeld to pour new flatteries upon. But Joseph, behind his counter, unaware of either the offense or the resentment, was blushing with pleasure before a visitor who had entered by the side door farthest from the company.

48

"Gentlemen," said Agricola, "h-my dear friends, you must not expect an old Creole to like anything in comparison with *la belle langue.*"

"Which language do you call *la belle?*" asked Doctor Keene, with pretended simplicity.

The old man bent upon him a look of unspeakable contempt, which nobody noticed. The gossips were one by one stealing a glance toward that which ever was, is and must be, an irresistible lodestone to the eyes of all the sons of Adam, to wit, a chaste and graceful complement of—skirts. Then in a lower tone they resumed their desultory conversation.

It was the seeker after basil who stood before the counter, holding in her hand, with her purse, the heavy veil whose folds had before concealed her features.

10 "Oo Dad Is, 'Sieur Frowenfel'?"

Whether the removal of the veil was because of the milder light of the evening, or the result of accident, or of haste, or both, or whether, by reason of some exciting or absorbing course of thought, the wearer had withdrawn it unconsciously, was a matter that occupied the apothecary as little as did Agricola's continued harangue. As he looked upon the fair face through the light gauze which still overhung but not obscured it, he readily perceived, despite the sprightly smile, something like distress, and as she spoke this became still more evident in her hurried undertone.

"'Sieur Frowenfel', I want you to sell me doze *basilic*."

As she slipped the rings of her purse apart her fingers trembled.

"It is waiting for you," said Frowenfeld; but the lady did not hear him; she was giving her attention to the loud voice of Agricola saying in the course of discussion:

"The Louisiana Creole is the noblest variety of enlightened man!"

"Oo dad is, 'Sieur Frowenfel'?" she asked, softly, but with an excited eye.

"That is Mr. Agricola Fusilier," answered Joseph in the same tone, his heart leaping inexplicably as he met her glance. With an angry flush she looked quickly around, scrutinized the old

50

man in an instantaneous, thorough way, and then glanced back at the apothecary again, as if asking him to fulfil her request the quicker.

He hesitated, in doubt as to her meaning.

"Wrap it yonder," she almost whispered.

He went, and in a moment returned, with the basil only partially hid in a paper covering.

But the lady, muffled again in her manifold veil had once more lost her eagerness for it; at least, instead of taking it, she moved aside, offering room for a masculine figure just entering. She did not look to see who it might be—plenty of time to do that by accident, by and by. There she made a mistake; for the newcomer, with a silent bow of thanks, declined the place made for him, moved across the shop, and occupied his eyes with the contents of the glass case, his back being turned to the lady and Frowenfeld. The apothecary recognized the Creole whom he had met under the live-oak.

The lady put forth her hand suddenly to receive the package. As she took it and turned to depart, another small hand was laid upon it and it was returned to the counter. Something was said in a low-pitched undertone, and the two sisters—if Frowenfeld's guess was right—confronted each other. For a single instant only they stood so; an earnest and hurried murmur of French words passed between them, and they turned together, bowed with great suavity, and were gone.

"The Cession is a mere temporary political manœuvre!" growled M. Fusilier.

Frowenfeld's merchant friend came from his place of waiting, and spoke twice before he attracted the attention of the bewildered apothecary.

"Good-day, Mr. Frowenfeld; I have been told that——"

Joseph gazed after the two ladies crossing the street, and felt uncomfortable that the group of gossips did the same. So did the black attendant who glanced furtively back.

"Good-day, Mr. Frowenfeld; I——"

"Oh! how do you do, sir?" exclaimed the apothecary, with great pleasantness of face. It seemed the most natural thing that they should resume their late conversation just where they had left off, and that would certainly be pleasant. But the man of more experience showed an unresponsive expression, that was as if he remembered no conversation of any note.

51

"I have been told that you might be able to replace the glass in this thing out of your private stock."

He presented a small, leather-covered case, evidently containing some optical instrument. "It will give me a pretext for going," he had said to himself, as he put it into his pocket in his counting-room. He was not going to let the apothecary know he had taken such a fancy to him.

"I do not know," replied Frowenfeld, as he touched the spring of the case; "I will see what I have."

He passed into the back room, more than willing to get out of sight till he might better collect himself.

"I do not keep these things for sale," said he as he went.

"Sir?" asked the Creole, as if he had not understood, and followed through the open door.

"Is this what that lady was getting?" he asked, touching the remnant of the basil in the box.

"Yes, sir," said the apothecary, with his face in the drawer of a table.

"They had no carriage with them." The Creole spoke with his back turned, at the same time running his eyes along a shelf of books. Frowenfeld made only the sound of rejecting bits of crystal and taking up others. "I do not know who they are," ventured the merchant.

Joseph still gave no answer, but a moment after approached, with the instrument in his extended hand.

"You had it? I am glad," said the owner, receiving it, but keeping one hand still on the books.

Frowenfeld put up his materials.

"Mr. Frowenfeld, are these your books? I mean do you use these books?"

"Yes, sir."

The Creole stepped back to the door.

"Agricola!"

"*Quoi!*"

"*Vien ici.*"

Citizen Fusilier entered, followed by a small volley of retorts from those with whom he had been disputing, and who rose as he did. The stranger said something very sprightly in French, running the back of one finger down the rank of books, and a lively dialogue followed.

52

"You must be a great scholar," said the unknown by and by, addressing the apothecary.

"He is a professor of chemistry," said the old man.

"I am nothing, as yet, but a student," said Joseph, as the three returned into the shop; "certainly not a scholar, and still less a professor." He spoke with a new quietness of manner that made the younger Creole turn upon him a pleasant look.

"H-my young friend," said the patriarch, turning toward Joseph with a tremendous frown, "when I, Agricola Fusilier, pronounce you a professor, you are a professor. Louisiana will not look to *you* for your credentials; she will look to me!"

He stumbled upon some slight impediment under foot. There were times when it took but little to make Agricola stumble.

Looking to see what it was, Joseph picked up a silken purse. There was a name embroidered on it.

11 Sudden Flashes of Light

The day was nearly gone. The company that had been chatting at the front door, and which in warmer weather would have tarried until bed-time, had wandered off; however, by stepping toward the light the young merchant could decipher the letters on the purse. Citizen Fusilier drew out a pair of spectacles, looked over his junior's shoulder, read aloud, "*Aurore De G. Nanca——*," and uttered an imprecation.

"Do not speak to me!" he thundered; "do not approach me! she did it maliciously!"

"Sir!" began Frowenfeld.

But the old man uttered another tremendous malediction and hurried into the street and away.

"Let him pass," said the other Creole calmly.

"What is the matter with him?" asked Frowenfeld.

"He is getting old." The Creole extended the purse carelessly to the apothecary. "Has it anything inside?"

"But a single pistareen."

"That is why she wanted the *basilic*, eh?"

"I do not understand you, sir."

"Do you not know what she was going to do with it?"

"With the basil? No sir."

"Maybe she was going to make a little *tisane*, eh?" said the Creole, forcing down a smile.

But a portion of the smile would come when Frowenfeld answered, with unnecessary resentment.

"She was going to make some *proper* use of it, which need not concern me."

"Without doubt."

The Creole quietly walked a step or two forward and back and looked idly into the glass-case. "Is this young man in love with her?" he asked himself. He turned around.

"Do you know those ladies, Mr. Frowenfeld? Do you visit them at home?"

He drew out his porte-monnaie.

"No, sir."

"I will pay you for the repair of this instrument; have you change for——"

"I will see," said the apothecary.

As he spoke he laid the purse on a stool, till he should light his shop and then went to his till without again taking it.

The Creole sauntered across to the counter and nipped the herb which still lay there.

"Mr. Frowenfeld, you know what some very excellent people do with this? They rub it on the sill of the door to make the money come into the house."

Joseph stopped aghast with the drawer half drawn.

"Not persons of intelligence and——"

"All kinds. It is only some of the foolishness which they take from the slaves. Many of our best people consult the voudou horses."

"Horses?"

"Priestesses, you might call them," explained the Creole, "like Momselle Marcelline or 'Zabeth Philosophe."

"Witches!" whispered Frowenfeld.

"Oh no," said the other with a shrug; "that is too hard a name; say fortune-tellers. But Mr. Frowenfeld, I wish you to lend me your good offices. Just supposing the possi*bi*lity that the lady may be in need of money, you know, and will send back or come back for the purse, you know, knowing that she most likely lost it here, I ask you the favor that you will not let her know I have filled it with gold. In fact, if she mentions my name——"

"To confess the truth, sir, I am not acquainted with your name."

The Creole smiled a genuine surprise.

"I thought you knew it." He laughed a little at himself. "We have nevertheless become very good friends—I believe? Well, in fact then, Mr. Frowenfeld, you might say you do not know who put the money in." He extended his open palm with the purse hanging across it. Joseph was about to object to this statement, but the Creole, putting on an expression of anxious desire, said: "I mean, not by name. It is somewhat important to me, Mr. Frowenfeld, that that lady should not know my present action. If you want to do those two ladies a favor, you may rest assured the way to do it is to say you do not know who put this gold." The Creole in his earnestness slipped in his idiom. "You will excuse me if I do not tell you my name; you can find it out at any time from Agricola. Ah! I am glad she did not see me! You must not tell anybody about this little event, eh?"

"No, sir," said Joseph, as he finally accepted the purse. "I shall say nothing to any one else, and only what I cannot avoid saying to the lady and her sister."

"*'Tis not her sister,*" responded the Creole, "*'tis her daughter.*"

The italics signify, not how the words were said, but how they sounded to Joseph. As if a dark lantern were suddenly turned full upon it, he saw the significance of Citizen Fusilier's transport. The fair strangers were the widow and daughter of the man whom Agricola had killed in duel—the ladies with whom Doctor Keene had desired to make him acquainted.

"Well, good-evening, Mr. Frowenfeld." The Creole extended his hand (his people are great hand-shakers). "Ah——" and then, for the first time, he came to the true object of his visit. "The conversation we had some weeks ago, Mr. Frowenfeld, has started a train of thought in my mind"—he began to smile as if to convey the idea that Joseph would find the subject a trivial one—"which has almost brought me to the——"

A light footfall accompanied with the soft sweep of robes cut short his words. There had been two or three entrances and exits during the time the Creole had tarried, but he had not allowed them to disturb him. Now, however, he had no sooner turned and fixed his glance upon this last comer, than without so much as the invariable Creole leave-taking of "Well, good-evening, sir," he hurried out.

12 The Philosophe

The apothecary felt an inward nervous start as there advanced
into the light of his hanging lamp and toward the spot where he
had halted, just outside the counter, a woman of the quadroon
caste, of superb stature and poise, severely handsome features,
clear, tawny skin and large, passionate black eyes.

"*Ben soï, Miché.*" [Monsieur.] A rather hard, yet not repellent
smile showed her faultless teeth.

Frowenfeld bowed.

"*Mo vien c'erc'er la bourse de Madame.*"

She spoke the best French at her command, but it was not
understood.

The apothecary could only shake his head.

"*La bourse,*" she repeated, softly smiling, but with a scintillation of the eyes in resentment of his scrutiny. "*La bourse,*" she
reiterated.

"Purse?"

"*Oui, Miché.*"

"You are sent for it?"

"*Oui, Miché.*"

He drew it from his breast pocket and marked the sudden
glisten of her eyes, reflecting the glisten of the gold in the silken
mesh.

"*Oui, c'est ça,*" said she, putting her hand out eagerly.

"I am afraid to give you this to-night," said Joseph.

"*Oui,*" ventured she, dubiously, the lightning playing deep back in her eyes.

"You might be robbed," said Frowenfeld. "It is very dangerous for you to be out alone. It will not be long, now, until gun-fire." (Eight o'clock P.M.—the gun to warn slaves to be in-doors, under pain of arrest and imprisonment.)

The object of this solicitude shook her head with a smile at its gratuitousness. The smile showed determination also.

"*Mo pas compren',*" she said.

"Tell the lady to send for it to-morrow."

She smiled helplessly and somewhat vexedly, shrugged and again shook her head. As she did so she heard footsteps and voices in the door at her back.

"*C'est ça,*" she said again with a hurried attempt at extreme amiability; "Dat it; *oui;*" and lifting her hand with some rapidity made a sudden eager reach for the purse, but failed.

"No!" said Frowenfeld, indignantly.

"Hello!" said Charlie Keene amusedly, as he approached from the door.

The woman turned, and in one or two rapid sentences in the Creole dialect offered her explanation.

"Give her the purse, Joe; I will answer for its being all right."

Frowenfeld handed it to her. She started to pass through the door in the rue Royale by which Doctor Keene had entered; but on seeing on its threshold Agricola frowning upon her, she turned quickly with evident trepidation, and hurried out into the darkness of the other street.

Agricola entered. Doctor Keene looked about the shop.

"I tell you, Agricole, you didn't have it with you; Frowenfeld, you haven't seen a big knotted walking-stick?"

Frowenfeld was sure no walking-stick had been left there.

"Oh yes, Frowenfeld," said Doctor Keene, with a little laugh, as the three sat down, "I'd a'most as soon trust that woman as if she was white."

The apothecary said nothing.

"How free," said Agricola, beginning with a meditative gaze at the sky without, and ending with a philosopher's smile upon his two companions,—"how free we people are from prejudice against the negro!"

58

"The white people," said Frowenfeld, half abstractedly, half inquiringly.

"H-my young friend, when we say, 'we people,' we *always* mean we white people. The non-mention of color always implies pure white; and whatever is not pure white is to all intents and purposes pure black. When I say the 'whole community,' I mean the whole white portion; when I speak of the 'undivided public sentiment,' I mean the sentiment of the white population. What else could I mean? Could you suppose, sir, the expression which you may have heard me use—'my down-trodden country' includes blacks and mulattoes? What is that up yonder in the sky? The moon. The new moon, or the old moon, or the moon in her third quarter, but always the moon! Which part of it? Why, the shining part—the white part, always and only! Not that there is a prejudice against the negro. By no means. Wherever he can be of any service in a strictly menial capacity we kindly and generously tolerate his presence."

Was the immigrant growing wise, or weak, that he remained silent?

Agricola rose as he concluded and said he would go home. Doctor Keene gave him his hand lazily, without rising.

"Frowenfeld," he said, with a smile, and in an undertone as Agricola's footsteps died away, "don't you know who that woman is?"

"No."

"Well, I'll tell you."

He told him.

On that lonely plantation at the Cannes Brulées, where Aurore Nancanou's childhood had been passed without brothers or sisters, there had been given her, according to the well-known custom of plantation life, a little quadroon slave-maid as her constant and only playmate. This maid began early to show herself in many ways remarkable. While yet a child she grew tall, lithe, agile; her eyes were large and black, and rolled and sparkled if she but turned to answer to her name. Her pale yellow forehead, low and shapely, with the jet hair above it, the heavily pencilled eyebrows and long lashes below, the faint red tinge that blushed with a kind of cold passion through the clear yellow skin of the cheek, the fullness of the red, voluptuous lips and the roundness of her perfect neck, gave her, even at fourteen, a barbaric and magnetic beauty, that startled the beholder like an unexpected drawing out of a jewelled sword. Such a type could have sprung only from high Latin ancestry on the one side and—we might venture—Jaloff African on the other. To these charms of person she added mental acuteness, conversational adroitness, concealed cunning and noiseless but visible strength of will; and to these, that rarest of gifts in one of her tincture, the purity of true womanhood.

At fourteen a necessity which had been parleyed with for two years or more became imperative and Aurore's maid was taken from her. Explanation is almost superfluous. Aurore was to become a lady and her playmate a lady's maid; but not *her* maid, because the maid had become, of the two, the ruling spirit. It was a question of grave debate in the mind of M. De Grapion what disposition to make of her.

About this time the Grandissimes and De Grapions, through certain efforts of Honoré's father (since dead) were making some feeble pretences of mutual good feeling, and one of those Kentuckian dealers in corn and tobacco whose flat-boat fleets were always drifting down the Mississippi, becoming one day M. De Grapion's transient guest, accidentally mentioned a wish of Agricola Fusilier. Agricola, it appeared, had commissioned him to buy the most beautiful lady's maid that in his extended journeyings he might be able to find; he wanted to make her a gift to his niece, Honoré's sister. The Kentuckians saw the demand met in Aurore's playmate. M. De Grapion would not sell her. (Trade with a Grandissime? Let them suspect he needed money?) No; but he would ask Agricola to accept the services of the waiting-maid for, say, ten years. The Kentuckian accepted the proposition on the spot and it was by and by carried out. She was never recalled to the Cannes Brulées, but in subsequent years received her freedom from her master, and in New Orleans became Palmyre la Philosophe, as they say in the corrupt French of the old Creoles, or Palmyre Philosophe, noted for her taste and skill as a hair-dresser, for the efficiency of her spells and the sagacity of her divinations, but most of all for the chaste austerity with which she practised the less baleful rites of the voudous.

"That's the woman," said Doctor Keene, rising to go, as he concluded the narrative,—"that's she, Palmyre Philosophe. Now you get a view of the vastness of Agricole's generosity; he tolerates her even though she does not present herself in the 'strictly menial capacity.' Reason why—*he's afraid of her.*"

Time passed, if that may be called time which we have to measure with a clock. The apothecary of the rue Royale found better ways of measurement. As quietly as a spider he was spinning information into knowledge and knowledge into what is supposed to be wisdom; whether it was or not we shall see. His unidentified merchant friend who had adjured him to become acclimated as "they all did" had also exhorted him to study the human mass of which he had become a unit; but whether that study, if pursued, was sweetening and ripening, or whether it was corrupting him, that friend did not come to see; it was the busy time of year. Certainly so young a solitary, coming among a people whose conventionalities were so at variance with his own door-yard ethics, was in sad danger of being unduly—as we might say—Timonized. His acquaintances continued to be few in number.

During this fermenting period he chronicled much wet and some cold weather. This may in part account for the uneventfulness of its passage; events do not happen rapidly among the Creoles in bad weather. However, trade was good.

But the weather cleared; and when it was getting well on into the Creole spring and approaching the spring of the almanacs, something did occur that extended Frowenfeld's acquaintance without Doctor Keene's assistance.

13 A Call from the Rent-Spectre

It is nearly noon of a balmy morning late in February. Aurore Nancanou and her daughter have only this moment ceased sewing, in the small front room of No. 19 rue Bienville. Number 19 is the right-hand half of a single-story, low-roofed tenement, washed with yellow ochre, which it shares generously with whoever leans against it. It sits as fast on the ground as a toad. There is a kitchen belonging to it somewhere among the weeds in the back yard, and besides this room, where the ladies are, there is directly behind it, a sleeping apartment. Somewhere back of this there is a little nook where in pleasant weather they eat. Their cook and housemaid is the plain person who attends them on the street. Her bed-chamber is the kitchen and her bed the floor. The house's only other protector is a hound, the aim of whose life is to get thrust out of the ladies' apartments every fifteen minutes.

Yet if you hastily picture to yourself a forlorn-looking establishment, you will be moving straight away from the fact. Neatness, order, excellence, are prevalent qualities in all the details of the main house's inward garniture. The furniture is old-fashioned, rich, French, imported. The carpets, if not new, are not cheap, either. Bits of crystal and silver, visible here and there, are as bright as they are antiquated; and one or two portraits, and the picture of Our Lady of Many Sorrows, are passably good productions. The brass work, of which there is much, is brilliantly burnished, and the front room is bright and cheery.

At the street door of this room somebody has just knocked. Aurore has risen from her seat. The other still sits on a low chair with her hands and sewing dropped into her lap, looking up steadfastly into her mother's face with a mingled expression of fondness and dismayed expectation. Aurore hesitates beside her chair, desirous of resuming her seat, even lifts her sewing from it; but tarries a moment, her alert suspense showing in her eyes. Her daughter still looks up into them. It is not strange that the dwellers round about dispute as to which is the fairer, nor that in the six months during which the two have occupied No. 19 the neighbors have reached no conclusion on this subject. If some young enthusiast compares the daughter—in her eighteenth year—to a bursting blush rosebud full of promise, some older one immediately retorts that the other—in her thirty-fifth—is the red, red, full-blown, faultless joy of the garden. If one says the maiden has the dew of youth,—"But!" cry two or three mothers in a breath, "that other one, child, will never grow old. With her it will always be morning. That woman is going to last forever; ha-a-a-a!—even longer!"

There was one direction in which the widow evidently had the advantage; you could see from the street or the opposite windows that she was a wise householder. On the day they moved into Number 19 she had been seen to enter in advance of all her other movables, carrying into the empty house a new broom, a looking-glass, and a silver coin. Every morning since, a little watching would have discovered her at the hour of sunrise sprinkling water from her side casement, and her opposite neighbors often had occasion to notice that, sitting at her sewing by the front window, she never pricked her finger but she quickly ran it up behind her ear, and then went on with her work. Would anybody but Joseph Frowenfeld ever have lived in and moved away from the two-story brick next them on the right and not have known of the existence of such a marvel?

"Ha!" they said, "she knows how to keep off bad luck, that Madame yonder. And the younger one seems not to like it. Girls think themselves so smart these days."

Ah, there was the knock again, right there on the street-door, as loud as if it had been given with a joint of sugar-cane!

The daughter's hand, which had just resumed the needle, stood

63

still in mid-course with the white thread half drawn. Aurore tiptoed slowly over the carpeted floor. There came a shuffling sound, and the corner of a folded white paper commenced appearing and disappearing under the door. She mounted a chair and peeped through that odd little *jalousie* which formerly was in almost all New Orleans street-doors; but the missive had meantime found its way across the sill, and she saw only the unpicturesque back of a departing errand-boy. But that was well. She had a pride, to maintain which—and a poverty, to conceal which—she felt to be necessary to her self-respect; and this made her of necessity a trifle unsocial in her own castle. Do you suppose she was going to put on the face of having been born or married to this degraded condition of things?

Who knows?—the knock might have been from 'Sieur Frowenfel'—ha, ha! He might be just silly enough to call so early; or it might have been from that *polisson* of a Grandissime,—which one didn't matter, they were all detestable,—coming to collect the rent. That was her original fear; or, worse still, it might have been, had it been softer, the knock of some possible lady-visitor. She had no intention of admitting any feminine eyes to detect this carefully covered up indigence. Besides, it was Monday. There is no sense in trifling with bad luck. The reception of Monday callers is a source of misfortune never known to fail, save in rare cases when good luck has already been secured by smearing the front walk or the banquette with Venetian red.

Before the daughter could dart up and disengage herself from her work her mother had pounced upon the paper. She was standing and reading, her rich black lashes curtaining their downcast eyes, her infant waist and round, close-fitted, childish arms harmonizing prettily with her mock frown of infantile perplexity, and her long, limp robe heightening the grace of her posture, when the younger started from her seat with the air of determining not to be left at a disadvantage.

But what is that on the dark eyelash? With a sudden additional energy the daughter dashes the sewing and chair to right and left, bounds up, and in a moment has Aurore weeping in her embrace and has snatched the note from her hand.

"Ah! maman! Ah! ma chère mère!"

The mother forced a laugh. She was not to be mothered by her daughter; so she made a dash at Clotilde's uplifted hand to recover the note, which was unavailing. Immediately there arose

64

in colonial French the loveliest of contentions, the issue of which was that the pair sat down side by side, like two sisters over one love-letter, and undertook to decipher the paper. It read as follows:

"New Orleans, 20 Feb're, 1804.

"*Madame Nancanou:* I muss oblige to ass you for rent of that house whare you living, it is at number 19 Bienville street whare I do not received thos rent from you not since tree mons and I demand you this is mabe thirteen time. And I give to you notice of 19 das writen in Anglish as the new law requi. That witch the law make necessare only for 15 das, and when you not pay me those rent in 19 das till the tense of Marh I will rekes you to move out. That witch make me to be very sorry. I have the honor to remain, Madam,

"Your humble servant,
"H. GRANDISSIME,
"*per* Z. F."

There was a short French postscript on the opposite page signed only by M. Zénon François, explaining that he, who had allowed them in the past to address him as their landlord and by his name, was but the landlord's agent; that the landlord was a far better-dressed man than he could afford to be; that the writing opposite was a notice for them to quit the premises they had rented (not leased), or pay up; that it gave the writer great pain to send it, although it was but the necessary legal form and he only an irresponsible drawer of an inadequate salary, with thirteen children to support; and that he implored them to tear off and burn up this postscript immediately they had read it.

"Ah, the miserable!" was all the comment made upon it as the two ladies addressed their energies to the previous English. They had never suspected him of being M. Grandissime.

Their eyes dragged slowly and ineffectually along the lines to the signature.

"H. Grandissime! Loog ad 'im!" cried the widow, with a sudden short laugh, that brought the tears after it like a wind-gust in a rose-tree. She held the letter out before them as if she was lifting something alive by the back of the neck, and to intensify her scorn spoke in the hated tongue prescribed by the new courts. "Loog ad 'im! dad ridge gen'leman oo give so mudge money to de 'ozpill!"

"Bud, *maman*," said the daughter, laying her hand appeasingly upon her mother's knee, "*ee* do nod know 'ow we is poor."

"Ah!" retorted Aurore, "*par example! Non?* Ee thingue we is ridge, eh? Ligue his oncle, eh? Ee thing so, too, eh?" She cast upon her daughter the look of burning scorn intended for Agricola Fusilier. "You wan' to tague the pard of dose Grandissime'?"

The daughter returned a look of agony.

"No," she said, "bud a man wad godd some 'ouses to rend, muz ee nod boun' to ged 'is rend?"

"Boun' to ged—ah! yez ee muz do 'is possible to ged 'is rend. Oh! certain*lee*. Ee is ridge, bud ee need a lill money, bad, bad. Fo' w'at?" The excited speaker rose to her feet under a sudden inspiration. "*Tenez, Mademoiselle!*" She began to make great show of unfastening her dress.

"*Mais, comment?*" demanded the suffering daughter.

"Yez!" continued Aurore, keeping up the demonstration, "you wand 'im to 'ave 'is rend so bad! An' I godd honely my cloze; so you juz tague diz to you' fine gen'lemen, 'Sieur Honoré Grandissime."

"Ah-h-h-h!" cried the martyr.

"An' you is righd," persisted the tormentor, still unfastening; but the daughter's tears gushed forth, and the repentant tease threw herself upon her knees, drew her child's head into her bosom and wept afresh.

Half an hour was passed in council; at the end of which they stood beneath their lofty mantel-shelf, each with a foot on a brazen fire-dog, and no conclusion reached.

"Ah, my child!"—they had come to themselves now and were speaking in their peculiar French—"if we had here in these hands but the tenth part of what your papa often played away in one night without once getting angry! But we have not. Ah! but your father was a fine fellow; if he could have lived for you to know him! So accomplished! Ha, ha, ha! I can never avoid laughing, when I remember him teaching me to speak English; I used to enrage him so!"

The daughter brought the conversation back to the subject of discussion. There were nineteen days yet allowed them. God knows—by the expiration of that time they might be able to pay. With the two music scholars whom she then had and three more whom she had some hope to get, she made bold to say they could pay the rent.

"Ah, Clotilde, my child," exclaimed Aurore, with sudden brightness, "you don't need a mask and costume to resemble your great-grandmother, the casket-girl!" Aurore felt sure, on her part, that with the one embroidery scholar then under her tutelage, and the three others who had declined to take lessons, they could easily pay the rent—and how kind it was of Monsieur, the aged father of that one embroidery scholar, to procure those invitations to the ball! The dear old man! He said he must see one more ball before he should die.

Aurore looked so pretty in the reverie into which she fell that her daughter was content to admire her silently.

"Clotilde," said the mother, presently looking up, "do you remember the evening you treated me so ill?"

The daughter smiled at the preposterous charge.

"I did not treat you ill."

"Yes, don't you know—the evening you made me lose my purse?"

"Certainly, I know!" The daughter took her foot from the andiron; her eyes lighted up aggressively. "For losing your purse blame yourself. For the way you found it again—which was far worse—thank Palmyre. If you had not asked her to find it and shared the gold with her we could have returned with it to 'Sieur Frowenfel'; but now we are ashamed to let him see us. I do not doubt he filled the purse."

"He? He never knew it was empty. It was Nobody who filled it. Palmyre says that Papa Lébat——"

"Ha!" exclaimed Clotilde at this superstitious mention.

The mother tossed her head and turned her back, swallowing the unendurable bitterness of being rebuked by her daughter. But the cloud hung over but a moment.

"Clotilde," she said, a minute after, turning with a look of sun-bright resolve, "I am going to see him."

"To see whom?" asked the other, looking back from the window, whither she had gone to recover from a reactionary trembling.

"To whom, my child? Why——"

"You do not expect mercy from Honoré Grandissime? You would not ask it?"

"No. There is no mercy in the Grandissime blood; but cannot I demand justice? Ha! it is justice that I shall demand!"

"And you will really go and see him?"

"You will see, Mademoiselle," replied Aurore, dropping a broom with which she had begun to sweep up some spilled buttons.

"And I with you?"

"No! To a counting-room? To the presence of the chief of that detestable race? No!"

"But you don't know where his office is."

"Anybody can tell me."

Preparation began at once. By and by——

"Clotilde."

Clotilde was stooping behind her mother, with a ribbon between her lips, arranging a flounce.

"M-m-m."

"You must not watch me go out of sight; do you hear? * * But it *is* dangerous. I knew of a gentleman who watched his wife go out of his sight and she never came back!"

"Hold still!" said Clotilde.

"But when my hand itches," retorted Aurore in a high key, "haven't I got to put it instantly into my pocket if I want the money to come there! Well, then!"

The daughter proposed to go to the kitchen and tell Alphonsina to put on her shoes.

"My child," cried Aurore, "you are crazy! Do you want Alphonsina to be seized for the rent?"

"But you cannot go alone—and on foot!"

"I must go alone; and—can you lend me your carriage? Ah, you have none? Certainly I must go alone and on foot if I am to say I cannot pay the rent. It is no indiscretion of mine. If anything happens to me it is M. Grandissime who is responsible."

Now she is ready for the adventurous errand. She darts to the mirror. The high-water marks are gone from her eyes. She wheels half around and looks over her shoulder. The flaring bonnet and loose ribbons give her a more girlish look than ever.

"Now which is the older, little old woman?" she chirrups, and smites her daughter's cheek softly with her palm.

"And you are not afraid to go alone?"

"No; but remember! look at that dog!"

The brute sinks apologetically to the floor. Clotilde opens the street door, hands Aurore the note, Aurore lays a frantic kiss upon her lips, pressing it on tight so as to get it again when she comes back, and—while Clotilde calls the cook to gather up the

68

buttons and take away the broom, and while the cook, to make one trip of it, gathers the hound into her bosom and carries broom and dog out together—Aurore sallies forth, leaving Clotilde to resume her sewing and await the coming of a guitar scholar.

"It will keep her fully an hour," thought the girl, far from imagining that Aurore had set about a little private business which she proposed to herself to accomplish before she even started in the direction of M. Grandissime's counting-rooms.

14 Before Sunset

In old times, most of the sidewalks of New Orleans not in the heart of town were only a rough, rank turf, lined on the side next the ditch with the gunwales of broken-up flat-boats—ugly, narrow, slippery objects. As Aurora—it sounds so much pleasanter to anglicize her name—as Aurora gained a corner where two of these gunwales met, she stopped and looked back to make sure that Clotilde was not watching her. That others had noticed her here and there she did not care; that was something beauty would have to endure, and it only made her smile to herself.

"Everybody sees I am from the country—walking on the street without a waiting-maid."

A boy passed, hushing his whistle, and gazing at the lone lady until his turning neck could twist no farther. She was so dewy fresh! After he had got across the street he turned to look again. Where could she have disappeared?

The only object to be seen on the corner from which she had vanished, was a small, yellow-washed house much like the one Aurora occupied, as it was like hundreds that then characterized and still characterize the town, only that now they are of brick instead of adobe. They showed in those days, even more than now, the wide contrast between their homely exteriors and the often elegant apartments within. However, in this house the front room was merely neat. The furniture was of rude, heavy pattern, Creole-made, and the walls were unadorned; the day of cheap pictures had not come. The lofty bedstead which filled one corner was spread and hung with a blue stuff showing through a web of white needlework. The brazen feet of the chairs were brightly burnished, as were the brass mountings of the bedstead and the brass globes on the cold andirons. Curtains of blue and white hung at the single window. The floor, from habitual scrubbing with the common weed which politeness has to call *Helenium autumnale*, was stained a bright, clean yellow. On it were here and there in places, white mats woven of bleached palmetto-leaf. Such were the room's appointments; there was but one thing more,—a singular bit of fantastic carving,—a small table of dark mahogany supported on the upward-writhing images of three scaly serpents.

Aurora sat down beside this table. A dwarf Congo woman, as black as soot, had ushered her in, and, having barred the door, had disappeared, and now the mistress of the house entered.

February though it was, she was dressed—and looked comfortable—in white. That barbaric beauty which had begun to bud twenty years before was now in perfect bloom. The united grace and pride of her movement was inspiring but—what shall we say?—feline? It was a femininity without humanity,—something that made her with all her superbness, a creature that one would want to find chained. It was the woman who had received the gold from Frowenfeld—Palmyre Philosophe.

The moment her eyes fell upon Aurora her whole appearance changed. A girlish smile lighted up her face, and as Aurora rose up reflecting it back, they simultaneously clapped hands, laughed and advanced joyously toward each other, talking rapidly without regard to each other's words.

"Sit down," said Palmyre, in the plantation French of their childhood, as they shook hands.

They took chairs and drew up face to face as close as they could come, then sighed and smiled a moment, and then looked grave and were silent. For in the nature of things, and notwithstanding the amusing familiarity common between Creole ladies and the menial class, the unprotected little widow should have had a very serious errand to bring her to the voudou's house.

"Palmyre," began the lady, in a sad tone.

"Momselle Aurore."

"I want you to help me." The former mistress not only cast her hands into her lap, lifted her eyes supplicatingly and dropped them again, but actually locked her fingers to keep them from trembling.

"Momselle Aurore——" began Palmyre, solemnly.

"Now, I know what you are going to say—but it is of no use to say it; do this much for me this one time and then I will let voudou alone as much as you wish—forever!"

"You have not lost your purse *again?*"

"Ah! foolishness, no."

Both laughed a little, the philosophe feebly, and Aurora with an excited tremor.

"Well?" demanded the quadroon, looking grave again.

Aurora did not answer.

"Do you wish me to work a spell for you?"

The widow nodded, with her eyes cast down.

Both sat quite still for some time; then the philosophe gently drew the landlord's letter from between Aurora's hands.

"What is this?" She could not read in any language.

"I must pay my rent within nineteen days."

"Have you not paid it?"

The delinquent shook her head.

"Where is the gold that came into your purse? All gone?"

"For rice and potatoes," said Aurora, and for the first time she uttered a genuine laugh, under that condition of mind which Latins usually substitute for fortitude. Palmyre laughed too, very properly.

Another silence followed. The lady could not return the quadroon's searching gaze.

"Momselle Aurore," suddenly said Palmyre, "you want me to work a spell for something else."

Aurora started, looked up for an instant in a frightened way, and then dropped her eyes and let her head droop, murmuring:

"No, I do not."

Palmyre fixed a long look upon her former mistress. She saw that though Aurora might be distressed about the rent, there was something else,—a deeper feeling, impelling her upon a course the very thought of which drove the color from her lips and made her tremble.

"You are wearing red," said the philosophe.

Aurora's hand went nervously to the red ribbon about her neck.

"It is an accident; I had nothing else convenient."

"Miché Agoussou loves red," persisted Palmyre. (Monsieur Agoussou is the demon upon whom the voudous call in matters of love.)

The color that came into Aurora's cheek ought to have suited Monsieur precisely.

"It is an accident," she feebly insisted.

"Well," presently said Palmyre, with a pretence of abandoning her impression, "then you want me to work you a spell for money, do you?"

Aurora nodded, while she still avoided the quadroon's glance.

"I know better," thought the philosophe. "You shall have the sort you want."

The widow stole an upward glance.

"Oh!" said Palmyre, with the manner of one making a decided digression, "I have been wanting to ask you something. That evening at the pharmacy—was there a tall handsome gentleman standing by the counter?"

"He was standing on the other side."

"Did you see his face?"

"No; his back was turned."

"Momselle Aurore," said Palmyre, dropping her elbows upon her knees and taking the lady's hand as if the better to secure the truth, "was that the gentleman you met at the ball?"

"My faith!" said Aurora, stretching her eyebrows upward. "I did not think to look. Who was it?"

But Palmyre Philosophe was not going to give more than she got, even to her old-time Momselle; she merely straightened back into her chair with an amiable face.

"Who do you think he is?" persisted Aurora, after a pause, smiling downward and toying with her rings.

The quadroon shrugged.

They both sat in reverie for a moment—a long moment for such sprightly natures—and Palmyre's mien took on a professional gravity. She presently pushed the landlord's letter under the lady's hands as they lay clasped in her lap, and a moment after drew Aurora's glance with her large, strong eyes and asked:

"What shall we do?"

73

The lady immediately looked startled and alarmed and again dropped her eyes in silence. The quadroon had to speak again.

"We will burn a candle."

Aurora trembled.

"No," she succeeded in saying.

"Yes," said Palmyre, "you must get your rent money." But the charm which she was meditating had no reference to rent money. "She knows that," thought the voudou.

As she rose and called her Congo slave-woman, Aurora made as if to protest further; but utterance failed her. She clenched her hands and prayed to Fate for Clotilde to come and lead her away as she had done at the apothecary's. And well she might.

The articles brought in by the servant were simply a little pound-cake and cordial, a tumbler half-filled with the *sirop naturelle* of the sugar-cane, and a small piece of candle of the kind made from the fragrant green wax of the candleberry myrtle. These were set upon the small table, the bit of candle standing, lighted, in the tumbler of sirup, the cake on a plate, the cordial in a wine-glass. This feeble child's play was all; except that as Palmyre closed out all daylight from the room and received the offering of silver that "paid the floor" and averted *guillons* (interferences of outside imps), Aurora,—alas! alas!— went down upon her knees with her gaze fixed upon the candle's flame, and silently called on Assonquer (the imp of good fortune) to cast his snare in her behalf around the mind and heart of—she knew not whom.

By and by her lips, which had moved at first, were still and she only watched the burning wax. When the flame rose clear and long it was a sign that Assonquer was enlisted in the coveted endeavor. When the wick sputtered, the devotee trembled in fear of failure. Its charred end curled down and twisted away from her and her heart sank; but the tall figure of Palmyre for a moment came between, the wick was snuffed, the flame tapered up again and for a long time burned a bright, tremulous cone. Again the wick turned down, but this time toward her,—a propitious omen,—and suddenly fell through the expended wax and went out in the sirup.

The daylight, as Palmyre let it once more into the apartment, showed Aurora sadly agitated. In evidence of the innocence of her fluttering heart, guilt, at least for the moment, lay on it, an appalling burden.

"That is all, Palmyre, is it not? I am sure that is all—it must be all. I cannot stay any longer. I wish I was with Clotilde; I have stayed too long."

"Yes; all for the present," replied the quadroon. "Here, here is some charmed basil; hold it between your lips as you walk——"

"But I am going to my landlord's office!"

"Office? Nobody is at his office now; it is too late. You would find that your landlord had gone to dinner. I will tell you, though, where you *must* go. First go home; eat your dinner; and this evening [the Creoles never say afternoon], about a half-hour before sunset, walk down Royale to the lower corner of the Place d'Armes, pass entirely around the square and return up Royale. Never look behind until you get into your house again."

Aurora blushed with shame.

"Alone?" she exclaimed, quite unnerved and tremulous.

"You will seem to be alone; but I will follow behind you when you pass here. Nothing shall hurt you. If you do that, the charm will certainly work; if you do not——"

The quadroon's intentions were good. She was determined to see who it was that could so infatuate her dear little Momselle; and, as on such an evening as the present afternoon promised to merge into, all New Orleans promenaded on the Place d'Armes and the levee, her charm was a very practical one.

"And that will bring the money, will it?" asked Aurora.

"It will bring anything you want."

"Possible?"

"These things that *you* want, Momselle Aurore, are easy to bring. You have no charms working against you. But, oh! I wish to God I could work the *curse I* want to work!" The woman's eyes blazed, her bosom heaved, she lifted her clenched hand above her head and looked upward, crying: "I would give this right hand off at the wrist to catch Agricola Fusilier where I could work him a curse! But I shall; I shall some day be revenged!" She pitched her voice still higher. "I cannot die till I have been! There is nothing that could kill me, I want my revenge so bad!" As suddenly as she had broken out, she hushed, unbarred the door, and with a stern farewell smile saw Aurora turn homeward.

"Give me something to eat, *chérie*," cried the exhausted lady, dropping into Clotilde's chair and trying to die.

"Ah! *maman,* what makes you look so sick?"

Aurora waved her hand contemptuously and gasped.

"Did you see him? What kept you so long—so long?"

"Ask me nothing; I am so enraged with disappointment. He was gone to dinner!"

"Ah! my poor mother!"

"And I must go back as soon as I can take a little *sieste*. I am determined to see him this very day."

"Ah! my poor mother!"

15 Rolled in the Dust

"No, Frowenfeld," said little Doctor Keene, speaking for the after-dinner loungers, "you must take a little human advice. Go, get the air on the Plaza. We will keep shop for you. Stay as long as you like and come home in any condition you think best." And Joseph, tormented into this course, put on his hat and went out.

"Hard to move as a cow in the moonlight," continued Doctor Keene, "and knows just about as much of the world. He wasn't aware, until I told him to-day, that there are two Honoré Grandissimes." [Laughter.]

"Why did you tell him?"

"I didn't give him anything but the bare fact. I want to see how long it will take him to find out the rest."

The Place d'Armes offered amusement to every one else rather than to the immigrant. The family relation, the most noticeable feature of its well-pleased groups, was to him too painful a reminder of his late losses, and, after an honest endeavor to flutter out of the inner twilight of himself into the outer glare of a moving world, he had given up the effort and had passed beyond the square and seated himself upon a rude bench which encircled the trunk of a willow on the levee.

The negress, who, resting near by with a tray of cakes before her, has been for some time contemplating the three-quarter face of her unconscious neighbor, drops her head at last with a small, Ethiopian, feminine laugh. It is a self-confession that, pleasant as the study of his countenance is, to resolve that study into knowledge is beyond her powers; and very pardonably so it is, she being but a *marchande des gâteaux* (an itinerant cake-vender), and he, she concludes, a man of parts. There is a purpose, too, as well as an admission, in the laugh. She would like to engage him in conversation. But he does not notice. Little supposing he is the object of even a cake-merchant's attention, he is lost in idle meditation.

One would guess his age to be as much as twenty-six. His face is beardless, of course, like almost everybody's around him, and of a German kind of seriousness. A certain diffidence in his look may tend to render him unattractive to careless eyes, the more so since he has a slight appearance of self-neglect. On a second glance, his refinement shows out more distinctly, and one also sees that he is not shabby. The little that seems lacking is woman's care, the brush of attentive fingers here and there, the turning of a fold in the high-collared coat, and a mere touch on the neckerchief and shirt-frill. He has a decidedly good forehead. His blue eyes, while they are both strong and modest, are noticeable, too, as betraying fatigue, and the shade of gravity in them is deepened by a certain worn look of excess—in books; a most unusual look in New Orleans in those days, and pointedly out of keeping with the scene which was absorbing his attention.

You might mistake the time for mid-May. Before the view lies the Place d'Armes in its green-breasted uniform of new spring grass crossed diagonally with white shell walks for facings, and dotted with the *élite* of the city for decorations. Over the line of shade-trees which marks its farther boundary, the white-topped twin turrets of St. Louis Cathedral look across it and beyond the bared site of the removed battery (built by the busy Carondelet to protect Louisiana from herself and Kentucky, and razed by his immediate successors) and out upon the Mississippi, the color of whose surface is beginning to change with the changing sky of this beautiful and now departing day. A breeze, which is almost early June, and which has been hovering over the bosom of the great river and above the turf-covered levee, ceases, as if it sank exhausted under its burden of spring odors, and in the profound calm the cathedral bell strikes the sunset hour. From its neighboring garden, the convent of the Ursulines responds in a tone of devoutness, while from the parapet of the less pious little Fort St. Charles, the evening gun sends a solemn ejaculation rumbling down the "coast"; a drum rolls, the air rises again from the water like a flock of birds, and many in the square and on the levee's crown turn and accept its gentle blowing. Rising over the levee willows, and sinking into the streets,— which are lower than the water,—it flutters among the balconies and in and out of dim Spanish arcades, and finally drifts away toward that part of the sky where the sun is sinking behind the low, unbroken line of forest. There is such seduction in the evening air, such sweetness of flowers on its every motion, such lack of cold, or heat, or dust, or wet, that the people have no heart to stay in-doors; nor is there any reason why they should. The levee road is dotted with horsemen, and the willow avenue on the levee's crown, the whole short mile between Terre aux Bœufs gate on the right and Tchoupitoulas gate on the left, is bright with promenaders, although the hour is brief and there will be no twilight; for, so far from being May, it is merely that same nineteenth of which we have already spoken,—the nineteenth of Louisiana's delicious February.

Among the throng were many whose names were going to be written large in history. There was Casa Calvo,—Sebastian de Casa Calvo de la Puerta y O'Farril, Marquis of Casa Calvo,—a man then at the fine age of fifty-three, elegant, fascinating, perfect in Spanish courtesy and Spanish diplomacy, rolling by in a showy equipage surrounded by a clanking body-guard of the Catholic king's cavalry. There was young Daniel Clark, already beginning to amass those riches which an age of litigation has not to this day consumed; it was he whom the French colonial prefect, Laussat, in a late letter to France, had extolled as a man whose "talents for intrigue were carried to a rare degree of excellence." There was Laussat himself, in the flower of his years, sour 'with pride, conscious of great official insignificance and full of petty spites—he yet tarried in a land where his beautiful wife was the "model of taste." There was that convivial old fox, Wilkinson, who had plotted for years with Miro and did not sell himself and his country to Spain because—as we now say—"he found he could do better"; who modestly confessed himself in a traitor's letter to the Spanish king as a man "whose head may err, but whose heart cannot deceive!" and who brought Governor Gayoso to an early death-bed by simply out-drinking him. There also was Edward Livingston, attorney-at-law, inseparably joined to the mention of the famous Batture cases—though that was later. There also was that terror of colonial peculators, the old ex-Intendant Morales, who, having quarrelled with every governor of Louisiana he ever saw, was now snarling at Casa Calvo from force of habit.

And the Creoles—the Knickerbockers of Louisiana—but time would fail us. The Villeres and Destrehans—patriots and patriots' sons; the De la Chaise family in mourning for young Auguste La Chaise of Kentuckian-Louisianian-San Domingan history; the Livaudaises, *père et fils,* of Haunted House fame, descendants of the first pilot of the Belize; the pirate brothers Lafitte, moving among the best; Marigny de Mandeville, afterward the marquis member of Congress; the Davezacs, the Mossys, the Boulignys, the Labatuts, the Bringiers, the De Trudeaus, the De Macartys, the De la Houssayes, the De Lavillebœuvres, the Grandprés, the Forstalls; and the proselyted Creoles: Etienne de Boré (he was the father of all such as handle the sugar-kettle); old man Pitot, who became mayor; Madame Pontalba and her unsuccessful suitor, John McDonough; the three Girods, the two Graviers, or the lone Julian Poydras, godfather of orphan girls. Besides these, and among them as shining fractions of the community, the numerous representatives of the not only noble, but noticeable and ubiquitous, family of Grandissime: Grandissimes simple and Grandissimes compound; Brahmins, Mandarins and Fusiliers. One, 'Polyte by name, a light, gay fellow, with classic features, hair turning gray, is standing and conversing with this group here by the mock-cannon inclosure of the grounds. Another, his cousin, Charlie Mandarin, a tall, very slender, bronzed gentleman in a flannel hunting-shirt and buckskin leggins, is walking, in moccasins, with a sweet lady in whose tasteful attire feminine scrutiny, but such only, might detect economy, but whose marked beauty of yesterday is retreating and re-appearing in the flock of children who are noisily running round and round them, nominally in the care of three fat and venerable black nurses. Another, yonder, Théophile Grandissime, is whipping his stockings with his cane, a lithe youngster in the height of the fashion (be it understood the fashion in New Orleans was five years or so behind Paris), with a joyous, noble face, a merry tongue and giddy laugh, and a confession of experiences which these pages, fortunately for their moral tone, need not recount. All these were there and many others.

This throng, shifting like the fragments of colored glass in the kaleidoscope, had its far-away interest to the contemplative Joseph. To them he was of little interest, or none. Of the many passers, scarcely an occasional one greeted him, and such only with an extremely polite and silent dignity which seemed to him like saying something of this sort: "Most noble alien, give you good-day—stay where you are. Profoundly yours——"

Two men came through the Place d'Armes on conspicuously fine horses. One it is not necessary to describe. The other, a man of perhaps thirty-three or thirty-four years of age, was extremely handsome and well dressed, the martial fashion of the day show-ing his tall and finely knit figure to much advantage. He sat his horse with an uncommon grace, and, as he rode beside his com-panion, spoke and gave ear by turns with an easy dignity suffi-cient of itself to have attracted popular observation. It was the apothecary's unknown friend. Frowenfeld noticed them while they were yet in the middle of the grounds. He could hardly have failed to do so, for some one close beside his bench in undoubted allusion to one of the approaching figures exclaimed:

"Here comes Honoré Grandissime."

Moreover, at that moment there was a slight unwonted stir on the Place d'Armes. It began at the farther corner of the square, hard by the Principal, and spread so quickly through the groups near about, that in a minute the entire company were quietly made aware of something going notably wrong in their immedi-ate presence. There was no running to see it. There seemed to be not so much as any verbal communication of the matter from mouth to mouth. Rather a consciousness appeared to catch noise-lessly from one to another as the knowledge of human intrusion comes to groups of deer in a park. There was the same elevating of the head here and there, the same rounding of beautiful eyes. Some stared, others slowly approached, while others turned and moved away; but a common indignation was in the breast of that thing dreadful everywhere, but terrible in Louisiana, the Major-ity. For there, in the presence of those good citizens, before the eyes of the proudest and fairest mothers and daughters of New Orleans, glaringly, on the open Plaza, the Creole whom Joseph had met by the graves in the field, Honoré Grandissime, the uttermost flower on the topmost branch of the tallest family tree ever transplanted from France to Louisiana, Honoré,—the worshiped, the magnificent,—in the broad light of the sun's going down, rode side by side with the Yankee governor and was not ashamed!

Joseph, on his bench, sat contemplating the two parties to this scandal as they came toward him. Their horses' flanks were damp from some pleasant gallop, but their present gait was the soft, mettlesome movement of animals who will even submit to walk if their masters insist. As they wheeled out of the broad diagonal path that crossed the square, and turned toward him in the highway, he fancied that the Creole observed him. He was not mistaken. As they seemed about to pass the spot where he sat, M. Grandissime interrupted the governor with a word and turning his horse's head, rode up to the bench, lifting his hat as he came.

"Good-evening, Mr. Frowenfeld."

Joseph, looking brighter than when he sat unaccosted, rose and blushed.

"Mr. Frowenfeld, you know my uncle very well, I believe—Agricole Fusilier—long beard?"

"Oh! yes, sir, certainly."

"Well, Mr. Frowenfeld, I shall be much obliged if you will tell him—that is, should you meet him this evening—that I wish to see him. If you will be so kind?"

"Oh! yes, sir, certainly."

Frowenfeld's diffidence made itself evident in this reiterated phrase.

"I do not know that you will see him, but if you should, you know——"

"Oh, certainly, sir!"

The two paused a single instant, exchanging a smile of amiable reminder from the horseman and of bashful but pleased acknowledgment from the one who saw his precepts being reduced to practice.

"Well, good-evening, Mr. Frowenfeld."

M. Grandissime lifted his hat and turned. Frowenfeld sat down.

"*Bou zou, Miché Honoré!*" called the *marchande*.

"*Comment to yé, Clemence?*"

The merchant waved his hand as he rode away with his companion.

"*Beau Miché, là,*" said the *marchande,* catching Joseph's eye.

He smiled his ignorance and shook his head.

"Dass one fine gen'leman," she repeated. "*Mo pa'lé Anglé,*" she added with a chuckle.

"You know him?"

"Oh! yass, sah; Mawse Honoré knows me, yass. All de gen'lemens knows me. I sell de *calas;* mawnin's sell *calas,* evenin's sell zinzer-cake. *You* know me" (a fact which Joseph had all along been aware of). "Dat me w'at pass in rue Royale ev'y mawnin' holl'in' '*Bé calas touts chauds,*' an' singin'; don't you know?"

The enthusiasm of an artist overcame any timidity she might have been supposed to possess, and, waiving the formality of an invitation, she began, to Frowenfeld's consternation, to sing, in a loud, nasal voice.

But the performance, long familiar, attracted no public attention, and he for whose special delight it was intended had taken an attitude of disclaimer and was again contemplating the quiet groups of the Place d'Armes and the pleasant hurry of the levee road.

"Don't you know?" persisted the woman. "Yass, sah, dass me; I's Clemence."

But Frowenfeld was looking another way.

"You know my boy," suddenly said she.

Frowenfeld looked at her.

"Yass, sah. Dat boy w'at bring you de box of *basilic* lass Chrismus; dass my boy."

She straightened her cakes on the tray and made some changes in their arrangement that possibly were important.

"I learned to speak English in Fijinny. Bawn dah."

She looked steadily into the apothecary's absorbed countenance for a full minute, then let her eyes wander down the highway. The human tide was turning cityward. Presently she spoke again.

"Folks comin' home a'ready, yass."

Her hearer looked down the road.

Suddenly a voice that, once heard, was always known,—deep and pompous, as if a lion roared,—sounded so close behind him as to startle him half from his seat.

83

"Is this a corporeal man, or must I doubt my eyes? Hah! Professor Frowenfeld!" it said.

"Mr. Fusilier!" exclaimed Frowenfeld in a subdued voice, while he blushed again and looked at the newcomer with that sort of awe which children experience in a menagerie.

"*Citizen* Fusilier," said the lion.

Agricola indulged to excess the grim hypocrisy of brandishing the catch-words of new-fangled reforms; they served to spice a breath that was strong with the praise of the "superior liberties of Europe,"—those old, cast-iron tyrannies to get rid of which America was settled.

Frowenfeld smiled amusedly and apologetically at the same moment.

"I am glad to meet you. I——"

He was going on to give Honoré Grandissime's message, but was interrupted.

"My young friend," rumbled the old man in his deepest key, smiling emotionally and holding and solemnly continuing to shake Joseph's hand, "I am sure you are. You ought to thank God that you have my acquaintance."

Frowenfeld colored to the temples.

"I must acknowledge——" he began.

"Ah!" growled the lion, "your beautiful modesty leads you to misconstrue me, sir. You pay my judgment no compliment. I know your worth, sir; I merely meant, sir, that in me—poor, humble me—you have secured a sympathizer in your tastes and plans. Agricola Fusilier, sir, is not a cock on a dunghill, to find a jewel and then scratch it aside."

The smile of diffidence, but not the flush, passed from the young man's face, and he sat down forcibly.

"You jest," he said.

The reply was a majestic growl.

"I *never* jest!" The speaker half sat down, then straightened up again. "Ah, the Marquis of Casa Calvo!—I must bow to him, though an honest man's bow is more than he deserves."

"More than he deserves?" was Frowenfeld's query.

"More than he deserves!" was the response.

"What has he done? I have never heard——"

The denunciator turned upon Frowenfeld his most royal frown, and retorted with a question which still grows wild in Louisiana:

"What"—he seemed to shake his mane—"what has he *not* done, sir?" and then he withdrew his frown slowly, as if to add, "You'll be careful next time how you cast doubt upon a public official's guilt."

The marquis's cavalcade came briskly jingling by. Frowenfeld saw within the carriage two men, one in citizen's dress, the other in a brilliant uniform. The latter leaned forward, and, with a cordiality which struck the young spectator as delightful, bowed. The immigrant glanced at Citizen Fusilier, expecting to see the greeting returned with great haughtiness; instead of which that person uncovered his leonine head, and, with a solemn sweep of his cocked hat, bowed half his length. Nay, he more than bowed, he bowed down—so that the action hurt Frowenfeld from head to foot.

"What large gentleman was that sitting on the other side?" asked the young man, as his companion sat down with the air of having finished an oration.

"No gentleman at all!" thundered the citizen. "That fellow" (beetling frown), "that *fellow* is Edward Livingston."

"The great lawyer?"

"The great villain!"

Frowenfeld himself frowned.

The old man laid a hand upon his junior's shoulder and growled benignantly:

"My young friend, your displeasure delights me!"

The patience with which Frowenfeld was bearing all this forced a chuckle and shake of the head from the *marchande*.

Citizen Fusilier went on speaking in a manner that might be construed either as address or soliloquy, gesticulating much and occasionally letting out a fervent word that made passers look around and Joseph inwardly wince. With eyes closed and hands folded on the top of the knotted staff which he carried but never used, he delivered an apostrophe to the "spotless soul of youth," enticed by the "spirit of adventure" to "launch away upon the unploughed sea of the future!" He lifted one hand and smote the back of the other solemnly, once, twice, and again, nodding his head faintly several times without opening his eyes, as who should say, "Very impressive; go on," and so resumed; spoke of this spotless soul of youth searching under unknown latitudes for the "sunken treasures of experience"; indulged, as the reporters of our day would say, in "many beautiful flights of rhetoric," and finally depicted the loathing with which the spotless soul of youth "recoils!"—suiting the action to the word so emphatically as to make a pretty little boy who stood gaping at him start back—"on encountering in the holy chambers of public office the vultures hatched in the nests of ambition and avarice!"

Three or four persons lingered carelessly near by with ears wide open. Frowenfeld felt that he must bring this to an end, and, like any young person who has learned neither deceit nor disrespect to seniors, he attempted to reason it down.

"You do not think many of our public men are dishonest!"

"Sir!" replied the rhetorician, with a patronizing smile, "h-you must be thinking of France!"

"No, sir; of Louisiana."

"Louisiana! Dishonest? All, sir, all. They are all as corrupt as Olympus, sir!"

"Well," said Frowenfeld, with more feeling than was called for, "there is one who, I feel sure, is pure. I know it by his face!"

The old man gave a look of stern interrogation.

"Governor Claiborne."

"Ye-e-e g-hods! Claiborne! *Claiborne!* Why, he is a Yankee!"

The lion glowered over the lamb like a thunder-cloud.

"He is a Virginian," said Frowenfeld.

"He is an American, and no American can be honest."

"You are prejudiced," exclaimed the young man.

Citizen Fusilier made himself larger.

"What is prejudice? I do not know."

"I am an American myself," said Frowenfeld, rising up with his face burning.

The citizen rose up also, but unruffled.

"My beloved young friend," laying his hand heavily upon the other's shoulder, "you are not. You were merely born in America."

But Frowenfeld was not appeased.

"Hear me through," persisted the flatterer. "You were merely born in America. I, too, was born in America; but will any man responsible for his opinion mistake me—Agricola Fusilier—for an American?"

He clutched his cane in the middle and glared around, but no person seemed to be making the mistake to which he so scornfully alluded, and he was about to speak again when an outcry

86

of alarm coming simultaneously from Joseph and the *marchande* directed his attention to a lady in danger.

The scene, as afterward recalled to the mind of the un-American citizen, included the figures of his nephew and the new governor returning up the road at a canter; but, at the time, he knew only that a lady of unmistakable gentility, her back toward him, had just gathered her robes and started to cross the road, when there was a general cry of warning, and the *marchande* cried *"garde choual!"* while the lady leaped directly into the danger and his nephew's horse knocked her to the earth!

Though there was a rush to the rescue from every direction, she was on her feet before any one could reach her, her lips compressed, nostrils dilated, cheek burning, and eyes flashing a lady's wrath upon a dismounted horseman. It was the governor. As the crowd had rushed in, the startled horses, from whom the two riders had instantly leaped, drew violently back, jerking their masters with them and leaving only the governor in range of the lady's angry eye.

"Mademoiselle!" he cried, striving to reach her.

She pointed him in gasping indignation to his empty saddle, and, as the crowd farther separated them, waved away all permission to apologize and turned her back.

"Hah!" cried the crowd, echoing her humor.

"Lady," interposed the governor, "do not drive us to the rudeness of leaving——"

"*Animal, vous!*" cried half a dozen, and the lady gave him such a look of scorn that he did not finish his sentence.

"Open the way, there," called a voice in French.

It was Honoré Grandissime. But just then he saw that the lady found the best of protectors, and the two horsemen, having no choice, remounted and rode away. As they did so, M. Grandissime called something hurriedly to Frowenfeld, on whose arm the lady hung, concerning the care of her; but his words were lost in the short yell of derision sent after himself and his companion by the crowd.

Old Agricola, meanwhile, was having a trouble of his own. He had followed Joseph's wake as he pushed through the throng; but as the lady turned her face he wheeled abruptly away. This brought again in view the bench he had just left, whereupon he, in turn, cried out, and, dashing through all obstructions, rushed back to it, lifting his ugly staff as he went and flourishing it in the face of Palmyre Philosophe.

She stood beside the seat with the smile of one foiled and intensely conscious of peril, but neither frightened nor suppliant, holding back with her eyes the execution of Agricola's threat against her life.

Presently she drew a short step backward, then another, then a third, and then turned and moved away down the avenue of willows, followed for a few steps by the lion and by the laughing comment of the *marchande*, who stood looking after them with her tray balanced on her head.

"*Ya, ya! ye connais voudou bien!*" *

The old man turned to rejoin his companion. The day was rapidly giving place to night and the people were withdrawing to their homes. He crossed the levee, passed through the Place d'Armes and on into the city without meeting the object of his search. For Joseph and the lady had hurried off together.

As the populace floated away in knots of three, four and five, those who had witnessed mademoiselle's (?) mishap told it to those who had not; explaining that it was the accursed Yankee governor who had designedly driven his horse at his utmost speed against the fair victim (some of them butted against their hearers by way of illustration); that the fiend had then maliciously laughed; that this was all the Yankees came to New Orleans for, and that there was an understanding among them—"Understanding, indeed!" exclaimed one. "They have instructions from the President!"—that unprotected ladies should be run down wherever overtaken. If you didn't believe it you could ask the tyrant, Claiborne, himself; he made no secret of it. One or two—but they were considered by others extravagant—testified that, as the lady fell, they had seen his face distorted with a horrid delight, and had heard him cry: "Daz de way to knog them!"

"But how came a lady to be out on the levee, at sun set, on foot and alone?" asked a citizen, and another replied—both using the French of the late province:

"As for being on foot"—a shrug. "But she was not alone; she had a *milatraisse* behind her."

"Ah! so; that was well."

"But—ha, ha!—the *milatraisse*, seeing her mistress out of dan-

* "They're up in the voudou arts."

88

ger, takes the opportunity to try to bring the curse upon Agricola Fusilier by sitting down where he had just risen up, and had to get away from him as quickly as possible to save her own skull."

"And left the lady?"

"Yes; and who took her to her home at last, but Frowenfeld, the apothecary!"

"Ho, ho! the astrologer! We ought to hang that fellow."

"With his books tied to his feet," suggested a third citizen. "It is no more than we owe to the community to go and smash his show-window. He had better behave himself. Come, gentlemen, a little *taffia* will do us good. When shall we ever get through these exciting times?"

16 Starlight in the Rue Chartres

"Oh! M'sieur Frowenfel', tague me ad home!"

It was Aurora, who caught the apothecary's arm vehemently in both her hands with a look of beautiful terror. And whatever Joseph's astronomy might have previously taught him to the contrary, he knew by his senses that the earth thereupon turned entirely over three times in two seconds.

His confused response, though unintelligible, answered all purposes, as the lady found herself the next moment hurrying across the Place d'Armes close to his side, and as they by-and-by passed its farther limits she began to be conscious that she was clinging to her protector as though she would climb up and hide under his elbow. As they turned up the rue Chartres she broke the silence.

"Oh!-h!"—breathlessly,—" 'h!—M'sieur Frowenf—you walkin' so faz!"

"Oh!" echoed Frowenfeld, "I did not know what I was doing."

"Ha, ha, ha," laughed the lady, "me, too, juz de sem lag you! *attendez;* wait."

They halted; a moment's deft manipulation of a veil turned it into a wrapping for her neck.

" 'Sieur Frowenfel', oo dad man was? You know 'im?"

She returned her hand to Frowenfeld's arm and they moved on.

90

"The one who spoke to you, or—you know the one who got near enough to apologize is not the one whose horse struck you!"

"I din know. But oo dad odder one? I saw h-only 'is back, bud I thing it is de sem——"

She identified it with the back that was turned to her during her last visit to Frowenfeld's shop; but finding herself about to mention a matter so nearly connected with the purse of gold, she checked herself; but Frowenfeld, eager to say a good word for his acquaintance, ventured to extol his character while he concealed his name.

"While I have never been introduced to him, I have some acquaintance with him, and esteem him a noble gentleman."

"W'ere you meet him?"

"I met him first," he said, "at the graves of my parents and sisters."

There was a kind of hush after the mention, and the lady made no reply.

"It was some weeks after my loss," resumed Frowenfeld.

"In wad *cimetière* dad was?"

"In no cemetery—being Protestants, you know——"

"Ah, yes, sir!" with a gentle sigh.

"The physician who attended me procured permission to bury them on some private land below the city."

"Not in de groun'?" *

"Yes; that was my father's expressed wish when he died."

"You 'ad de fivver? Oo nurse you w'en you was sick?"

"An old hired negress."

"Dad was all?"

"Yes."

"Hm-m-m!" she said piteously, and laughed in her sleeve.

Who could hope to catch and reproduce the continuous lively thrill which traversed the frame of the escaped book-worm as every moment there was repeated to his consciousness the knowledge that he was walking across the vault of heaven with the evening star on his arm—at least, that he was, at her instigation, killing time along the dim, ill-lighted *trottoirs* of the rue Chartres, with Aurora listening sympathetically at his side. But let it go; also the sweet broken English with which she now and then interrupted him; also the inward, hidden sparkle of her dancing

* Only Jews and paupers are buried in the ground in New Orleans.

Gallic blood; her low, merry laugh; the roguish mental reservation that lurked behind her graver speeches; the droll bravados she uttered against the powers that be, as with timid fingers he brushed from her shoulder a little remaining dust of the late encounter—these things, we say, we let go,—as we let butterflies go rather than pin them to paper.

They had turned into the rue Bienville, and were walking toward the river, Frowenfeld in the midst of a long sentence, when a low cry of tearful delight sounded in front of them, some one in long robes glided forward, and he found his arm relieved of its burden and that burden transferred to the bosom and passionate embrace of another—we had almost said a fairer—Creole, amid a bewildering interchange of kisses and a pelting shower of Creole French.

A moment after, Frowenfeld found himself introduced to "my dotter, Clotilde," who all at once ceased her demonstrations of affection and bowed to him with a majestic sweetness, that seemed one instant grateful and the next, distant.

"I can hardly understand that you are not sisters," said Frowenfeld, a little awkwardly.

"Ah! *ecoutez!*" exclaimed the younger.

"Ah! *par exemple!*" cried the elder, and they laughed down each other's throats, while the immigrant blushed.

This encounter was presently followed by a silent surprise when they stopped and turned before the door of No. 19, and Frowenfeld contrasted the women with their painfully humble dwelling. But therein is where your true Creole was, and still continues to be, properly, yea, delightfully un-American; the outside of his house may be as rough as the outside of a bird's nest; it is the inside that is for the birds; and the front room of this house, when the daughter presently threw open the batten shutters of its single street door, looked as bright and happy, with its candelabras glittering on the mantel, and its curtains of snowy lace, as its bright-eyed tenants.

"'Sieur Frowenfel', if you pliz to come in," said Aurora, and the timid apothecary would have bravely accepted the invitation, but for a quick look which he saw the daughter give the mother; whereupon he asked, instead, permission to call at some future day, and received the cordial leave of Aurora and another bow from Clotilde.

17 That Night

Do we not fail to accord to our nights their true value? We are ever giving to our days the credit and blame of all we do and mis-do, forgetting those silent, glimmering hours when plans—and sometimes plots—are laid; when resolutions are formed or changed; when heaven, and sometimes heaven's enemies, are invoked; when anger and evil thoughts are recalled, and sometimes hate made to inflame and fester; when problems are solved, riddles guessed, and things made apparent in the dark, which day refused to reveal. Our nights are the keys to our days. They explain them. They are also the day's correctors. Night's leisure untangles the mistakes of day's haste. We should not attempt to comprise our pasts in the phrase, "in those days"; we should rather say "in those days and nights."

That night was a long-remembered one to the apothecary of the rue Royale. But it was after he had closed his shop, and in his back room sat pondering the unusual experiences of the evening, that it began to be, in a higher degree, a night of events to most of those persons who had a part in its earlier incidents.

That Honoré Grandissime whom Frowenfeld had only this day learned to know as *the* Honoré Grandissime and the young governor-general were closeted together.

"What can you expect, my-de-seh?" the Creole was asking, as they confronted each other in the smoke of their choice tobacco. "Remember, they are citizens by compulsion. You say your best and wisest law is that one prohibiting the slave-trade; my-de-seh, I assure you, privately, I agree with you; but they abhor your law!

"Your principal danger—at least, I mean difficulty—is this: that the Louisianais themselves, some in pure lawlessness, some through loss of office, some in a vague hope of preserving the old condition of things, will not only hold off from all participation in your government, but will make all sympathy with it, all advocacy of its principles, and especially all office-holding under it, odious—disreputable—infamous. You may find yourself constrained to fill your offices with men who can face down the contumely of a whole people. You know what such men generally are. One out of a hundred may be a moral hero—the ninety-nine will be scamps; and the moral hero will most likely get his brains blown out early in the day.

"Count O'Reilly, when he established the Spanish power here thirty-five years ago, cut a similar knot with the executioner's sword; but, my-de-seh, you are here to establish a *free* government; and how can you make it freer than the people wish it? There is your riddle! They hold off and say, 'Make your government as free as you can, but do not ask us to help you'; and before you know it you have no retainers but a gang of shameless mercenaries, who will desert you whenever the indignation of this people overbalances their indolence; and you will fall the victim of what you may call our mutinous patriotism."

The governor made a very quiet, unappreciative remark about a "patriotism that lets its government get choked up with corruption and then blows it out with gunpowder!"

The Creole shrugged.

"And repeats the operation indefinitely," he said.

The governor said something often heard, before and since, to the effect that communities will not sacrifice themselves for mere ideas.

"My-de-seh," replied the Creole, "you speak like a true Anglo-Saxon; but, sir! how many, many communities have *committed suicide*. And this one?—why, it is *just* the kind to do it!"

"Well," said the governor, smilingly, "you have pointed out

what you consider to be the breakers, now can you point out the channel?"

"Channel? There is none! And you, nor I, cannot dig one. Two great forces *may* ultimately do it, Religion and Education —as I was telling you I said to my young friend, the apothecary, —but still I am free to say what would be my first and principal step, if I was in your place—as I thank God I am not."

The listener asked him what that was.

"Wherever I could find a Creole that I could venture to trust, my-de-seh, I would put him in office. Never mind a little political heterodoxy, you know; almost any man can be trusted to shoot away from the uniform he has on. And then——"

"But," said the other, "I have offered you——"

"Oh!" replied the Creole, like a true merchant, "me, I am too busy; it is impossible! But, I say, I would *compel*, my-de-seh, this people to govern themselves!"

"And pray, how would you give a people a free government and then compel them to administer it?"

"My-de-seh, you should not give one poor Creole the puzzle which belongs to your whole Congress; but you may depend on this, that the worst thing for all parties—and I say it only because it is worst for all—would be a feeble and dilatory punishment of bad faith."

When this interview finally drew to a close the governor had made a memorandum of some fifteen or twenty Grandissimes, scattered through different cantons of Louisiana, who, their kinsman Honoré thought, would not decline appointments.

Certain of the Muses were abroad that night. Faintly audible to the apothecary of the rue Royale through that deserted stillness which is yet the marked peculiarity of New Orleans streets by night, came from a neighboring slave-yard the monotonous chant and machine-like tune-beat of an African dance. There our lately met *marchande* (albeit she was but a guest, fortified against the street-watch with her master's written "pass") led the ancient Calinda dance and that well-known song of derision, in whose ever multiplying stanzas the helpless satire of a feeble race still continues to celebrate the personal failings of each newly prominent figure among the dominant caste. There was a new distich to the song to-night, signifying that the pride of the Grandissimes must find his friends now among the Yankees:

"Miché Hon'ré, allé! h-allé!
Trouvé to zamis parmi les Yankis.
Dancé calinda, bou-joum! bou-joum!
Dancé calinda, bou-joum! bou-joum!"

Frowenfeld, as we have already said, had closed his shop, and was sitting in the room behind it with one arm on his table and the other on his celestial globe, watching the flicker of his small fire and musing upon the unusual experiences of the evening. Upon every side there seemed to start away from his turning glance the multiplied shadows of something wrong. The melancholy face of that Honoré Grandissime, his landlord, at whose mention Dr. Keene had thought it fair to laugh without explaining; the tall, bright-eyed *milatraisse;* old Agricola; the lady of the basil; the newly-identified merchant friend, now the more satisfactory Honoré,—they all came before him in his meditation, provoking among themselves a certain discord, faint but persistent, to which he strove to close his ear. For he was brain-weary. Even in the bright recollection of the lady and her talk he became involved among shadows, and going from bad to worse, seemed at length almost to gasp in an atmosphere of hints, allusions, faint unspoken admissions, ill-concealed antipathies, unfinished speeches, mistaken identities and whisperings of hidden strife. The cathedral clock struck twelve and was answered again from the convent tower; and as the notes died away he suddenly became aware that the weird, drowsy throb of the African song and dance had been swinging drowsily in his brain for an unknown lapse of time.

The apothecary nodded once or twice, and thereupon rose up and prepared for bed, thinking to sleep till morning.

Aurora and her daughter had long ago put out their chamber light. Early in the evening the younger had made favorable mention of retiring, to which the elder replied by asking to be left awhile to her own thoughts. Clotilde, after some tender protestations, consented, and passed through the open door that showed, beyond it, their couch. The air had grown just cool and humid enough to make the warmth of one small brand on the hearth acceptable, and before this the fair widow settled herself to gaze beyond her tiny, slippered feet into its wavering flame, and think. Her thoughts were such as to bestow upon her

96

face that enhancement of beauty that comes of pleasant reverie, and to make it certain that that little city afforded no fairer sight,—unless, indeed, it was the figure of Clotilde just beyond the open door, as in her white night-dress enriched with the work of a diligent needle, she knelt upon the low *prie-Dieu* before the little family altar, and committed her pure soul to the Divine keeping.

Clotilde could have been many minutes asleep when Aurora changed her mind and decided to follow. The shade upon her face had deepened for a moment into a look of trouble; but a bright philosophy, which was part of her paternal birthright, quickly chased it away, and she passed to her room, disrobed, lay softly down beside the beauty already there and smiled herself to sleep,—

> *"Blinded alike from sunshine and from rain,*
> *As though a rose should shut, and be a bud again."*

But she also wakened again, and lay beside her unconscious bed-mate, occupied with the company of her own thoughts. "Why should these little concealments ruffle my bosom? Does not even Nature herself practice wiles? Look at the innocent birds; do they build where everybody can count their eggs? And shall a poor human creature try to be better than a bird? Didn't I say my prayers under the blanket just now?"

Her companion stirred in her sleep, and she rose upon one elbow to bend upon the sleeper a gaze of ardent admiration. "Ah, beautiful little chick! how guileless! indeed, how deficient in that respect!" She sat up in the bed and hearkened; the bell struck for midnight. Was that the hour? The fates were smiling! Surely M. Assonquer himself must have waked her to so choice an opportunity. She ought not to despise it. Now, by the application of another and easily wrought charm, that darkened hour lately spent with Palmyre would have, as it were, its colors set.

The night had grown much cooler. Stealthily, by degrees, she rose and left the couch. The openings of the room were a window and two doors, and these, with much caution, she contrived to open without noise. None of them exposed her to the possibility of public view. One door looked into the dim front room; the window let in only a flood of moonlight over the top of a high house, which was without openings on that side; the other door revealed a weed-grown back yard and that invaluable protector, the cook's hound, lying fast asleep.

In her night-clothes as she was, she stood a moment in the centre of the chamber, then sank upon one knee, rapped the floor gently but audibly thrice, rose, drew a step backward, sank upon the other knee, rapped thrice, rose again, stepped backward, knelt the third time, the third time rapped, and then, rising, murmured a vow to pour upon the ground next day an oblation of champagne—then closed the doors and window and crept back to bed. Then she knew how cold she had become. It seemed as though her very marrow was frozen. She was seized with such an uncontrollable shivering that Clotilde presently opened her eyes, threw her arm about her mother's neck, and said:

"Ah! my sweet mother, are you so cold?"

"The blanket was all off of me," said the mother, returning the embrace, and the two sank into unconsciousness together.

Into slumber sank almost at the same moment Joseph Frowenfeld. He awoke, not a great while later, to find himself standing in the middle of the floor. Three or four men had shouted at once, and three pistol-shots, almost in one instant, had resounded just outside his shop. He had barely time to throw himself into half his garments when the knocker sounded on his street door, and when he opened it Agricola Fusilier entered, supported by his nephew Honoré on one side and Doctor Keene on the other. The latter's right hand was pressed hard against a bloody place in Agricola's side.

"Give us plenty of light, Frowenfeld," said the doctor, "and a chair and some lint, and some Castile soap, and some towels and sticking-plaster, and anything else you can think of. Agricola's about scared to death——"

"Professor Frowenfeld," groaned the aged citizen, "I am basely and mortally stabbed!"

"Right on, Frowenfeld," continued the doctor, "right on into the back room. Fasten that front door. Here, Agricola, sit down here. That's right, Frow, stir up a little fire. Give me—never mind, I'll just cut the cloth open."

There was a moment of silent suspense while the wound was being reached, and then the doctor spoke again.

"Just as I thought; only a safe and comfortable gash that will

98

keep you in-doors a while with your arm in a sling. You are more scared than hurt, I think, old gentleman."

"You think an infernal falsehood, sir!"

"See here, sir," said the doctor, without ceasing to ply his dexterous hands in his art, "I'll jab these scissors into your back if you say that again."

"I suppose," growled the "citizen," "it is just the thing your professional researches have qualified you for, sir!"

"Just stand here, Mr. Frowenfeld," said the little doctor, settling down to a professional tone, "and hand me things as I ask for them. Honoré, please hold this arm; so." And so, after a moderate lapse of time, the treatment that medical science of those days dictated was applied—whatever that was. Let those who do not know give thanks.

M. Grandissime explained to Frowenfeld what had occurred.

"You see, I succeeded in meeting my uncle, and we went together to my office. My uncle keeps his accounts with me. Sometimes we look them over. We stayed until midnight; I dismissed my carriage. As we walked homeward we met some friends coming out of the rooms of the Bagatelle Club; five or six of my uncles and cousins, and also Doctor Keene. We all fell a-talking of my grandfather's *fête de grandpère* of next month, and went to have some coffee. When we separated, and my uncle and my cousin Achille Grandissime, and Doctor Keene and myself came down Royal street, out from that dark alley behind your shop jumped a little man and stuck my uncle with a knife. If I had not caught his arm he would have killed my uncle."

"And he escaped," said the apothecary.

"No, sir!" said Agricola, with his back turned.

"I think he did. I do not think he was struck."

"And Mr. ——, your cousin?"

"Achille? I have sent him for a carriage."

"Why, Agricola," said the doctor, snipping the loose ravellings from his patient's bandages, "an old man like you should not have enemies."

"I am *not* an old man, sir!"

"I said *young* man."

"I am not a *young* man, sir!"

"I wonder who the fellow was," continued Doctor Keene, as he re-adjusted the ripped sleeve.

"That is *my* affair, sir; I know who it was."

"And yet she insists," M. Grandissime was asking Frowenfeld, standing with his leg thrown across the celestial globe, "that I knocked her down intentionally?"

Frowenfeld, about to answer, was interrupted by a knock on the door.

"That is my cousin, with the carriage," said M. Grandissime, following the apothecary into the shop.

Frowenfeld opened to a young man,—a rather poor specimen of the Grandissime type, deficient in stature but not in stage manner.

"*Est il mort?*" he cried at the threshold.

"Mr. Frowenfeld, let me make you acquainted with my cousin, Achille Grandissime."

Mr. Achille Grandissime gave Frowenfeld such a bow as we see now only in pictures.

"Ve'y 'appe to meck yo' acquaintenz!"

Agricola entered, followed by the doctor, and demanded in indignant thunder-tones, as he entered:

"Who—ordered—that—carriage?"

"I did," said Honoré. "Will you please get into it at once."

"Ah! dear Honoré!" exclaimed the old man, "always too kind! I go in it purely to please you."

Good-night was exchanged; Honoré entered the vehicle and Agricola was helped in. Achille touched his hat, bowed and waved his hand to Joseph, and shook hands with the doctor, and saying, "Well, good-night, Doctor Keene," he shut himself out of the shop with another low bow. "Think I am going to shake hands with an apothecary?" thought M. Achille.

Doctor Keene had refused Honoré's invitation to go with them.

"Frowenfeld," he said, as he stood in the middle of the shop wiping a ring with a towel and looking at his delicate, freckled hand, "I propose, before going to bed with you, to eat some of your bread and cheese. Aren't you glad?"

"I shall be, Doctor," replied the apothecary, "if you will tell me what all this means."

"Indeed I will not,—that is, not to-night. What? Why, it would take until breakfast to tell what 'all this means,'—the story of that pestiferous darky Bras Coupé, with the rest? Oh, no, sir. I would sooner not have any bread and cheese. What on earth has waked your curiosity so suddenly, anyhow?"

"Have you any idea who stabbed Citizen Fusilier?" was Joseph's response.

"Why, at first I thought it was the other Honoré Grandissime; but when I saw how small the fellow was, I was at a loss, completely. But, whoever it is, he has my bullet in him, whatever Honoré may think."

"Will Mr. Fusilier's wound give him much trouble?" asked Joseph, as they sat down to a luncheon at the fire.

"Hardly; he has too much of the blood of Lufki-Humma in him. But I need not say that; for the Grandissime blood is just as strong. A wonderful family, those Grandissimes! They are an old, illustrious line, and the strength that was once in the intellect and will is going down into the muscles. I have an idea that their greatness began, hundreds of years ago, in ponderosity of arm,—of frame, say,—and developed from generation to generation, in a rising scale, first into fineness of sinew, then, we will say, into force of will, then into power of mind, then into subtleties of genius. Now they are going back down the incline. Look at Honoré; he is high up on the scale, intellectual and sagacious. But look at him physically, too. What an exquisite mould! What compact strength! I should not wonder if he gets that from the Indian Queen. What endurance he has! He will probably go to his business by and by and not see his bed for seventeen or eighteen hours. He is the flower of the family, and possibly the last one. Now, old Agricola shows the downward grade better. Seventy-five, if he is a day, with, maybe, one-fourth the attainments he pretends to have, and still less good sense; but strong—as an orang-outang. Shall we go to bed?"

18 New Light upon Dark Places

When the long, wakeful night was over, and the doctor gone, Frowenfeld seated himself to record his usual observations of the weather; but his mind was elsewhere—here, there, yonder. There are understandings that expand, not imperceptibly hour by hour, but as certain flowers do, by little explosive ruptures, with periods of quiescence between. After this night of experiences it was natural that Frowenfeld should find the circumference of his perceptions consciously enlarged. The daylight shone, not into his shop alone, but into his heart as well. The face of Aurora, which had been the dawn to him before, was now a perfect sunrise, while in pleasant timeliness had come in this Apollo of a Honoré Grandissime. The young immigrant was dazzled. He felt a longing to rise up and run forward in this flood of beams. He was unconscious of fatigue, or nearly so— would have been wholly so but for the return by and by of that same, dim shadow, or shadows, still rising and darting across every motion of the fancy that grouped again the actors in last night's scenes; not such shadows as naturally go with sunlight to make it seem brighter, but a something which qualified the light's perfection and the air's freshness.

Wherefore, resolved: that he would compound his life, from this time forward, by a new formula: books, so much; observa-

102

tion, so much; social intercourse, so much; love—as to that, time enough for that in the future (if he was in love with anybody, he certainly did not know it); of love, therefore, amount not yet necessary to state, but probably (when it should be introduced), in the generous proportion in which physicians prescribe *aqua*. Resolved, in other words, without ceasing to be Frowenfeld the studious, to begin at once the perusal of this newly found book, the Community of New Orleans. True, he knew he should find it a difficult task—not only that much of it was in a strange tongue, but that it was a volume whose displaced leaves would have to be lifted tenderly, blown free of much dust, re-arranged, some torn fragments laid together again with much painstaking, and even the purport of some pages guessed out. Obviously, the place to commence at was that brightly illuminated title-page, the ladies Nancanou.

As the sun rose and diffused its beams in an atmosphere whose temperature had just been recorded as 50° F., the apothecary stepped half out of his shop-door to face the bracing air that came blowing upon his tired forehead from the north. As he did so, he said to himself:

"How are these two Honoré Grandissimes related to each other, and why should one be thought capable of attempting the life of Agricola?"

The answer was on its way to him.

There is left to our eyes, but a poor vestige of the picturesque view presented to those who looked down the rue Royale before the garish day that changed the rue Enghien into Ingine street, and dropped the 'e' from Royale. It was a long, narrowing perspective of arcades, lattices, balconies, *zaguans*, dormer windows, and blue sky—of low, tiled roofs, red and wrinkled, huddled down into their own shadows; of canvas awnings with fluttering borders, and of grimy lamp-posts twenty feet in height, each reaching out a gaunt iron arm over the narrow street and dangling a lamp from its end. The human life which dotted the view displayed a variety of tints and costumes such as a painter would be glad to take just as he found them: the gayly feathered Indian, the slashed and tinselled Mexican, the leather-breeched raftsmen, the blue- or yellow-turbaned *négresse*, the sugar-planter in white flannel and moccasins, the average townsman in the last suit of clothes of the lately deceased century, and now and then a fashionable man in that costume whose union of tight-buttoned martial severity, swathed throat, and effeminate superabundance of fine linen seemed to offer a sort of state's evidence against the pompous tyrannies and frivolities of the times.

The *marchande des calas* was out. She came toward Joseph's shop, singing in a high-pitched nasal tone this new song:

> "Dé 'tit zozos—yé té assis—
> Dé 'tit zozos—si la barrier.
> De 'tit zozos, qui zabotté;
> Qui ça yé di' mo pas conné.

> "Manzeur-poulet vini simin,
> Croupé si yé et croqué yé;
> Personn' pli' 'tend' yé zabotté—
> Dé 'tit zozos si la barrier."

"You lak dat song?" she asked, with a chuckle, as she let down from her turbaned head a flat Indian basket of warm rice cakes.

"What does it mean?"

She laughed again—more than the questioner could see occasion for.

"Dat mean—two lill birds; dey was sittin' on de fence an' gabblin' togeddah, you know, lak you see two young gals sometime', an' you can't mek out w'at dey sayin', even ef dey know demself? H-ya! Chicken-hawk come 'long dat road an' jes' set down an' munch 'em, an' nobody can't no mo' hea' deir lill gabblin' on de fence, you know."

Here she laughed again.

Joseph looked at her with severe suspicion, but she found refuge in benevolence.

"Honey, you ought to be asleep dis werry minit; look lak folks been a-worr'in' you. I's gwine to pick out de werry bes' *calas* I's got for you."

As she delivered them she courtesied, first to Joseph and then, lower and with hushed gravity, to a person who passed into the shop behind him, bowing and murmuring politely as he passed. She followed the newcomer with her eyes, hastily accepted the price of the cakes, whispered, "Dat's my mawstah," lifted her basket to her head and went away. Her master was Frowenfeld's landlord.

Frowenfeld entered after him, *calas* in hand, and with a grave "good-morning, sir."

"——m'sieu'," responded the landlord, with a low bow.

Frowenfeld waited in silence.

The landlord hesitated, looked around him, seemed about to speak, smiled, and said, in his soft, solemn voice, feeling his way word by word through the unfamiliar language:

"Ah lag to teg you apar'."

"See me alone?"

The landlord recognized his error by a fleeting smile.

"Alone," said he.

"Shall we go into my room?"

"*S'il vous plait, m'sieu'.*"

Frowenfeld's breakfast, furnished by contract from a neighboring kitchen, stood on the table. It was a frugal one, but more comfortable than formerly, and included coffee, that subject of just pride in Creole cookery. Joseph deposited his *calas* with these things and made haste to produce a chair, which his visitor, as usual, declined.

"Idd you' bregfuz, m'sieu'."

"I can do that afterward," said Frowenfeld; but the landlord insisted and turned away from him to look up at the books on the wall, precisely as that other of the same name had done a few weeks before.

Frowenfeld, as he broke his loaf, noticed this, and, as the landlord turned his face to speak, wondered that he had not before seen the common likeness.

"Dez stog," said the sombre man.

"What, sir? Oh—dead stock? But how can the materials of an education be dead stock?"

The landlord shrugged. He would not argue the point. One American trait which the Creole is never entirely ready to encounter is this gratuitous Yankee way of going straight to the root of things.

"Dead stock in a mercantile sense, you mean," continued the apothecary; "but are men right in measuring such things only by their present market value?"

The landlord had no reply. It was little to him, his manner

intimated; his contemplation dwelt on deeper flaws in human right and wrong; yet—but it was needless to discuss it. However, he did speak.

"Ah was elevade in Pariz."

"Educated in Paris," exclaimed Joseph, admiringly. "Then you certainly cannot find *your* education dead stock."

The grave, not amused, smile which was the landlord's only rejoinder, though perfectly courteous, intimated that his tenant was sailing over depths of the question that he was little aware of. But the smile in a moment gave way for the look of one who was engrossed with another subject.

"M'sieu'," he began; but just then Joseph made an apologetic gesture and went forward to wait upon an inquirer after "Godfrey's Cordial"; for that comforter was known to be obtainable at "Frowenfeld's." The business of the American drug-store was daily increasing. When Frowenfeld returned his landlord stood ready to address him, with the air of having decided to make short of a matter.

"M'sieu'——"

"Have a seat, sir," urged the apothecary.

His visitor again declined, with his uniform melancholy grace. He drew close to Frowenfeld.

"Ah wand you mague me one *ouangan*," he said.

Joseph shook his head. He remembered Doctor Keene's expressed suspicion concerning the assault of the night before.

"I do not understand you, sir; what is that?"

"You know."

The landlord offered a heavy, persuading smile.

"An unguent? Is that what you mean—an ointment?"

"M'sieu'," said the applicant, with a not-to-be-deceived expression, "*vous êtes astrologue—magicien*——"

"God forbid!"

The landlord was grossly incredulous.

"You godd one 'P'tit Albert.'"

He dropped his forefinger upon an iron-clasped book on the table, whose title much use had effaced.

"That is the Bible. I do not know what the Tee Albare is!"

Frowenfeld darted an aroused glance into the ever-courteous eyes of his visitor, who said without a motion:

"You di'n't gave Agricola Fusilier *une ouangan, la nuit passé?*"

"Sir?"

"Ee was yeh?—laz nighd?"

"Mr. Fusilier was here last night—yes. He had been attacked by an assassin and slightly wounded. He was accompanied by his nephew, who, I suppose, is your cousin; he has the same name."

Frowenfeld, hoping he had changed the subject, concluded with a propitiatory smile, which, however, was not reflected.

"Ma bruzzah," said the visitor.

"Your brother!"

"Ma whide bruzzah; ah ham nod whide, m'sieu'."

Joseph said nothing. He was too much awed to speak; the ejaculation that started toward his lips turned back and rushed into his heart, and it was the quadroon who, after a moment, broke the silence:

"Ah ham de holdez son of Numa Grandissime."

"Yes—yes," said Frowenfeld, as if he would wave away something terrible.

"Nod sell me—*ouangan?*" asked the landlord, again.

"Sir," exclaimed Frowenfeld, taking a step backward, "pardon me if I offend you; that mixture of blood which draws upon you the scorn of this community, is to me nothing—nothing! And every invidious distinction made against you on that account I despise! But, sir, whatever may be either your private wrongs, or the wrongs you suffer in common with your class, if you have it in your mind to employ any manner of secret art against the interests or person of any one——"

The landlord was making silent protestations, and his tenant, lost in a wilderness of indignant emotions, stopped.

"M'sieu'," began the quadroon, but ceased and stood with an expression of annoyance every moment deepening on his face, until he finally shook his head slowly, and said with a baffled smile: "Ah can nod spig Engliss."

"Write it," said Frowenfeld, lifting forward a chair.

The landlord, for the first time in their acquaintance, accepted a seat, bowing low as he did so, with a demonstration of profound gratitude that just perceptibly heightened his even dignity. Paper, quills, and ink were handed down from a shelf and Joseph retired into the shop.

Honoré Grandissime, f. m. c. (these initials could hardly have come into use until some months later but the convenience covers the sin of the slight anachronism), Honoré Grandissime, free man of color, entered from the rear room so silently that Joseph was first made aware of his presence by feeling him at his elbow. He handed the apothecary—but a few words in time, lest we misjudge.

The father of the two Honorés was that Numa Grandissime —that mere child—whom the Grand Marquis, to the great chagrin of the De Grapions, had so early cadetted. The commission seems not to have been thrown away. While the province was still in first hands, Numa's was a shining name in the annals of Kerlerec's unsatisfactory Indian wars; and in 1768 (when the colonists, ill-informed, inflammable, and long ill-governed, resisted the transfer of Louisiana to Spain), at a time of life when most young men absorb all the political extravagances of their day, he had stood by the side of law and government, though the popular cry was a frenzied one for "liberty." Moreover, he had held back his whole chafing and stamping tribe from a precipice of disaster, and had secured valuable recognition of their office-holding capacities from that really good governor and princely Irishman whose one act of summary vengeance upon a few insurgent office-coveters has branded him in history as Cruel O'Reilly. But the experience of those days turned Numa gray, and withal he was not satisfied with their outcome. In the midst of the struggle he had weakened in one manly resolve— against his will he married. The lady was a Fusilier, Agricola's sister, a person of rare intelligence and beauty, whom, from early childhood, the secret counsels of his seniors had assigned to him. Despite this, he had said he would never marry; he made, he said, no pretensions to severe conscientiousness, or to being better than others, but—as between his Maker and himself —he had forfeited the right to wed, they all knew how. But the Fusiliers had become very angry and Numa, finding strife about to ensue just when without unity he could not bring an undivided clan through the torrent of the revolution, had "nobly sacrificed a little sentimental feeling," as his family defined it, by breaking faith with the mother of the man now standing at Joseph Frowenfeld's elbow, and who was then a little toddling boy. It was necessary to save the party—nay, that was a slip; we should say, to save the family; this is not a parable. Yet Numa loved his wife. She bore him a boy and a girl, twins; and as her son grew in physical, intellectual, and moral symmetry, he indulged the

108

hope that—the ambition and pride of all the various Grandissimes now centering in this lawful son, and all strife being lulled, he should yet see this Honoré right the wrongs which he had not quite dared to uproot. And Honoré inherited the hope and began to make it an intention and aim even before his departure (with his half-brother the other Honoré) for school in Paris, at the early age of fifteen. Numa soon after died, and Honoré, after various fortunes in Paris, London, and elsewhere, in the care, or at least company, of a pious uncle in holy orders, returned to the ancestral mansion. The father's will—by the law they might have set it aside, but that was not their way—left the darker Honoré the bulk of his fortune, the younger a competency. The latter—instead of taking office as an ancient Grandissime should have done—to the dismay and mortification of his kindred, established himself in a prosperous commercial business. The elder bought houses and became a *rentier.*

The landlord handed the apothecary the following writing:

MR. JOSEPH FROWENFELD:

Think not that anybody is to be either poisoned by me nor yet to be made a sufferer by the exercise of anything by me of the character of what is generally known as grigri, otherwise magique. This, sir, I do beg your permission to offer my assurance to you of the same. Ah, no! it is not for that! I am the victim of another entirely and a far differente and dissimilar passion, *i.e.,* Love. Esteemed sir, speaking or writing to you as unto the only man of exclusively white blood whom I believe is in Louisiana willing to do my dumb, suffering race the real justice, I love Palmyre la Philosophe with a madness which is by the human lips or tongues not possible to be exclaimed (as, I may add, that I have in the same like manner since exactley nine years and seven months and some days). Alas! heavens! I can't help it in the least particles at all! What, what shall I do, for ah! it is pitiful! She loves me not at all, but, on the other hand, is (if I suspicion not wrongfully) wrapped up head and ears in devotion of one who does not love her, either, so cold and incapable of appreciation is he. I allude to Honoré Grandissime.

Ah! well do I remember the day when we returned—he and me— from the France. She was there when we landed on that levee, she was among that throng of kindreds and domestiques, she shind like the evening star as she stood there (it was the first time I saw her, but she was known to him when at fifteen he left his home, but I resided, not under my own white father's roof—not at all—far from that). She cried out *"A la fin to vini!"* and leap herself with both resplendant arm around his neck and kist him twice on the one cheek and the other, and her resplendant eyes shining with a so great beauty.

If you will give me a *poudre d'amour* such as I doubt not your great knowledge enable you to make of a power that cannot to be resist, while still at the same time of a harmless character toward the life or the health of such that I shall succeed in its use to gain the affections of that emperice of my soul, I hesitate not to give you such price as it may please you to nominate up as high as to $1,000—nay, more. Sir, will you do that?

I have the honor to remain, sir,

Very respectfully, your obedient servant,

H. GRANDISSIME.

Frowenfeld slowly transferred his gaze from the paper to his landlord's face. Dejection and hope struggled with each other in the gaze that was returned; but when Joseph said, with a countenance full of pity, "I have no power to help you," the disappointed lover merely gazed fixedly for a moment in the direction of the street, then lifted his hat toward his head, bowed, and departed.

19 Art and Commerce

It was some two or three days after the interview just related that the apothecary of the rue Royale found it necessary to ask a friend to sit in the shop a few minutes while he should go on a short errand. He was kept away somewhat longer than he had intended to stay, for, as they were coming out of the cathedral, he met Aurora and Clotilde. Both the ladies greeted him with a cordiality which was almost inebriating. Aurora even extending her hand. He stood but a moment, responding blushingly to two or three trivial questions from Aurora; yet even in so short a time, and although Clotilde gave ear with the sweetest smiles and loveliest changes of countenance, he experienced a lively renewal of a conviction that this young lady was most unjustly harboring toward him a vague disrelish, if not a positive distrust. That she had some mental reservation was certain.

"'Sieur Frowenfel'," said Aurora, as he raised his hat for good-day, "you din come home yet."

He did not understand until he had crimsoned and answered he knew not what—something about having intended every day. He felt lifted he knew not where, Paradise opened, there was a flood of glory, and then he was alone; the ladies, leaving adieux sweeter than the perfume they carried away with them, floated into the south and were gone. Why was it that the elder, though plainly regarded by the younger with admiration, dependence, and overflowing affection, seemed sometimes to be, one might almost say, watched by her? He liked Aurora the better.

On his return to the shop his friend remarked that if he received many such visitors as the one who had called during his absence, he might be permitted to be vain. It was Honoré Grandissime, and he had left no message.

"Frowenfeld," said his friend, "it would pay you to employ a regular assistant."

Joseph was in an abstracted mood.

"I have some thought of doing so."

Unlucky slip! As he pushed open his door next morning, what was his dismay to find himself confronted by some forty men. Five of them leaped up from the door-sill, and some thirty-five from the edge of the *trottoir*, brushed that part of their wearing-apparel which always fits with great neatness on a Creole, and trooped into the shop. The apothecary fell behind his defences, that is to say, his prescription desk, and explained to them in a short and spirited address that he did not wish to employ any of them on any terms. Nine tenths of them understood not a word of English; but his gesture was unmistakable. They bowed gratefully, and said good-day.

Now Frowenfeld did these young men an injustice; and though they were far from letting him know it, some of them felt it and interchanged expressions of feeling reproachful to him as they stopped on the next corner to watch a man painting a sign. He had treated them as if they all wanted situations. Was this so? Far from it. Only twenty men were applicants; the other twenty were friends who had come to see them get the place. And again, though, as the apothecary had said, none of them knew anything about the drug business—no, nor about any other business under the heavens—they were all willing that he should teach them—except one. A young man of patrician softness and costly apparel tarried a moment after the general exodus, and quickly concluded that on Frowenfeld's account it was probably as well that he could not qualify, since he was expecting from France an important government appointment as soon as these troubles should be settled and Louisiana restored to her former happy condition. But he had a friend—a cousin—whom he would recommend, just the man for the position; a splendid fellow; popular, accomplished—what? the best trainer of dogs that M. Frowenfeld might ever hope to look upon; a "so good fisherman as I never saw!"—the marvel of the ball-room—could handle a partner of twice his weight; the speaker had seen him take a lady so tall that his head hardly came up to her bosom, whirl her in the waltz from right to left—this way! and then, as quick as lightning, turn and whirl her this way, from left to right—"so grezful ligue a peajohn! He could read and write, and knew more comig song!"—the speaker would hasten to secure him before he should take some other situation.

The wonderful waltzer never appeared upon the scene; yet Joseph made shift to get along, and by and by found a man who partially met his requirements. The way of it was this: With his forefinger in a book which he had been reading, he was one day pacing his shop floor in deep thought. There were two loose threads hanging from the web of incident weaving around him which ought to connect somewhere; but where? They were the two visits made to his shop by the young merchant, Honoré Grandissime. He stopped still to think; what "train of thought" could he have started in the mind of such a man?

He was about to resume his walk, when there came in, or, more strictly speaking, there shot in, a young, auburn-curled, blue-eyed man, whose adolescent buoyancy, as much as his delicate, silver-buckled feet and clothes of perfect fit, pronounced him all-pure-Creole. His name, when it was presently heard, accounted for the blond type by revealing a Franco-Celtic origin.

" 'Sieur Frowenfel'," he said, advancing like a boy coming in after recess, "I 'ave somet'ing beauteeful to place into yo' window."

He wheeled half around as he spoke and seized from a naked black boy, who at that instant entered, a rectangular object enveloped in paper.

Frowenfeld's window was fast growing to be a place of art exposition. A pair of statuettes, a golden tobacco-box, a costly jewel-casket, or a pair of richly gemmed horse-pistols—the property of some ancient gentleman or dame of emaciated fortune, and which must be sold to keep up the bravery of good clothes and pomade that hid slow starvation, went into the shop-window of the ever-obliging apothecary, to be disposed of by *tombola*. And it is worthy of note in passing, concerning the moral education of one who proposed to make no conscious compromise with any sort of evil, that in this drivelling species of gambling he saw nothing hurtful or improper. But "in Frowenfeld's window" appeared also articles for simple sale or mere transient exhibition; as, for instance, the wonderful tapestries of a blind widow of ninety; tremulous little bunches of flowers, proudly stated to have been made entirely of the bones of the ordinary catfish; others, large and spreading, the sight of which would make any botanist fall down "and die as mad as the wild waves be," whose ticketed merit was that they were composed exclusively of materials produced upon Creole soil; a picture of the Ursulines' convent and chapel, done in forty-five minutes by a child of ten years, the daughter of the widow Felicie Grandissime; and the siege of Troy, in ordinary ink, done entirely with the pen, the labor of twenty years, by "a citizen of New Orleans." It was natural that these things should come to "Frowenfeld's corner," for there, oftener than elsewhere, the critics were gathered together. Ah! wonderful men, those critics; and, fortunately, we have a few still left.

The young man with auburn curls rested the edge of his burden upon the counter, tore away its wrappings and disclosed a painting.

He said nothing—with his mouth; but stood at arm's length balancing the painting and casting now upon it and now upon Joseph Frowenfeld a look more replete with triumph than Cæsar's three-worded dispatch.

The apothecary fixed upon it long and silently the gaze of a somnambulist. At length he spoke:

"What is it?"

"Louisiana rif-using to hanter de h-Union!" replied the Creole, with an ecstasy that threatened to burst forth in hip-hurrahs.

Joseph said nothing, but silently wondered at Louisiana's anatomy.

"Gran' subjec'!" said the Creole.

"Allegorical," replied the hard-pressed apothecary.

"Allegoricon? No, sir! Allegoricon never saw that pigshoe. If you insist to know who make dat pigshoe—de hartis' stan' bif-ore you!"

"It is your work?"

" 'Tis de work of me, Raoul Innerarity, cousin to de distingwish Honoré Grandissime. I swear to you, sir, on stack of Bible' as 'igh as yo' head!"

114

He smote his breast.

"Do you wish to put it in the window?"

"Yes, seh."

"For sale?"

M. Raoul Innerarity hesitated a moment before replying:

"'Sieur Frowenfel', I think it is a foolishness to be too proud, eh? I want you to say, 'My frien', 'Sieur Innerarity, never care to sell anything; 'tis for egshibbyshun'; *mais*—when somebody look at it, so," the artist cast upon his work a look of languishing covetousness, "'you say, *foudre tonnerre!* what de dev'!—I take dat ris-pon-sibble-ty—you can have her for two hun'red fifty dollah!' Better not be too proud, eh, 'Sieur Frowenfel'?"

"No, sir," said Joseph, proceeding to place it in the window, his new friend following him about, spaniel-wise; "but you had better let me say plainly that it is for sale."

"Oh—I don't care—*mais*—my rillation' will never forgive me! *Mais*—go-ahead-I-don't-care! 'Tis for sale."

"'Sieur Frowenfel'," he resumed, as they came away from the window, "one week ago"—he held up one finger—"what I was doing? Makin' bill of ladin', my faith!—for my cousin Honoré! an' now, I ham a hartis'! So soon I foun' dat, I say, 'Cousin Honoré,'"—the eloquent speaker lifted his foot and administered to the empty air a soft, polite kick—"'I never goin' to do anoder lick o' work so long I live; adieu!'"

He lifted a kiss from his lips and wafted it in the direction of his cousin's office.

"Mr. Innerarity," exclaimed the apothecary, "I fear you are making a great mistake."

"You tink I hass too much?"

"Well, sir, to be candid, I do; but that is not your greatest mistake."

"What she's worse?"

The apothecary simultaneously smiled and blushed.

"I would rather not say; it is a passably good example of Creole art; there is but one way by which it can ever be worth what you ask for it."

"What dat is?"

The smile faded and the blush deepened as Frowenfeld replied:

"If it could become the means of reminding this community that crude ability counts next to nothing in art, and that nothing else in this world ought to work so hard as genius, it would be worth thousands of dollars!"

"You tink she is worse a t'ousand dollah?" asked the Creole, shadow and sunshine chasing each other across his face.

"No, sir."

The unwilling critic strove unnecessarily against his smile.

"'Ow much you t'ink?"

"Mr. Innerarity, as an exercise it is worth whatever truth or skill it has taught you; to a judge of paintings it is ten dollars' worth of paint thrown away; but as an article of sale it is worth what it will bring without misrepresentation."

"Two—hun-rade an'—fifty—dollahs or—not'in'!" said the indignant Creole, clenching one fist, and with the other hand lifting his hat by the front corner and slapping it down upon the counter. "Ha, ha, ha! a pase of waint—a wase of paint! 'Sieur Frowenfel', you don' know not'in' 'bout it! You har a jedge of painting?" he added cautiously.

"No, sir."

"*Eh, bien! foudre tonnerre!*—look yeh! you know? 'Sieur Frowenfel'? Dat de way de publique halways talk about a hartis's firs' pigshoe. But, I hass you to pardon me, Monsieur Frowenfel', if I 'ave speak a lill too warm."

"Then you must forgive me if, in my desire to set you right, I have spoken with too much liberty. I probably should have said only what I first intended to say, that unless you are a person of independent means——"

"You t'ink I would make bill of ladin'? Ah! Hm-m!"

"——that you had made a mistake in throwing up your means of support——"

"But 'e 'as fill de place an' don' want me no mo'. You want a clerk?—one what can speak fo' lang-widge—French, Eng-lish, Spanish, an' Italienne? Come! I work for you in de mawnin' an' paint in de evenin'; come!"

Joseph was taken unaware. He smiled, frowned, passed his hand across his brow, noticed, for the first time since his delivery of the picture, the naked little boy standing against the edge of a door, said, "Why——," and smiled again.

"I riffer you to my cousin Honoré," said Innerarity.

"Have you any knowledge of this business?"

"I 'ave."

"Can you keep shop in the forenoon or afternoon indifferently, as I may require?"

"Eh? Forenoon—afternoon?" was the reply.

"Can you paint sometimes in the morning and keep shop in the evening?"

"Yes, seh."

Minor details were arranged on the spot. Raoul dismissed the black boy, took off his coat and fell to work decanting something, with the understanding that his salary, a microscopic one, should begin from date if his cousin should recommend him.

"'Sieur Frowenfel'," he called from under the counter, later in the day, "you t'ink it would be hanny disgrace to paint de pigshoe of a niggah?"

"Certainly not."

"Ah, my soul! what a pigshoe I could paint of Bras-Coupé!"

We have the afflatus in Louisiana, if nothing else.

20 A Very Natural Mistake

Mr. Raoul Innerarity proved a treasure. The fact became patent in a few hours. To a student of the community he was a key, a lamp, a lexicon, a microscope, a tabulated statement, a book of heraldry, a city directory, a glass of wine, a Book of Days, a pair of wings, a comic almanac, a diving bell, a Creole *veritas*. Before the day had had time to cool, his continual stream of words had done more to elucidate the mysteries in which his employer had begun to be befogged than half a year of the apothecary's slow and scrupulous guessing. It was like showing how to carve a strange fowl. The way he dovetailed story into story and drew forward in panoramic procession Lufki-Humma and Epaminondas Fusilier, Zephyr Grandissime and the lady of the *lettre de cachet*, Demosthenes De Grapion and the *fille à l'hôpital*, Georges De Grapion and the *fille à la cassette*, Numa Grandissime, father of the two Honorés, young Nancanou and old Agricola,—the way he made them

> "*Knit hands and beat the ground*
> *In a light, fantastic round,*"

would have shamed the skilled volubility of Sheharazade.

"Look!" said the story-teller, summing up; "you take hanny

'istory of France an' see the hage of my familie. Pipple talk about de Boulignys, de Sauvés, de Grandprès, de Lemoynes, de St. Maxents,—bla-a-a! De Grandissimes is as hole as de dev'! What? De mose of de Creole families is not so hold as plenty of my yallah kinfolks!"

The apothecary found very soon that a little salt improved M. Raoul's statements.

But here he was, a perfect treasure, and Frowenfeld, fleeing before his illimitable talking power in order to digest in seclusion the ancestral episodes of the Grandissimes and De Grapions, laid pleasant plans for the immediate future. To-morrow morning he would leave the shop in Raoul's care and call on M. Honoré Grandissime to advise with him concerning the retention of the born artist as a drug-clerk. To-morrow evening he would pluck courage and force his large but bashful feet up to the door-step of Number 19 rue Bienville. And the next evening he would go and see what might be the matter with Doctor Keene, who had looked ill on last parting with the evening group that lounged in Frowenfeld's door, some three days before. The intermediate hours were to be devoted, of course, to the prescription desk and his "dead stock."

And yet after this order of movement had been thus compactly planned, there all the more seemed still to be that abroad which, now on this side, and now on that, was urging him in a nervous whisper to make haste. There had escaped into the air, it seemed, and was gliding about, the expectation of a crisis.

Such a feeling would have been natural enough to the tenants of Number 19 rue Bienville, now spending the tenth of the eighteen days of grace allowed them in which to save their little fortress. For Palmyre's assurance that the candle-burning would certainly cause the rent-money to be forthcoming in time was to Clotilde unknown, and to Aurora it was poor stuff to make peace of mind of. But there was a degree of impractibility in these ladies, which, if it was unfortunate, was, nevertheless, a part of their Creole beauty, and made the absence of any really brilliant outlook what the galaxy makes a moonless sky. Perhaps they had not been as diligent as they might have been in canvassing all possible ways and means for meeting the pecuniary emergency so fast bearing down upon them. From a Creole standpoint, they were not bad managers. They could dress delightfully on an incredibly small outlay; could wear a well-to-do

119

smile over an inward sigh of stifled hunger; could tell the parents of their one or two scholars to consult their convenience, and then come home to a table that would make any kind soul weep; but as to estimating the velocity of bills payable in their orbits, such trained sagacity was not theirs. Their economy knew how to avoid what the Creole-African apothegm calls *commerce Man Lizon—qui asseté pou' trois picaillons et vend' pou' ein escalin* (bought for three picayunes and sold for two); but it was an economy that made their very hound a Spartan; for, had that economy been half as wise as it was heroic, his one meal a day would not always have been the cook's leavings of cold rice and the lickings of the gumbo plates.

On the morning fixed by Joseph Frowenfeld for calling on M. Grandissime, on the banquette of the rue Toulouse, directly in front of an old Spanish archway and opposite a blacksmith's shop,—this blacksmith's shop stood between a jeweller's store and a large, balconied and dormer-windowed wine-warehouse—Aurore Nancanou, closely veiled, had halted in a hesitating way and was inquiring of a gigantic negro cartman the whereabouts of the counting-room of M. Honoré Grandissime.

Before he could respond she descried the name upon a stair-case within the archway, and, thanking the cartman as she would have thanked a prince, hastened to ascend. An inspiring smell of warm rusks, coming from a bakery in the paved court below, rushed through the archway and up the stair and accompanied her into the cemetery-like silence of the counting-room. There were in the department some fourteen clerks. It was a den of Grandissimes. More than half of them were men beyond middle life, and some were yet older. One or two are so handsome, under their noble silvery locks, that almost any woman—Clotilde, for instance,—would have thought, "No doubt that one, or that one, is the head of the house." Aurora approached the railing which shut in the silent toilers and directed her eyes to the farthest corner of the room. There sat there at a large desk a thin, sickly-looking man with very sore eyes and two pairs of spectacles, plying a quill with a privileged loudness.

"H-h-m-m!" said she, very softly.

A young man laid down his rule and stepped to the rail with a silent bow. His face showed a jaded look. Night revelry, rather than care or years, had wrinkled it; but his bow was high-bred.

"Madame,"—in an undertone.

"Monsieur, it is M. Grandissime whom I wish to see," she said, in French.

But the young man responded in English.

"You har one tenant, ent it?"

"Yes, seh."

"Zen eet ees M. De Brahmin zat you 'ave to see."

"No, seh; M. Grandissime."

"M. Grandissime nevva see one tenant."

"I muz see M. Grandissime."

Aurora lifted her veil and laid it up on her bonnet.

The clerk immediately crossed the floor to the distant desk. The quill of the sore-eyed man scratched louder—scratch, scratch —as though it were trying to scratch under the door of Number 19 rue Bienville—for a moment, and then ceased. The clerk, with one hand behind him and one touching the desk, murmured a few words, to which the other, after glancing under his arm at Aurora, gave a short, low reply and resumed his pen. The clerk returned, came through a gate-way in the railing, led the way into a rich inner room, and turning with another courtly bow, handed her a cushioned armchair and retired.

"After eighteen years," thought Aurora, as she found herself alone. It had been eighteen years since any representative of the De Grapion line had met a Grandissime face to face, so far as she knew; even that representative was only her deceased husband, a mere connection by marriage. How many years it was since her grandfather, Georges De Grapion, captain of dragoons, had had his fatal meeting with a Mandarin de Grandissime, she did not remember. There, opposite her on the wall, was the portrait of a young man in a corslet who might have been M. Mandarin himself. She felt the blood of her race growing warmer in her veins. "Insolent tribe," she said, without speaking, "we have no more men left to fight you; but now wait. See what a woman can do."

These thoughts ran through her mind as her eye passed from one object to another. Something reminded her of Frowenfeld, and, with mingled defiance at her inherited enemies and amusement at the apothecary, she indulged in a quiet smile. The smile was still there as her glance in its gradual sweep reached a small mirror.

She almost leaped from her seat.

Not because that mirror revealed a recess which she had not

previously noticed; not because behind a costly desk therein sat a youngish man, reading a letter; not because he might have been observing her, for it was altogether likely that, to avoid premature interruption, he had avoided looking up; nor because this was evidently Honoré Grandissime; but because Honoré Grandissime, if this were he, was the same person whom she had seen only with his back turned in the pharmacy—the rider whose horse ten days ago had knocked her down, the Lieutenant of Dragoons who had unmasked and to whom she had unmasked at the ball! Fly! But where? How? It was too late; she had not even time to lower her veil. M. Grandissime looked up at the glass, dropped the letter with a slight start of consternation and advanced quickly toward her. For an instant her embarrassment showed itself in a mantling blush and a distressful yearning to escape; but the next moment she rose, all a-flutter within, it is true, but with a face as nearly sedate as the inborn witchery of her eyes would allow.

He spoke in Parisian French:

"Please be seated, madame."

She sank down.

"Do you wish to see me?"

"No, sir."

She did not see her way out of this falsehood, but—she couldn't say yes.

Silence followed.

"Whom do——"

"I wish to see M. Honoré Grandissime."

"That is my name, madame."

"Ah!"—with an angelic smile; she had collected her wits now, and was ready for war. "You are not one of his clerks?"

M. Grandissime smiled softly, while he said to himself: "You little honey-bee, you want to sting me, eh?" and then he answered her question.

"No, madame; I am the gentleman you are looking for."

"The gentleman she was look—" her pride resented the fact. "Me!"—thought she—"I am the lady whom, I have not a doubt, you have been longing to meet ever since the ball;" but her look was unmoved gravity. She touched her handkerchief to her lips and handed him the rent notice.

"I received that from your office the Monday before last."

There was a slight emphasis in the announcement of the time; it was the day of the run over.

Honoré Grandissime, stopping with the rent-notice only half unfolded, saw the advisability of calling up all the resources of his sagacity and wit in order to answer wisely; and as they answered his call a brighter nobility so overspread face and person that Aurora inwardly exclaimed at it even while she exulted in her thrust.

"Monday before last?"

She slightly bowed.

"A serious misfortune befell me that day," said M. Grandissime.

"Ah?" replied the lady, raising her brows with polite distress, "but you have entirely recovered, I suppose."

"It was I, madame, who that evening caused you a mortification for which I fear you will accept no apology."

"On the contrary," said Aurora, with an air of generous protestation, "it is I who should apologize; I fear I injured your horse."

M. Grandissime only smiled, and opening the rent-notice dropped his glance upon it while he said in a preoccupied tone:

"My horse is very well, I thank you."

But as he read the paper, his face assumed a serious air and he seemed to take an unnecessary length of time to reach the bottom of it.

"He is trying to think how he will get rid of me," thought Aurora; "he is making up some pretext with which to dismiss me, and when the tenth of March comes we shall be put into the street."

M. Grandissime extended the letter toward her, but she did not lift her hands.

"I beg to assure you, madame, I could never have permitted this notice to reach you from my office; I am not the Honoré Grandissime for whom this is signed."

Aurora smiled in a way to signify clearly that that was just the subterfuge she had been anticipating. Had she been at home she would have thrown herself, face downward, upon the bed; but she only smiled meditatively upward at the picture of an East Indian harbor and made an unnecessary re-arrangement of her handkerchief under her folded hands.

"There are, you know,"—began Honoré, with a smile which changed the meaning to "You know very well there are"—"two Honoré Grandissimes. This one who sent you this letter is a man of color——"

"Oh!" exclaimed Aurora, with a sudden malicious sparkle.

"If you will entrust this paper to me," said Honoré, quietly, "I will see him and do now engage that you shall have no further trouble about it. Of course, I do not mean that I will pay it, myself; I dare not offer to take such a liberty."

Then he felt that a warm impulse had carried him a step too far.

Aurora rose up with a refusal as firm as it was silent. She neither smiled nor scintillated now, but wore an expression of amiable practicality as she presently said, receiving back the rent-notice as she spoke:

"I thank you, sir, but it might seem strange to him to find his notice in the hands of a person who can claim no interest in the matter. I shall have to attend to it myself."

"Ah! little enchantress," thought her grave-faced listener, as he gave attention, "this, after all—ball and all—is the mood in which you look your very, very best"—a fact which nobody knew better than the enchantress herself.

He walked beside her toward the open door leading back into the counting-room, and the dozen and more clerks, who, each by some ingenuity of his own, managed to secure a glimpse of them, could not fail to feel that they had never before seen quite so fair a couple. But she dropped her veil, bowed M. Grandissime a polite "No farther," and passed out.

M. Grandissime walked once up and down his private office, gave the door a soft push with his foot and lighted a cigar.

The clerk who had before acted as usher came in and handed him a slip of paper with a name written on it. M. Grandissime folded it twice, gazed out the window, and finally nodded. The clerk disappeared, and Joseph Frowenfeld paused an instant in the door and then advanced, with a buoyant good-morning.

"Good-morning," responded M. Grandissime.

He smiled and extended his hand, yet there was a mechanical and preoccupied air that was not what Joseph felt justified in expecting.

"How can I serve you, Mr. Frhowenfeld?" asked the merchant, glancing through into the counting-room. His coldness was al-

124

most all in Joseph's imagination, but to the apothecary it seemed such that he was nearly induced to walk away without answering. However, he replied:

"A young man whom I have employed refers to you to recommend him."

"Yes, sir? Prhay, who is that?"

"Your cousin, I believe, Mr. Raoul Innerarity."

M. Grandissime gave a low, short laugh, and took two steps toward his desk.

"Rhaoul? Oh yes, I rhecommend Rhaoul to you. As an assistant in yo' sto'?—the best man you could find."

"Thank you, sir," said Joseph, coldly. "Good-morning!" he added, turning to go.

"Mr. Frhowenfeld," said the other, "do you evva rhide?"

"I used to ride," replied the apothecary, turning, hat in hand, and wondering what such a question could mean.

"If I send a saddle-hoss to yo' do' on day aftah tomorrhow evening at fo' o'clock, will you rhide out with me for-h about a hour-h and a half—just for a little pleasu'e?"

Joseph was yet more astonished than before. He hesitated, accepted the invitation, and once more said good-morning.

21 Doctor Keene Recovers His Bullet

It early attracted the apothecary's notice, in observing the civilization around him, that it kept the flimsy false bottoms in its social errors only by incessant reiteration. As he re-entered the shop, dissatisfied with himself for accepting M. Grandissime's invitation to ride, he knew by the fervent words which he overheard from the lips of his employee that the f. m. c. had been making one of his reconnoissances, and possibly had ventured in to inquire for his tenant.

"I t'ink, me, dat hanny w'ite man is a gen'leman; but I don't care if a man are good like a h-angel, if 'e had not pu'e w'ite, 'ow can 'e be a gen'leman?"

Raoul's words were addressed to a man who, as he rose up and handed Frowenfeld a note, ratified the Creole's sentiment by a spurt of tobacco juice and an affirmative "Hm-m."

The note was a lead-pencil scrawl, without date.

"DEAR JOE: Come and see me some time this evening. I am on my back in bed. Want your help in a little matter.

Yours,

KEENE

I have found out who —— ——"

Frowenfeld pondered: "I have found out who —— ——" Ah! Doctor Keene had found out who stabbed Agricola.

Some delays occurred in the afternoon, but toward sunset the apothecary dressed and went out. From the doctor's bedside in the rue St. Louis, if not delayed beyond all expectation, he would proceed to visit the ladies at Number 19 rue Bienville. The air was growing cold and threatening bad weather.

He found the Doctor prostrate, wasted, hoarse, cross, and almost too weak for speech. He could only whisper, as his friend approached his pillow:

"These vile lungs!"

"Hemorrhage?"

The invalid held up three small, freckled fingers.

Joseph dared not show pity in his gaze, but it seemed savage not to express some feeling, so after standing a moment he began to say:

"I am very sorry——"

"You needn't bother yourself!" whispered the Doctor, who lay frowning upward. By and by he whispered again.

Frowenfeld bent his ear, and the little man, so merry when well, repeated, in a savage hiss:

"Sit down!"

It was some time before he again broke the silence.

"Tell you what I want—you to do—for me."

"Well, sir——"

"Hold on!" gasped the invalid, shutting his eyes with impatience,—"till I get through."

He lay a little while motionless, and then drew from under his pillow a wallet, and from the wallet a pistol-ball.

"Took that out—a badly neglected wound—last day I saw you." Here a pause, an appalling cough, and by and by a whisper: "knew the bullet in an instant." He smiled wearily. "Peculiar size." He made a feeble motion. Frowenfeld guessed the meaning of it and handed him a pistol from a small table. The ball slipped softly home. "Refused two hundred dollars—those pistols"—with a sigh and closed eyes. By and by again—"Patient had smart fever—but it will be gone—time you get—there. Want you to—take care—t' I get up."

"But, Doctor——"

The sick man turned away his face with a petulant frown;

but presently, with an effort at self-control, brought it back and whispered:

"You mean you—not physician?"

"Yes."

"No. No more are half—doc's. You can do it. Simple gun-shot wound in the shoulder." A rest. "Pretty wound; ranges"—he gave up the effort to describe it. "You'll see it." Another rest. "You see—this matter has been kept quiet so far. I don't want any one —else to know—anything about it." He sighed audibly and looked as though he had gone to sleep, but whispered again, with his eyes closed—"'specially on culprit's own account."

Frowenfeld was silent: but the invalid was waiting for an answer, and, not getting it, stirred peevishly.

"Do you wish me to go to-night?" asked the apothecary.

"To-morrow morning. Will you——?"

"Certainly, Doctor."

The invalid lay quite still for several minutes, looking steadily at his friend, and finally let a faint smile play about his mouth,— a wan reminder of his habitual roguery.

"Good boy," he whispered.

Frowenfeld rose and straightened the bed-clothes, took a few steps about the room, and finally returned. The Doctor's restless eye had followed him at every movement.

"You'll go?"

"Yes," replied the apothecary, hat in hand; "where is it?"

"Corner Bienville and Bourbon,—upper river corner,—yellow one-story house, door-steps on street. You know the house?"

"I think I do."

"Good-night. Here!—I wish you would send that black girl in here—as you go out—make me better fire—Joe!" the call was a ghostly whisper.

Frowenfeld paused in the door.

"You don't mind my—bad manners, Joe?"

The apothecary gave one of his infrequent smiles.

"No, Doctor."

He started toward No. 19 rue Bienville; but a light, cold sprinkle set in, and he turned back toward his shop. No sooner had the rain got him there than it stopped, as rain sometimes will do.

22 Wars within the Breast

The next morning came in frigid and gray. The unseasonable numerals which the meteorologist recorded in his tables might have provoked a superstitious lover of better weather to suppose that Monsieur Danny, the head imp of discord, had been among the aërial currents. The passionate southern sky, looking down and seeing some six thousand to seventy-five hundred of her favorite children disconcerted and shivering, tried in vain, for two hours, to smile upon them with a little frozen sunshine, and finally burst into tears.

In thus giving way to despondency, it is sad to say, the sky was closely imitating the simultaneous behavior of Aurora Nancanou. Never was pretty lady in cheerier mood than that in which she had come home from Honoré's counting-room. Hard would it be to find the material with which to build again the castles-in-air that she founded upon two or three little discoveries there made. Should she tell them to Clotilde? Ah! and for what? No, Clotilde was a dear daughter—ha! few women were capable of having such a daughter as Clotilde; but there were things about which she was entirely too scrupulous. So, when she came in from that errand, profoundly satisfied that she would in future hear no more about the rent than she might choose to hear, she had been too shrewd to expose herself to her daughter's catechising. She would save her little revelations for disclosure when they might be used to advantage. As she threw her bonnet upon the bed, she exclaimed, in a tone of gentle and wearied reproach:

"Why did you not remind me that M. Honoré Grandissime, that precious somebody-great, has the honor to rejoice in a quadroon half-brother of the same illustrious name? Why did you not remind me, eh?"

"Ah! and you know it as well as A, B, C," playfully retorted Clotilde.

"Well, guess which one is our landlord?"

"Which one?"

"*Ma foi!* how do *I* know? I had to wait a shameful long time to see *Monsieur le prince,*—just because I am a De Grapion, I know. When at last I saw him, he says, 'Madame, this is the other Honoré Grandissime.' There, you see we are the victims of a conspiracy; if I go to the other, he will send me back to the first. But, Clotilde, my darling," cried the beautiful speaker, beamingly, "dismiss all fear and care; we shall have no more trouble about it."

"And how, indeed, do you know that?"

"Something tells it to me in my ear. I feel it! Trust in Providence, my child. Look at me, how happy I am; but you—you never trust in Providence. That is why we have so much trouble, —because you don't trust in Providence. Oh! I am so hungry, let us have dinner."

"What sort of a person is M. Grandissime in his appearance?" asked Clotilde, over their feeble excuse for a dinner.

"What sort? Do you imagine I had nothing better to do than notice whether a Grandissime is good-looking or not? For all I know to the contrary, he is—some more rice, please, my dear."

But this light-heartedness did not last long. It was based on an unutterable secret, all her own, about which she still had trembling doubts; this, too, notwithstanding her consultation of the dark oracles. She was going to stop that. In the long run, these charms and spells themselves bring bad luck. Moreover, the practice, indulged in to excess, was wicked, and she had promised Clotilde,—that droll little saint,—to resort to them no more. Hereafter, she should do nothing of the sort, except, to be sure, to take such ordinary precautions against misfortune as casting upon the floor a little of whatever she might be eating or drinking to propitiate M. Assonquer. She would have liked, could she have done it without fear of detection, to pour upon the front door-sill an oblation of beer sweetened with black molasses to Papa Lébat, who keeps the invisible keys of all the doors that admits suitors, but she dared not; and then, the hound would surely have licked it up. Ah me! was she forgetting that she was a widow?

She was in poor plight to meet the all but icy gray morning; and, to make her misery still greater, she found, on dressing, that an accident had overtaken her, which she knew to be a trustworthy sign of love grown cold. She had lost—alas! how can we communicate it in English!—a small piece of lute-string ribbon, about *so long*, which she used for—not a necktie exactly, but——

And she hunted and hunted, and couldn't bear to give up the search, and sat down to breakfast and ate nothing, and rose up and searched again (not that she cared for the omen), and struck the hound with the broom, and broke the broom, and hunted again, and looked out the front window, and saw the rain beginning to fall, and dropped into a chair—crying "Oh! Clotilde, my child, my child! the rent collector will be here Saturday and turn us into the street!" and so fell a-weeping.

A little tear-letting lightened her unrevealable burden, and she rose, rejoicing that Clotilde had happened to be out of eye-and-ear-shot. The scanty fire in the fireplace was ample to warm the room; the fire within her made it too insufferably hot! Rain or no rain, she parted the window-curtains and lifted the sash. What a mark for Love's arrow she was, as, at the window, she stretched her two arms upward! And, "right so," who should chance to come cantering by, the big drops of rain pattering after him, but the knightliest man in that old town, and the fittest to perfect the fine old-fashioned poetry of the scene!

"Clotilde," said Aurora, turning from her mirror, whither she had hastened to see if her face showed signs of tears (Clotilde was entering the room), "we shall never be turned out of this house by Honoré Grandissime!"

"Why?" asked Clotilde, stopping short in the floor, forgetting Aurora's trust in Providence, and expecting to hear that M. Grandissime had been found dead in his bed.

"Because I saw him just now; he rode by on horseback. A man with that noble face could never *do such a thing!*"

The astonished Clotilde looked at her mother searchingly. This

131

sort of speech about a Grandissime? But Aurora was the picture of innocence.

Clotilde uttered a derisive laugh.

"*Impertinente!*" exclaimed the other, laboring not to join in it.

"Ah-h-h!" cried Clotilde, in the same mood, "and what face had he when he wrote that letter?"

"What face?"

"Yes, what face?"

"I do not know what face you mean," said Aurora.

"What face," repeated Clotilde, "had Monsieur Honoré de Grandissime on the day that he wrote——"

"Ah, f-fah!" cried Aurora, and turned away, "you don't know what you are talking about! You make me wish sometimes that I were dead!"

Clotilde had gone and shut down the sash, as it began to rain hard and blow. As she was turning away, her eye was attracted by an object at a distance.

"What is it?" asked Aurora, from a seat before the fire.

"Nothing," said Clotilde, weary of the sensational,—"a man in the rain."

It was the apothecary of the rue Royale, turning from that street toward the rue Bourbon, and bowing his head against the swirling norther.

23 Frowenfeld Keeps His Appointment

Doctor Keene, his ill-humor slept off, lay in bed in a quiescent state of great mental enjoyment. At times he would smile and close his eyes, open them again and murmur to himself, and turn his head languidly and smile again. And when the rain and wind, all tangled together, came against the window with a whirl and a slap, his smile broadened almost to laughter.

"He's in it," he murmured, "he's just reaching there. I would give fifty dollars to see him when he first gets into the house and sees where he is."

As this wish was finding expression on the lips of the little sick man, Joseph Frowenfeld was making room on a narrow door-step for the outward opening of a pair of small batten doors, upon which he had knocked with the vigorous haste of a man in the rain. As they parted, he hurriedly helped them open, darted within, heedless of the odd black shape which shuffled out of his way, wheeled and clapped them shut again, swung down the bar and then turned, and with the good-natured face that properly goes with a ducking, looked to see where he was.

One object—around which everything else instantly became nothing—set his gaze. On the high bed, whose hangings of blue we already described, silently regarding the intruder with a pair of eyes that sent an icy thrill through him and fastened

133

him where he stood, lay Palmyre Philosophe. Her dress was a long, snowy morning-gown, wound loosely about at the waist with a cord and tassel of scarlet silk; a bright-colored woollen shawl covered her from the waist down, and a necklace of red coral heightened to its utmost her untamable beauty.

An instantaneous indignation against Doctor Keene set the face of the speechless apothecary on fire, and this, being as instantaneously comprehended by the philosophe, was the best of introductions. Yet, her gaze did not change.

The Congo negress broke the spell with a bristling protest, all in African b's and k's, but hushed and drew off at a single word of command from her mistress.

In Frowenfeld's mind an angry determination was taking shape, to be neither trifled with nor contemned. And this again the quadroon discerned, before he was himself aware of it.

"Doctor Keene"——he began, but stopped, so uncomfortable were her eyes.

She did not stir or reply.

Then he bethought him with a start, and took off his dripping hat.

At this a perceptible sparkle of imperious approval shot along her glance; it gave the apothecary speech.

"The doctor is sick, and he asked me to dress your wound."

She made the slightest discernible motion of the head, remained for a moment silent, and then, still with the same eye, motioned her hand toward a chair near a comfortable fire.

He sat down. It would be well to dry himself. He drew near the hearth and let his gaze fall into the fire. When he presently lifted his eyes and looked full upon the woman with a steady, candid glance, she was regarding him with apparent coldness, but with secret diligence and scrutiny, and a yet more inward and secret surprise and admiration. Hard rubbing was bringing out the grain of the apothecary. But she presently suppressed the feeling. She hated men.

But Frowenfeld, even while his eyes met hers, could not resent her hostility. This monument of the shame of two races—this poisonous blossom of crime growing out of crime—this final, unanswerable white man's accuser—this would-be murderess—what ranks and companies would have to stand up in the Great Day with her and answer as accessory before the fact! He looked again into the fire.

134

The patient spoke:

"*Eh bi'n, Miché?*" Her look was severe, but less aggressive. The shuffle of the old negress's feet was heard and she appeared bearing warm and cold water and fresh bandages; after depositing them she tarried.

"Your fever is gone," said Frowenfeld, standing by the bed. He had laid his fingers on her wrist. She brushed them off and once more turned full upon him the cold hostility of her passionate eyes.

The apothecary, instead of blushing, turned pale.

"You—" he was going to say, "you insult me"; but his lips came tightly together. Two big cords appeared between his brows, and his blue eyes spoke for him. Then, as the returning blood rushed even to his forehead, he said, speaking his words one by one:

"Please understand that you must trust me."

She may not have understood his English, but she comprehended, nevertheless. She looked up fixedly for a moment, then passively closed her eyes. Then she turned, and Frowenfeld put out one strong arm, helped her to a sitting posture on the side of the bed and drew the shawl about her.

"Zizi," she said, and the negress, who had stood perfectly still since depositing the water and bandages, came forward and proceeded to bare the philosophe's superb shoulder. As Frowenfeld again put forward his hand, she lifted her own as if to prevent him, but he kindly and firmly put it away and addressed himself with silent diligence to his task; and by the time he had finished, his womanly touch, his commanding gentleness, his easy despatch, had inspired Palmyre not only with a sense of safety, comfort, and repose, but with a pleased wonder.

This woman had stood all her life with dagger drawn, on the defensive against what certainly was to her an unmerciful world. With possibly one exception, the man now before her was the only one she had ever encountered whose speech and gesture were clearly keyed to that profound respect which is woman's first, foundation claim on man. And yet by inexorable decree, she belonged to what we used to call "the happiest people under the sun." We ought to stop saying that.

So far as Palmyre knew, the entire masculine wing of the mighty and exalted race, three-fourths of whose blood bequeathed her none of its prerogatives, regarded her as legitimate

135

prey. The man before her did not. There lay the fundamental difference that, in her sight, as soon as she discovered it, glorified him. Before this assurance the cold fierceness of her eyes gave way, and a friendlier light from them rewarded the apothecary's final touch. He called for more pillows, made a nest of them, and, as she let herself softly into it, directed his next consideration toward his hat and the door.

It was many an hour after he had backed out into the trivial remains of the rain-storm before he could replace with more tranquillizing images the vision of the philosophe reclining among her pillows, in the act of making that uneasy movement of her fingers upon the collar button of her robe, which women make when they are uncertain about the perfection of their dishabille, and giving her inaudible adieu with the majesty of an empress.

24 Frowenfeld Makes an Argument

On the afternoon of the same day on which Frowenfeld visited the house of the philosophe, the weather, which had been so unfavorable to his late plans, changed; the rain ceased, the wind drew around to the south, and the barometer promised a clear sky. Wherefore he decided to leave his business, when he should have made his evening weather notes, to the care of M. Raoul Innerarity, and venture to test both Mademoiselle Clotilde's repellent attitude and Aurora's seeming cordiality at No. 19 rue Bienville.

Why he should go was a question which the apothecary felt himself but partially prepared to answer. What necessity called him, what good was to be effected, what was to happen next, were points he would have liked to be clear upon. That he should be going merely because he was invited to come—merely for the pleasure of breathing their atmosphere—that he should be supinely gravitating toward them—this conclusion he positively could not allow; no, no; the love of books and the fear of women alike protested.

True, they were a part of that book which is pronounced "the proper study of mankind,"—indeed, that was probably the reason which he sought: he was going to contemplate them as a frontispiece to that unwriteable volume which he had undertaken to

137

con. Also, there was a charitable motive. Doctor Keene, months before, had expressed a deep concern regarding their lack of protection and even of daily provision; he must quietly look into that. Would some unforeseen circumstance shut him off this evening again from this very proper use of time and opportunity?

As he was sitting at the table in his back room, registering his sunset observations, and wondering what would become of him if Aurora should be out and that other in, he was startled by a loud, deep voice exclaiming, close behind him:

"*Eh, bien! Monsieur le Professeur!*"

Frowenfeld knew by the tone, before he looked behind him, that he would find M. Agricola Fusilier very red in the face; and when he looked, the only qualification he could make was that the citizen's countenance was not so ruddy as the red handkerchief in which his arm was hanging.

"What have you there?" slowly continued the patriarch, taking his free hand off his fettered arm and laying it upon the page as Frowenfeld hurriedly rose, and endeavored to shut the book.

"Some private memoranda," answered the metereologist, managing to get one page turned backward, reddening with confusion and indignation, and noticing that Agricola's spectacles were upside down.

"Private! Eh? No such thing, sir! Professor Frowenfeld, allow me" (a classic oath) "to say to your face, sir, that you are the most brilliant and the most valuable man—of your years—in afflicted Louisiana! Ha!" (reading): "'Morning observation; Cathedral clock, 7 A.M. Thermometer 70 degrees.' Ha! 'Hygrometer 15'—but this is not to-day's weather? Ah! no. Ha! 'Barometer 30.380.' Ha! 'Sky cloudy, dark; wind, south, light.' Ha! 'River rising.' Ha! Professor Frowenfeld, when will you give your splendid services to your section? You must tell me, my son, for I ask you, my son, not from curiosity, but out of impatient interest."

"I cannot say that I shall ever publish my tables," replied the "son," pulling at the book.

"Then, sir, in the name of Louisiana," thundered the old man, clinging to the book, "I can! They shall be published! Ah! yes, dear Frowenfeld. The book, of course, will be in French, eh? You would not so affront the most sacred prejudices of the noble people to whom you owe everything as to publish it in English? You—ah! have we torn it?"

138

"I do not write French," said the apothecary, laying the torn edges together.

"Professor Frowenfeld, men are born for each other. What do I behold before me? I behold before me, in the person of my gifted young friend, a supplement to myself! Why has Nature strengthened the soul of Agricola to hold the crumbling fortress of this body until these eyes—which were once, my dear boy, as proud and piercing as the battled steed's—have become dim?"

Joseph's insurmountable respect for gray hairs kept him standing, but he did not respond with any conjecture as to Nature's intentions, and there was a stern silence.

The crumbling fortress resumed, his voice pitched low like the beginning of the long roll. He knew Nature's design.

"It was in order that you, Professor Frowenfeld, might become my vicar! Your book shall be in French! We must give it a wide scope! It shall contain valuable geographical, topographical, biographical, and historical notes. It shall contain complete lists of all the officials in the province (I don't say territory, I say province) with their salaries and perquisites; ah! we will expose that! And—ha! I will write some political essays for it. Raoul shall illustrate it. Honoré shall give you money to publish it. Ah! Professor Frowenfeld, the star of your fame is rising out of the waves of oblivion! Come—I dropped in purposely to ask you—come across the street and take a glass of *taffia* with Agricola Fusilier."

This crowning honor the apothecary was insane enough to decline, and Agricola went away with many professions of endearment, but secretly offended because Joseph had not asked about his wound.

All the same the apothecary, without loss of time, departed for the yellow-washed cottage, No. 19 rue Bienville.

"To-morrow, at four P.M.," he said to himself, "if the weather is favorable, I ride with M. Grandissime."

He almost saw his books and instruments look up at him reproachfully.

The ladies were at home. Aurora herself opened the door, and Clotilde came forward from the bright fireplace with a cordiality never before so unqualified. There was something about these ladies—in their simple, but noble grace, in their half-Gallic, half-classic beauty, in a jocund buoyancy mated to an amiable dignity—that made them appear to the scholar as though they had just

139

bounded into life from the garlanded procession of some old fresco. The resemblance was not a little helped on by the costume of the late Revolution (most acceptably chastened and belated by the distance from Paris). Their black hair, somewhat heavier on Clotilde's head, where it rippled once or twice, was knotted *en Grecque,* and adorned only with the spoils of a nosegay given to Clotilde by a chivalric small boy in the home of her music scholar.

"We was expectin' you since several days," said Clotilde, as the three sat down before the fire, Frowenfeld in a cushioned chair whose moth-holes had been carefully darned.

Frowenfeld intimated, with tolerable composure, that matters beyond his control had delayed his coming beyond his intention.

"You gedd'n' ridge," said Aurora, dropping her wrists across each other.

Frowenfeld, for once, laughed outright, and it seemed so odd in him to do so that both the ladies followed his example. The ambition to be rich had never entered his thought, although in an unemotional, German way, he was prospering in a little city where wealth was daily pouring in, and a man had only to keep step, so to say, to march into possessions.

"You hought to 'ave a mo' larger sto' an' some clerque," pursued Aurora.

The apothecary answered that he was contemplating the enlargement of his present place or removal to a roomier, and that he had already employed an assistant.

"Oo it is, 'Sieur Frowenfel'?"

Clotilde turned toward the questioner a remonstrative glance.

"His name," replied Frowenfeld, betraying a slight embarrassment, "is—Innerarity; Mr. Raoul Innerarity; he is——"

"Ee pain' dad pigtu' w'at 'angin' in yo' window?"

Clotilde's remonstrance rose to a slight movement and a murmur.

Frowenfeld answered in the affirmative, and possibly betrayed the faint shadow of a smile. The response was a peal of laughter from both ladies.

"He is an excellent drug clerk," said Frowenfeld, defensively.

Whereat Aurora laughed again, leaning over and touching Clotilde's knee with one finger.

"An' excellen' drug cl'—ha, ha, ha! oh!"

"You muz podden uz, M'sieu' Frowenfel'," said Clotilde, with forced gravity.

Aurora sighed her participation in the apology; and, a few moments later, the apothecary and both ladies (the one as fond of the abstract as the other two were ignorant of the concrete) were engaged in an animated, running discussion on art, society, climate, education,—all those large, secondary *desiderata* which seem of first importance to young ambition and secluded beauty, flying to and fro among these subjects with all the liveliness and uncertainty of a game of pussy-wants-a-corner.

Frowenfeld had never before spent such an hour. At its expiration, he had so well held his own against both the others, that the three had settled down to this sort of entertainment: Aurora would make an assertion, or Clotilde would ask a question; and Frowenfeld, moved by that frankness and ardent zeal for truth which had enlisted the early friendship of Doctor Keene, amused and attracted Honoré Grandissime, won the confidence of the f. m. c., and tamed the fiery distrust and enmity of Palmyre, would present his opinions without the thought of a reservation either in himself or his hearers. On their part, they would sit in deep attention, shielding their faces from the fire, and responding to enunciations directly contrary to their convictions with an occasional "yes-seh," or "ceddenly," or "of coze," or,—prettier affirmation still,—a solemn drooping of the eyelids, a slight compression of the lips, and a low, slow declination of the head.

"The bane of all Creole art-effort"—(we take up the apothecary's words at a point where Clotilde was leaning forward and slightly frowning in an honest attempt to comprehend his condensed English)—"the bane of all Creole art-effort, so far as I have seen it, is amateurism."

"Amateu—" murmured Clotilde, a little beclouded on the main word and distracted by a French difference of meaning, but planting an elbow on one knee in the genuineness of her attention, and responding with a bow.

"That is to say," said Frowenfeld, apologizing for the homeliness of his further explanation by a smile, "a kind of ambitious indolence that lays very large eggs, but can neither see the necessity for building a nest beforehand, nor command the patience to hatch the eggs afterward."

"Of coze," said Aurora.

"It is a great pity," said the sermonizer, looking at the face of Clotilde, elongated in the brass andiron; and, after a pause: "Nothing on earth can take the place of hard and patient labor. But that, in this community, is not esteemed; most sorts of it are contemned; the humbler sorts are despised, and the higher are regarded with mingled patronage and commiseration. Most of those who come to my shop with their efforts at art, hasten to explain, either that they are merely seeking pastime, or else that they are driven to their course by want; and if I advise them to take their work back and finish it, they take it back and never return. Industry is not only despised, but has been degraded and disgraced, handed over into the hands of African savages."

"Doze Creole' is *lezzy*," said Aurora.

"That is a hard word to apply to those who do not *consciously* deserve it," said Frowenfeld; "but if they could only wake up to the fact,—find it out themselves——"

"Ceddenly," said Clotilde.

" 'Sieur Frowenfel'," said Aurora, leaning her head on one side, "some pipple thing it is doze climade; 'ow you lag doze climade?"

"I do not suppose," replied the visitor, "there is a more delightful climate in the world."

"Ah-h-h!"—both ladies at once, in a low, gracious tone of acknowledgment.

"I thing Louisiana is a paradize-me!" said Aurora. "W'ere you goin' fin' sudge a h-air?" She respired a sample of it. "W'ere you goin' fin' sudge a so ridge groun'? De weed' in my bag yard is twenny-five feet 'igh!"

"Ah! maman!"

"Twenty-six!" said Aurora, correcting herself. "W'ere you fin' sudge a reever lag dad Mississippi? *On dit*," she said, turning to Clotilde, "*que ses eaux ont la propriété de contribuer même à multiplier l'espèce humaine*—ha, ha, ha!"

Clotilde turned away an unmoved countenance to hear Frowenfeld.

Frowenfeld had contracted a habit of falling into meditation whenever the French language left him out of the conversation.

"Yes," he said, breaking a contemplative pause, "the climate is *too* comfortable and the soil too rich,—though I do not think it is entirely on their account that the people who enjoy them are so sadly in arrears to the civilized world." He blushed with the fear that his talk was bookish, and felt grateful to Clotilde for seeming to understand his speech.

"W'ad you fin' de rizzon is, 'Sieur Frowenfel'?" she asked.

"I do not wish to philosophize," he answered.

"*Mais*, go hon." "*Mais*, go ahade," said both ladies, settling themselves.

142

"It is largely owing," exclaimed Frowenfeld, with sudden fervor, "to a defective organization of society, which keeps this community, and will continue to keep it for an indefinite time to come, entirely unprepared and disinclined to follow the course of modern thought."

"Of coze," murmured Aurora, who had lost her bearings almost at the first word.

"One great general subject of thought now is human rights,— universal human rights. The entire literature of the world is becoming tinctured with contradictions of the dogmas upon which society in this section is built. Human rights is, of all subjects, the one upon which this community is most violently determined to hear no discussion. It has pronounced that slavery and caste are right, and sealed up the whole subject. What, then, will they do with the world's literature? They will coldly decline to look at it, and will become, more and more as the world moves on, a comparatively illiterate people."

"Bud, 'Sieur Frowenfel'," said Clotilde, as Frowenfeld paused —Aurora was stunned to silence,—"de Unitee State' goin' pud doze nigga' free, aind it?"

Frowenfeld pushed his hair hard back. He was in the stream now, and might as well go through.

"I have heard that charge made, even by some Americans. I do not know. But there is a slavery that no legislation can abolish,—the slavery of caste. That, like all the slaveries on earth, is a double bondage. And what a bondage it is which compels a community, in order to preserve its established tyrannies, to walk behind the rest of the intelligent world! What a bondage is that which incites a people to adopt a system of social and civil distinctions, possessing all the enormities and none of the advantages of those systems which Europe is learning to despise! This system, moreover, is only kept up by a flourish of weapons. We have here what you may call an armed aristocracy. The class over which these instruments of main force are held is chosen for its servility, ignorance, and cowardice; hence, indolence in the ruling class. When a man's social or civil standing is not dependent on his knowing how to read, he is not likely to become a scholar."

"Of coze," said Aurora, with a pensive respiration, "I thing id is doze climade," and the apothecary stopped, as a man should who finds himself unloading large philosophy in a little parlor.

"I thing, me, dey hought to pud doze quadroon' free?" It was

143

Clotilde who spoke, ending with the rising inflection to indicate the tentative character of this daringly premature declaration.

Frowenfeld did not answer hastily.

"The quadroons," said he, "want a great deal more than mere free papers can secure them. Emancipation before the law, though it may be a right which man has no right to withhold, is to them little more than a mockery until they achieve emancipation in the minds and good will of the people—'the people,' did I say? I mean the ruling class." He stopped again. One must inevitably feel a little silly, setting up tenpins for ladies who are too polite, even if able, to bowl them down.

Aurora and the visitor began to speak simultaneously; both apologized, and Aurora said:

"'Sieur Frowenfel', w'en I was a lill' girl,"—and Frowenfeld knew that he was going to hear the story of Palmyre. Clotilde moved, with the obvious intention to mend the fire, Aurora asked, in French, why she did not call the cook to do it, and Frowenfeld said, "Let me,"—threw on some wood, and took a seat nearer Clotilde. Aurora had the floor.

25 Aurora as a Historian

Alas! the phonograph was invented three-quarters of a century too late. If type could entrap one-half the pretty oddities of Aurora's speech,—the arch, the pathetic, the grave, the earnest, the matter-of-fact, the ecstatic tones of her voice,—nay, could it but reproduce the movement of her hands, the eloquence of her eyes, or the shapings of her mouth,—ah! but type—even the phonograph—is such an inadequate thing! Sometimes she laughed; sometimes Clotilde, unexpectedly to herself, joined her; and twice or thrice she provoked a similar demonstration from the ox-like apothecary,—to her own intense amusement. Sometimes she shook her head in solemn scorn; and, when Frowenfeld, at a certain point where Palmyre's fate locked hands for a time with that of Bras-Coupé, asked a fervid question concerning that strange personage, tears leaped into her eyes, as she said:

"Ah! 'Sieur Frowenfel', iv I tra to tell de sto'y of Bras-Coupé, I goin' to cry lag a lill bebby."

The account of the childhood days upon the plantation at Cannes Brulée may be passed by. It was early in Palmyre's fifteenth year that that Kentuckian, 'mutual friend' of her master and Agricola, prevailed with M. de Grapion to send her to the paternal Grandissime mansion,—a complimentary gift, through Agricola, to Mademoiselle, his niece,—returnable ten years after date.

The journey was made in safety; and, by and by, Palmyre was presented to her new mistress. The occasion was notable. In a great chair in the centre sat the *grandpère*, a Chevalier de Grandissime, whose business had narrowed down to sitting on the front veranda and wearing his decorations,—the cross of St. Louis being one; on his right, Colonel Numa Grandissime, with one arm dropped around Honoré, then a boy of Palmyre's age, expecting to be off in sixty days for France; and on the left, with Honoré's fair sister nestled against her, "Madame Numa," as the Creoles would call her, a stately woman and beautiful, a great admirer of her brother Agricola. (Aurora took pains to explain that she received these minutiæ from Palmyre herself in later years.) One other member of the group was a young don of some twenty years' age, not an inmate of the house, but only a cousin of Aurora on her deceased mother's side. To make the affair complete, and as a seal to this tacit Grandissime-de-Grapion treaty, this sole available representative of the "other side" was made a guest for the evening. Like the true Spaniard that he was, Don José Martinez fell deeply in love with Honoré's sister. Then there came Agricola leading in Palmyre. There were others, for the Grandissime mansion was always full of Grandissimes; but this was the central group.

In this house Palmyre grew to womanhood, retaining without interruption the place into which she seemed to enter by right of indisputable superiority over all competitors,—the place of favorite attendant to the sister of Honoré. Attendant, we say, for servant she never seemed. She grew tall, arrowy, lithe, imperial, diligent, neat, thorough, silent. Her new mistress, though scarcely at all her senior, was yet distinctly her mistress; she had that through her Fusilier blood; experience was just then beginning to show that the Fusilier Grandissime was a superb variety; she was a mistress one could wish to obey. Palmyre loved her, and through her contact ceased, for a time at least, to be the pet leopard she had been at the Cannes Brulée.

Honoré went away to Paris only sixty days after Palmyre entered the house. But even that was not soon enough.

"'Sieur Frowenfel'," said Aurora, in her recital, "Palmyre, she never tole me dad, *mais* I am shoe, *shoe* dad she fall in love wid Honoré Grandissime. 'Sieur Frowenfel', I thing dad Honoré Grandissime is one bad man, ent it? Whad you thing, 'Sieur Frowenfel'?"

"I think, as I said to you the last time, that he is one of the best, as I know that he is one of the kindest and most enlightened gentlemen in the city," said the apothecary.

"Ah, 'Sieur Frowenfel'! ha, ha!"

"That is my conviction."

The lady went on with her story.

"Hanny'ow, I know she *continue* in love wid 'im all doze ten year' w'at 'e been gone. She baig Mademoiselle Grandissime to wrad dad ledder to my papa to ass to kip her two years mo'."

Here Aurora carefully omitted that episode which Doctor Keene had related to Frowenfeld,—her own marriage and removal to Fausse Rivière, the visit of her husband to the city, his unfortunate and finally fatal affair with Agricola, and the surrender of all her land and slaves to that successful duelist.

M. de Grapion, through all that, stood by his engagement concerning Palmyre; and, at the end of ten years, to his own astonishment, responded favorably to a letter from Honoré's sister, irresistible for its goodness, good sense, and eloquent pleading, asking leave to detain Palmyre two years longer; but this response came only after the old master and his pretty, stricken Aurora had wept over it until they were weak and gentle,—and was not a response either, but only a silent consent.

Shortly before the return of Honoré—and here it was that Aurora took up again the thread of her account—while his mother, long-widowed, reigned in the paternal mansion, with Agricola for her manager, Bras-Coupé appeared. From that advent and the long and varied mental sufferings which its consequences brought upon her, sprang that second change in Palmyre, which made her finally untamable, and ended in a manumission, granted her more for fear than for conscience' sake. When Aurora attempted to tell those experiences, even leaving Bras-Coupé as much as might be out of the recital, she choked with tears at the very start, stopped, laughed, and said:

"*C'est tout*—daz all. 'Sieur Frowenfel', oo you fine dad pigtu' to loog lag, yonnah, hon de wall?"

She spoke as if he might have overlooked it, though twenty times, at least, in the last hour, she had seen him glance at it.

"It is a good likeness," said the apothecary, turning to Clotilde, yet showing himself somewhat puzzled in the matter of the costume.

The ladies laughed.

"Daz ma grade-gran'-mamma," said Clotilde.

"Dass one *fille à la cassette*," said Aurora, "my gran'-muzzah; *mais,* ad de sem tam id is Clotilde." She touched her daughter under the chin with a ringed finger. "Clotilde is my gran'-mamma."

Frowenfeld rose to go.

"You muz come again, 'Sieur Frowenfel'," said both ladies, in a breath.

What could he say?

26 A Ride and a Rescue

"Douane or Bienville?"

Such was the choice presented by Honoré Grandissime to Joseph Frowenfeld, as the former on a lively brown colt and the apothecary on a nervy chestnut, fell into a gentle, preliminary trot while yet in the rue Royale, looked after by that great admirer of both, Raoul Innerarity.

"Douane?" said Frowenfeld. (It was the street we call Custom-House.)

"It has mud-holes," objected Honoré.

"Well, then, the rue du Canal?"

"The canal—I can smell it from here. Why not rue Bienville?"

Frowenfeld said he did not know. (We give the statement for what it is worth.)

Notice their route. A spirit of perversity seems to have entered into the very topography of this quarter. They turned up the rue Bienville (up is toward the river); reaching the levee, they took their course up the shore of the Mississippi (almost due south), and broke into a lively gallop on the Tchoupitoulas road, which in those days skirted that margin of the river nearest the sunsetting, namely, the *eastern* bank.

Conversation moved sluggishly for a time, halting upon trite topics or swinging easily from polite inquiry to mild affirmation, and back again. They were men of thought, these two, and one of them did not fully understand why he was in his present position; hence some reticence. It was one of those afternoons in early March that make one wonder how the rest of the world avoids emigrating to Louisiana in a body.

"Is not the season early?" asked Frowenfeld.

M. Grandissime believed it was; but then the Creole spring always seemed so, he said.

The land was an inverted firmament of flowers. The birds were an innumerable, busy, joy-compelling multitude, darting and fluttering hither and thither, as one might imagine the babes do in heaven. The orange-groves were in blossom; their dark green boughs seemed snowed upon from a cloud of incense, and a listening ear might catch an incessant, whispered trickle of falling petals, dropping "as the honey-comb." The magnolia was beginning to add to its dark and shining evergreen foliage, frequent sprays of pale new leaves and long, slender, buff buds of others yet to come. The oaks, both the bare-armed and the "green-robed senators," the willows, and the plaqueminiers, were putting out their subdued florescence as if they smiled in grave participation with the laughing gardens. The homes that gave perfection to this beauty were those old, large, belvedered colonial villas, of which you may still here and there see one standing, battered into half ruin, high and broad, among foundries, cotton and tobacco-sheds, junk-yards, and longshoremen's hovels, like one unconquered elephant in a wreck of artillery. In Frowenfeld's day the "smell of their garments was like Lebanon." They were seen by glimpses through chance openings in lofty hedges of Cherokee rose or bois-d'arc, under boughs of cedar or pride-of-China, above their groves of orange or down their long, overarched avenues of oleander; and the lemon and the pomegranate, the banana, the fig, the shaddock, and at times even the mango and the guava, joined "hands around" and tossed their fragrant locks above the lilies and roses. Frowenfeld forgot to ask himself further concerning the probable intent of M. Grandissime's invitation to ride; these beauties seemed rich enough in good reasons. He felt glad and grateful.

At a certain point the two horses turned of their own impulse, as by force of habit, and with a few clambering strides mounted to the top of the levee and stood still, facing the broad, dancing, hurrying, brimming river.

150

The Creole stole an amused glance at the elated, self-forgetful look of his immigrant friend.

"Mr. Frowenfeld," he said, as the delighted apothecary turned with unwonted suddenness and saw his smile, "I believe you like this better than discussion. You find it easier to be in harmony with Louisiana than with Louisianians, eh?"

Frowenfeld colored with surprise. Something unpleasant had lately occurred in his shop. Was this to signify that M. Grandissime had heard of it?

"I am a Louisianian," replied he, as if this were a point assailed.

"I would not insinuate otherwise," said M. Grandissime, with a kindly gesture. "I would like you to feel so. We are citizens now of a different government to that under which we lived the morning we first met. Yet"—the Creole paused and smiled—"you are not and I am glad you are not, what we call a Louisianian."

Frowenfeld's color increased. He turned quickly in his saddle as if to say something very positive, but hesitated, restrained himself and asked:

"Mr. Grandissime, is not your Creole 'we' a word that does much damage?"

The Creole's response was at first only a smile, followed by a thoughtful countenance; but he presently said, with some suddenness:

"My-de'-seh, yes. Yet you see I am, even this moment, forgetting we are not a separate people. Yes, our Creole 'we' does damage, and our Creole 'you' does more. I assure you, sir, I try hard to get my people to understand that it is time to stop calling those who come and add themselves to the community, aliens, interlopers, invaders. That is what I hear my cousins, 'Polyte and Sylvestre, in the heat of discussion, called you the other evening; is it so?"

"I brought it upon myself," said Frowenfeld. "I brought it upon myself."

"Ah!" interrupted M. Grandissime, with a broad smile, "excuse me—I am fully prepared to believe it. But the charge is a false one. I told them so. My-de'-seh—I know that a citizen of the United States in the United States has a right to become, and to be called, under the laws governing the case, a Louisianian, a Vermonter, or a Virginian, as it may suit his whim; and even if he should be found dishonest or dangerous, he has a right to be

151

treated just exactly as we treat the knaves and ruffians who are native born! Every discreet man must admit that."

"But if they do not enforce it, Mr. Grandissime," quickly responded the sore apothecary, "if they continually forget it—if one must surrender himself to the errors and crimes of the community as he finds it——"

The Creole uttered a low laugh.

"Party differences, Mr. Frowenfeld; they have them in all countries."

"So your cousins said," said Frowenfeld.

"And how did you answer them?"

"Offensively," said the apothecary, with sincere mortification.

"Oh! that was easy," replied the other, amusedly; "but how?"

"I said that, having here only such party differences as are common elsewhere, we do not behave as they elsewhere do; that in most civilized countries the immigrant is welcome, but here he is not. I am afraid I have not learned the art of courteous debate," said Frowenfeld, with a smile of apology.

" 'Tis a great art," said the Creole, quietly, stroking his horse's neck. "I suppose my cousins denied your statement with indignation, eh?"

"Yes; they said the honest immigrant is always welcome."

"Well, do you not find that true?"

"But, Mr. Grandissime, that is requiring the immigrant to prove his innocence!" Frowenfeld spoke from the heart. "And even the honest immigrant is welcome only when he leaves his peculiar opinions behind him. Is that right, sir?"

The Creole smiled at Frowenfeld's heat.

"My-de'-seh, my cousins complain that you advocate measures fatal to the prevailing order of society."

"But," replied the unyielding Frowenfeld, turning redder than ever, "that is the very thing that American liberty gives me the right—peaceably—to do! Here is a structure of society defective, dangerous, erected on views of human relations which the world is abandoning as false; yet the immigrant's welcome is modified with the warning not to touch these false foundations with one of his fingers!"

"Did you tell my cousins the foundations of society here are false?"

"I regret to say I did, very abruptly. I told them they were privately aware of the fact."

152

"You may say," said the ever-amiable Creole, "that you allowed debate to run into controversy, eh?"

Frowenfeld was silent; he compared the gentleness of this Creole's rebukes with the asperity of his advocacy of right and felt humiliated. But M. Grandissime spoke with a rallying smile.

"Mr. Frowenfeld, you never make pills with eight corners, eh?"

"No, sir." The apothecary smiled.

"No, you make them round; cannot you make your doctrines the same way? My-de'-seh, you will think me impertinent; but the reason I speak is because I wish very much that you and my cousins would not be offended with each other. To tell you the truth, my-de'-seh, I hoped to use you with them—pardon my frankness."

"If Louisiana had more men like you, M. Grandissime," cried the untrained Frowenfeld, "society would be less sore to the touch."

"My-de'-seh," said the Creole, laying his hand out toward his companion and turning his horse in such a way as to turn the other also, "do me one favor; remember that it *is* sore to the touch."

The animals picked their steps down the inner face of the levee and resumed their course up the road at a walk.

"Did you see that man just turn the bend of the road, away yonder?" the Creole asked.

"Yes."

"Did you recognize him?"

"It was—my landlord, wasn't it?"

"Yes. Did he not have a conversation with you lately, too?"

"Yes, sir; why do you ask?"

"It has had a bad effect on him. I wonder why he is out here on foot?"

The horses quickened their paces. The two friends rode along in silence. Frowenfeld noticed his companion frequently cast an eye up along the distant sunset shadows of the road with a new anxiety. Yet, when M. Grandissime broke the silence it was only to say:

"I suppose you find the blemishes in our state of society can all be attributed to one main defect, Mr. Frowenfeld?"

Frowenfeld was glad of the chance to answer:

"I have not overlooked that this society has disadvantages as well as blemishes; it is distant from enlightened centres; it has a language and religion different from that of the great people of which it is now called to be a part. That it has also positive blemishes of organism——"

"Yes," interrupted the Creole, smiling at the immigrant's sudden magnanimity, "its positive blemishes; do they all spring from one main defect?"

"I think not. The climate has its influence, the soil has its influence—dwellers in swamps cannot be mountaineers."

"But after all," persisted the Creole, "the greater part of our troubles comes from——"

"Slavery," said Frowenfeld, "or rather caste."

"Exactly," said M. Grandissime.

"You surprise me, sir," said the simple apothecary. "I supposed you were——"

"My-de'-seh," exclaimed M. Grandissime, suddenly becoming very earnest, "I am nothing, nothing! There is where you have the advantage of me. I am but a *dilettante*, whether in politics, in philosophy, morals, or religion. I am afraid to go deeply into anything, lest it should make ruin in my name, my family, my property."

He laughed unpleasantly.

The question darted into Frowenfeld's mind, whether this might not be a hint of the matter that M. Grandissime had been trying to see him about.

"Mr. Grandissime," he said, "I can hardly believe you would neglect a duty either for family, property, or society."

"Well, you mistake," said the Creole, so coldly that Frowenfeld colored.

They galloped on. M. Grandissime brightened again, almost to the degree of vivacity. By and by they slackened to a slow trot and were silent. The gardens had been long left behind, and they were passing between continuous Cherokee rose-hedges on the right, and on the left along the bend of the Mississippi where its waters, glancing off three miles above from the old De Macarty levee (now Carrollton), at the slightest opposition in the breeze go whirling and leaping like a herd of dervishes across to the ever-crumbling shore, now marked by the little yellow depot-house of Westwego. Miles up the broad flood the sun was disappearing gorgeously. From their saddles, the two horsemen feasted on the scene without comment.

But presently, M. Grandissime uttered a low ejaculation and

spurred his horse toward a tree hard by, preparing, as he went, to fasten his rein to an overhanging branch. Frowenfeld, agreeable to his beckon, imitated the movement.

"I fear he intends to drown himself," whispered M. Grandissime, as they hurriedly dismounted.

"Who? Not——"

"Yes, your landlord, as you call him. He is on the flat; I saw his hat over the levee. When we get on top the levee, we must get right into it. But do not follow him into the water in front of the flat; it is certain death; no power of man could keep you from going under it."

The words were quickly spoken; they scrambled to the levee's crown. Just abreast of them lay a "flatboat," emptied of its cargo and moored to the levee. They leaped into it. A human figure swerved from the onset of the Creole and ran toward the bow of the boat, and in an instant more would have been in the river.

"Stop!" said Frowenfeld, seizing the unresisting f. m. c. firmly by the collar.

Honoré Grandissime smiled, partly at the apothecary's brief speech, but much more at his success.

"Let him go, Mr. Frowenfeld," he said, as he came near.

The silent man turned away his face with a gesture of shame.

M. Grandissime, in a gentle voice, exchanged a few words with him, and he turned and walked away, gained the shore, descended the levee, and took a foot-path which soon hid him behind a hedge.

"He gives his pledge not to try again," said the Creole, as the two companions proceeded to resume the saddle. "Do not look after him." (Joseph had cast a searching look over the hedge.)

They turned homeward.

"Ah! Mr. Frowenfeld," said the Creole, suddenly, "if the *immigrant* has cause of complaint, how much more has *that* man! True, it is only love for which he would have just now drowned himself; yet what an accusation, my-de'-seh, is his whole life against that 'caste' which shuts him up within its narrow and almost solitary limits! And yet, Mr. Frowenfeld, this people esteem this very same crime of caste the holiest and most precious of their virtues. My-de'-seh, it never occurs to us that in this matter we are interested, and therefore disqualified, witnesses. We say we are not understood; that the jury (the civilized world) renders its decision without viewing the body; that we

155

are judged from a distance. We forget that we ourselves are too *close* to see distinctly, and so continue, a spectacle to civilization, sitting in a horrible darkness, my-de'-seh!" He frowned.

"The shadow of the Ethiopian," said the grave apothecary.

M. Grandissime's quick gesture implied that Frowenfeld had said the very word.

"Ah! my-de'-seh, when I try sometimes to stand outside and look at it, I am *ama-aze* at the length, the blackness of that shadow!" (He was so deep in earnest that he took no care of his English.) "It is the *Némésis* w'ich, instead of coming afteh, glides along by the side of this morhal, political, commercial, social mistake! It blanches, my-de'-seh, ow whole civilization! It drhags us a centurhy behind the rhes' of the world! It rhetahds and poisons everhy industrhy we got!—mos' of all our-h immense agrhicultu'e! It brheeds a thousan' cusses that nevva leave home but jus' flutter-h up an' rhoost, my-de'-seh, on ow *heads;* an' we nevva know it!—yes, sometimes some of us know it."

He changed the subject.

They had repassed the ruins of Fort St. Louis, and were well within the precincts of the little city, when, as they pulled up from a final gallop, mention was made of Doctor Keene. He was improving; Honoré had seen him that morning; so, at another hour, had Frowenfeld. Doctor Keene had told Honoré about Palmyre's wound.

"You was at her house again this morning?" asked the Creole.

"Yes," said Frowenfeld.

M. Grandissime shook his head warningly.

" 'Tis a dangerous business. You are almost sure to become the object of slander. You ought to tell Doctor Keene to make some other arrangement, or presently you, too, will be under the—" he lowered his voice, for Frowenfeld was dismounting at the shop door, and three or four acquaintances stood around—"under the 'shadow of the Ethiopian.' "

27 The Fête de Grandpère

Sojourners in New Orleans who take their afternoon drive down Esplanade street will notice, across on the right, between it and that sorry streak once fondly known as Champ Elysées, two or three large, old houses, rising above the general surroundings and displaying architectural features which identify them with an irrevocable past—a past when the faithful and true Creole could, without fear of contradiction, express his religious belief that the antipathy he felt for the Américain invader was an inborn horror laid lengthwise in his ante-natal bones by a discriminating and appreciative Providence. There is, for instance, or was until lately, one house which some hundred and fifteen years ago was the suburban residence of the old sea-captain governor, Kerlerec. It stands up among the oranges as silent and gray as a pelican, and, so far as we know, has never had one cypress plank added or subtracted since its master was called to France and thrown into the Bastile. Another has two dormer windows looking out westward, and, when the setting sun strikes the panes, reminds one of a man with spectacles standing up in an audience, searching for a friend who is not there and will never come back. These houses are the last remaining—if, indeed, they were not pulled down yesterday—of a group that once marked from afar the direction of the old highway between the city's walls and the suburb St. Jean. Here clustered the earlier aristocracy of the colony; all that pretty crew of counts, chevaliers, marquises, colonels, dons, etc., who loved their kings, and especially their kings' moneys, with an *abandon* which affected the accuracy of nearly all their accounts.

Among these stood the great mother-mansion of the Grandissimes. Do not look for it now; it is quite gone. The round, white-plastered brick pillars which held the house fifteen feet up from the reeking ground and rose on loftily to sustain the great overspreading roof, or clustered in the cool, paved basement; the lofty halls, with their multitudinous glitter of gilded brass and twinkle of sweet-smelling wax-candles; the immense encircling veranda, where twenty Creole girls might walk abreast; the great front stairs, descending from the veranda to the garden, with a lofty palm on either side, on whose broad steps forty Grandissimes could gather on a birthday afternoon; and the belvedere, whence you could see the cathedral, the Ursulines', the governor's mansion, and the river, far away, shining between the villas of Tchoupitoulas Coast—all have disappeared as entirely beyond recall as the flowers that bloomed in the gardens on the day of this *fête de grandpère.*

Odd to say, it was not the grandpère's birthday that had passed. For weeks the happy children of the many Grandissime branches—the Mandarins, the St. Blancards, the Brahmins—had been standing with their uplifted arms apart, awaiting the signal to clap hands and jump, and still, from week to week, the appointed day had been made to fall back, and fall back before—what think you?—an inability to understand Honoré.

It was a sad paradox in the history of this majestic old house that her best child gave her the most annoyance; but it had long been so. Even in Honoré's early youth, a scant two years after she had watched him over the tops of her green myrtles and white and crimson oleanders, go away, a lad of fifteen, supposing he would of course come back a Grandissime of the Grandissimes—an inflexible of the inflexibles, he was found "inciting" (so the stately dames and officials who graced her front veranda called it) a Grandissime-De Grapion reconciliation by means of transatlantic letters, and reducing the flames of the old feud, rekindled by the Fusilier-Nancanou duel, to a little foul smoke. The main difficulty seemed to be that Honoré could not be satisfied with a clean conscience as to his own deeds and the peace

158

and fellowships of single households; his longing was, and had ever been—he had inherited it from his father—to see one unbroken and harmonious Grandissime family gathering yearly under his venerated roof without reproach before all persons, classes, and races with whom they had ever had to do. It was not hard for the old mansion to forgive him once or twice; but she had had to do it often. It seems no overstretch of fancy to say she sometimes gazed down upon his erring ways with a look of patient sadness in her large and beautiful windows.

And how had that forbearance been rewarded? Take one short instance: when, seven years before this present *fête de grand-père,* he came back from Europe, and she (this old home which we cannot help but personify), though in trouble then—a trouble than sent up the old feud flames again—opened her halls to rejoice in him with the joy of all her gathered families, he presently said such strange things in favor of indiscriminate human freedom that for very shame's sake she hushed them up, in the fond hope that he would outgrow such heresies. But he? On top of all the rest, he declined a military commission and engaged in commerce—"shop-keeping, *parbleu!*"

However, therein was developed a grain of consolation. Honoré became—as he chose to call it—more prudent. With much tact, Agricola was amiably crowded off the dictator's chair, to become, instead, a sort of seneschal. For a time the family peace was perfect, and Honoré, by a touch here to-day and a word there to-morrow, was ever lifting the name, and all who bore it, a little and a little higher; when suddenly, as in his father's day—that dear Numa who knew how to sacrifice his very soul, as a sort of Iphigenia for the propitiation of the family gods— as in Numa's day came the cession to Spain, so now fell this other cession, like an unexpected tornado, threatening the wreck of her children's slave-schooners and the prostration alike of their slave-made crops and their Spanish liberties; and just in the fateful moment where Numa would have stood by her, Honoré had let go. Ah, it was bitter!

"See what foreign education does!" cried a Mandarin de Grandissime of the Baton Rouge Coast. "I am sorry now"— derisively—"that I never sent *my* boy to France, am I not? No! No-o-o! I would rather my son should never know how to read, than that he should come back from Paris repudiating the sentiments and prejudices of his own father. Is education better than family peace? Ah, bah! My son make friends with Américains and tell me they—that call a negro 'monsieur'—are as good as his father? But that is what we get for letting Honoré become a merchant. Ha! the degradation! Shaking hands with men who do not believe in the slave trade! Shake hands? Yes; associate—fraternize! with apothecaries and negrophiles. And now we are invited to meet at the *fête de grandpère,* in the house where he is really the chief—the *caçique!*"

No! The family would not come together on the first appointment; no, nor on the second; no, not if the grandpapa did express his wish; no, nor on the third—nor on the fourth.

"Non, Messieurs!" cried both youth and reckless age; and, sometimes, also, the stronger heads of the family, the men of means, of force and of influence, urged on from behind by their proud and beautiful wives and daughters.

Arms, generally, rather than heads, ruled there in those days, and sentiments (which are the real laws) took shape in accordance with the poetry, rather than the reason, of things, and the community recognized the supreme domination of the "gentleman" in questions of right and of "the ladies" in matters of sentiment. Under such conditions strength establishes over weakness a showy protection which is the subtlest of tyrannies, yet which, in the very moment of extending its arm over woman, confers upon her a power which a truer freedom would only diminish; constitutes her in a large degree an autocrat of public sentiment and thus accepts her narrowest prejudices and most belated errors as a very need-be's of social life.

The clans classified easily into three groups: there were those who boiled, those who stewed, and those who merely steamed under a close cover. The men in the first two groups were, for the most part, those who were holding office under old Spanish commissions, and were daily expecting themselves to be displaced and Louisiana thereby ruined. The steaming ones were a goodly fraction of the family—the timid, the apathetic, the "conservative." The conservatives found ease better than exactitude, the trouble of thinking great, the agony of deciding harrowing, and the alternative of smiling cynically and being liberal so much easier—and the warm weather coming on with a rapidity wearying to contemplate.

"The Yankee was an inferior animal."

"Certainly."

"But Honoré had a right to his convictions."

"Yes, that was so, too."

"It looked very traitorous, however."

"Yes, so it did."

"Nevertheless, it might turn out that Honoré was advancing the true interests of his people."

"Very likely."

"It would not do to accept office under the Yankee government."

"Of course not."

"Yet it would never do to let the Yankees get the offices, either."

"That was true; nobody could deny that."

"If Spain or France got the country back, they would certainly remember and reward those who had held out faithfully."

"Certainly! That was an old habit with France and Spain."

"But if they did not get the country back——"

"Yes, that is so; Honoré is a very good fellow, and——"

And, one after another, under the mild coolness of Honoré's amiable disregard, their indignation trickled back from steam to water, and they went on drawing their stipends, some in Honoré's counting-room, where they held positions, some from the provisional government, which had as yet made but few changes, and some, secretly, from the cunning Casa-Calvo; for, blow the wind east or blow the wind west, the affinity of the average Grandissime for a salary abideth forever.

Then, at the right moment, Honoré made a single happy stroke, and even the hot Grandissimes, they of the interior parishes and they of Agricola's squadron, slaked and crumbled when he wrote each a letter saying that the governor was about to send them appointments, and that it would be well, if they wished to *evade* them, to write the governor at once, surrendering their present commissions. Well! Evade? They would evade nothing! Do you think they would so belittle themselves as to write to the usurper? They would submit to keep the positions first.

But the next move was Honoré's making the whole town aware of his apostasy. The great mansion, with the old grandpère sitting out in front, shivered. As we have seen, he had ridden through the Place d'Armes with the arch-usurper himself. Yet, after all, a Grandissime would be a Grandissime still; whatever he did he did openly. And wasn't that glorious—never to be ashamed of anything, no matter how bad? It was not every one who could ride with the governor.

And blood was so much thicker than vinegar that the family that would not meet either in January or February, met in the first week of March, every constituent one of them.

The feast has been eaten. The garden now is joyous with children and the veranda resplendent with ladies. From among the latter the eye quickly selects one. She is perceptibly taller than the others; she sits in their midst near the great hall entrance; and as you look at her there is no claim of ancestry the Grandissimes can make which you would not allow. Her hair, once black, now lifted up into a glistening snow-drift, augments the majesty of a still beautiful face, while her full stature and stately bearing suggest the finer parts of Agricola, her brother. It is Madame Grandissime, the mother of Honoré.

One who sits at her left, and is very small, is a favorite cousin. On her right is her daughter, the widowed señora of José Martinez; she has wonderful black hair and a white brow as wonderful. The commanding carriage of the mother is tempered in her to a gentle dignity and calm, contrasting pointedly with the animated manners of the courtly matrons among whom she sits, and whose continuous conversation takes this direction or that, at the pleasure of Madame Grandissime.

But if you can command your powers of attention, despite those children who are shouting Creole French and sliding down the rails of the front stair, turn the eye to the laughing squadron of beautiful girls, which every few minutes, at an end of the veranda, appears, wheels and disappears, and you note, as it were by flashes, the characteristics of face and figure that mark the Louisianaises in the perfection of the new-blown flower. You see that blondes are not impossible; there, indeed, are two sisters who might be undistinguishable twins but that one has blue eyes and golden hair. You note the exquisite pencilling of their eyebrows, here and there some heavier and more velvety, where a less vivacious expression betrays a share of Spanish blood. As Grandissimes, you mark their tendency to exceed the medium Creole stature, an appearance heightened by the fashion of their robes. There is scarcely a rose in all their cheeks and a full red-ripeness of the lips would hardly be in keeping; but there is plenty of life in their eyes, which glance out between the curtains of their long lashes with a merry dancing that keeps time to the prattle of tongues. You are not able to get a straight look into them, and if you could you would see only your own image cast back in pitiful miniature; but you turn away and feel, as you fortify yourself with an inward smile, that they know you, you man, through and through, like a little song. And in turning, your sight is glad to rest again on the face of Honoré's mother. You see, this time, that she *is* his mother, by a charm you had overlooked, a candid, serene and lovable smile. It is the wonder of those who see that smile that she can ever be harsh.

The playful, mock-martial tread of the delicate Creole feet is all at once swallowed up by the sound of many heavier steps in the hall, and the fathers, grandfathers, sons, brothers, uncles and nephews of the great family come out, not a man of them that cannot, with a little care, keep on his feet. Their descendants of the present day sip from shallower glasses and with less marked results.

The matrons, rising, offer the chief seat to the first comer, the great-grandsire—the oldest living Grandissime—Alcibiade, a shaken but unfallen monument of early colonial days, a browned and corrugated souvenir of De Vaudreuil's pomps, of O'Reilly's iron rule, of Galvez' brilliant wars—a man who had seen Bienville and Zephyr Grandissime. With what splendor of manner Madame Fusilier de Grandissime offers, and he accepts, the place of honor! Before he sits down he pauses a moment to hear out the companion on whose arm he had been leaning. But Théophile, a dark, graceful youth of eighteen, though he is recounting something with all the oblivious ardor of his kind, becomes instantly silent, bows with grave deference to the ladies, hands the aged forefather gracefully to his seat, and turning, recommences the recital to one who listens with the same perfect courtesy to all—his beloved cousin Honoré.

Meanwhile, the gentlemen throng out. Gallant crew! These are they who have been pausing proudly week after week in an endeavor (?) to understand the opaque motives of Numa's son.

In the middle of the veranda pauses a tall, muscular man of fifty, with the usual smooth face and an iron-gray queue. That is Colonel Agamemnon Brahmin de Grandissime, purveyor to the family's military pride, conservator of its military glory, and, after Honoré, the most admired of the name. Achille Grandissime, he who took Agricola away from Frowenfeld's shop in the carriage, essays to engage Agamemnon in conversation, and the colonel, with a glance at his kinsman's nether limbs and another at his own, and, with that placid facility with which the graver sort of Creoles take up the trivial topics of the lighter, grapples the subject of boots. A tall, bronzed, slender young man, who prefixes to Grandissime the maternal St. Blancard, asks where his wife is, is answered from a distance, throws her a kiss and sits down on a step, with Jean Baptiste de Grandissime, a piratical-looking black-beard, above him, and Alphonse Mandarin, an olive-skinned boy, below. Valentine Grandissime, of Tchoupitoulas, goes quite down to the bottom of the steps and leans against the balustrade. He is a large, broad-shouldered, well-built man, and, as he stands smoking a cigar, with his black-stockinged legs crossed, he glances at the sky with the eye of a hunter—or, it may be, of a sailor.

"Valentine will not marry," says one of two ladies who lean over the rail of the veranda above. "I wonder why."

The other fixes on her a meaning look, and she twitches her shoulders and pouts, seeing she has asked a foolish question, the answer to which would only put Valentine in a numerous class and do him no credit.

Such were the choice spirits of the family. Agricola had retired. Raoul was there; his pretty auburn head might have been seen about half-way up the steps, close to one well sprinkled with premature gray.

"No such thing!" exclaimed his companion.

(The conversation was entirely in Creole French.)

"I give you my sacred word of honor!" cried Raoul.

"That Honoré is having all his business carried on in English?" asked the incredulous Sylvestre. (Such was his name.)

"I swear—" replied Raoul, resorting to his favorite pledge— "on a stack of Bibles that high!"

"Ah-h-h-h, pf-f-f-f-f!"

This polite expression of unbelief was further emphasized by a spasmodic flirt of one hand, with the thumb pointed outward.

"Ask him! ask him!" cried Raoul.

"Honoré!" called Sylvestre, rising up. Two or three persons passed the call around the corner of the veranda.

Honoré came with a chain of six girls on either arm. By the time he arrived, there was a Babel of discussion.

"Raoul says you have ordered all your books and accounts to be written in English," said Sylvestre.

"Well?"

"It is not true, is it?"

"Yes."

The entire veranda of ladies raised one long-drawn, deprecatory "Ah!" except Honoré's mother. She turned upon him a look of silent but intense and indignant disappointment.

"Honoré!" cried Sylvestre, desirous of repairing his defeat, "Honoré!"

But Honoré was receiving the clamorous abuse of the two half dozens of girls.

"Honoré!" cried Sylvestre again, holding up a torn scrap of writing-paper which bore the marks of the counting-room floor and of a boot-heel, "how do you spell 'la-dee'?"

There was a moment's hush to hear the answer.

"Ask Valentine," said Honoré.

Everybody laughed aloud. That taciturn man's only retort was to survey the company above him with an unmoved countenance, and to push the ashes slowly from his cigar with his little finger. M. Valentine Grandissime, of Tchoupitoulas, could not read.

"Show it to Agricola," cried two or three, as that great man came out upon the veranda, heavy-eyed, and with tumbled hair.

Sylvestre, spying Agricola's head beyond the ladies, put the question.

"How is it spelled on that paper?" retorted the king of beasts.

"L-a-y——"

"Ignoramus!" growled the old man.

"I did not spell it," cried Raoul, and attempted to seize the paper. But Sylvestre throwing his hand behind him, a lady snatched the paper, two or three cried "Give it to Agricola!" and a pretty boy, whom the laughter and excitement had lured from the garden, scampered up the steps and handed it to the old man.

"Honoré!" cried Raoul, "it must not be read. It is one of your private matters."

But Raoul's insinuation that anybody would entrust him with a private matter brought another laugh.

Honoré nodded to his uncle to read it out, and those who could not understand English, as well as those who could, listened. It was a paper Sylvestre had picked out of a wastebasket on the day of Aurore's visit to the counting-room. Agricola read:

165

"What is that layde want in thare with Honoré?"

"Honoré is goin giv her bac that property—that is Aurore De-Grapion what Agricola kill the husband."

That was the whole writing, but Agricola never finished. He was reading aloud—"that is Aurore De Grap——"

At that moment he dropped the paper and blackened with wrath; a sharp flash of astonishment ran through the company; an instant of silence followed and Agricola's thundering voice rolled down upon Sylvestre in a succession of terrible imprecations.

It was painful to see the young man's face as speechless he received this abuse. He stood pale and frightened, with a smile playing about his mouth, half of distress and half of defiance, that said as plain as a smile could say, "Uncle Agricola, you will have to pay for this mistake."

As the old man ceased, Sylvestre turned and cast a look downward to Valentine Grandissime; then walked up the steps and passing with a courteous bow through the group that surrounded Agricola, went into the house. Valentine looked at the zenith, then at his shoe-buckles, tossed his cigar quietly into the grass and passed around a corner of the house to meet Sylvestre in the rear.

Honoré had already nodded to his uncle to come aside with him, and Agricola had done so. The rest of the company, save a few male figures down in the garden, after some feeble efforts to keep up their spirits on the veranda, remarked the growing coolness or the waning daylight, and singly or in pairs withdrew. It was not long before Raoul, who had come up upon the veranda, was left alone. He seemed to wait for something, as, leaning over the rail while the stars came out, he sang to himself, in a soft undertone, a snatch of a Creole song:

"La pluie—le pluie tombait,
    Crapaud criait,
    Moustique chantait——"

The moon shone so brightly that the children in the garden did not break off their hide-and-seek, and now and then Raoul suspended the murmur of his song, absorbed in the fate of some little elf gliding from one black shadow to crouch in another. He was himself in the deep shade of a magnolia, over whose outer boughs the moonlight was trickling, as if the whole tree had been dipped in quicksilver.

166

In the broad walk running down to the garden gate some six or seven dark forms sat in chairs, not too far away for the light of their cigars to be occasionally seen and their voices to reach his ear; but he did not listen. In a little while there came a light footstep, and a soft, mock-startled "Who is that?" and one of that same sparkling group of girls that had lately hung upon Honoré came so close to Raoul, in her attempt to discern his lineaments, that their lips accidentally met. They had but a moment of hand-in-hand converse before they were hustled forth by a feminine scouting party and thrust along into one of the great rooms of the house, where the youth and beauty of the Grandissimes were gathered in an expansive semicircle around a languishing fire, waiting to hear a story, or a song, or both, or half a dozen of each, from that master of narrative and melody, Raoul Innerarity.

"But mark," they cried unitedly, "you have got to wind up with the story of Bras-Coupé!"

"A song! A song!"

"*Une chanson Créole! Une chanson des nègres!*"

"Sing 'Yé tolé dancé la doung y doung doung!'" cried a black-eyed girl.

Raoul explained that it had too many objectionable phrases.

"Oh, just hum the objectionable phrases and go right on."

But instead he sang them this:

"*La prémier' fois mo té 'oir li,*
Li té posé au bord so lit;
Mo di', Bouzon, bel n'amourèse!
L'aut' fois li té si' so la saise
Comme viê Madam dans so fauteil,
Quand li vivé côté soleil.
So giés yé té plis noir passé la nouitte,
So dé la lev' plis doux passe la quitte!
Tou' mo la vie, zamein mo oir
Ein n'amourèse zoli comme ça!
   Mo' blié manzé—mo' blié boir'—
   Mo' blié tout dipi ç' temps-là—
   Mo' blié parlé—mo' blié dormi,
   Quand mo pensê aprés zami!"

"And you have heard Bras-Coupé sing that, yourself?"

"Once upon a time," said Raoul, warming with his subject, "we were coming down from Pointe Macarty in three pirogues. We had been three days fishing and hunting in Lake Salvador. Bras-Coupé had one pirogue with six paddles——"

"Oh, yes!" cried a youth named Baltazar; "sing that, Raoul!" And he sang that.

"But oh, Raoul, sing that song the negroes sing when they go out in the bayous at night, stealing pigs and chickens!"

"That boat song, do you mean, which they sing as a signal to those on shore?" He hummed.

"*Dé zabs, dé zabs, dé counou ouaïe ouaïe,*
Dé zabs, dé zabs, dé counou ouaïe ouaïe,
Counou ouaïe ouaïe ouaïe ouaïe,
Counou ouaïe ouaïe ouaïe ouaïe,
Counou ouaïe ouaïe ouaïe, momza,
Momza, momza, momza, momza,
Roza roza, roza-et—momza."

This was followed by another and still another, until the hour began to grow late. And then they gathered closer round him and heard the promised story. At the same hour, Honoré Grandissime, wrapping himself in a great-coat and giving himself up to sad and somewhat bitter reflections, had wandered from the paternal house, and by and by from the grounds, not knowing why or whither, but after a time soliciting, at Frowenfeld's closing door, the favor of his company. He had been feeling a kind of suffocation. This it was that made him seek and prize the presence and hand-grasp of the inexperienced apothecary. He led him out to the edge of the river. Here they sat down, and with a laborious attempt at a hard and jesting mood, Honoré told the same dark story.

168

28 The Story of Bras-Coupé

"A very little more than eight years ago," began Honoré—but not only Honoré, but Raoul also; and not only they, but another, earlier on the same day,—Honoré, the f. m. c. But we shall not exactly follow the words of any one of these.

Bras-Coupé, they said, had been, in Africa and under another name, a prince among his people. In a certain war of conquest, to which he had been driven by *ennui*, he was captured, stripped of his royalty, marched down upon the beach of the Atlantic, and, attired as a true son of Adam, with two goodly arms intact, became a commodity. Passing out of first hands in barter for a looking-glass, he was shipped in good order and condition on board the good schooner *Egalité*, whereof Blank was master, to be delivered without delay at the port of Nouvelle Orleans (the dangers of fire and navigation excepted), unto Blank Blank. In witness whereof, He that made men's skins of different colors, but all blood of one, hath entered the same upon His book, and sealed it to the day of judgment.

Of the voyage little is recorded—here below; the less the better. Part of the living merchandise failed to keep; the weather was rough, the cargo large, the vessel small. However, the captain discovered there was room over the side, and there—all flesh is grass—from time to time during the voyage he jettisoned the unmerchantable.

Yet, when the reopened hatches let in the sweet smell of the land, Bras-Coupé had come to the upper—the favored—the buttered side of the world; the anchor slid with a rumble of relief down through the muddy fathoms of the Mississippi, and the prince could hear through the schooner's side the savage current of the river, leaping and licking about the bows, and whimpering low welcomes home. A splendid picture to the eyes of the royal captive, as his head came up out of the hatchway, was the little Franco-Spanish-American city that lay on the low, brimming bank. There were little forts that showed their whitewashed teeth; there was a green parade-ground, and yellow barracks, and cabildo, and hospital, and cavalry stables, and custom-house, and a most inviting jail, convenient to the cathedral—all of dazzling white and yellow, with a black stripe marking the track of the conflagration of 1794, and here and there among the low roofs a lofty one with round-topped dormer windows and a breezy belvedere looking out upon the plantations of coffee and indigo beyond the town.

When Bras-Coupé staggered ashore, he stood but a moment among a drove of "likely boys," before Agricola Fusilier, managing the business adventures of the Grandissime estate, as well as the residents thereon, and struck with admiration for the physical beauties of the chieftain (a man may even fancy a negro—as a negro), bought the lot, and loth to resell him with the rest to some unappreciative 'Cadian, induced Don José Martinez' overseer to become his purchaser.

Down in the rich parish of St. Bernard (whose boundary line now touches that of the distended city) lay the plantation, known before Bras-Coupé passed away, as La Renaissance. Here it was that he entered at once upon a chapter of agreeable surprises. He was humanely met, presented with a clean garment, lifted into a cart drawn by oxen, taken to a whitewashed cabin of logs, finer than his palace at home, and made to comprehend that it was a free gift. He was also given some clean food, whereupon he fell sick. At home it would have been the part of piety for the magnate next the throne to launch him heavenward at once; but now, healing doses were administered, and to his amazement he recovered. It reminded him that he was no longer king.

His name, he replied to an inquiry touching that subject, was —— ——, something in the Jaloff tongue, which he by and by

170

condescended to render into Congo: Mioko-Koanga, in French Bras-Coupé, the Arm Cut Off. Truly it would have been easy to admit, had this been his meaning, that his tribe, in losing him, had lost its strong right arm close off at the shoulder; not so easy for his high-paying purchaser to allow, if this other was his intent; that the arm which might no longer shake the spear or swing the wooden sword, was no better than a useless stump never to be lifted for aught else. But whether easy to allow or not, that was his meaning. He made himself a type of all Slavery, turning into flesh and blood the truth that all Slavery is maiming.

He beheld more luxury in a week than all his subjects had seen in a century. Here Congo girls were dressed in cottons and flannels worth, where he came from, an elephant's tusk apiece. Everybody wore clothes—children and lads alone excepted. Not a lion had invaded the settlement since his immigration. The serpents were as nothing; an occasional one coming up through the floor—that was all. True, there was more emaciation than unassisted conjecture could explain—a profusion of enlarged joints and diminished muscles, which, thank God, was even then confined to a narrow section and disappeared with Spanish rule. He had no experimental knowledge of it; nay, regular meals, on the contrary, gave him anxious concern, yet had the effect— spite of his apprehension that he was being fattened for a purpose—of restoring the herculean puissance which formerly in Africa had made him the terror of the battle.

When one day he had come to be quite himself, he was invited out into the sunshine, and escorted by the driver (a sort of foreman to the overseer), went forth dimly wondering. They reached a field where some men and women were hoeing. He had seen men and women—subjects of his—labor—a little—in Africa. The driver handed him a hoe; he examined it with silent interest— until by signs he was requested to join the pastime.

"What?"

He spoke, not with his lips, but with the recoil of his splendid frame and the ferocious expansion of his eyes. This invitation was a cataract of lightning leaping down an ink-black sky. In one instant of all-pervading clearness he read his sentence—WORK.

Bras-Coupé was six feet five. With a sweep as quick as instinct the back of the hoe smote the driver full in the head. Next, the prince lifted the nearest Congo crosswise, brought thirty-two teeth together in his wildly kicking leg and cast him away as a bad morsel; then, throwing another into the branches of a willow, and a woman over his head into a draining-ditch, he made one bound for freedom, and fell to his knees, rocking from side to side under the effect of a pistol-ball from the overseer. It had struck him in the forehead, and running around the skull in search of a penetrable spot, tradition—which sometimes jests —says came out despairingly, exactly where it had entered.

It so happened that, except the overseer, the whole company were black. Why should the trivial scandal be blabbed? A plaster or two made everything even in a short time, except in the driver's case—for the driver died. The woman whom Bras-Coupé had thrown over his head lived to sell *calas* to Joseph Frowenfeld.

Don José, young and austere, knew nothing about agriculture and cared as much about human nature. The overseer often thought this, but never said it; he would not trust even himself with the dangerous criticism. When he ventured to reveal the foregoing incidents to the señor he laid all the blame possible upon the man whom death had removed beyond the reach of correction, and brought his account to a climax by hazarding the assertion that Bras-Coupé was an animal that could not be whipped.

"Caramba!" exclaimed the master, with gentle emphasis, "how so?"

"Perhaps señor had better ride down to the quarters," replied the overseer.

It was a great sacrifice of dignity, but the master made it.

"Bring him out."

They brought him out—chains on his feet, chains on his wrists, an iron yoke on his neck. The Spanish-Creole master had often seen the bull, with his long, keen horns and blazing eye, standing in the arena; but this was as though he had come face to face with a rhinoceros.

"This man is not a Congo," he said.

"He is a Jaloff," replied the encouraged overseer. "See his fine, straight nose; moreover, he is a *candio*—a prince. If I whip him he will die."

The dauntless captive and fearless master stood looking into each other's eyes until each recognized in the other his peer in physical courage, and each was struck with an admiration for

172

the other which no after difference was sufficient entirely to destroy. Had Bras-Coupé's eye quailed but once—just for one little instant—he would have got the lash; but, as it was——

"Get an interpreter," said Don José; then, more privately, "and come to an understanding. I shall require it of you."

Where might one find an interpreter—one not merely able to render a Jaloff's meaning into Creole French, or Spanish, but with such a turn for diplomatic correspondence as would bring about an "understanding" with this African buffalo? The overseer was left standing and thinking, and Clemence, who had not forgotten who threw her into the draining-ditch, cunningly passed by.

"Ah, Clemence——"

"*Mo pas capabe! Mo pas capabe!* (I cannot, I cannot!) *Ya, ya, ya! 'oir Miché Agricol' Fusilier! ouala yune bon monture, oui!*"—which was to signify that Agricola could interpret the very Papa Lébat.

"Agricola Fusilier! The last man on earth to make peace."

But there seemed to be no choice, and to Agricola the overseer went. It was but a little ride to the Grandissime place.

"I, Agricola Fusilier, stand as an interpreter to a negro? H-sir!"

"But I thought you might know of some person," said the weakening applicant, rubbing his ear with his hand.

"Ah!" replied Agricola, addressing the surrounding scenery, "if I did not—who would? You may take Palmyre."

The overseer softly smote his hands together at the happy thought.

"Yes," said Agricola, "take Palmyre; she has picked up as many negro dialects as I know European languages."

And she went to the don's plantation as interpretess, followed by Agricola's prayer to Fate that she might in some way be overtaken by disaster. The two hated each other with all the strength they had. He knew not only her pride, but her passion for the absent Honoré. He hated her, also, for her intelligence, for the high favor in which she stood with her mistress, and for her invincible spirit, which was more offensively patent to him than to others, since he was himself the chief object of her silent detestation.

It was Palmyre's habit to do nothing without painstaking. "When Mademoiselle comes to be Señora," thought she—she knew that her mistress and the don were affianced—"it will be well to have Señor's esteem. I shall endeavor to succeed." It was from this motive, then, that with the aid of her mistress she attired herself in a resplendence of scarlet and beads and feathers that could not fail the double purpose of connecting her with the children of Ethiopia and commanding the captive's instant admiration.

Alas for those who succeed too well! No sooner did the African turn his tiger glance upon her than the fire of his eyes died out; and when she spoke to him in the dear accents of his native tongue, the matter of strife vanished from his mind. He loved.

He sat down tamely in his irons and listened to Palmyre's argument as a wrecked mariner would listen to ghostly church-bells. He would give a short assent, feast his eyes, again assent, and feast his ears; but when at length she made bold to approach the actual issue, and finally uttered the loathed word, *Work*, he rose up, six feet five, a statue of indignation in black marble.

And then Palmyre, too, rose up, glorying in him, and went to explain to master and overseer. Bras-Coupé understood, she said, that he was a slave—it was the fortune of war, and he was a warrior; but, according to a generally recognized principle in African international law, he could not reasonably be expected to work.

"As señor will remember I told him," remarked the overseer; "how can a man expect to plow with a zebra?"

Here he recalled a fact in his early experience. An African of this stripe had been found to answer admirably as a "driver" to make others work. A second and third parley, extending through two or three days, were held with the prince, looking to his appointment to the vacant office of driver; yet what was the master's amazement to learn at length that his Highness declined the proffered honor.

"Stop!" spoke the overseer again, detecting a look of alarm in Palmyre's face as she turned away, "he doesn't do any such thing. If Señor will let me take the man to Agricola——"

"No!" cried Palmyre, with an agonized look, "I will tell. He will take the place and fill it if you will give me to him for his own—but oh, messieurs, for the love of God—I do not want to be his wife!"

The overseer looked at the Señor, ready to approve whatever he should decide. Bras-Coupé's intrepid audacity took the Spaniard's heart by irresistible assault.

"I leave it entirely with Señor Fusilier," he said.

"But he is not my master; he has no right——"

"Silence!"

And she was silent; and so, sometimes, is fire in the wall.

Agricola's consent was given with malicious promptness, and as Bras-Coupé's fetters fell off it was decreed that, should he fill his office efficiently, there should be a wedding on the rear veranda of the Grandissime mansion simultaneously with the one already appointed to take place in the grand hall of the same house six months from that present day. In the meanwhile Palmyre should remain with Mademoiselle, who had promptly but quietly made up her mind that Palmyre should not be wed unless she wished to be. Bras-Coupé made no objection, was royally worthless for a time, but learned fast, mastered the "gumbo" dialect in a few weeks, and in six months was the most valuable man ever bought for gourde dollars. Nevertheless, there were but three persons within as many square miles who were not most vividly afraid of him.

The first was Palmyre. His bearing in her presence was ever one of solemn, exalted respect, which, whether from pure magnanimity in himself, or by reason of her magnetic eye, was something worth being there to see. "It was royal!" said the overseer.

The second was not that official. When Bras-Coupé said—as, at stated intervals, he did say—"*Mo courri c'ez Agricole Fusilier 'pou oir' n'amourouse* (I go to Agricola Fusilier to see my betrothed,)" the overseer would sooner have intercepted a score of painted Chickasaws than that one lover. He would look after him and shake a prophetic head. "Trouble coming; better not deceive that fellow"; yet that was the very thing Palmyre dared do. Her admiration for Bras-Coupé was almost boundless. She rejoiced in his stature; she revelled in the contemplation of his untamable spirit; he seemed to her the gigantic embodiment of her own dark, fierce will, the expanded realization of her lifetime longing for terrible strength. But the single deficiency in all this impassioned regard was—what so many fairer loves have found impossible to explain to so many gentler lovers—an entire absence of preference; her heart she could not give him—she did not have it. Yet after her first prayer to the Spaniard and his overseer for deliverance, to the secret surprise and chagrin of her young mistress, she stimulated content. It was artifice; she

175

knew Agricola's power, and to seem to consent was her one chance with him. He might thus be beguiled into withdrawing his own consent. That failing, she had Mademoiselle's promise to come to the rescue, which she could use at the last moment; and that failing, there was a dirk in her bosom, for which a certain hard breast was not too hard. Another element of safety, of which she knew nothing, was a letter from the Cannes Brulée. The word had reached there that love had conquered—that, despite all hard words, and rancor, and positive injury, the Grandissime hand—the fairest of Grandissime hands—was about to be laid into that of one who without much stretch might be called a De Grapion; that there was, moreover, positive effort being made to induce a restitution of old gaming-table spoils. Honoré and Mademoiselle, his sister, one on each side of the Atlantic, were striving for this end. Don José sent this intelligence to his kinsman as glad tidings (a lover never imagines there are two sides to that which makes him happy), and, to add a touch of humor, told how Palmyre, also, was given to the chieftain. The letter that came back to the young Spaniard did not blame him so much: *he* was ignorant of all the facts; but a very formal one to Agricola begged to notify him that if Palmyre's union with Bras-Coupé should be completed, as sure as there was a God in heaven, the writer would have the life of the man who knowingly had thus endeavored to dishonor one who *shared the blood of the De Grapions*. Thereupon Agricola, contrary to his general character, began to drop hints to Don José that the engagement of Bras-Coupé and Palmyre need not be considered irreversible; but the don was not desirous of disappointing his terrible pet. Palmyre, unluckily, played her game a little too deeply. She thought the moment had come for herself to insist on the match, and thus provoke Agricola to forbid it. To her incalculable dismay she saw him a second time reconsider and become silent.

The second person who did not fear Bras-Coupé was Mademoiselle. On one of the giant's early visits to see Palmyre he obeyed the summons which she brought him, to appear before the lady. A more artificial man might have objected on the score of dress, his attire being a single gaudy garment tightly enveloping the waist and thighs. As his eyes fell upon the beautiful white lady he prostrated himself upon the ground, his arms outstretched before him. He would not move till she was gone. Then

176

he arose like a hermit who has seen a vision. *"Bras-Coupé 'n pas oulé oir zombis* (Bras-Coupé dares not look upon a spirit)." From that hour he worshipped. He saw her often; every time, after one glance at her countenance, he would prostrate his gigantic length with his face in the dust.

The third person who did not fear him was—Agricola? Nay, it was the Spaniard—a man whose capability to fear anything in nature or beyond had never been discovered.

Long before the end of his probation Bras-Coupé would have slipped the entanglements of bondage, though as yet he felt them only as one feels a spider's web across the face, had not the master, according to a little affectation of the times, promoted him to be his game-keeper. Many a day did these two living magazines of wrath spend together in the dismal swamps and on the meagre intersecting ridges, making war upon deer and bear and wildcat; or on the Mississippi after wild goose and pelican; when even a word misplaced would have made either the slayer of the other. Yet the months ran smoothly round and the wedding night drew nigh.* A goodly company had assembled. All things were ready. The bride was dressed, the bridegroom had come. On the great back piazza, which had been inclosed with sail-cloth and lighted with lanterns, was Palmyre, full of a new and deep design and playing her deceit to the last, robed in costly garments to whose beauty was added the charm of their having been worn once, and once only, by her beloved Mademoiselle.

But where was Bras-Coupé?

The question was asked of Palmyre by Agricola with a gaze that meant in English, "No tricks, girl!"

Among the servants who huddled at the windows and door to see the inner magnificence a frightened whisper was already going round.

"We have made a sad discovery, Miché Fusilier," said the overseer. "Bras-Coupé is here; we have him in a room just yonder. But—the truth is, sir, Bras-Coupé is a voudou."

"Well, and suppose he is; what of it? Only hush; do not let

---

* An over-zealous Franciscan once complained bitterly to the bishop of Havana, that people were being married in Louisiana in their own houses after dark and thinking nothing of it. It is not certain that he had reference to the Grandissime mansion; at any rate he was tittered down by the whole community.

his master know it. It is nothing; all the blacks are voudous, more or less."

"But he declines to dress himself—has painted himself all rings and stripes, antelope fashion."

"Tell him Agricola Fusilier says, 'dress immediately!'"

"Oh, Miché, we have said that five times already, and his answer—you will pardon me—his answer is—spitting on the ground—that you are a contemptible *dotchian* (white trash)."

There is nothing to do but privily to call the very bride—the lady herself. She comes forth in all her glory, small, but oh, so beautiful! Slam! Bras-Coupé is upon his face, his finger-tips touching the tips of her snowy slippers. She gently bids him go and dress, and at once he goes.

Ah! now the question may be answered without whispering. There is Bras-Coupé, towering above all heads, in ridiculous red and blue regimentals, but with a look of savage dignity upon him that keeps every one from laughing. The murmur of admiration that passed along the thronged gallery leaped up into a shout in the bosom of Palmyre. Oh, Bras-Coupé—heroic soul! She would not falter. She would let the silly priest say his say—then her cunning should help her *not to be* his wife, yet to show his mighty arm how and when to strike.

"He is looking for Palmyre," said some, and at that moment he saw her.

"Ho-o-o-o-o!"

Agricola's best roar was a penny trumpet to Bras-Coupé's note of joy. The whole masculine half of the in-door company flocked out to see what the matter was. Bras-Coupé was taking her hand in one of his and laying his other upon her head; and as some one made an unnecessary gesture for silence, he sang, beating slow and solemn time with his naked foot and with the hand that dropped hers to smite his breast:

> "'En haut la montagne, zami,
> Mo pé coupé canne, zami,
> Pou' fé i'a'zen' zami,
> Pou' mo baille Palmyre.
> Ah! Palmyre, Palmyre mo c'ere,
> Mo l'aimé ou'—mo l'aimé ou'.'"

"*Montagne?*" asked one slave of another, "*qui ce çà, montagne?*
178

gnia pas quiç' ose comme çà dans la Louisiana? (What's a mountain? We haven't such things in Louisiana.)"

"*Mein ye gagnein plein montagnes dans l'Afrique,* listen!"

> " '*Ah! Palmyre, Palmyre, mo' piti zozo,*
> *Mo l'aimé'ou'—mo l'aimé, l'aimé'ou.*' "

"Bravissimo!—" but just then a counter-attraction drew the white company back into the house. An old French priest with sandalled feet and a dirty face had arrived. There was a moment of hand-shaking with the good father, then a moment of palpitation and holding of the breath, and then—you would have known it by the turning away of two or three feminine heads in tears—the lily hand became the don's, to have and to hold, by authority of the Church and the Spanish king. And all was merry, save that outside there was coming up as villainous a night as ever cast black looks in through snug windows.

It was just as the newly wed Spaniard, with Agricola and all the guests, were concluding the by-play of marrying the darker couple, that the hurricane struck the dwelling. The holy and jovial father had made faint pretence of kissing this second bride; the ladies, colonels, dons, etc.,—though the joke struck them as a trifle coarse—were beginning to laugh and clap hands again and the gowned jester to bow to right and left, when Bras-Coupé, tardily realizing the consummation of his hopes, stepped forward to embrace his wife.

"Bras-Coupé!"

The voice was that of Palmyre's mistress. She had not been able to comprehend her maid's behavior, but now Palmyre had darted upon her an appealing look.

The warrior stopped as if a javelin had flashed over his head and stuck in the wall.

"Bras-Coupé must wait till I give him his wife."

He sank, with hidden face, slowly to the floor.

"Bras-Coupé hears the voice of zombis; the voice is sweet, but the words are very strong; from the same sugar-cane comes *sirop* and *tafia;* Bras-Coupé says to zombis, 'Bras-Coupé will wait; but if the *dotchians* deceive Bras-Coupé—'" he rose to his feet with his eyes closed and his great black fist lifted over his head—"Bras-Coupé will call Voudou-Magnan!"

The crowd retreated and the storm fell like a burst of infernal

179

applause. A whiff like fifty witches flouted up the canvas curtain of the gallery and a fierce black cloud, drawing the moon under its cloak, belched forth a stream of fire that seemed to flood the ground; a peal of thunder followed as if the sky had fallen in, the house quivered, the great oaks groaned, and every lesser thing bowed down before the awful blast. Every lip held its breath for a minute—or an hour, no one knew—there was a sudden lull of the wind, and the floods came down. Have you heard it thunder and rain in those Louisiana lowlands? Every clap seems to crack the world. It has rained a moment; you peer through the black pane—your house is an island, all the land is sea.

However, the supper was spread in the hall and in due time the guests were filled. Then a supper was spread in the big hall in the basement, below stairs, the sons and daughters of Ham came down like the fowls of the air upon a rice-field, and Bras-Coupé, throwing his heels about with the joyous carelessness of a smutted Mercury, for the first time in his life tasted the blood of the grape. A second, a fifth, a tenth time he tasted it, drinking more deeply each time, and would have taken it ten times more had not his bride cunningly concealed it. It was like stealing a tiger's kittens.

The moment quickly came when he wanted his eleventh bumper. As he presented his request a silent shiver of consternation ran through the dark company; and when, in what the prince meant as a remonstrative tone, he repeated the petition—splitting the table with his fist by way of punctuation—there ensued a hustling up staircases and a cramming into dim corners that left him alone at the banquet.

Leaving the table, he strode upstairs and into the chirruping and dancing of the grand salon. There was a halt in the cotillion and a hush of amazement like the shutting off of steam. Bras-Coupé strode straight to his master, laid his paw upon his fellow-bridegroom's shoulder and in a thunder-tone demanded:

"More!"

The master swore a Spanish oath, lifted his hand and—fell, beneath the terrific fist of his slave, with a bang that jingled the candelabras. Dolorous stroke!—for the dealer of it. Given, apparently to him—poor, tipsy savage—in self-defence, punishable, in a white offender, by a small fine or a few days' imprisonment, it assured Bras-Coupé the death of a felon; such was the old

180

Code Noir. (We have a *Code Noir* now, but the new one is a mental reservation, not an enactment.)

The guests stood for an instant as if frozen, smitten stiff with the instant expectation of insurrection, conflagration and rapine (just as we do to-day whenever some poor swaggering Pompey rolls up his fist and gets a ball through his body), while, single-handed and naked-fisted in a room full of swords, the giant stood over his master, making strange signs and passes and rolling out in wrathful words of his mother tongue what it needed no interpreter to tell his swarming enemies was a voudou malediction.

"*Nous sommes grigis!*" screamed two or three ladies, "we are bewitched!"

"Look to your wives and daughters!" shouted a Brahmin-Mandarin.

"Shoot the black devils without mercy!" cried a Mandarin-Fusilier, unconsciously putting into a single outflash of words the whole Creole treatment of race troubles.

With a single bound Bras-Coupé reached the drawing-room door; his gaudy regimentals made a red and blue streak down the hall; there was a rush of frilled and powdered gentlemen to the rear veranda, an avalanche of lightning with Bras-Coupé in the midst making for the swamp, and then all without was blackness of darkness and all within was a wild commingled chatter of Creole, French, and Spanish tongues,—in the midst of which the reluctant Agricola returned his dress-sword to its scabbard.

While the wet lanterns swung on crazily in the trees along the way by which the bridegroom was to have borne his bride; while Madame Grandissime prepared an impromptu bridal-chamber; while the Spaniard bathed his eye and the blue gash on his cheek-bone; while Palmyre paced her room in a fever and wild tremor of conflicting emotions throughout the night and the guests splashed home after the storm as best they could, Bras-Coupé was practically declaring his independence on a slight rise of ground hardly sixty feet in circumference and lifted scarce above the water in the inmost depths of the swamp.

And what surroundings! Endless colonnades of cypresses; long, motionless drapings of gray moss; broad sheets of noisome waters, pitchy black, resting on bottomless ooze; cypress knees studding the surface; patches of floating green, gleaming brilliantly here and there; yonder where the sunbeams wedge them-

181

selves in, constellations of water-lilies, the many-hued iris, and a multitude of flowers that no man had named; here, too, serpents great and small, of wonderful colorings, and the dull and loathsome moccasin sliding warily off the dead tree; in dimmer recesses the cow alligator, with her nest hard by; turtles a century old; owls and bats, racoons, opossums, rats, centipedes and creatures of like vileness; great vines of beautiful leaf and scarlet fruit in deadly clusters; maddening mosquitoes, parasitic insects, gorgeous dragon-flies and pretty water-lizards: the blue heron, the snowy crane, the red-bird, the moss-bird, the night-hawk and the chuckwill's widow; a solemn stillness and stifled air only now and then disturbed by the call or whir of the summer duck, the dismal ventriloquous note of the rain-crow, or the splash of a dead branch falling into the clear but lifeless bayou.

The pack of Cuban hounds that howl from Don José's kennels cannot snuff the trail of the stolen canoe that glides through the sombre blue vapors of the African's fastnesses. His arrows send no tell-tale reverberations to the distant clearing. Many a wretch in his native wilderness has Bras-Coupé himself, in palmier days, driven to just such an existence, to escape the chains and horrors of the barracoons; therefore not a whit broods he over man's inhumanity, but, taking the affair as a matter of course, casts about him for a future.

29 The Story of Bras-Coupé, *continued*

Bras-Coupé let the autumn pass, and wintered in his den.

Don José, in a majestic way, endeavored to be happy. He took his señora to his hall, and under her rule it took on for a while a look and feeling which turned it from a hunting-lodge into a home. Wherever the lady's steps turned—or it is as correct to say wherever the proud tread of Palmyre turned—the features of bachelor's hall disappeared; guns, dogs, oars, saddles, nets, went their way into proper banishment, and the broad halls and lofty chambers—the floors now muffled with mats of palmetto-leaf—no longer re-echoed the tread of a lonely master, but breathed a redolence of flowers and a rippling murmur of well-contented song.

But the song was not from the throat of Bras-Coupé's *"piti zozo."* Silent and severe by day, she moaned away whole nights heaping reproaches upon herself for the impulse—now to her, because it had failed, inexplicable in its folly—which had permitted her hand to lie in Bras-Coupé's and the priest to bind them together.

For in the audacity of her pride, or, as Agricola would have said, in the immensity of her impudence, she had held herself consecrate to a hopeless love. But now she was a black man's wife; and even he unable to sit at her feet and learn the lesson she had hoped to teach him. She had heard of San Domingo, and for months the fierce heart within her silent bosom had been leaping and shouting and seeing visions of fire and blood, and when she brooded over the nearness of Agricola and the remoteness of Honoré these visions got from her a sort of mad consent. The lesson she would have taught the giant was Insurrection. But it was too late. Letting her dagger sleep in her bosom, and with an undefined belief in imaginary resources, she had consented to join hands with her giant hero before the priest; and when the wedding had come and gone, like a white sail, she was seized with a lasting, fierce despair. A wild aggressiveness that had formerly characterized her glance in moments of anger— moments which had grown more and more infrequent under the softening influence of her Mademoiselle's nature—now came back intensified and blazed in her eye perpetually. Whatever her secret love may have been in kind, its sinking beyond hope below the horizon had left her fifty times the mutineer she had been before—the mutineer who has nothing to lose.

"She loves her *candio*," said the negroes.

"Simple creatures!" said the overseer, who prided himself on his discernment, "she loves nothing; she hates Agricola; it's a case of hate at first sight—the strongest kind."

Both were partly right; her feelings were wonderfully knit to the African; and she now dedicated herself to Agricola's ruin.

The señor, it has been said, endeavored to be happy; but now his heart conceived and brought forth its first-born fear, sired by superstition—the fear that he was bewitched. The negroes said that Bras-Coupé had cursed the land. Morning after morning the master looked out with apprehension toward his fields, until one night the worm came upon the indigo and between sunset and sunrise every green leaf had been eaten up, and there was nothing left for either insect or apprehension, to feed upon.

And then he said—and the echo came back from the Cannes Brulées—that the very bottom culpability of this thing rested on the Grandissimes, and specifically on their fugleman Agricola, through his putting the hellish African upon him. Moreover, fever and death, to a degree unknown before, fell upon his slaves. Those to whom life was spared—but to whom strength did not return—wandered about the place like scarecrows, looking for shelter, and made the very air dismal with the reiteration, *"No' ouanga* (we are bewitched), *Bras-Coupé fe moi des grigis* (the

184

voudou's spells are on me)." The ripple of song was hushed and the flowers fell upon the floor.

"I have heard an English maxim," wrote Colonel De Grapion to his kinsman, "which I would recommend you to put into practice—'Fight the devil with fire.'"

No, he would not recognize devils as belligerents.

But if Rome commissioned exorcists, could not he employ one?

No, he would not! If his hounds could not catch Bras-Coupé, why, let him go. The overseer tried the hounds once more and came home with the best one across his saddle-bow, an arrow run half through its side.

Once the blacks attempted by certain familiar rum-pourings and nocturnal charm-singing to lift the curse; but the moment the master heard the wild monotone of their infernal worship, he stopped it with a word.

Early in February came the spring, and with it some resurrection of hope and courage. It may have been—it certainly was, in part—because young Honoré Grandissime had returned. He was like the sun's warmth wherever he went; and the other Honoré was like his shadow. The fairer one quickly saw the meaning of these things, hastened to cheer the young don with hopes of a better future, and to effect, if he could, the restoration of Bras-Coupé to his master's favor. But this latter effort was an idle one. He had long sittings with his uncle Agricola to the same end, but they always ended fruitless and often angrily.

His dark half-brother had seen Palmyre and loved her. Honoré would gladly have solved one or two riddles by effecting their honorable union in marriage. The previous ceremony on the Grandissime back piazza need be no impediment; all slave-owners understood those things. Following Honoré's advice, the f. m. c., who had come into possession of his paternal portion, sent to Cannes Brulées a written offer, to buy Palmyre at any price that her master might name, stating his intention to free her and make her his wife. Colonel De Grapion could hardly hope to settle Palmyre's fate more satisfactorily, yet he could not forego an opportunity to indulge his pride by following up the threat he had hung over Agricola to kill whosoever should give Palmyre to a black man. He referred the subject and the would-be purchaser to him. It would open up to the old braggart a line of retreat, thought the planter of the Cannes Brulées.

But the idea of retreat had left Citizen Fusilier.

"She is already married," said he to M. Honoré Grandissime, f. m. c. "She is the lawful wife of Bras-Coupé; and what God has joined together let no man put asunder. You know it, sirrah. You did this for impudence, to make a show of your wealth. You intended it as an insinuation of equality. I overlook the impertinence for the sake of the man whose white blood you carry; but h-mark you, if ever you bring your Parisian airs and self-sufficient face on a level with mine again, h-I will slap it."

The quadroon, three nights after, was so indiscreet as to give him the opportunity, and he did it—at that quadroon ball, to which Dr. Keene alluded in talking to Frowenfeld.

But Don José, we say, plucked up new spirit.

"Last year's disasters were but fortune's freaks," he said. "See, others' crops have failed all about us."

The overseer shook his head.

"C'est ce maudit cocodri' là bas (It is that accursed alligator, Bras-Coupé, down yonder in the swamp)."

And by and by the master was again smitten with the same belief. He and his neighbors put in their crops afresh. The spring waned, summer passed, the fevers returned, the year wore round, but no harvest smiled. "Alas!" cried the planters, "we are all poor men!" The worst among the worst were the fields of Bras-Coupé's master—parched and shrivelled. "He does not understand planting," said his neighbors; "neither does his overseer. Maybe, too, it is true as he says, that he is voudoued."

One day at high noon the master was taken sick with fever.

The third noon after—the sad wife sitting by the bedside—suddenly, right in the centre of the room, with the open door behind him, stood the magnificent, half-nude form of Bras-Coupé. He did not fall down as the mistress's eyes met his, though all his flesh quivered. The master was lying with his eyes closed. The fever had done a fearful three days' work.

"Mioko-koanga oulé so' femme (Bras-Coupé wants his wife)."

The master started wildly and stared upon his slave.

"Bras-Coupé oulé so' femme!" repeated the black.

"Seize him!" cried the sick man, trying to rise.

But, though several servants had ventured in with frightened faces, none dared molest the giant. The master turned his entreating eyes upon his wife, but she seemed stunned, and only covered her face with her hands and sat as if paralyzed by a foreknowledge of what was coming.

186

Bras-Coupé lifted his great, black palm and commenced:

"*Mo cé voudrai que la maison ci là et tout ça qui pas femme'
ici s'raient encore maudits!* (May this house and all in it who are
not women be accursed)."

The master fell back upon his pillow with a groan of helpless
wrath.

The African pointed his finger through the open window.

"May its fields not know the plough nor nourish the cattle
that overrun it."

The domestics, who had thus far stood their ground, suddenly
rushed from the room like stampeded cattle, and at that moment appeared Palmyre.

"Speak to him," faintly cried the panting invalid.

She went firmly up to her husband and lifted her hand. With
an easy motion, but quick as lightning, as a lion sets foot on a
dog, he caught her by the arm.

"*Bras-Coupé oulé so' femme,*" he said, and just then Palmyre
would have gone with him to the equator.

"You shall not have her!" gasped the master.

The African seemed to rise in height, and still holding his
wife at arm's length, resumed his malediction:

"May weeds cover the ground until the air is full of their
odor and the wild beasts of the forest come and lie down under
their cover."

With a frantic effort the master lifted himself upon his elbow
and extended his clenched fist in speechless defiance; but his
brain reeled, his sight went out, and when again he saw, Palmyre and her mistress were bending over him, the overseer stood
awkwardly by, and Bras-Coupé was gone.

The plantation became an invalid camp. The words of the
voudou found fulfilment on every side. The plough went not
out; the herds wandered through broken hedges from field to
field and came up with staring bones and shrunken sides; a
frenzied mob of weeds and thorns wrestled and throttled each
other in a struggle for standing-room—rag-weed, smart-weed,
sneeze-weed, bind-weed, iron-weed—until the burning skies of
mid-summer checked their growth and crowned their unshorn
tops with rank and dingy flowers.

"Why in the name of—St. Francis," asked the priest of the
overseer, "didn't the señora use her power over the black scoun-
drel when he stood and cursed, that day?"

"Why, to tell you the truth, father," said the overseer, in a discreet whisper, "I can only suppose she thought Bras-Coupé had half a right to do it."

"Ah, ah, I see; like her brother Honoré—looks at both sides of a question—a miserable practice; but why couldn't Palmyre use *her* eyes? They would have stopped him."

"Palmyre? Why Palmyre has become the best *mon ture* (Plutonian medium) in the parish. Agricola Fusilier himself is afraid of her. Sir, I think sometimes Bras-Coupé is dead and his spirit has gone into Palmyre. She would rather add to his curse than take from it."

"Ah!" said the jovial divine, with a fat smile, "castigation would help her case; the whip is a great sanctifier. I fancy it would even make a Christian of the inexpugnable Bras-Coupé."

But Bras-Coupé kept beyond the reach alike of the lash and of the Latin Bible.

By and by came a man with a rumor, whom the overseer brought to the master's sick-room, to tell that an enterprising Frenchman was attempting to produce a new staple in Louisiana, one that worms would not annihilate. It was that year of history when the despairing planters saw ruin hovering so close over them that they cried to heaven for succor. Providence raised up Etienne de Boré. "And if Etienne is successful," cried the newsbearer, "and gets the juice of the sugar-cane to crystallize, so shall all of us, after him, and shall yet save our lands and homes. Oh, Señor, it will make you strong again to see these fields all cane and the long rows of negroes and negresses cutting it, while they sing their song of those droll African numerals, counting the canes they cut," and the bearer of good tidings sang them for very joy:

An - o - qué, An - o - bia, Bia - tail - la, Que - re - que, Nal - le - oua,

Au - mon-dé, Au - tap - o - té, Au - pa - to - té, Au-qué - ré - qué, Bo.

"And Honoré Grandissime is going to introduce it on his lands," said Don José.

"That is true," said Agricola Fusilier, coming in. Honoré, the indefatigable peace-maker, had brought his uncle and his brother-in-law for the moment not only to speaking but to friendly terms.

The señor smiled.

"I have some good tidings, too," he said; "my beloved lady has borne me a son."

"Another scion of the house of Grand——I mean Martinez!" exclaimed Agricola. "And now, Don José, let me say that *I* have an item of rare intelligence!"

The don lifted his feeble head and opened his inquiring eyes with a sudden, savage light in them.

"No," said Agricola, "he is not exactly taken yet, but they are on his track."

"Who?"

"The police. We may say he is virtually in our grasp."

It was on a Sabbath afternoon that a band of Choctaws having just played a game of racquette behind the city and a similar game being about to end between the white champions of two rival faubourgs, the beating of tom-toms, rattling of mules' jawbones and sounding of wooden horns drew the populace across the fields to a spot whose present name of Congo Square still preserves a reminder of its old barbaric pastimes. On a grassy plain under the ramparts, the performers of these hideous discords sat upon the ground facing each other, and in their midst the dancers danced. They gyrated in couples, a few at a time, throwing their bodies into the most startling attitudes and the wildest contortions, while the whole company of black lookers-on, incited by the tones of the weird music and the violent posturing of the dancers, swayed and writhed in passionate sympathy, beating their breasts, palms and thighs in time with the bones and drums, and at frequent intervals lifting, in that wild African unison no more to be described than forgotten, the unutterable songs of the Babouille and Counjaille dances, with their ejaculatory burdens of *"Aie! Aie! Voudou Magnan!"* and *"Aie Calinda! Dancé Calinda!"* The volume of sound rose and fell with the augmentation or diminution of the dancers' extravagances. Now a fresh man, young and supple, bounding into the ring, revived the flagging rattlers, drummers and trumpeters; now a wearied dancer, finding his strength going, gathered all his force at the cry of *"Dancé zisqu'a mort!"* rallied to grand finale and with one magnificent antic, fell, foaming at the mouth.

The amusement had reached its height. Many participants had been lugged out by the neck to avoid their being danced on, and the enthusiasm had risen to a frenzy, when there bounded into the ring the blackest of black men, an athlete of superb figure, in breeches of "Indienne"—the stuff used for slave women's best dresses—jingling with bells, his feet in moccasins, his tight, crisp hair decked out with feathers, a necklace of alligator's teeth rattling on his breast and a living serpent twined about his neck.

It chanced that but one couple was dancing. Whether they had been sent there by advice of Agricola is not certain. Snatching a tambourine from a bystander as he entered, the stranger thrust the male dancer aside, faced the woman and began a series of saturnalian antics, compared with which all that had gone before was tame and sluggish; and as he finally leaped, with tinkling heels, clean over his bewildered partner's head, the multitude howled with rapture.

Ill-starred Bras-Coupé. He was in that extra-hazardous and irresponsible condition of mind and body known in the undignified present as "drunk again."

By the strangest fortune, if not, as we have just hinted, by some design, the man whom he had once deposited in the willow bushes, and the woman Clemence, were the very two dancers, and no other, whom he had interrupted. The man first stupidly regarded, next admiringly gazed upon, and then distinctly recognized, his whilom driver. Five minutes later the Spanish police were putting their heads together to devise a quick and permanent capture; and in the midst of the sixth minute, as the wonderful fellow was rising in a yet more astounding leap than his last, a lasso fell about his neck and brought him, crashing like a burnt tree, face upward upon the turf.

"The runaway slave," said the old French code, continued in force by the Spaniards, "the runaway slave who shall continue to be so for one month from the day of his being denounced to the officers of justice, shall have his ears cut off and shall be branded with the flower de luce on the shoulder; and on a second offence of the same nature, persisted in during one month of his being denounced, he shall be hamstrung, and be marked with the flower de luce on the other shoulder. On the third offence he shall die." Bras-Coupé had run away only twice. "But," said Agricola, "these 'bossals' must be taught their place. Besides,

190

there is Article 27 of the same code: 'The slave who, having struck his master, shall have produced a bruise, shall suffer capital punishment'—a very necessary law!" He concluded with a scowl upon Palmyre, who shot back a glance which he never forgot.

The Spaniard showed himself very merciful—for a Spaniard; he spared the captive's life. He might have been more merciful still; but Honoré Grandissime said some indignant things in the African's favor, and as much to teach the Grandissimes a lesson as to punish the runaway, he would have repented his clemency, as he repented the momentary truce with Agricola, but for the tearful pleading of the señora and the hot, dry eyes of her maid. Because of these he overlooked the offence against his person and estate, and delivered Bras-Coupé to the law to suffer only the penalties of the crime he had committed against society by attempting to be a free man.

We repeat it for the credit of Palmyre, that she pleaded for Bras-Coupé. But what it cost her to make that intercession, knowing that his death would leave her free, and that if he lived she must be his wife, let us not attempt to say.

In the midst of the ancient town, in a part which is now crumbling away, stood the Calaboza, with its humid vaults, grated cells, iron cages and its whips; and there, soon enough, they strapped Bras-Coupé face downward and laid on the lash. And yet not a sound came from the mutilated but unconquered African to annoy the ear of the sleeping city.

("And you suffered this thing to take place?" asked Joseph Frowenfeld of Honoré Grandissime.

"My-de'-seh!" exclaimed the Creole, "they lied to me—said they would not harm him!")

He was brought at sunrise to the plantation. The air was sweet with the smell of the weed-grown fields. The long-horned oxen that drew him and the naked boy that drove the team stopped before his cabin.

"You cannot put that creature in there," said the thoughtful overseer. "He would suffocate under a roof—he has been too long out-of-doors for that. Put him on my cottage porch." There, at last, Palmyre burst into tears and sank down, while before her on a soft bed of dry grass, rested the helpless form of the captive giant, a cloth thrown over his galled back, his ears shorn from his head, and the tendons behind his knees severed. His eyes were dry, but there was in them that unspeakable despair that fills the eye of the charger when, fallen in battle, he gazes with sidewise-bended neck upon the ruin wrought upon him. His eye turned sometimes slowly to his wife. He need not demand her now—she was always by him.

There was much talk over him—much idle talk; no power or circumstance has ever been found that will keep a Creole from talking. He merely lay still under it with a fixed frown; but once some incautious tongue dropped the name of Agricola. The black man's eyes came so quickly round to Palmyre that she thought he would speak; but no; his words were all in his eyes. She answered their gleam with a fierce affirmative glance, whereupon he slowly bent his head and spat upon the floor.

There was yet one more trial of his wild nature. The mandate came from his master's sick-bed that he must lift the curse.

Bras-Coupé merely smiled. God keep thy enemy from such a smile!

The overseer, with a policy less Spanish than his master's, endeavored to use persuasion. But the fallen prince would not so much as turn one glance from his parted hamstrings. Palmyre was then besought to intercede. She made one poor attempt, but her husband was nearer doing her an unkindness than ever he had been before; he made a slow sign for silence—with his fist; and every mouth was stopped.

At midnight following, there came, on the breeze that blew from the mansion, a sound of running here and there, of wailing and sobbing—another Bridegroom was coming, and the Spaniard, with much such a lamp in hand as most of us shall be found with, neither burning brightly nor wholly gone out, went forth to meet Him.

"Bras-Coupé," said Palmyre, next evening, speaking low in his mangled ear, "the master is dead; he is just buried. As he was dying, Bras-Coupé, he asked that you would forgive him."

The maimed man looked steadfastly at his wife. He had not spoken since the lash struck him, and he spoke not now; but in those large, clear eyes, where his remaining strength seemed to have taken refuge as in a citadel, the old fierceness flared up for a moment, and then, like an expiring beacon, went out.

"Is your mistress well enough by this time to venture here?" whispered the overseer to Palmyre. "Let her come. Tell her not to fear, but to bring the babe—in her own arms, tell her—quickly!"

The lady came, her infant boy in her arms, knelt down beside the bed of sweet grass and set the child within the hollow of the African's arm. Bras-Coupé turned his gaze upon it; it smiled, its mother's smile, and put its hand upon the runaway's face, and the first tears of Bras-Coupé's life, the dying testimony of his humanity, gushed from his eyes and rolled down his cheek upon the infant's hand. He laid his own tenderly upon the babe's forehead, then removing it, waved it abroad, inaudibly moved his lips, dropped his arm, and closed his eyes. The curse was lifted.

"*Le pauv' dgiab'!*" said the overseer, wiping his eyes and looking fieldward. "Palmyre, you must get the priest."

The priest came, in the identical gown in which he had appeared the night of the two weddings. To the good father's many tender questions Bras-Coupé turned a failing eye that gave no answers; until, at length:

"Do you know where you are going?" asked the holy man.

"Yes," answered his eyes, brightening.

"Where?"

He did not reply; he was lost in contemplation, and seemed looking far away.

So the question was repeated.

"Do you know where you are going?"

And again the answer of the eyes. He knew.

"Where?"

The overseer at the edge of the porch, the widow with her babe, and Palmyre and the priest bending over the dying bed, turned an eager ear to catch the answer.

"To—" the voice failed a moment; the departing hero essayed again; again it failed; he tried once more, lifted his hand, and with an ecstatic, upward smile, whispered, "To—Africa"—and was gone.

30 Paralysis

As we have said, the story of Bras-Coupé was told that day three times: to the Grandissime beauties once, to Frowenfeld twice. The fair Grandissimes all agreed, at the close, that it was pitiful. Specially, that it was a great pity to have hamstrung Bras-Coupé, a man who even in his cursing had made an exception in favor of the ladies. True, they could suggest no alternative; it was undeniable that he had deserved his fate; still, it seemed a pity. They dispersed, retired and went to sleep confirmed in this sentiment. In Frowenfeld the story stirred deeper feelings.

On this same day, while it was still early morning, Honoré Grandissime, f. m. c., with more than even his wonted slowness of step and propriety of rich attire, had reappeared in the shop of the rue Royale. He did not need to say he desired another private interview. Frowenfeld ushered him silently and at once into his rear room, offered him a chair (which he accepted), and sat down before him.

In his labored way the quadroon stated his knowledge that Frowenfeld had been three times to the dwelling of Palmyre Philosophe. Why, he further intimated, he knew not, nor would he ask; but *he*—when *he* had applied for admission—had been refused. He had laid open his heart to the apothecary's eyes—"It may have been unwisely——"

Frowenfeld interrupted him; Palmyre had been ill for several days; Doctor Keene—who, Mr. Grandissime probably knew, was her physician——

The landlord bowed, and Frowenfeld went on to explain that Doctor Keene, while attending her, had also fallen sick and had asked him to take the care of this one case until he could himself resume it. So there, in a word, was the reason why Joseph had, and others had not, been admitted to her presence.

As obviously to the apothecary's eyes as anything intangible could be, a load of suffering was lifted from the quadroon's mind, as this explanation was concluded. Yet he only sat in meditation before his tenant, who regarded him long and sadly. Then, seized with one of his energetic impulses, he suddenly said:

"Mr. Grandissime, you are a man of intelligence, accomplishments, leisure and wealth; why" (clenching his fists and frowning), "why do you not give yourself—your time—wealth—attainments—energies—everything—to the cause of the down-trodden race with which this community's scorn unjustly compels you to rank yourself?"

The quadroon did not meet Frowenfeld's kindled eyes for a moment, and when he did, it was slowly and dejectedly.

"He canno' be," he said, and then, seeing his words were not understood, he added: "He 'ave no Cause. Dad peop' 'ave no Cause." He went on from this with many pauses and gropings after words and idiom, to tell with a plaintiveness that seemed to Frowenfeld almost unmanly, the reasons why the people a little of whose blood had been enough to blast his life, would never be free by the force of their own arm. Reduced to the meanings which he vainly tried to convey in words, his statement was this: that that people was not a people. Their cause—was in Africa. They upheld it there—they lost it there—and to those that are here the struggle was over; they were, one and all, prisoners of war.

"You speak of them in the third person," said Frowenfeld.

"Ah ham nod a slev."

"Are you certain of that?" asked the tenant.

His landlord looked at him.

"It seems to me," said Frowenfeld, "that you—your class—the free quadroons—are the saddest slaves of all. Your men, for a little property, and your women, for a little amorous attention,

195

let themselves be shorn even of the virtue of discontent, and for a paltry bait of sham freedom have consented to endure a tyrannous contumely which flattens them into the dirt like grass under a slab. I would rather be a runaway in the swamps than content myself with such a freedom. As your class stands before the world to-day—free in form but slaves in spirit—you are—I do not know but I was almost ready to say—a warning to philanthropists!"

The free man of color slowly arose.

"I trust you know," said Frowenfeld, "that I say nothing in offence."

"Havery word is tru'," replied the sad man.

"Mr. Grandissime," said the apothecary, as his landlord sank back again into his seat, "I know you are a broken-hearted man."

The quadroon laid his fist upon his heart and looked up.

"And being broken hearted, you are thus specially fitted for a work of patient and sustained self-sacrifice. You have only those things to lose which grief has taught you to despise—ease, money, display. Give yourself to your people—to those, I mean, who groan, or should groan, under the degraded lot which is theirs and yours in common."

The quadroon shook his head, and after a moment's silence, answered:

"Ah cannod be one Toussaint l'Ouverture. Ah cannod trah to be. Hiv I trah, I h-only s'all soogceed to be one Bras-Coupé."

"You entirely misunderstand me," said Frowenfeld in quick response. "I have no stronger disbelief than my disbelief in insurrection. I believe that to every desirable end there are two roads, the way of strife and the way of peace. I can imagine a man in your place, going about among his people, stirring up their minds to a noble discontent, laying out his means, sparingly here and bountifully there, as in each case might seem wisest, for their enlightenment, their moral elevation, their training in skilled work; going, too, among the men of the prouder caste, among such as have a spirit of fairness, and seeking to prevail with them for a public recognition of the rights of all; using all his cunning to show them the double damage of all oppression, both great and petty——"

The quadroon motioned "enough." There was a heat in his eyes which Frowenfeld had never seen before.

"M'sieu'," he said, "waid till Agricola Fusilier ees keel."

196

"Do you mean 'dies'?"

"No," insisted the quadroon; "listen." And with slow, painstaking phrase this man of strong feeling and feeble will (the trait of his caste) told—as Frowenfeld felt he would do the moment he said "listen"—such part of the story of Bras-Coupé as showed how he came by his deadly hatred of Agricola.

"Tale me," said the landlord, as he concluded the recital, "w'y deen Bras-Coupé mague dad curze on Agricola Fusilier? Becoze Agricola ees one sorcier! Elz 'e bin dade sinz long tamm."

The speaker's gestures seemed to imply that his own hand, if need be, would have brought the event to pass.

As he rose to say adieu, Frowenfeld, without previous intention, laid a hand upon his visitor's arm.

"Is there no one who can make peace between you?"

The landlord shook his head.

" 'Tis impossib'; we don' wand."

"I mean," insisted Frowenfeld, "is there no man who can stand between you and those who wrong you, and effect a peaceful reparation?"

The landlord slowly moved away, neither he nor his tenant speaking, but each knowing that the one man in the minds of both, as a possible peace-maker, was Honoré Grandissime.

"Should the opportunity offer," continued Joseph, "may I speak a word for you myself?"

The quadroon paused a moment, smiled politely though bitterly, and departed repeating again:

" 'Tis impossib'. We don' wand."

"Palsied," murmured Frowenfeld, looking after him, regretfully,—"like all of them."

Frowenfeld's thoughts were still on the same theme when, the day having passed, the hour was approaching wherein Raoul Innerarity was exhorted to tell his good-night story in the merry circle at the distant Grandissime mansion. As the apothecary was closing his last door for the night, the fairer Honoré called him out into the moonlight.

"Withered," the student was saying audibly to himself, "not in the shadow of the Ethiopian, but in the glare of the white man."

"Who is withered?" pleasantly demanded Honoré.

The apothecary started slightly.

"Did I speak? How do you do, sir? I meant the free quadroons."

"Including the gentleman from whom you rent your store?"

"Yes, him especially; he told me this morning the story of Bras-Coupé."

M. Grandissime laughed. Joseph did not see why, nor did the laugh sound entirely genuine.

"Do not open your door, Mr. Frowenfeld," said the Creole. "Get your great-coat and cane and come take a walk with me; I will tell you the same story."

It was two hours before they approached this door again on their return. Just before they reached it, Honoré stopped under the huge street-lamp, whose light had gone out, where a large stone lay before him on the ground in the narrow, moonlit street. There was a tall, unfinished building at his back.

"Mr. Frowenfeld,"—he struck the stone with his cane,—"this stone is Bras-Coupé—we cast it aside because it turns the edge of our tools."

He laughed. He had laughed to-night more than was comfortable to a man of Frowenfeld's quiet mind.

As the apothecary thrust his shop-key into the lock and so paused to hear his companion, who had begun again to speak, he wondered what it could be—for M. Grandissime had not disclosed it—that induced such a man as he to roam aimlessly, as it seemed, in deserted streets at such chill and dangerous hours. "What does he want with me?" The thought was so natural that it was no miracle the Creole read it.

"Well," said he, smiling and taking an attitude, "you are a great man for causes, Mr. Frowenfeld; but me, I am for results, ha, ha! You may ponder the philosophy of Bras-Coupé in your study, but *I* have got to get rid of his results, me. You know them."

"You tell me it revived a war where you had made a peace," said Frowenfeld.

"Yes—yes—that is his results; but good-night, Mr. Frowenfeld."

"Good-night, sir."

31 Another Wound in a New Place

Each day found Doctor Keene's strength increasing, and on the morning following the incidents last recorded he was imprudently projecting an out-door promenade. An announcement from Honoré Grandissime, who had paid an early call, had, to that gentleman's no small surprise, produced a sudden and violent effect on the little man's temper.

He was sitting alone by his window, looking out upon the levee, when the apothecary entered the apartment.

"Frowenfeld," he instantly began, with evident displeasure most unaccountable to Joseph, "I hear you have been visiting the Nancanous."

"Yes, I have been there."

"Well, you had no business to go!"

Doctor Keene smote the arm of his chair with his fist.

Frowenfeld reddened with indignation, but suppressed his retort. He stood still in the middle of the floor, and Doctor Keene looked out of the window.

"Doctor Keene," said the visitor, when this attitude was no longer tolerable, "have you anything more to say to me before I leave you?"

"No, sir."

"It is necessary for me, then, to say that in fulfilment of my

199

promise, I am going from here to the house of Palmyre, and that she will need no further attention after to-day. As to your present manner toward me, I shall endeavor to suspend judgment until I have some knowledge of its cause."

The doctor made no reply, but went on looking out of the window, and Frowenfeld turned and left him.

As he arrived in the Philosophe's sick-chamber—where he found her sitting in a chair set well back from a small fire—she half whispered "Miché" with a fine, greeting smile, as if to a brother after a week's absence. To a person forced to lie abed, shut away from occupation and events, a day is ten, three are a month: not merely in the wear and tear upon the patience, but also in the amount of thinking and recollecting done. It was to be expected, then, that on this, the apothecary's fourth visit, Palmyre would have learned to take pleasure in his coming.

But the smile was followed by a faint, momentary frown, as if Frowenfeld had hardly returned it in kind. Likely enough, he had not. He was not distinctively a man of smiles; and as he engaged in his appointed task she presently thought of this.

"This wound is doing so well," said Joseph, still engaged with the bandages, "that I shall not need to come again." He was not looking at her as he spoke, but he felt her give a sudden start. "What is this?" he thought, but presently said very quietly: "With the assistance of your slave woman, you can now attend to it yourself."

She made no answer.

When, with a bow, he would have bade her good-morning, she held out her hand for his. After a barely perceptible hesitation, he gave it, whereupon she held it fast, in a way to indicate that there was something to be said which he must stay and hear.

She looked up into his face. She may have been merely framing in her mind the word or two of English she was about to utter; but an excitement shone through her eyes and reddened her lips, and something sent out from her countenance a look of wild distress.

"You goin' tell 'im?" she asked.

"Who? Agricola?"

"*Non!*"

He spoke the next name more softly.

"Honoré?"

Her eyes looked deeply into his for a moment, then dropped, and she made a sign of assent.

He was about to say that Honoré knew already, but saw no necessity for doing so, and changed his answer.

"I will never tell any one."

"You know?" she asked, lifting her eyes for an instant. She meant to ask if he knew the motive that had prompted her murderous intent.

"I know your whole sad history."

She looked at him for a moment, fixedly; then, still holding his hand with one of hers, she threw the other to her face and turned away her head. He thought she moaned.

Thus she remained for a few moments, then suddenly she turned, clasped both hands about his, her face flamed up and she opened her lips to speak, but speech failed. An expression of pain and supplication came upon her countenance, and the cry burst from her:

"Meg 'im to love me!"

He tried to withdraw his hand, but she held it fast, and, looking up imploringly with her wide, electric eyes, cried:

"*Vous pouvez le faire, vous pouvez le faire* (you can do it, you can do it); *êtes sorcier, mo conné bien vous êtes sorcier* (you are a sorcerer, I know)."

However harmless or healthful Joseph's touch might be to the Philosophe, he felt now that hers, to him, was poisonous. He dared encounter her eyes, her touch, her voice, no longer. The better man in him was suffocating. He scarce had power left to liberate his right hand with his left, to seize his hat and go.

Instantly she rose from her chair, threw herself on her knees in his path, and found command of his language sufficient to cry as she lifted her arms, bared of their drapery:

"Oh, my God! don' rif-used me—don' rif-used me!"

There was no time to know whether Frowenfeld wavered or not. The thought flashed into his mind that in all probability all the care and skill he had spent upon the wound was being brought to naught in this moment of wild posturing and excitement; but before it could have effect upon his movements, a stunning blow fell upon the back of his head, and Palmyre's slave woman, the Congo dwarf, under the impression that it was the most timely of strokes, stood brandishing a billet of pine and preparing to repeat the blow.

He hurled her, snarling and gnashing like an ape, against the farther wall, cast the bar from the street-door and plunged out, hatless, bleeding, and stunned.

32 Interrupted Preliminaries

About the same time of day, three gentlemen (we use the term gentlemen in its petrified state) were walking down the rue Royale from the direction of the Faubourg Ste. Marie.

They were coming down toward Palmyre's corner. The middle one, tall and shapely, might have been mistaken at first glance for Honoré Grandissime, but was taller and broader, and wore a cocked hat, which Honoré did not. It was Valentine. The short, black-bearded man in buckskin breeches on his right was Jean-Baptiste Grandissime, and the slight one on the left, who, with the prettiest and most graceful gestures and balancings, was leading the conversation, was Hippolyte Brahmin Mandarin, a cousin and counterpart of that sturdy-hearted challenger of Agricola, Sylvestre.

"But after all," he was saying in Louisiana French, "there is no spot comparable, for comfortable seclusion, to the old orange grove under the levee on the Point; twenty minutes in a skiff, five minutes for preliminaries—you would not want more, the ground has been measured off five hundred times—'are you ready?'——"

"Ah, bah!" said Valentine, tossing his head, "the Yankees would be down on us before you could count one."

"Well, then, behind the Jesuits' warehouses, if you insist. I don't care. Perdition take such a government! I am almost sorry I went to the governor's reception."

"It was quiet, I hear; a sort of quiet ball, all promenading and no contra-dances. One quadroon ball is worth five of such."

This was the opinion of Jean-Baptiste.

"No, it was fine, anyhow. There was a contra-dance. The music was—tárata joonc, tará, tará—tá ta joonc, tarárata joonc, tará—oh! it was the finest thing—and composed here. They compose as fine things here as they do anywhere in the——look there! That man came out of Palmyre's house; see how he staggered just then!"

"Drunk," said Jean-Baptiste.

"No, he seems to be hurt. He has been struck on the head. Oho, I tell you, gentlemen, that same Palmyre is a wonderful animal! Do you see? She not only defends herself and ejects the wretch, but she puts her mark upon him; she identifies him, ha, ha, ha! Look at the high art of the thing; she keeps his hat as a small souvenir and gives him a receipt for it on the back of his head. Ah! but hasn't she taught him a lesson? Why, gentlemen,—it is— if it isn't that sorcerer of an apothecary!"

"What?" exclaimed the other two; "well, well, but this is too good! Caught at last, ha, ha, ha, the saintly villain! Ah, ha, ha! Will not Honoré be proud of him now? *Ah! voilà un joli Joseph!* What did I tell you? Didn't I *always* tell you so?"

"But the beauty of it is, he is caught so cleverly. No escape— no possible explanation. There he is, gentlemen, as plain as a rat in a barrel, and with as plain a case. Ha, ha, ha! Isn't it just glorious?"

And all three laughed in such an ecstasy of glee that Frowenfeld looked back, saw them, and knew forthwith that his good name was gone. The three gentlemen, with tears of merriment still in their eyes, reached a corner and disappeared.

"Mister," said a child, trotting along under Frowenfeld's elbow, —the odd English of the New Orleans street-urchin was at that day just beginning to be heard—"Mister, dey got some blood on de back of you' hade!"

But Frowenfeld hurried on groaning with mental anguish.

33 Unkindest Cut of All

It was the year 1804. The world was trembling under the tread of the dread Corsican. It was but now that he had tossed away the whole Valley of the Mississippi, dropping it overboard as a little sand from a balloon, and Christendom in a pale agony of suspense was watching the turn of his eye; yet when a gibbering black fool here on the edge of civilization merely swings a pine-knot, the swinging of that pine-knot becomes to Joseph Frowenfeld, student of man, a matter of greater moment than the destination of the Boulogne Flotilla. For it now became for the moment the foremost necessity of his life to show, to that minute fraction of the earth's population which our terror misnames "the world," that a man may leap forth hatless and bleeding from the house of a New Orleans quadroon into the open street and yet be pure white within. Would it answer to tell the truth? Parts of that truth he was pledged not to tell; and even if he could tell it all it was incredible—bore all the features of a flimsy lie.

"Mister," repeated the same child who had spoken before, reinforced by another under the other elbow, "dey got some *blood* on de back of you' hade."

And the other added the suggestion:

"Dey got one drug-sto', yondah."

Frowenfeld groaned again. The knock had been a hard one,

the ground and sky went round not a little, but he retained withal a white hot process of thought that kept before him his hopeless inability to explain. He was coffined alive. The world (so-called) would bury him in utter loathing, and write on his head-stone the one word—hypocrite. And he should lie there and helplessly contemplate Honoré pushing forward those purposes which he had begun to hope he was to have had the honor of furthering. But instead of so doing he would now be the by-word of the street.

"Mister," interposed the child once more, spokesman this time for a dozen blacks and whites of all sizes trailing along before and behind, "*dey got some blood* on de back of you' *hade.*"

That same morning Clotilde had given a music-scholar her appointed lesson, and at its conclusion had borrowed of her patroness (how pleasant it must have been to have such things to lend!) a little yellow maid, in order that, with more propriety, she might make a business call. It was that matter of the rent— one that had of late occasioned her great secret distress. "It is plain," she had begun to say to herself, unable to comprehend Aurora's peculiar trust in Providence, "that if the money is to be got I must get it." A possibility had flashed upon her mind; she had nurtured it into a project, had submitted it to her father-confessor in the cathedral, and received his unqualified approval of it, and was ready this morning to put it into execution. A great merit of the plan was its simplicity. It was merely to find for her heaviest bracelet a purchaser in time, and a price sufficient, to pay to-morrow's "maturities." See there again!—to her, her little secret was of greater import than the collision of almost any pine-knot with almost any head.

It must not be accepted as evidence either of her unwillingness to sell or of the amount of gold in the bracelet, that it took the total of Clotilde's moral and physical strength to carry it to the shop where she hoped—against hope—to dispose of it.

'Sieur Frowenfeld, M. Innerarity said, was out, but would certainly be in in a few minutes, and she was persuaded to take a chair against the half-hidden door at the bottom of the shop with the little borrowed maid crouched at her feet.

She had twice or thrice felt a regret that she had undertaken to wait, and was about to rise and go, when suddenly she saw before her Joseph Frowenfeld, wiping the sweat of anguish from his brow and smeared with blood from his forehead down. She rose quickly and silently, turned sick and blind, and laid her hand upon the back of the chair for support. Frowenfeld stood an instant before her, groaned, and disappeared through the door. The little maid, retreating backward against her from the direction of the street-door, drew to her attention a crowd of sight-seers which had rushed up to the doors and against which Raoul was hurriedly closing the shop.

34 Clotilde as a Surgeon

Was it worse to stay, or to fly? The decision must be instantaneous. But Raoul made it easy by crying in their common tongue,
as he slammed a massive shutter and shot its bolt:

"Go to him! he is down—I heard him fall. Go to him!"

At this rallying cry she seized her shield—that is to say, the
little yellow attendant, and hurried into the room. Joseph lay just
beyond the middle of the apartment, face downward. She found
water and a basin, wet her own handkerchief, and dropped to her
knees beside his head; but the moment he felt the small, feminine
hands he stood up. She took him by the arm.

"*Asseyez-vous, Monsieu'*—pliz to give you'sev de pens to see
down, 'Sieu' Frowenfel'."

She spoke with a nervous tenderness in contrast with her
alarmed and entreating expression of face, and gently pushed
him into a chair.

The child ran behind the bed and burst into frightened sobs,
but ceased when Clotilde turned for an instant and glared at her.

"Mague yo' 'ead back," said Clotilde, and with tremulous tenderness she softly pressed back his brow and began wiping off
the blood. "W'ere you is 'urted?"

But while she was asking her question she had found the gash
and was growing alarmed at its ugliness, when Raoul, having
made everything fast, came in with:

"W'at's de mattah, 'Sieur Frowenfel'? w'at's de mattah wid you? Oo done dat, 'Sieur Frowenfel'?"

Joseph lifted his head and drew away from it the small hand and wet handkerchief, and without letting go the hand, looked again into Clotilde's eyes, and said:

"Go home; oh, go home!"

"Oh! no," protested Raoul, whereupon Clotilde turned upon him with a perfectly amiable, nurse's grimace for silence.

"I goin' rad now," she said.

Raoul's silence was only momentary.

"W'ere you lef' you' hat, 'Sieur Frowenfel'?" he asked, and stole an artist's glance at Clotilde, while Joseph straightened up, and nerving himself to a tolerable calmness of speech, said:

"I have been struck with a stick of wood by a halfwitted person under a misunderstanding of my intentions; but the circumstances are such as to blacken my character hopelessly; but I am innocent!" he cried, stretching forward both arms and quite losing his momentary self-control.

" 'Sieu' Frowenfel'!" cried Clotilde, tears leaping to her eyes, "I am shoe of it!"

"I believe you! I believe you, 'Sieur Frowenfel'!" exclaimed Raoul with sincerity.

"You will not believe me," said Joseph. "You will not; it will be impossible."

"*Mais,*" cried Clotilde, "id shall nod be impossib'!"

But the apothecary shook his head.

"All I can be suspected of will seem probable; the truth only is incredible."

His head began to sink and a pallor to overspread his face.

"*Allez, monsieur, allez,*" cried Clotilde to Raoul, a picture of beautiful terror which he tried afterward to paint from memory, "*appelez* Doctah Kin!"

Raoul made a dash for his hat, and the next moment she heard, with unpleasant distinctness, his impetuous hand slam the shop door and lock her in.

"*Baille ma do l'eau,*" she called to the little mulattress, who responded by searching wildly for a cup and presently bringing a measuring-glass full of water.

Clotilde gave it to the wounded man, and he rose at once and stood on his feet.

"Raoul."

"'E gone at Doctah Kin."

"I do not need Doctor Keene; I am not badly hurt. Raoul should not have left you here in this manner. You must not stay."

"Bud, 'Sieur Frowenfel', I am afred to trah to paz dad gangue!"

A new distress seized Joseph in view of this additional complication. But, unmindful of this suggestion, the fair Creole suddenly exclaimed:

"'Sieu' Frowenfel', you har a hinnocen' man! Go, hopen yo' do's an' stan' juz as you har ub biffo dad crowd and sesso! My God! 'Sieu' Frowenfel', iv you cannod stan' ub by you'sev——"

She ceased suddenly with a wild look, as if another word would have broken the levees of her eyes, and in that instant Frowenfeld recovered the full stature of a man.

"God bless you!" he cried. "I will do it!" He started, then turned again toward her, dumb for an instant, and said: "And God reward you! You believe in me, and you do not even know me."

Her eyes became wilder still as she looked up into his face with the words:

"*Mais*, I does know you—betteh 'n you know annyt'in' boud it!" and turned away, blushing violently.

Frowenfeld gave a start. She had given him too much light. He recognized her, and she knew it. For another instant he gazed at her averted face, and then with forced quietness said:

"Please go into the shop."

The whole time that had elapsed since the shutting of the doors had not exceeded five minutes; a sixth sufficed for Clotilde and her attendant to resume their original position in the nook by the private door and for Frowenfeld to wash his face and hands. Then the alert and numerous ears without heard a drawing of bolts at the door next to that which Raoul had issued, its leaves opened outward, and first the pale hands and then the white, weakened face and still bloody hair and apparel of the apothecary made their appearance. He opened a window and another door. The one locked by Raoul, when unbolted, yielded without a key, and the shop stood open.

"My friends," said the trembling proprietor, "if any of you wishes to buy anything, I am ready to serve him. The rest will please move away."

The invitation, though probably understood, was responded to by only a few at the banquette's edge, where a respectable face or two wore scrutinizing frowns. The remainder persisted in silently standing and gazing in at the bloody man.

Frowenfeld bore the gaze. There was one element of emphatic satisfaction in it—it drew their observation from Clotilde at the other end of the shop. He stole a glance backward; she was not there. She had watched her chance, safely escaped through the side door, and was gone.

Raoul returned.

"'Sieur Frowenfel', Doctor Keene is took worse ag'in. 'E is in bed; but 'e say to tell you in dat lill troubl' of dis mawnin' it is himseff w'at is inti'lie wrong, an' 'e hass you poddon. 'E says sen' fo' Doctor Conrotte, but I din go fo' him; dat ole scoun'rel—he believe in puttin' de niggas fre'."

Frowenfeld said he would not consult professional advisers; with a little assistance from Raoul, he could give the cut the slight attention it needed. He went back into his room, while Raoul turned back to the door and addressed the public.

"Pray, Messieurs, come in and be seated." He spoke in the Creole French of the gutters. "Come in. M. Frowenfeld is dressing, and desires that you will have a little patience. Come in. Take chairs. You will not come in? No? Nor you, Monsieur? No? I will set some chairs outside, eh? No?"

They moved by twos and threes away, and Raoul, retiring, gave his employer such momentary aid as was required. When Joseph, in changed dress, once more appeared, only a child or two lingered to see him, and he had nothing to do but sit down and, as far as he felt at liberty to do so, answer his assistant's questions.

During the recital, Raoul was obliged to exercise the severest self-restraint to avoid laughing,—a feeling which was modified by the desire to assure his employer that he understood this sort of thing perfectly, had run the same risks himself, and thought no less of a man, *providing he was a gentleman,* because of an unlucky retributive knock on the head. But he feared laughter would overclimb speech; and, indeed, with all expression of sympathy stifled, he did not succeed so completely in hiding the conflicting emotion but that Joseph did once turn his pale, grave face surprisedly, hearing a snuffling sound, suddenly stifled in a drawer of corks. Said Raoul, with an unsteady utterance, as he slammed the drawer:

"H-h-dat makes me dat I can't 'elp to laugh w'en I t'ink of dat fool yesse'dy w'at want to buy my pigshoe for honly one 'undred dolla'—ha, ha, ha, ha!"

He laughed almost indecorously.

"Raoul," said Frowenfeld, rising and closing his eyes, "I am going back for my hat. It would make matters worse for that person to send it to me, and it would be something like a vindication for me to go back to the house and get it."

Mr. Innerarity was about to make strenuous objection, when there came in one whom he recognized as an attaché of his cousin Honoré's counting-room, and handed the apothecary a note. It contained Honoré's request that if Frowenfeld was in his shop he would have the goodness to wait there until the writer could call and see him.

"I will wait," was the reply.

35 "Fo' Wad You Cryne?"

Clotilde, a step or two from home, dismissed her attendant, and as Aurora, with anxious haste, opened to her familiar knock, appeared before her pale and trembling.

"*Ah, ma fille*——"

The overwrought girl dropped her head and wept without restraint upon her mother's neck. She let herself be guided to a chair, and there, while Aurora nestled close to her side, yielded a few moments to reverie before she was called upon to speak. Then Aurora first quietly took possession of her hands, and after another tender pause asked in English, which was equivalent to whispering:

"W'ere you was, *chérie?*"

" 'Sieur Frowenfel'——"

Aurora straightened up with angry astonishment and drew in her breath for an emphatic speech, but Clotilde, liberating her own hands, took Aurora's, and hurriedly said, turning still paler as she spoke:

" 'E godd his 'ead strigue! 'Tis all knog in be'ine! 'E come in blidding——"

"In w'ere?" cried Aurora.

"In 'is shob."

"You was in dad shob of 'Sieur Frowenfel'?"

212

"I wend ad 'is shob to pay doze rend."

"How—you wend ad 'is shob to pay——"

Clotilde produced the bracelet. The two looked at each other in silence for a moment, while Aurora took in without further explanation Clotilde's project and its failure.

"An' 'Sieur Frowenfel'—dey kill 'im? Ah! *ma chère,* fo' wad you mague me to hass all doze question?"

Clotilde gave a brief account of the matter, omitting only her conversation with Frowenfeld.

"*Mais,* oo strigue 'im?" demanded Aurora, impatiently.

"Addunno!" replied the other. "Bud I does know 'e is hinnocen'!"

A small scouting-party of tears reappeared on the edge of her eyes.

"Innocen' from wad?"

Aurora betrayed a twinkle of amusement.

"Hev'ryt'in', iv you pliz!" exclaimed Clotilde, with most uncalled for warmth.

"An' you crah bic-ause 'e is nod guiltie?"

"Ah! foolish!"

"Ah, non, mie chile, I know fo' wad you cryne: 'tis h-only de sighd of de blood."

"Oh, sighd of blood!"

Clotilde let a little nervous laugh escape through her dejection.

"Well, then,"—Aurora's eyes twinkled like stars,—"id muz be bic-ause 'Sieur Frowenfel' bump 'is 'ead—ha, ha, ha!"

"'T is nod true!" cried Clotilde; but, instead of laughing, as Aurora had supposed she would, she sent a double flash of light from her eyes, crimsoned, and retorted, as the tears again sprang from their lurking-place, "You wand to mague ligue you don't kyah! But *I* know! I know verrie well! You kyah fifty time' as mudge as me! I know you! I know you! I bin wadge you!"

Aurora was quite dumb for a moment, and gazed at Clotilde, wondering what could have made her so unlike herself. Then she half rose up, and, as she reached forward an arm, and laid it tenderly about her daughter's neck, said:

"Ma lill dotter, wad dad meggin you cry? Iv you will tell me wad dad mague you cry, I will tell you—on ma *second word of honor*"—she rolled up her fist—"juz wad I thing about dad 'Sieur Frowenfel'!"

"I don't kyah wad de whole worl' thing aboud 'im!"

213

"*Mais,* anny'ow, tell me fo' wad you cryne?"

Clotilde gazed aside for a moment and then confronted her questioner consentingly.

"I tole 'im I knowed 'e war h-innocen'."

"*Eh, bien,* dad was h-only de poli-i-idenez. Wad 'e said?"

" 'E said I din knowed 'im 'tall."

"An' you," exclaimed Aurora, "it is nod pozzyble dad you——"

"I tole 'im I know 'im bette'n 'e know annyt'in' 'boud id!"

The speaker dropped her face into her mother's lap.

"Ha, ha!" laughed Aurora, "an' wad of dad? I would say dad, me, fo' time' a day. I gi'e you mie word 'e don godd dad sens' to know wad dad mean."

"Ah! don godd sens'!" cried Clotilde, lifting her head up suddenly with a face of agony. " 'E reg—'e reggo-ni-i-ize me!"

Aurora caught her daughter's cheeks between her hands and laughed all over them.

"*Mais,* don you see 'ow dad was luggy? Now, you know?—'e goin' fall in love wid you an' you goin' 'ave dad sadizfagzion to rif-use de biggis' hand in Noo-'leans. An' you will be h-even, ha, ha! Bud me—you wand to know wad I thing aboud 'im? I thing 'e is one—egcellen' drug-cl—ah, ha, ha!"

Clotilde replied with a smile of grieved incredulity.

"De bez in de ciddy!" insisted the other. She crossed the forefinger of one hand upon that of the other and kissed them, reversed the cross and kissed them again. "*Mais,* ad de sem tam," she added, giving her daughter time to smile, "I thing 'e is one *noble gen'leman.* Nod to sood me, of coze, *mais, çà fait rien*—daz nott'n; me, I am now a h'ole woman, you know, eh? Noboddie can' nevva sood me no mo', nod ivven dad Govenno' Cleb-orne."

She tried to look old and jaded.

"Ah, Govenno' Cleb-orne!" exclaimed Clotilde.

"Yass!—Ah, you!—you thing iv a man is nod a Creole 'e bown to be no 'coun'! I assu' you dey don' godd no boddy wad I fine a so nize gen'leman lag Govenno' Cleb-orne! Ah! Clotilde, you godd no lib'ral'ty!"

The speaker rose, cast a discouraged parting look upon her narrow-minded companion and went to investigate the slumbrous silence of the kitchen.

36 Aurora's Last Picayune

Not often in Aurora's life had joy and trembling so been mingled in one cup as on this day. Clotilde wept; and certainly the mother's heart could but respond; yet Clotilde's tears filled her with a secret pleasure which fought its way up into the beams of her eyes and asserted itself in the frequency and heartiness of her laugh despite her sincere participation in her companion's distresses and a fearful looking forward to to-morrow.

Why these flashes of gladness? If we do not know, it is because we have overlooked one of her sources of trouble. From the night of the *bal masqué* she had—we dare say no more than that she had been haunted; she certainly would not at first have admitted even so much to herself. Yet the fact was not thereby altered, and first the fact and later the feeling had given her much distress of mind. Who he was whose image would not down, for a long time she did not know. This, alone, was torture; not merely because it was mystery, but because it helped to force upon her consciousness that her affections, spite of her, were ready and waiting for him and he did not come after them. That he loved her, she knew; she had achieved at the ball an overwhelming victory, to her certain knowledge, or, depend upon it, she never would have unmasked—never.

But with this torture was mingled not only the ecstasy of loving, but the fear of her daughter. This is a world that allows nothing without its obverse and reverse. Strange differences are often seen between the two sides; and one of the strangest and most inharmonious in this world of human relations is that coinage which a mother sometimes finds herself offering to a daughter, and which reads on one side, Bridegroom, and on the other, Step-father.

Then, all this torture to be hidden under smiles! Worse still, when by and by Messieurs Agoussou, Assonquer, Danny and others had been appealed to and a Providence boundless in tender compassion had answered in their stead, she and her lover had simultaneously discovered each other's identity only to find that he was a Montague to her Capulet. And the source of her agony must be hidden, and falsely attributed to the rent deficiency and their unprotected lives. Its true nature must be concealed even from Clotilde. What a secret—for what a spirit—to keep from what a companion!—a secret yielding honey to her, but, it might be, gall to Clotilde. She felt like one locked in the Garden of Eden all alone—alone with all the ravishing flowers, alone with all the lions and tigers. She wished she had told the secret when it was small and had let it increase by gradual accretions in Clotilde's knowledge day by day. At first it had been but a garland, then it had become a chain, now it was a ball and chain; and it was oh! and oh! if Clotilde would only fall in love herself. How that would simplify matters! More than twice or thrice she had tried to reveal her overstrained heart in broken sections; but on her approach to the very outer confines of the matter, Clotilde had always behaved so strangely, so nervously, in short, so beyond Aurora's comprehension, that she invariably failed to make any revelation.

And now, here in the very central darkness of this cloud of troubles, comes in Clotilde, throws herself upon the defiant little bosom so full of hidden suffering, and weeps tears of innocent confession that in a moment lay the dust of half of Aurora's perplexities. Strange world! The tears of the orphan making the widow weep for joy, if she only dared.

The pair sat down opposite each other at their little dinner-table. They had a fixed hour for dinner. It is well to have a fixed hour; it is in the direction of system. Even if you have not the dinner, there is the hour. Alphonsina was not in perfect harmony with this fixed-hour idea. It was Aurora's belief, often expressed in hungry moments with the laugh of a vexed Creole lady (a laugh worthy of study), that on the day when dinner should really be served at the appointed hour, the cook would drop dead of apoplexy and she of fright. She said it to-day, shutting her arms down to her side, closing her eyes with her eyebrows raised, and dropping into her chair at the table like a dead bird from its perch. Not that she felt particularly hungry; but there is a certain desultoriness allowable at table more than elsewhere, and which suited the hither-thither movement of her conflicting feelings. This is why she had wished for dinner.

Boiled shrimps, rice, claret-and-water, bread—they were dining well the day before execution. Dining is hardly correct, either, for Clotilde, at least, did not eat; they only sat. Clotilde had, too, if not her unknown, at least her unconfessed emotions. Aurora's were tossed by the waves, hers were sunken beneath them. Aurora had a faith that the rent would be paid—a faith which was only a vapor, but a vapor gilded by the sun—that is, by Apollo, or, to be still more explicit, by Honoré Grandissime. Clotilde, deprived of this confidence, had tried to raise means wherewith to meet the dread obligation, or, rather, had tried to try and had failed. Today was the ninth, to-morrow, the street. Joseph Frowenfeld was hurt; her dependence upon his good offices was gone. When she thought of him suffering under public contumely, it seemed to her as if she could feel the big drops of blood dropping from her heart; and when she recalled her own actions, speeches, and demonstrations in his presence, exaggerated by the groundless fear that he had guessed into the deepest springs of her feelings, then she felt those drops of blood congeal. Even if the apothecary had been duller of discernment than she supposed, here was Aurora on the opposite side of the table, reading every thought of her inmost soul. But worst of all was 'Sieur Frowenfel's indifference. It is true that, as he had directed upon her that gaze of recognition, there was a look of mighty gladness, if she dared believe her eyes. But no, she dared not; there was nothing there for her, she thought,—probably (when this anguish of public disgrace should by any means be lifted) a benevolent smile at her and her betrayal of interest. Clotilde felt as though she had been laid entire upon a slide of his microscope.

Aurora at length broke her reverie.

"Clotilde,"—she spoke in French—"the matter with you is that you have no heart. You never did have any. Really and truly, you do not care whether 'Sieur Frowenfel' lives or dies. You do not care how he is or where he is this minute. I wish you had some of my too large heart. I not only have the heart, as I tell you, to think kindly of our enemies, doze Grandissime, for example"—she waved her hand with the air of selecting at random —"but I am burning up to know what is the condition of that poor, sick, noble 'Sieur Frowenfel', and I am going to do it!"

The heart which Clotilde was accused of not having gave a stir of deep gratitude. Dear, pretty little mother! Not only knowing full well the existence of this swelling heart and the significance, to-day, of its every warm pulsation, but kindly covering up the discovery with make-believe reproaches. The tears started in her eyes; that was her reply.

"Oh, now! it is the rent again, I suppose," cried Aurora, "always the rent. It is not the rent that worries *me*, it is 'Sieur Frowenfel', poor man. But very well, Mademoiselle Silence, I will match you for making me do all the talking." She was really beginning to sink under the labor of carrying all the sprightliness for both. "Come," she said, savagely, "propose something."

"Would you think well to go and inquire?"

"Ah, listen! Go and what? No, Mademoiselle, I think not."

"Well, send Alphonsina."

"What? And let him know that I am anxious about him? Let me tell you, my little girl, I shall not drag upon myself the responsibility of increasing the self-conceit of any of that sex."

"Well, then, send to buy a picayune's worth of something."

"Ah, ha, ha! An emetic, for instance. Tell him we are poisoned on mushrooms, ha, ha, ha!"

Clotilde laughed too.

"Ah, no," she said. "Send for something he does not sell."

Aurora was laughing while Clotilde spoke; but as she caught these words she stopped with open-mouthed astonishment, and, as Clotilde blushed, laughed again.

"Oh, Clotilde, Clotilde, Clotilde!"—she leaned forward over the table, her face beaming with love and laughter—"you rowdy! you rascal! You are just as bad as your mother, whom you think so wicked! I accept your advice. Alphonsina!"

"Momselle!"

The answer came from the kitchen.

"Come go—or, rather,—*vini'ci courri dans boutique de l'apothecaire.* Clotilde," she continued, in better French, holding up the coin to view, "Look!"

"What?"

"The last picayune we have in the world—ha, ha, ha!"

37 Honoré Makes Some Confessions

"*Comment çà va, Raoul?*" said Honoré Grandissime; he had come to the shop according to the proposal contained in his note. "Where is Mr. Frowenfeld?"

He found the apothecary in the rear room, dressed, but just rising from the bed at sound of his voice. He closed the door after him; they shook hands and took chairs.

"You have fever," said the merchant. "I have been troubled that way myself, some, lately." He rubbed his face all over, hard, with one hand, and looked at the ceiling. "Loss of sleep, I suppose, in both of us; in your case voluntary—in pursuit of study, most likely; in my case—effect of anxiety." He smiled a moment and then suddenly sobered as after a pause he said:

"But I hear you are in trouble; may I ask——"

Frowenfeld had interrupted him with almost the same words:

"May I venture to ask, Mr. Grandissime, what——"

And both were silent for a moment.

"Oh," said Honoré, with a gesture. "My trouble—I did not mean to mention it; 'tis an old matter—in part. You know, Mr. Frowenfeld, there is a kind of tree not dreamed of in botany, that lets fall its fruit every day in the year—you know? We call it—with reverence—'our dead father's mistakes.' I have had to eat much of that fruit; a man who has to do that must expect to have now and then a little fever."

219

"I have heard," replied Frowenfeld, "that some of the titles under which your relatives hold their lands are found to be of the kind which the State's authorities are pronouncing worthless. I hope this is not the case."

"I wish they had never been put into my custody," said M. Grandissime.

Some new thought moved him to draw his chair closer.

"Mr. Frowenfeld, those two ladies whom you went to see the other evening——"

His listener started a little:

"Yes."

"Did they ever tell you their history?"

"No, sir; but I have heard it."

"And you think they have been deeply wronged, eh? Come Mr. Frowenfeld, take right hold of the acacia-bush."

M. Grandissime did not smile.

Frowenfeld winced.

"I think they have."

"And you think restitution should be made them, no doubt, eh?"

"I do."

"At any cost?"

The questioner showed a faint, unpleasant smile, that stirred something like opposition in the breast of the apothecary.

"Yes," he answered.

The next question had a tincture even of fierceness:

"You think it right to sink fifty or a hundred people into poverty to lift one or two out?"

"Mr. Grandissime," said Frowenfeld, slowly, "you bade me study this community."

"I adv—yes; what is it you find?"

"I find—it may be the same with other communities, I suppose it is, more or less—that just upon the culmination of the moral issue it turns and asks the question which is behind it, instead of the question which is before it."

"And what is the question before me?"

"I know it only in the abstract."

"Well?"

The apothecary looked distressed.

"You should not make me say it," he objected.

"Nevertheless," said the Creole, "I take that liberty."

"Well, then," said Frowenfeld, "the question behind is Expediency and the question in front, Divine Justice. You are asking yourself——"

He checked himself.

"Which I ought to regard," said M. Grandissime, quickly. "Expediency, of course, and be like the rest of mankind." He put on a look of bitter humor. "It is all easy enough for you, Mr. Frowenfeld, my-de'-seh; you have the easy part—the theorizing."

He saw the ungenerousness of his speech as soon as it was uttered, yet he did not modify it.

"True, Mr. Grandissime," said Frowenfeld; and after a pause —"but you have the noble part—the doing."

"Ah, my-de'-seh!" exclaimed Honoré; "the noble part! There is the bitterness of the draught! The opportunity to act is pushed upon me, but the opportunity to act nobly has passed by."

He again drew his chair closer, glanced behind him and spoke low:

"Because for years I have had a kind of custody of all my kinsmen's property interests, Agricola's among them, it is supposed that he has always kept the plantation of Aurore Nancanou (or rather of Clotilde—who, you know, by our laws is the real heir). That is a mistake. Explain it as you please, call it remorse, pride, love—what you like—while I was in France and he was managing my mother's business, unknown to me he gave me that plantation. When I succeeded him I found it and all its revenues kept distinct—as was but proper—from all other accounts, and belonging to me. 'Twas a fine, extensive place, had a good overseer on it and—I kept it. Why? Because I was a coward. I did not want it or its revenues; but, like my father, I would not offend my people. Peace first and justice afterwards —that was the principle on which I quietly made myself the trustee of a plantation and income which you would have given back to their owners, eh?"

Frowenfeld was silent.

"My-de'-seh, recollect that to us the Grandissime name is a treasure. And what has preserved it so long? Cherishing the unity of our family; that has done it; that is how my father did it. Just or unjust, good or bad, needful or not, done elsewhere or not, I do not say; but it is a Creole trait. See, even now" (the speaker smiled on one side of his mouth) "in a certain section of the territory certain men, Creoles" (he whispered, gravely), *"some Grandissimes among them,* evading the United States revenue laws and even beating and killing some of the officials: well! Do the people at large repudiate those men? My-de'-seh, in no wise, seh! No; if they were *Americains*—but a Louisianian —is a Louisianian; touch him not; when you touch him you touch all Louisiana! So with us Grandissimes; we are legion, but we are one. Now, my-de'-seh, the thing you ask me to do is to cast overboard that old traditional principle which is the secret of our existence."

"I ask you?"

"Ah, bah! you know you expect it. Ah! but you do not know the uproar such an action would make. And no 'noble part' in it, my-de'-seh, either. A few months ago—when we met by those graves—if I had acted then, my action would have been one of pure—even violent—*self*-sacrifice. Do you remember—on the levee, by the Place d'Armes—me asking you to send Agricola to me? I tried then to speak of it. He would not let me. Then, my people felt safe in their land-titles and public offices; this restitution would have hurt nothing but pride. Now, titles in doubt, government appointments uncertain, no ready capital in reach for any purpose except that which would have to be handed over with the plantation (for to tell you the fact, my-de'-seh, no other account on my books has prospered), with matters changed in this way, I become the destroyer of my own flesh and blood! Yes, seh! and lest I might still find some room to boast, another change moves me into a position where it suits me, my-de'-seh, to make the restitution so fatal to those of my name. When you and I first met, those ladies were as much strangers to me as to you—as far as I *knew.* Then, if I had done this thing——but now—now, my-de'-seh, I find myself in love with one of them!"

M. Grandissime looked his friend straight in the eye with the frowning energy of one who asserts an ugly fact.

Frowenfeld, regarding the speaker with a gaze of respectful attention, did not falter; but his fevered blood, with an impulse that started him half from his seat, surged up into his head and face; and then—

M. Grandissime blushed.

In the few silent seconds that followed, the glances of the two friends continued to pass into each other's eyes, while about Honoré's mouth hovered the smile of one who candidly surrenders his innermost secret, and the lips of the apothecary set themselves together as though he were whispering to himself behind them, "Steady."

"Mr. Frowenfeld," said the Creole, taking a sudden breath and waving a hand, "I came to ask about *your* trouble; but if you think you have any reason to withhold your confidence——"

"No, sir; no! But can I be no help to you in this matter?"

The Creole leaned back smilingly in his chair and knit his fingers.

"No, I did not intend to say all this; I came to offer my help to you; but my mind is full—what do you expect? My-de'-seh, the foam must come first out of the bottle. You see"—he leaned forward again, laid two fingers in his palm and deepened his tone—"I will tell you: this tree—'our dead father's mistakes'—is about to drop another rotten apple. I spoke just now of the uproar this restitution would make; why, my-de'-seh, just the mention of the lady's name at my house, when we lately held the *fête de grandpère*, has given rise to a quarrel which is likely to end in a duel."

"Raoul was telling me," said the apothecary.

M. Grandissime made an affirmative gesture.

"Mr. Frowenfeld, if you—if any one—could teach my people —I mean my family—the value of peace (I do not say the duty, my-de'-seh, a merchant talks of values); if you could teach them the value of peace, I would give you, if that was your price"—he ran the edge of his left hand knife-wise around the wrist of his right—"that. And if you would teach it to the whole community —well—I think I would not give my head; maybe you would." He laughed.

"There is a peace which is bad," said the contemplative apothecary.

"Yes," said the Creole, promptly, "the very kind that I have been keeping all this time—and my father before me!"

He spoke with much warmth.

"Yes," he said again, after a pause which was not a rest, "I often see that we Grandissimes are a good example of the Creoles at large; we have one element that makes for peace; that—pardon the self-consciousness—is myself; and another element that makes for strife—led by my uncle Agricola; but, my-de'-seh, the peace element is that which ought to make the strife, and the strife element is that which ought to be made to keep the peace! Mr. Frowenfeld, I propose to become the strifemaker;

how, then, can I be a peacemaker at the same time? There is my diffycultie."

"Mr. Grandissime," exclaimed Frowenfeld, "if you have any design in view founded on the high principles which I know to be the foundations of all your feelings, and can make use of the aid of a disgraced man, use me."

"You are very generous," said the Creole, and both were silent. Honoré dropped his eyes from Frowenfeld's to the floor, rubbed his knee with his palm, and suddenly looked up.

"You are innocent of wrong?"

"Before God."

"I feel sure of it. Tell me in a few words all about it. I ought to be able to extricate you. Let me hear it."

Frowenfeld again told as much as he thought he could, consistently with his pledges to Palmyre, touching with extreme lightness upon the part taken by Clotilde.

"Turn around," said M. Grandissime at the close; "let me see the back of your head. And it is that that is giving you this fever, eh?"

"Partly," replied Frowenfeld: "but how shall I vindicate my innocence? I think I ought to go back openly to this woman's house and get my hat. I was about to do that when I got your note; yet it seems a feeble—even if possible—expedient."

"My friend," said Honoré, "leave it to me. I see your whole case, both what you tell and what you conceal. I guess it with ease. Knowing Palmyre so well, and knowing (what you do not) that all the voudous in town think you a sorcerer, I know just what she would drop down and beg you for—a *ouangan*, ha, ha! You see? Leave it all to me—and your hat with Palmyre, take a febrifuge and a nap, and await word from me."

"And may I offer you no help in your difficulty?" asked the apothecary, as the two rose and grasped hands.

"Oh!" said the Creole, with a little shrug, "you may do anything you can—which will be nothing."

38 Tests of Friendship

Frowenfeld turned away from the closing door, caught his head between his hands and tried to comprehend the new wildness of the tumult within. Honoré Grandissime avowedly in love with one of them—*which one?* Doctor Keene visibly in love with one of them—*which one?* And he! What meant this bounding joy that, like one gorgeous moth among innumerable bats, flashed to and fro among the wild distresses and dismays swarming in and out of his distempered imagination? He did not answer the question; he only knew the confusion in his brain was dreadful. Both hands could not hold back the throbbing of his temples; the table did not steady the trembling of his hands; his thoughts went hither and thither, heedless of his call. Sit down as he might, rise up, pace the room, stand, lean his forehead against the wall—nothing could quiet the fearful disorder, until at length he recalled Honoré's neglected advice and resolutely lay down and sought sleep; and, long before he had hoped to secure it, it came.

In the distant Grandissime mansion, Agricola Fusilier was casting about for ways and means to rid himself of the heaviest heart that ever had throbbed in his bosom. He had risen at sunrise from slumber worse than sleeplessness, in which his dreams had anticipated the duel of to-morrow with Sylvestre.

He was trying to get the unwonted quaking out of his hands and the memory of the night's heart-dissolving phantasms from before his inner vision. To do this he had resort to a very familiar, we may say time-honored, prescription—rum. He did not use it after the voudou fashion; the voudous pour it on the ground— Agricola was an anti-voudou. It finally had its effect. By eleven o'clock he seemed, outwardly at least, to be at peace with everything in Louisiana that he considered Louisianian, properly so-called; as to all else he was ready for war, as in peace one should be. While in this mood, and performing at a side-board the solemn rite of *las onze,* news incidentally reached him, by the mouth of his busy second, Hippolyte, of Frowenfeld's trouble, and despite 'Polyte's protestations against the principal in a pending "affair" appearing on the street, he ordered the carriage and hurried to the apothecary's.

When Frowenfeld awoke, the fingers of his clock were passing the meridian. His fever was gone, his brain was calm, his strength in good measure had returned. There had been dreams in his sleep, too: he had seen Clotilde standing at the foot of his bed. He lay now, for a moment, lost in retrospection.

"There can be no doubt about it," said he, as he rose up, looking back mentally at something in the past.

The sound of carriage-wheels attracted his attention by ceasing before his street door. A moment later the voice of Agricola was heard in the shop greeting Raoul. As the old man lifted the head of his staff to tap on the inner door, Frowenfeld opened it.

"Fusilier to the rescue!" said the great Louisianian, with a grasp of the apothecary's hand and a gaze of brooding admiration.

Joseph gave him a chair, but with magnificent humility he insisted on not taking it until "Professor Frowenfeld" had himself sat down.

The apothecary was very solemn. It seemed to him as if in this little back room his dead good name was lying in state, and these visitors were coming in to take their last look. From time to time he longed for more light, wondering why the gravity of his misadventure should seem so great.

"H-m-h-y dear Professor!" began the old man. Pages of print could not comprise all the meanings of his smile and accent;

226

benevolence, affection, assumed knowledge of the facts, disdain of results, remembrance of his own youth, charity for pranks, patronage—these were but a few. He spoke very slowly and deeply and with this smile of a hundred meanings. "Why did you not send for me, Joseph? Sir, whenever you have occasion to make a list of the friends who will stand by you, *right or wrong*—h-write the name of Citizen Agricola Fusilier at the top! Write it large and repeat it at the bottom! You understand me, Joseph?—and, mark me,—right or wrong!"

"Not wrong," said Frowenfeld, "at least not in defence of wrong; I could not do that; but, I assure you, in this matter I have done——"

"No worse than any one else would have done under the circumstances, my dear boy!—Nay, nay, do not interrupt me; I understand you, I understand you. H-do you imagine there is anything strange to me in this—at my age?"

"But I am——"

"——all right, sir! that is *what* you are. And you are under the wing of Agricola Fusilier, the old eagle; that is *where* you are. And you are one of my brood; that is *who* you are. Professor, listen to your old father. *The—man—makes—the—crime!* The wisdom of mankind never brought forth a maxim of more gigantic beauty. If the different grades of race and society did not have corresponding moral and civil liberties, varying in degree as they vary—h-why! *this* community, at least, would go to pieces! See here! Professor Frowenfeld is charged with misdemeanor. Very well, who is he? Foreigner or native? Foreigner by sentiment and intention, or only by accident of birth? Of our mental fibre—our aspirations—our delights—our indignations? I answer for you, Joseph, yes!—yes! What then? H-why then the decision! Reached how? By apologetic reasonings? By instinct, sir! h-h-that guide of the nobly proud! And what is the decision? Not guilty. Professor Frowenfeld, *absolvo te!*"

It was in vain that the apothecary repeatedly tried to interrupt this speech. "Citizen Fusilier, do you know me no better?"—"Citizen Fusilier, if you will but listen!"—such were the fragments of his efforts to explain. The old man was not so confident as he pretended to be that Frowenfeld was that complete proselyte which alone satisfies a Creole; but he saw him in a predicament and cast to him this life-buoy, which if a man should refuse, he would deserve to drown.

Frowenfeld tried again to begin.

"Mr. Fusilier——"

"*Cit*izen Fusilier!"

"Citizen, candor demands that I undeceive——"

"Candor demands—h-my dear Professor, let me tell you exactly what she demands. She demands that in here—within this apartment—we understand each other. That demand is met."

"But——" Frowenfeld frowned impatiently.

"That demand, Joseph, is fully met! I understand the whole matter like an eye-witness! Now there is another demand to be met, the demand of friendship! In here, candor; outside, friendship; in here, one of our brethren has been adventurous and unfortunate; outside"—the old man smiled a smile of benevolent mendacity—"outside, nothing has happened."

Frowenfeld insisted savagely on speaking; but Agricola raised his voice, and gray hairs prevailed.

"At least, what *has* happened? The most ordinary thing in the world; Professor Frowenfeld lost his footing on a slippery gunwale, fell, cut his head upon a protruding spike, and went into the house of Palmyre to bathe his wound; but finding it worse than he had at first supposed it, immediately hurried out again and came to his store. He left his hat where it had fallen, too muddy to be worth recovery. Hippolyte Brahmin-Mandarin and others, passing at the time, thought he had met with violence in the house of the hairdresser, and drew some natural inferences, but have since been better informed; and the public will please understand that Professor Frowenfeld is a white man, a gentleman, and a Louisianian, ready to vindicate his honor, and that Citizen Agricola Fusilier is his friend!"

The old man looked around with the air of a bull on a hill-top.

Frowenfeld, vexed beyond degree, restained himself only for the sake of an object in view, and contented himself with repeating for the fourth or fifth time,—

"I cannot accept any such deliverance."

"Professor Frowenfeld, friendship—society—demands it; our circle must be protected in all its members. You have nothing to do with it. You will leave it with me, Joseph."

"No, no," said Frowenfeld, "I thank you, but——"

"Ah! my dear boy, thank me not; I cannot help these impulses; I belong to a warm-hearted race. But"—he drew back in his chair sidewise and made great pretence of frowning—"you decline the offices of that precious possession, a Creole friend?"

"I only decline to be shielded by a fiction."

"Ah-h!" said Agricola, further nettling his victim by a gaze of stagy admiration. "'Sans peur et sans reproche'—and yet you disappoint me. Is it for naught, that I have sallied forth from home, drawing the curtains of my carriage to shield me from the gazing crowd? It was to rescue my friend—my vicar—my coadjutor—my son, from the laughs and finger-points of the vulgar mass. H-I might as well have stayed at home—or better, for my peculiar position to-day rather requires me to keep in——"

"No, citizen," said Frowenfeld, laying his hand upon Agricola's arm, "I trust it is not in vain that you have come out. There *is* a man in trouble whom only you can deliver."

The old man began to swell with complacency.

"H-why, really——"

"*He*, citizen, is truly of your kind——"

"He must be delivered, Professor Frowenfeld——"

"He is a native Louisianian, not only by accident of birth but by sentiment and intention," said Frowenfeld.

The old man smiled a benign delight, but the apothecary now had the upper hand, and would not hear him speak.

"His aspirations," continued the speaker, "his indignations— mount with his people's. His pulse beats with yours, sir. He is a part of your circle. He is one of your caste."

Agricola could not be silent.

"Ha-a-a-ah! Joseph, h-h-you make my blood tingle! Speak to the point; who——"

"I believe him, moreover, Citizen Fusilier, innocent of the charge laid——"

"H-innocent? H-of course he is innocent, sir! We will *make* him inno——"

"Ah! Citizen, he is already under sentence of death!"

"*What?* A Creole under sentence!" Agricola swore a heathen oath, set his knees apart and grasped his staff by the middle. "Sir, we will liberate him if we have to overturn the government!"

Frowenfeld shook his head.

"You have got to overturn something stronger than government."

"And pray what——"

"A conventionality," said Frowenfeld, holding the old man's eye.

"Ha, ha! my b-hoy, h-you are right. But we will overturn—eh?"

"I say I fear your engagements will prevent. I hear you take part to-morrow morning in——"

Agricola suddenly stiffened.

"Professor Frowenfeld, it strikes me, sir, you are taking something of a liberty."

"For which I ask pardon," exclaimed Frowenfeld. "Then I may not expect——"

The old man melted again.

"But who is this person in mortal peril?"

Frowenfeld hesitated.

"Citizen Fusilier," he said, looking first down at the floor and then up into the inquirer's face, "on my assurance that he is not only a native Creole, but a Grandissime——"

"It is not possible!" exclaimed Agricola.

"——a Grandissime of the purest blood, will you pledge me your aid to liberate him from his danger, 'right or wrong?'"

"*Will* I? H-why, certainly! Who is he?"

"Citizen——it is Sylves——"

Agricola sprang up with a thundering oath.

The apothecary put out a pacifying hand, but it was spurned.

"Let me go! How dare you, sir? How dare you, sir?" bellowed Agricola.

He started toward the door, cursing furiously and keeping his eye fixed on Frowenfeld with a look of rage not unmixed with terror.

"Citizen Fusilier," said the apothecary, following him with one palm uplifted, as if that would ward off his abuse, "don't go! I adjure you, don't go! Remember your pledge, Citizen Fusilier!"

Agricola did not pause a moment; but when he had swung the door violently open the way was still obstructed. The painter of "Louisiana refusing to enter the Union" stood before him, his head elevated loftily, one foot set forward and his arm extended like a tragedian's.

"Stan' bag-sah!"

"Let me pass! Let me pass, or I will kill you!"

Mr. Innerarity smote his bosom and tossed his hand aloft.

"Kill me-firse an' pass aftah!"

"Citizen Fusilier," said Frowenfeld, "I beg you to hear me."

230

"Go away! Go away!"

The old man drew back from the door and stood in the corner against the book-shelves as if all the horrors of the last night's dreams had taken bodily shape in the person of the apothecary. He trembled and stammered:

"Ke—keep off! Keep off! My God! Raoul, he has insulted me!" He made a miserable show of drawing a weapon. "No man may insult me and live! If you are a man, Professor Frowenfeld, you will defend yourself!"

Frowenfeld lost his temper, but his hasty reply was drowned by Raoul's vehement speech.

" 'Tis not de trute!" cried Raoul. "He try to save you from hell-'n'-damnation w'en 'e h-ought to give you a good cuss'n!"— and in the ecstasy of his anger burst into tears.

Frowenfeld, in an agony of annoyance, waved him away and he disappeared, shutting the door.

Agricola, moved far more from within than from without, had sunk into a chair under the shelves. His head was bowed, a heavy grizzled lock fell down upon his dark, frowning brow, one hand clenched the top of his staff, the other his knee, and both trembled violently. As Frowenfeld, with every demonstration of beseeching kindness, began to speak, he lifted his eyes and said, piteously:

"Stop! Stop!"

"Citizen Fusilier, it is you who must stop. Stop before God Almighty stops you, I beg you. I do not presume to rebuke you. I *know* you want a clear record. I know it better to-day than I ever did before. Citizen Fusilier, I honor your intentions——"

Agricola roused a little and looked up with a miserable attempt at his habitual patronizing smile.

"H-my dear boy, I overlook"—but he met in Frowenfeld's eyes a spirit so superior to his dissimulation that the smile quite broke down and gave way to another of deprecatory and apologetic distress. He reached up an arm.

"I could easily convince you, Professor, of your error"—his eyes quailed and dropped to the floor—"but I—your arm, my dear Joseph; age is creeping upon me." He rose to his feet. "I am feeling really indisposed to-day—not at all bright; my solicitude for you, my dear b——"

He took two or three steps forward, tottered, clung to the apothecary, moved another step or two, and grasping the edge of the table stumbled into a chair which Frowenfeld thrust under him. He folded his arms on the edge of the board and rested his forehead on them, while Frowenfeld sat down quickly on the opposite side, drew paper and pen across the table and wrote.

"Are you writing something, Professor?" asked the old man, without stirring. His staff tumbled to the floor. The apothecary's answer was a low, preoccupied one. Two or three times over he wrote and rejected what he had written.

Presently he pushed back his chair, came around the table, laid the writing he had made before the bowed head, sat down again and waited.

After a long time the old man looked up, trying in vain to conceal his anguish under a smile.

"I have a sad headache."

He cast his eyes over the table and took mechanically the pen which Frowenfeld extended toward him.

"What can I do for you, Professor? Sign something? There is nothing I would not do for Professor Frowenfeld. What have you written, eh?"

He felt helplessly for his spectacles.

Frowenfeld read:

"Mr. Sylvestre Grandissime: I spoke in haste."

He felt himself tremble as he read. Agricola fumbled with the pen, lifted his eyes with one more effort at the old look, said:

"My dear boy, I do this purely to please you," and to Frowenfeld's delight and astonishment wrote:

"Your affectionate uncle, Agricola Fusilier."

39 Louisiana States Her Wants

" 'Sieur Frowenfel'," said Raoul as that person turned in the front door of the shop after watching Agricola's carriage roll away— he had intended to unburden his mind to the apothecary with all his natural impetuosity; but Frowenfeld's gravity as he turned, with the paper in his hand, induced a different manner. Raoul had learned, despite all the impulses of his nature, to look upon Frowenfeld with a sort of enthusiastic awe. He dropped his voice and said—asking like a child a question he was perfectly able to answer—

"What de matta wid Agricole?"

Frowenfeld, for the moment well-nigh oblivious of his own trouble, turned upon his assistant a look in which elation was oddly blended with solemnity, and replied as he walked by:

"Rush of truth to the heart."

Raoul followed a step.

" 'Sieur Frowenfel'——"

The apothecary turned once more. Raoul's face bore an expression of earnest practicability that invited confidence.

" 'Sieur Frowenfel', Agricola writ'n' to Sylvestre to stop dat dool?"

"Yes."

"You goin' take dat lett' to Sylvestre?"

"Yes."

" 'Sieur Frowenfel', dat de wrong g-way. You got to take it to 'Polyte Brahmin-Mandarin, an' 'e got to take it to Valentine Grandissime, an' 'e got to take it to Sylvestre. You see, you got to know de manner to make. Once 'pon a time I had a diffycultie wid——"

"I see," said Frowenfeld; "where may I find Hippolyte Brahmin-Mandarin at this time of day?"

Raoul shrugged.

"If the pre-parish ions are not complitted, you will not find 'im; but if they har complitted—you know 'im?"

"By sight."

"Well, you may fine him at Maspero's, or helse in de front of de Veau-qui-tête, or helse at the Café Louis Quatorze—mos' likely in front of de Veau-qui-tête. You know, dat diffycultie I had, dat arise itseff from de discush'n of one of de mil-littery mov'ments of ca-valry; you know, I——"

"Yes," said the apothecary; "here, Raoul, is some money; please go and buy me a good, plain hat."

"All right." Raoul darted behind the counter and got his hat out of a drawer. "We're at you buy your hats?"

"Anywhere."

"I will go at *my* hatter."

As the apothecary moved about his shop awaiting Raoul's return, his own disaster became once more the subject of his anxiety. He noticed that almost every person who passed looked in. "This is the place,"—"That is the man,"—how plainly the glances of passers sometimes speak! The people seemed, moreover, a little nervous. Could even so little a city be stirred about such a petty, private trouble as this of his? No; the city was having tribulations of its own.

New Orleans was in that state of suppressed excitement which, in later days, a frequent need of reassuring the outer world has caused to be described by the phrase "never more peaceable." Raoul perceived it before he had left the shop twenty paces behind. By the time he reached the first corner he was in the swirl of the popular current. He enjoyed it like a strong swimmer. He even drank of it. It was better than wine and music mingled.

"Twelve weeks next Thursday, and no sign of re-cession!" said one of two rapid walkers just in front of him. Their talk was in the French of the province.

"Oh, re-cession!" exclaimed the other angrily. "The cession is a reality. That, at least, we have got to swallow. Incredulity is dead."

The first speaker's feelings could find expression only in profanity.

"The cession—we wash our hands of it!" He turned partly around upon his companion, as they hurried along, and gave his hands a vehement dry washing. "If Incredulity is dead, Nonparticipation reigns in its stead, and Discontent is prime minister!" He brandished his fist as they turned a corner.

"If we must change, let us be subjects of the First Consul!" said one of another pair whom Raoul met on a crossing.

There was a gathering of boys and vagabonds at the door of a gun-shop. A man inside was buying a gun. That was all.

A group came out of a "coffee-house." The leader turned about upon the rest:

"*Ah, bah! cette* Amayrican libetty!"

"See! see! it is this way!" said another of the number, taking two others by their elbows, to secure an audience, "we shall do nothing ourselves; we are just watching that vile Congress. It is going to tear the country all to bits!"

"Ah, my friend, you haven't got the *inside* news," said still another—Raoul lingered to hear him—"Louisiana is going to state her wants! We have the liberty of free speech and are going to use it!"

His information was correct; Louisiana, no longer incredulous of her Americanization, had laid hold of her new liberties and was beginning to run with them, like a boy dragging his kite over the clods. She was about to state her wants, he said.

"And her don't-wants," volunteered one whose hand Raoul shook heartily. "We warn the world. If Congress doesn't take heed, we will not be responsible for the consequences!"

Raoul's hatter was full of the subject. As Mr. Innerarity entered, he was saying good-day to a customer in his native tongue, English, and so continued:

"Yes, under Spain we had a solid, quiet government—Ah! Mr. Innerarity, overjoyed to see you! We were speaking of these political troubles. I wish we might see the last of them. It's a terrible bad mess; corruption to-day—I tell you what—it will be disruption to-morrow. Well, it is no work of ours; we shall merely stand off and see it."

"Mi-frien'," said Raoul, with mingled pity and superiority, "you haven't got doze *inside* nooz; Louisiana is goin' to state w'at she want."

On his way back toward the shop Mr. Innerarity easily learned Louisiana's wants and don't-wants by heart. She wanted a Creole governor; she did not want Casa Calvo invited to leave the country; she wanted the provisions of the Treaty of Cession hurried up; "as soon as possible," that instrument said; she had waited long enough; she did not want "dat trile bi-ju'y"—execrable trash! she wanted an *unwatched import trade!* she did not want a single additional Américain appointed to office; she wanted the slave trade.

Just in sight of the bare-headed and anxious Frowenfeld, Raoul let himself be stopped by a friend.

The remark was exchanged that the times were exciting.

"And yet," said the friend, "the city was never more peaceable. It is exasperating to see that coward governor looking so diligently after his police and hurrying on the organization of the Américain volunteer militia!" He pointed savagely here and there. "M. Innerarity, I am lost in admiration at the all but craven patience with which our people endure their wrongs! Do my pistols show *too* much through my coat? Well, good-day; I must go home and clean my gun; my dear friend, one don't know how soon he may have to encounter the Recorder and Register of Land-titles."

Raoul finished his errand.

"'Sieur Frowenfel', excuse me—I take dat lett' to 'Polyte for you if you want." There are times when mere shop-keeping—any peaceful routine—is torture.

But the apothecary felt so himself; he declined his assistant's offer and went out toward the Veau-qui-tête.

40 Frowenfeld Finds Sylvestre

The Veau-qui-tête restaurant occupied the whole ground floor of a small, low, two-story, tile-roofed, brick-and-stucco building which still stands on the corner of Chartres and St. Peter streets, in company with the well-preserved old Cabildo and the young Cathedral, reminding one of the shabby and swarthy Creoles whom we sometimes see helping better kept kinsmen to murder time on the banquettes of the old French Quarter. It was a favorite rendezvous of the higher classes, convenient to the court-rooms and municipal bureaus. There you found the choicest legal and political gossips, with the best the market afforded of meat and drink.

Frowenfeld found a considerable number of persons there. He had to move about among them to some extent, to make sure he was not overlooking the object of his search.

As he entered the door, a man sitting near it stopped talking, gazed rudely as he passed, and then leaned across the table and smiled and murmured to his companion. The subject of his jest felt their four eyes on his back.

There was a loud buzz of conversation throughout the room, but wherever he went a wake of momentary silence followed him, and once or twice he saw elbows nudged. He perceived that there was something in the state of mind of these good citizens that made the present sight of him particularly discordant.

Four men, leaning or standing at a small bar, were talking excitedly in the Creole patois. They made frequent anxious, yet amusedly defiant, mention of a certain *Pointe Canadienne*. It was a portion of the Mississippi River "coast" not far above New Orleans, where the merchants of the city met the smugglers who came up from the Gulf by way of Barrataria bay and the bayou. These four men did not call it by the proper title just given; there were commercial gentlemen in the Creole city, Englishmen, Scotchmen, Yankees, as well as French and Spanish Creole, who in public indignantly denied, and in private tittered over, their complicity with the pirates of Grand Isle, and who knew their trading rendezvous by the sly nickname of "Little Manchar." As Frowenfeld passed these four men they, too, ceased speaking and looked after him, three with offensive smiles and one with a stare of contempt.

Farther on, some Creoles were talking rapidly to an Américain, in English.

"And why?" one was demanding; "because money is scarce. Under other governments we had any quantity!"

"Yes," said the venturesome Américain in retort, "such as it was; *assignats, liberanzas, bons*—Claiborne will give us better money than that when he starts his bank."

"Hah, his bank, yes! John Law once had a bank, too; ask my old father. What do we want with a bank? Down with banks!" The speaker ceased; he had not finished, but he saw the apothecary. Frowenfeld heard a muttered curse, an inarticulate murmur, and then a loud burst of laughter.

A tall, slender young Creole whom he knew, and who had always been greatly pleased to exchange salutations, brushed against him without turning his eyes.

"You know," he was saying to a companion, "everybody in Louisiana is to be a citizen, except the negroes and mules; that is the kind of liberty they give us—all eat out of one trough."

"What we want," said a dark, ill-looking, but finely-dressed man, setting his claret down, "and what we have got to have, is"—he was speaking in French, but gave the want in English— "Representesh'n wizout Taxa——" There his eye fell upon Frowenfeld and followed him with a scowl.

"Mah frang," he said to his table companion, "wass you sink

of a mane w'at hask-a one nee-grow to 'ave-a one shair wiz 'im, eh?—in ze sem room?"

The apothecary found that his fame was far wider and more general than he had supposed. He turned to go out, bowing as he did so, to an Américain merchant with whom he had some acquaintance.

"Sir?" asked the merchant, with severe politeness, "wish to see me? I thought you—— As I was saying, gentlemen, what, after all, does it sum up?"

A Creole interrupted him with an answer:

"Leetegash'n, Spoleeash'n, Pahtitsh'n, Disintegrhash'n!"

The voice was like Honoré's. Frowenfeld looked; it was Agamemnon Grandissime.

"I must go to Maspero's," thought the apothecary, and he started up the rue Chartres. As he turned into the rue St. Louis, he suddenly found himself one of a crowd standing before a newly-posted placard, and at a glance saw it to be one of the inflammatory publications which were a feature of the times, appearing both daily and nightly on walls and fences.

"One Amerry-can pull' it down, an' Camille Brahmin 'e pas'e it back," said a boy at Frowenfeld's side.

Exchange Alley was once *Passage de la Bourse,* and led down (as it now does to the State House—late St. Louis Hotel) to an establishment which seems to have served for a long term of years as a sort of merchants' and auctioneers' coffee-house, with a minimum of china and a maximum of glass: Maspero's—certainly Maspero's as far back as 1810, and, we believe, Maspero's the day the apothecary entered it, March 9, 1804. It was a livelier spot than the Veau-qui-tête; it was to that what commerce is to litigation, what standing and quaffing is to sitting and sipping. Whenever the public mind approached that sad state of public sentiment in which sanctity signs politicians' memorials and chivalry breaks into the gun-shops, a good place to feel the thump of the machinery was in Maspero's.

The first man Frowenfeld saw as he entered was M. Valentine Grandissime. There was a double semi-circle of gazers and listeners in front of him; he was talking, with much show of unconcern, in Creole French.

"Policy? I care little about policy." He waved his hand. "I know my rights—and Louisiana's. We have a right to our opinions. We have"—with a quiet smile and an upward turn of his

239

extended palm—"a right to protect them from the attack of interlopers, even if we have to use gunpowder. I do not propose to abridge the liberties of even this army of fortune-hunters. *Let them think.*" He half laughed. "Who cares whether they share our opinions or not? Let them have their own. I had rather they would. But let them hold their tongues. Let them remember they are Yankees. Let them remember they are unbidden guests." All this without the least warmth.

But the answer came aglow with passion, from one of the semicircle, whom two or three seemed disposed to hold in check. It also was in French, but the apothecary was astonished to hear his own name uttered.

"But this fellow Frowenfeld"—the speaker did not see Joseph —"has never held his tongue. He has given us good reason half a dozen times, with his too free speech and his high moral whine, to hang him with the lamp-post rope! And now, when we have borne and borne and borne and borne with him, and he shows up, all at once, in all his rottenness, you say let him alone! One would think you were defending Honoré Grandissime!" The back of one of the speaker's hands fluttered in the palm of the other.

Valentine smiled.

"Honoré Grandissime? Boy, you do not know what you are talking about. Not Honoré, ha, ha! A man who, upon his own avowal, is guilty of affiliating with the Yankees. A man whom we have good reason to suspect of meditating his family's dishonor and embarrassment!" Somebody saw the apothecary and laid a cautionary touch on Valentine's arm, but he brushed it off. "As for Professor Frowenfeld, he must defend himself."

"Ha-a-a-ah!"—a general cry of derision from the listeners.

"Defend himself?" exclaimed their spokesman; "shall I tell you again what he is?" In his vehemence, the speaker wagged his chin and held his clenched fists stiffly toward the floor. "He is— he is—he is——"

He paused, breathing like a fighting dog. Frowenfeld, large, white, and immovable, stood close before him.

"Dey 'ad no bizniz led 'im come oud to-day," said a bystander, edging toward a pillar.

The Creole, a small young man not unknown to us, glared upon the apothecary; but Frowenfeld was far above his blush-

240

ing mood, and was not disconcerted. This exasperated the Creole beyond bound; he made a sudden, angry change of attitude, and demanded:

"Do you interrup' two gen'lemen in dey conve'sition, you Yankee clown? Do you igno' dad you 'ave insult me, off-scow'-ing?"

Frowenfeld's first response was a stern gaze. When he spoke, he said:

"Sir, I am not aware that I have ever offered you the slightest injury or affront; if you wish to finish your conversation with this gentleman, I will wait till you are through."

The Creole bowed, as a knight who takes up the gage. He turned to Valentine.

"Valentine, I was sayin' to you dad diz pusson is a cowa'd and a sneak; I repead thad! I repead id! I spurn you! Go f'om yeh!"

The apothecary stood like a cliff.

It was too much for Creole forbearance. His adversary, with a long snarl of oaths, sprang forward and with a great sweep of his arm slapped the apothecary on the cheek. And then—

What a silence!

Frowenfeld had advanced one step; his opponent stood half turned away, but with his face toward the face he had just struck and his eyes glaring up into the eyes of the apothecary. The semicircle was dissolved, and each man stood in neutral isolation, motionless and silent. For one instant objects lost all natural proportion, and to the expectant on-lookers the largest thing in the room was the big, upraised, white fist of Frowenfeld. But in the next—how was this? Could it be that that fist had not descended?

The imperturbable Valentine, with one preventing arm laid across the breast of the expected victim and an open hand held restrainingly up for truce, stood between the two men and said:

"Professor Frowenfeld—one moment—"

Frowenfeld's face was ashen.

"Don't speak, sir!" he exclaimed. "If I attempt to parley I shall break every bone in his body. Don't speak! I can guess your explanation—he is drunk. But take him away."

Valentine, as sensible as cool, assisted by the kinsman who had laid a hand on his arm, shuffled his enraged companion out. Frowenfeld's still swelling anger was so near getting the better of him that he unconsciously followed a quick step or two; but as Valentine looked back and waved him to stop, he again stood still.

"*Proffesseur*—you know,—" said a stranger, "daz Sylvestre Grandissime."

Frowenfeld rather spoke to himself than answered:

"If I had not known that, I should have——" He checked himself and left the place.

While the apothecary was gathering these experiences, the free spirit of Raoul Innerarity was chafing in the shop like an eagle in a hen-coop. One moment after another brought him straggling evidences, now of one sort, now of another, of the "never more peaceable" state of affairs without. If only some pretext could be conjured up, plausible or flimsy, no matter; if only some man would pass with a gun on his shoulder, were it only a blow-gun; or if his employer were any one but his beloved Frowenfeld, he would clap up the shutters as quickly as he had already done once to-day, and be off to the wars. He was just trying to hear imaginary pistol-shots down toward the Place d'Armes, when the apothecary returned.

"D' you fin' him?"

"I found Sylvestre."

" 'E took de lett'?"

"I did not offer it." Frowenfeld, in a few compact sentences, told his adventure.

Raoul was ablaze with indignation.

" 'Sieur Frowenfel', gimmy dat lett'!" He extended his pretty hand.

Frowenfeld pondered.

"Gimmy 'er!" persisted the artist; "befo' I lose de sight from dat lett' she goin' to be hanswer by Sylvestre Grandissime, an' 'e goin' to wrat you one appo-logie! Oh! I goin' mek 'im crah fo' shem!"

"If I could know you would do only as I——"

"I do it!" cried Raoul, and sprang for his hat; and in the end Frowenfeld let him have his way.

"I had intended seeing him——" the apothecary said.

"Nevvamine to see; I goin' tell him!" cried Raoul, as he crowded his hat fiercely down over his curls and plunged out.

41 To Come to the Point

It was equally a part of Honoré Grandissime's nature and of his art as a merchant to wear a look of serene leisure. With this look on his face he re-entered his counting-room after his morning visit to Frowenfeld's shop. He paused a moment outside the rail, gave the weak-eyed gentleman who presided there a quiet glance equivalent to a beckon, and, as that person came near, communicated two or three items of intelligence or instruction concerning office details, by which that invaluable diviner of business meanings understood that he wished to be let alone for an hour. Then M. Grandissime passed on into his private office, and, shutting the door behind him, walked briskly to his desk and sat down.

He dropped his elbows upon a broad paper containing some recently written, unfinished memoranda that included figures in column, cast his eyes quite around the apartment, and then covered his face with his palms—a gesture common enough for a tired man of business in a moment of seclusion; but just as the face disappeared in the hands, the look of serene leisure gave place to one of great mental distress. The paper under his elbows, to the consideration of which he seemed about to return, was in the handwriting of his manager, with additions by his own pen. Earlier in the day he had come to a pause in the making of these additions, and, after one or two vain efforts to proceed, had laid down his pen, taken his hat, and gone to see the unlucky apothecary. Now he took up the broken thread. To come to a decision; that was the task which forced from him his look of distress. He drew his face slowly through his palms, set his lips, cast up his eye, knit his knuckles, and then opened and struck his palms together, as if to say: "Now, come; let me make up my mind."

There may be men who take every moral height at a dash; but to the most of us there must come moments when our wills can but just rise and walk in their sleep. Those who in such moments wait for clear views, find, when the issue is past, that they were only yielding to the devil's chloroform.

Honoré Grandissime bent his eyes upon the paper. But he saw neither its figures nor its words. The interrogation, "Surrender Fausse Rivière?" appeared to hang between his eyes and the paper, and when his resolution tried to answer "Yes," he saw red flags; he heard the auctioneer's drum; he saw his kinsmen handing house-keys to strangers; he saw the old servants of the great family standing in the market-place; he saw kinswomen pawning their plate; he saw his clerks (Brahmins, Mandarins, Grandissimes) standing idle and shabby in the arcade of the Cabildo and on the banquette of Maspero's and the Veau-qui-tête; he saw red-eyed young men in the Exchange denouncing a man who, they said, had, ostensibly for conscience's sake, but really for love, forced upon the woman he had hoped to marry a fortune filched from his own kindred. He saw the junto of doctors in Frowenfeld's door charitably deciding him insane; he saw the more vengeful of his family seeking him with half-concealed weapons; he saw himself shot at in the rue Royale, in the rue Toulouse, and in the Place d'Armes; and, worst of all, missed.

But he wiped his forehead, and the writing on the paper became, in a measure, visible. He read:

Total mortgages on the lands of all the Grandissimes $—
Total present value of same, titles at buyers' risk —
Cash, goods, and account —
Fausse Rivière Plantation account —

There were other items, but he took up the edge of the paper mechanically, pushed it slowly away from him, leaned back in his chair and again laid his hands upon his face.

"Suppose I retain Fausse Rivière," he said to himself, as if he had not said it many times before.

Then he saw memoranda that were not on any paper before him—such a mortgage to be met on such a date; so much from Fausse Rivière Plantation account retained to protect that mortgage from foreclosure; such another to be met on such a date—so much more of same account to protect it. He saw Aurora and Clotilde Nancanou, with anguished faces, offering woman's pleadings to deaf constables. He saw the remainder of Aurora's plantation account thrown to the lawyers to keep the question of the Grandissime titles languishing in the courts. He saw the meanwhile-rallied fortunes of his clan coming to the rescue, himself and kindred growing independent of questionable titles, and even Fausse Rivière Plantation account restored, but Aurora and Clotilde nowhere to be found. And then he saw the grave, pale face of Joseph Frowenfeld.

He threw himself forward, drew the paper nervously toward him, and stared at the figures. He began at the first item and went over the whole paper, line by line, testing every extension, proving every addition, noting if possibly any transposition of figures had been made and overlooked, if something was added that should have been subtracted, or subtracted that should have been added. It was like a prisoner trying the bars of his cell.

Was there no way to make things happen differently? Had he not overlooked some expedient? Was not some financial manœuvre possible which might compass both desired ends? He left his chair and walked up and down, as Joseph at that very moment was doing in the room where he had left him, came back, looked at the paper, and again walked up and down. He murmured now and then to himself: "*Self*-denial—that is not the hard work. Penniless myself—*that* is play," and so on. He turned by and by and stood looking up at that picture of the man in the cuirass which Aurora had once noticed. He looked at it, but he did not see it. He was thinking—"Her rent is due to-morrow. She will never believe I am not her landlord. She will never go to my half-brother." He turned once more and mentally beat his breast as he muttered: "Why do I not decide?"

Somebody touched the door-knob. Honoré stepped forward and opened it. It was a mortgager.

"*Ah! entrez, Monsieur.*"

He retained the visitor's hand, leading him in and talking

245

pleasantly in French until both had found chairs. The conversation continued in that tongue through such pointless commercial gossip as this:

"So the brig *Equinox* is aground at the head of the Passes," said M. Grandissime.

"I have just heard she is off again."

"Aha?"

"Yes; the Fort Plaquemine canoe is just up from below. I understand John McDonough has bought the entire cargo of the schooner *Freedom*."

"No, not all; Blanque et Fils bought some twenty boys and women out of the lot. Where is she lying?"

"Right at the head of the Basin."

And much more like this; but by and by the mortgager came to the point with the casual remark:

"The excitement concerning land-titles seems to increase rather than subside."

"They must have *something* to be excited about, I suppose," said M. Grandissime, crossing his legs and smiling. It was tradesman's talk.

"Yes," replied the other; "there seems to be an idea current to-day that all holders under Spanish titles are to be immediately dispossessed, without even process of court. I believe a very slight indiscretion on the part of the Governor-General would precipitate a riot."

"He will not commit any," said M. Grandissime with a quiet gravity, changing his manner to that of one who draws upon a reserve of private information. "There will be no outbreak."

"I suppose not. We do not know, really, that the American Congress will throw any question upon titles; but still——"

"What are some of the shrewdest Americans among us doing?" asked M. Grandissime.

"Yes," replied the mortgagor, "it is true they are buying these very titles; but they may be making a mistake?"

Unfortunately for the speaker, he allowed his face an expression of argumentative shrewdness as he completed this sentence, and M. Grandissime, the merchant, caught an instantaneous full view of his motive; he wanted to buy. He was a man whose known speculative policy was to "go in" in moments of panic.

M. Grandissime was again face to face with the question of the morning. To commence selling must be to go on selling. This, as a plan, included restitution to Aurora; but it meant also dissolution to the Grandissimes, for should their *sold* titles be pronounced bad, then the titles of other lands would be bad; many an asset among M. Grandissime's memoranda would shrink into nothing, and the meagre proceeds of the Grandissime estates, left to meet the strain without the aid of Aurora's accumulated fortune, would founder in a sea of liabilities; while should these titles, after being parted with, turn out good, his incensed kindred, shutting their eyes to his memoranda and despising his exhibits, would see in him only the family traitor, and he would go about the streets of his town the subject of their implacable denunciation, the community's obloquy, and Aurora's cold evasion. So much, should he sell. On the other hand, to decline to sell was to enter upon that disingenuous scheme of delays which would enable him to avail himself and his people of that favorable wind and tide of fortune which the Cession had brought. Thus the estates would be lost, if lost at all, only when the family could afford to lose them, and Honoré Grandissime would continue to be Honoré the Magnificent, the admiration of the city and the idol of his clan. But Aurora—and Clotilde—would have to eat the crust of poverty, while their fortunes, even in his hands, must bear all the jeopardy of the scheme. That was all. Retain Fausse Rivière and its wealth, and save the Grandissimes; surrender Fausse Rivière, let the Grandissime estates go, and save the Nancanous. That was the whole dilemma.

"Let me see," said M. Grandissime. "You have a mortgage on one of our Golden Coast plantations. Well, to be frank with you, I was thinking of that when you came in. You know I am partial to prompt transactions—I thought of offering you either to take up that mortgage or to sell you the plantation, as you may prefer. I have ventured to guess that it would suit you to own it."

And the speaker felt within him a secret exultation in the idea that he had succeeded in throwing the issue off upon a Providence that could control this mortgagor's choice.

"I would prefer to leave that choice with you," said the coy would-be purchaser; and then the two went coquetting again for another moment.

"I understand that Nicholas Girod is proposing to erect a four-story brick building on the corner of Royale and St. Pierre. Do you think it practicable? Do you think our soil will support such a structure?"

"Pitot thinks it will. Boré says it is perfectly feasible."

So they dallied.

"Well," said the mortgagor, presently rising, "you will make up your mind and let me know, will you?"

The chance repetition of those words "make up your mind" touched Honoré Grandissime like a hot iron. He rose with the visitor.

"Well, sir, what would you give us for our title in case we should decide to part with it?"

The two men moved slowly, side by side, toward the door, and in the half-open door-way, after a little further trifling, the title was sold.

"Well, good-day," said M. Grandissime. "M. de Brahmin will arrange the papers for us to-morrow."

He turned back toward his private desk.

"And now," thought he, "I am acting without resolving. No merit; no strength of will; no clearness of purpose; no emphatic decision; nothing but a yielding to temptation."

And M. Grandissime spoke true; but it is only whole men who so yield—yielding to the temptation to do right.

He passed into the counting-room, to M. de Brahmin, and standing there talked in an inaudible tone, leaning over the upturned spectacles of his manager, for nearly an hour. Then, saying he would go to dinner, he went out. He did not dine at home nor at the Veau-qui-tête, nor at any of the clubs; so much is known; he merely disappeared for two or three hours and was not seen again until late in the afternoon, when two or three Brahmins and Grandissimes, wandering about in search of him, met him on the levee near the head of the rue Bienville, and with an exclamation of wonder and a look of surprise at his dusty shoes, demanded to know where he had hid himself while they had been ransacking the town in search of him.

"We want you to tell us what you will do about our titles."

He smiled pleasantly, the picture of serenity, and replied:

"I have not fully made up my mind yet; as soon as I do so I will let you know."

There was a word or two more exchanged, and then, after a moment of silence, with a gentle "Eh, bien," and a gesture to which they were accustomed, he stepped away backward, they resumed their hurried walk and talk, and he turned into the rue Bienville.

42 An Inheritance of Wrong

"I tell you," Doctor Keene used to say, "that old woman's a thinker." His allusion was to Clemence, the *marchande des calas.* Her mental activity was evinced not more in the cunning aptness of her songs than in the droll wisdom of her sayings. Not the melody only, but the often audacious, epigrammatic philosophy of her tongue as well, sold her *calas* and ginger-cakes.

But in one direction her wisdom proved scant. She presumed too much on her insignificance. She was a "study," the gossiping circle at Frowenfeld's used to say; and any observant hearer of her odd aphorisms could see that she herself had made a life-study of herself and her conditions; but she little thought that others—some with wits and some with none—young hare-brained Grandissimes, Mandarins and the like—were silently, and for her most unluckily, charging their memories with her knowing speeches; and that of every one of those speeches she would ultimately have to give account.

Doctor Keene, in the old days of his health, used to enjoy an occasional skirmish with her. Once, in the course of chaffering over the price of *calas,* he enounced an old current conviction which is not without holders even to this day; for we may still hear it said by those who will not be decoyed down from the mountain fastnesses of the old Southern doctrines, that their slaves were "the happiest people under the sun." Clemence had

made bold to deny this with argumentative indignation, and
was courteously informed in retort that she had promulgated a
falsehood of magnitude.

"W'y, Mawse Chawlie," she replied, "does you s'pose one po'
nigga kin tell a big lie? No, sah! But w'en de whole people
tell w'at ain' so—if dey know it, aw if dey don' know it—den
dat *is* a big lie!" And she laughed to contortion.

"What is that you say?" he demanded, with mock ferocity.
"You charge white people with lying?"

"Oh, sakes, Mawse Chawlie, no! De people don't mek up dat
ah; de debble pass it on 'em. Don' you know de debble ah de
grett cyount'feiteh? Ev'y piece o' money he mek he tek an' put
some debblemen' on de under side, an' one o' his pootiess lies
on top; an' 'e gilt dat lie, and 'e rub dat lie on 'is elbow, an' 'e
shine dat lie, an' 'e put 'is bess licks on dat lie; entel ev'ybody
say: 'Oh, how pooty!' An' dey tek it fo' good money, yass—and
pass it! Dey b'lieb it!"

"Oh," said some one at Doctor Keene's side, disposed to
quiz, "you niggers don't know when you are happy."

"Dass so, Mawse—*c'est vrai, oui!*" she answered quickly: "we
donno no mo'n white folks!"

The laugh was against him.

"Mawse Chawlie," she said again, "w'a's dis I yeh 'bout dat
Eu'ope country? 's dat true de niggas is all free in Eu'ope?"

Doctor Keene replied that something like that was true.

"Well, now, Mawse Chawlie, I gwan t' ass you a riddle. If dat
is *so*, den fo' w'y I yeh folks bragg'n 'bout de 'stayt o' s'iety in
Eu'ope'?"

The mincing drollery with which she used this fine phrase
brought another peal of laughter. Nobody tried to guess.

"I gwan tell you," said the *marchande;* " 'tis becyaze dey got a
'fixed wuckin' class.' " She sputtered and giggled with the general
ha, ha. "Oh, ole Clemence kin talk proctah, yass!"

She made a gesture for attention.

"D'y' ebber yeh w'at de cya'ge-hoss say w'en 'e see de cyaht-
hoss tu'n losse in de sem pawstu'e wid he, an' knowed dat
some'ow de cyaht gotteh be haul'? W'y 'e jiz snawt an' kick up 'is
heel' "—she suited the action to the word—"an' tah' roun' de fiel'
an' prance up to de fence an' say: 'Whoopy! shoo! shoo! dis yeh
country gittin' *too* free!'

"Oh," she resumed, as soon as she could be heard, "white folks
is werry kine. Dey wants us to b'lieb we happy—dey *wants to*
250

b'lieb we is. W'y, you know, dey 'bleeged to b'lieb it—fo' dey own cyumfut. 'Tis de sem weh wid de preache's; dey buil' we ow own sep'ate meet'n-houses; dey b'leebs us lak it de bess, an' dey *knows* dey lak it de bess."

The laugh at this was mostly her own. It is not a laughable sight to see the comfortable fractions of Christian communities everywhere striving, with sincere, pious, well-meant, criminal benevolence, to make their poor brethren contented with the ditch. Nor does it become so to see these efforts meet, or seem to meet, some degree of success. Happily man cannot so place his brother that his misery will continue unmitigated. You may dwarf a man to the mere stump of what he ought to be, and yet he will put out green leaves. "Free from care," we benignly observe of the dwarfed classes of society; but we forget, or have never thought, what a crime we commit when we rob men and women of their cares.

To Clemence the order of society was nothing. No upheaval could reach to the depth to which she was sunk. It is true, she was one of the population. She had certain affections toward people and places; but they were not of a consuming sort.

As for us, our feelings, our sentiments, affections, etc., are fine and keen, delicate and many; what we call refined. Why? Because we get them as we get our old swords and gems and laces—from our grandsires, mothers, and all. Refined they are— after centuries of refining. But the feelings handed down to Clemence had come through ages of African savagery; through fires that do not refine, but that blunt and blast and blacken and char; starvation, gluttony, drunkenness, thirst, drowning, nakedness, dirt, fetichism, debauchery, slaughter, pestilence and the rest— she was their heiress; they left her the cinders of human feelings. She remembered her mother. They had been separated in her childhood, in Virginia when it was a province. She remembered, with pride, the price her mother had brought at auction, and remarked, as an additional interesting item, that she had never seen or heard of her since. She had had children, assorted colors —had one with her now, the black boy that brought the basil to Joseph; the others were here and there, some in the Grandissime households or field-gangs, some elsewhere within occasional sight, some dead, some not accounted for. Husbands—like the Samaritan woman's. We know she was a constant singer and laugher.

And so on that day, when Honoré Grandissime had advised

the Governor-General of Louisiana to be very careful to avoid demonstration of any sort if he wished to avert a street-war in his little capital, Clemence went up one street and down another, singing her song and laughing her professional merry laugh. How could it be otherwise? Let events take any possible turn, how could it make any difference to Clemence? What could she hope to gain? What could she fear to lose? She sold some of her goods to Casa Calvo's Spanish guard and sang them a Spanish song; some to Claiborne's soldiers and sang them Yankee Doodle with unclean words of her own inspiration, which evoked true soldiers' laughter; some to a priest at his window, exchanging with him a pious comment or two upon the wickedness of the times generally and their Américain-Protestant-poisoned community in particular; and (after going home to dinner and coming out newly furnished) she sold some more of her wares to the excited groups of Creoles to which we have had occasion to allude, and from whom, insensible as she was to ribaldry, she was glad to escape. The day now drawing to a close, she turned her steps toward her wonted crouching-place, the willow avenue on the levee, near the Place d'Armes. But she had hardly defined this decision clearly in her mind, and had but just turned out of the rue St. Louis, when her song attracted an ear in a second-story room under whose window she was passing. As usual it was fitted to the passing event:

"*Apportez moi mo' sabre,*
Ba boum, ba boum, boum, boum."

"Run, fetch that girl here," said Dr. Keene to the slave woman who had just entered his room with a pitcher of water.

"Well, old eaves-dropper," he said, as Clemence came, "what is the scandal to-day?"

Clemence laughed.

"You know, Mawse Chawlie, I dunno noth'n' 'tall 'bout nobody. I'se a nigga w'at mine my own business."

"Sit down there on that stool, and tell me what is going on outside."

"I d'no noth'n' 'bout no goin's on; got no time fo' sit down, me; got sell my cakes. I don't goin' git mix' in wid no white folks's doin's."

"Hush, you old hypocrite; I will buy all your cakes. Put them out there on the table."

The invalid, sitting up in bed, drew a purse from behind his pillow and tossed her a large price. She tittered, courtesied and received the money.

"Well, well, Mawse Chawlie, 'f you ain' de funni'st gen'leman I knows, to be sho!"

"Have you seen Joseph Frowenfeld to-day?" he asked.

"He, he, he! W'at I got do wid Mawse Frowenfel'? I goes on de off side o' sich folks—folks w'at cann' 'have deyself no bette'n dat—he, he, he! At de same time I did happen, jis chancin' by accident, to see 'im."

"How is he?"

Dr. Keene made plain by his manner that any sensational account would receive his instantaneous contempt, and she answered within bounds.

"Well, now, tellin' the simple trufe, he ain' much hurt."

The doctor turned slowly and cautiously in bed.

"Have you seen Honoré Grandissime?"

"W'y—das funny you ass me dat. I jis now see 'im dis werry minnit."

"Where?"

"Jis gwine into de house wah dat laydy live w'at 'e runned over dat ah time."

"Now, you old hag," cried the sick man, his weak, husky voice trembling with passion, "you know you're telling me a lie."

"No, Mawse Chawlie," she protested with a coward's frown, "I swah I tellin' you de God's trufe!"

"Hand me my clothes off that chair."

"Oh! but, Mawse Chawlie——"

The little doctor cursed her. She did as she was bid, and made as if to leave the room.

"Don't you go away."

"But Mawse Chawlie, you' undress'—he, he!"

She was really abashed and half frightened.

"I know that; and you have got to help me put my clothes on."

"You gwan kill yo'se'f, Mawse Chawlie," she said, handling a garment.

"Hold your black tongue."

She dressed him hastily, and he went down the stairs of his lodging-house and out into the street. Clemence went in search of her master.

43 The Eagle
Visits the Doves in Their Nest

Alphonsina—only living property of Aurora and Clotilde—was called upon to light a fire in the little parlor. Elsewhere, although the day was declining, few persons felt such a need; but in No. 19 rue Bienville there were two chilling influences combined requiring an artificial offset. One was the ground under the floor, which was only three inches distant, and permanently saturated with water; the other was despair.

Before this fire the two ladies sat down together like watchers, in that silence and vacuity of mind which come after an exhaustive struggle ending in the recognition of the inevitable; a torpor of thought, a stupefaction of feeling, a purely negative state of joylessness sequent to the positive state of anguish. They were now both hungry, but in want of some present friend acquainted with the motions of mental distress who could guess this fact and press them to eat. By their eyes it was plain they had been weeping much; by the subdued tone, too, of their short and infrequent speeches.

Alphonsina, having made the fire, went out with a bundle. It was Aurora's last good dress. She was going to try to sell it.

"It ought not to be so hard," began Clotilde, in a quiet manner of contemplating some one else's difficulty, but paused with the saying uncompleted, and sighed under her breath.

254

"But it *is* so hard," responded Aurora.

"No, it ought not to be so hard——"

"How, not so hard?"

"It is not so hard to live," said Clotilde; "but it is hard to be ladies. You understand——" she knit her fingers, dropped them into her lap and turned her eyes toward Aurora, who responded with the same motions, adding the crossing of her silk-stockinged ankles before the fire.

"No," said Aurora, with a scintillation of irrepressible mischief in her eyes.

"After all," pursued Clotilde, "what troubles us is not how to make a living, but how to get a living without making it."

"Ah! that would be magnificent!" said Aurora, and then added, more soberly: "but we are compelled to make a living."

"No."

"No-o? Ah! what do you mean with your no?"

"I mean it is just the contrary; we are compelled not to make a living. Look at me: I can cook, but I must not cook; I am skillful with the needle, but I must not take in sewing; I could keep accounts; I could nurse the sick; but I must not. I could be a confectioner, a milliner, a dressmaker, a vest-maker, a cleaner of gloves and laces, a dyer, a bird-seller, a mattress-maker, an upholsterer, a dancing-teacher, a florist——"

"Oh!" softly exclaimed Aurora, in English, "you could be— you know w'ad?—an egcellen' drug-cl'—ah, ha, ha!"

"Now——"

But the threatened irruption was averted by a look of tender apology from Aurora, in reply to one of martyrdom from Clotilde.

"My angel daughter," said Aurora, "if society has decreed that ladies must be ladies, then that is our first duty; our second is to live. Do you not see why it is that this practical world does not permit ladies to make a living? Because if they could, none of them would ever consent to be married. Ha! women talk about marrying for love; but society is too sharp to trust them, yet! It makes it *necessary* to marry. I will tell you the honest truth; some days when I get very, very hungry, and we have nothing but rice—all because we are ladies without male protectors—I think society could drive even me to marriage!—for your sake, though, darling; of course, only for your sake!"

"Never!" replied Clotilde; "for my sake, never; for your own sake if you choose. I should not care. I should be glad to see you do so if it would make you happy; but never for my sake and never for hunger's sake; but for love's sake, yes; and God bless thee, pretty maman."

"Clotilde, dear," said the unconscionable widow, "let me assure you, once for all,—starvation is preferable. I mean for me, you understand, simply for me; that is my feeling on the subject."

Clotilde turned her saddened eyes with a steady scrutiny upon her deceiver, who gazed upward in apparently unconscious reverie, and sighed softly as she laid her head upon the high chair-back and stretched out her feet.

"I wish Alphonsina would come back," she said. "Ah!" she added, hearing a footfall on the step outside the street-door, "there she is."

She arose and drew the bolt. Unseen to her, the person whose footsteps she had heard stood upon the doorstep with a hand lifted to knock, but pausing to "make up his mind." He heard the bolt shoot back, recognized the nature of the mistake, and, feeling that here again he was robbed of volition, rapped.

"That is not Alphonsina!"

The two ladies looked at each other and turned pale.

"But you must open it," whispered Clotilde, half rising.

Aurora opened the door, and changed from white to crimson. Clotilde rose up quickly. The gentleman lifted his hat.

"Madame Nancanou."

"M. Grandissime?"

"Oui, Madame."

For once, Aurora was in an uncontrollable flutter. She stammered, lost her breath, and even spoke worse French than she needed to have done.

"Be pl—pleased, sir—to enter. Clotilde, my daughter—Monsieur Grandissime. P-please be seated, sir. Monsieur Grandissime,"—she dropped into a chair with an air of vivacity pitiful to behold,—"I suppose you have come for the rent." She blushed even more violently than before, and her hand stole upward upon her heart to stay its violent beating. "Clotilde, dear, I should be glad if you would put the fire before the screen; it is so much too warm." She pushed her chair back and shaded her face with her hand. "I think the warmer is growing weather outside, is it—is it not?"

The struggles of a wounded bird could not have been more

piteous. Monsieur Grandissime sought to speak. Clotilde, too, nerved by the sight of her mother's embarrassment, came to her support, and she and the visitor spoke in one breath.

"Maman, if Monsieur—pardon——"

"Madame Nancanou, the—pardon, Mademoiselle."

"I have presumed to call upon you," resumed M. Grandissime, addressing himself now to both ladies at once, "to see if I may enlist you in a purely benevolent undertaking in the interest of one who has been unfortunate—a common acquaintance——"

"Common acquaint—" interrupted Aurora, with a hostile lighting of her eyes.

"I believe so—Professor Frowenfeld." M. Grandissime saw Clotilde start, and in her turn falsely accuse the fire by shading her face: but it was no time to stop. "Ladies," he continued, "please allow me, for the sake of the good it may effect, to speak plainly and to the point."

The ladies expressed acquiescence by settling themselves to hear.

"Professor Frowenfeld had the extraordinary misfortune this morning to incur the suspicion of having entered a house for the purpose of—at least, for a bad design——"

"He is innocent!" came from Clotilde, against her intention; Aurora covertly put out a hand, and Clotilde clutched it nervously.

"As, for example, robbery," said the self-recovered Aurora, ignoring Clotilde's look of protestation.

"Call it so," responded M. Grandissime. "Have you heard at whose house this was?"

"No, sir."

"It was at the house of Palmyre Philosophe."

"Palmyre Philosophe!" exclaimed Aurora, in low astonishment. Clotilde let slip, in a tone of indignant incredulity, a soft "Ah!" Aurora turned, and with some hope that M. Grandissime would not understand, ventured to say in Spanish, quietly:

"Come, come, this will never do."

And Clotilde replied in the same tongue:

"I know it, but he is innocent."

"Let us understand each other," said their visitor. "There is not the faintest idea in the mind of one of us that Professor Frowenfeld is guilty of even an intention of wrong; otherwise I should not be here. He is a man simply incapable of anything ignoble."

Clotilde was silent. Aurora answered promptly, with the air of one not to be excelled in generosity:

"Certainly, he is very incapabl'."

"Still," resumed the visitor, turning especially to Clotilde, "the known facts are these, according to his own statement: he was in the house of Palmyre on some legitimate business which, unhappily, he considers himself on some account bound not to disclose, and by some mistake of Palmyre's old Congo woman, was set upon by her and wounded, barely escaping with a whole skull into the street, an object of public scandal. Laying aside the consideration of his feelings, his reputation is at stake and likely to be ruined unless the affair can be explained clearly and satisfactorily, and at once, by his friends."

"And you undertake——" began Aurora.

"Madame Nancanou," said Honoré Grandissime, leaning toward her earnestly, "you know—I must beg leave to appeal to your candor and confidence—you know everything concerning Palmyre that I know. You know me, and who I am; you know it is not for me to undertake to confer with Palmyre. I know, too, her old affection for you; she lives but a little way down this street upon which you live; there is still daylight enough at your disposal; if you will, you can go to see her, and get from her a full and complete exoneration of this young man. She cannot come to you; she is not fit to leave her room."

"Cannot leave her room?"

"I am, possibly, violating confidence in this disclosure, but it is unavoidable—you have to know; she is not fully recovered from a pistol-shot wound received between two and three weeks ago."

"Pistol-shot wound!"

Both ladies started forward with open lips and exclamations of amazement.

"Received from a third person—not myself and not Professor Frowenfeld—in a desperate attempt made by her to avenge the wrongs which she has suffered, as you, Madame, as well as I, are aware, at the hands of——"

Aurora rose up with a majestic motion for the speaker to desist.

"If it is to mention the person of whom your allusion reminds me, that you have honored us with a call this evening, Monsieur——"

Her eyes were flashing as he had seen them flash in front of the Place d'Armes.

"I beg you not to suspect me of meanness," he answered, gently, and with a remonstrative smile. "I have been trying all day, in a way unnecessary to explain, to be generous."

"I suppose you are incapabl'," said Aurora, following her double meaning with that combination of mischievous eyes and unsmiling face of which she was master. She resumed her seat, adding: "It is generous for you to admit that Palmyre has suffered wrongs."

"It *would* be," he replied, "to attempt to repair them, seeing that I am not responsible for them, but this I cannot claim yet to have done. I have asked of you, Madame, a generous act. I might ask another of you both, jointly. It is to permit me to say without offence, that there is one man, at least, of the name of Grandissime who views with regret and mortification the yet deeper wrongs which you are even now suffering."

"Oh!" exclaimed Aurora, inwardly ready for fierce tears, but with no outward betrayal save a trifle too much grace and an overbright smile, "Monsieur is much mistaken; we are quite comfortable and happy, wanting nothing, eh, Clotilde?—not even our rights, ha, ha!"

She rose and let Alphonsina in. The bundle was still in the negress's arms, and passed through the room and disappeared in the direction of the kitchen.

"Oh! no, sir, not at all," repeated Aurora, as she once more sat down.

"You ought to want your rights," said M. Grandissime. "You ought to have them."

"You think so?"

Aurora was really finding it hard to conceal her growing excitement, and turned, with a faint hope of relief, toward Clotilde.

Clotilde, looking only at their visitor, but feeling her mother's glance, with a tremulous and half-choked voice, said eagerly:

"Then why do you not give them to us?"

"Ah!" interposed Aurora, "we shall get them tomorrow, when the sheriff comes."

And, thereupon, what did Clotilde do but sit bolt upright, with her hands in her lap, and let the tears roll, tear after tear, down her cheeks.

"Yes, Monsieur," said Aurora, smiling still, "those that you see are really tears. Ha, ha, ha! excuse me, I really have to laugh; for I just happened to remember our meeting at the masked ball last September. We had such a pleasant evening and were so much indebted to you for our enjoyment,—particularly myself,—little thinking, you know, that you were one of that great family which believes we ought to have our rights, you know. There are many people who ought to have their rights. There was Bras-Coupé; indeed, he got them—found them in the swamp. Maybe Clotilde and I shall find ours in the street. When we unmasked in the theatre, you know, I did not know you were my landlord, and you did not know that I could not pay a few picayunes of rent. But you must excuse those tears; Clotilde is generally a brave little woman, and would not be so rude as to weep before a stranger; but she is weak to-day—we are both weak to-day, from the fact that we have eaten nothing since early morning, although we have abundance of food—for want of appetite, you understand. You must sometimes be affected the same way, having the care of so much wealth *of all sorts.*"

Honoré Grandissime had risen to his feet and was standing with one hand on the edge of the lofty mantel, his hat in the other dropped at his side and his eye fixed upon Aurora's beautiful face, whence her small nervous hand kept dashing aside the tears through which she defiantly talked and smiled. Clotilde sat with clenched hands buried in her lap, looking at Aurora and still weeping.

And M. Grandissime was saying to himself:

"If I do this thing now—if I do it here—I do it on an impulse; I do it under constraint of woman's tears; I do it because I love this woman; I do it to get out of a corner; I do it in weakness, not in strength; I do it without having made up my mind whether or not it is the best thing to do."

And then without intention, with scarcely more consciousness of movement than belongs to the undermined tree which settles, roots and all, into the swollen stream, he turned and moved toward the door.

Clotilde rose.

"Monsieur Grandissime."

He stopped and looked back.

"We will see Palmyre at once, according to your request."

He turned his eyes toward Aurora.

"Yes," said she, and she buried her face in her handkerchief and sobbed aloud.

She heard his footstep again; it reached the door; the door opened—closed; she heard his footstep again; was he gone?

He was gone.

The two women threw themselves into each other's arms and wept. Presently Clotilde left the room. She came back in a moment from the rear apartment, with a bonnet and veil in her hands.

"No," said Aurora, rising quickly, "I must do it."

"There is no time to lose," said Clotilde. "It will soon be dark."

It was hardly a minute before Aurora was ready to start. A kiss, a sorrowful look of love exchanged, the veil dropped over the swollen eyes, and Aurora was gone.

A minute passed, hardly more, and—what was this?—the soft patter of Aurora's knuckles on the door.

"Just here at the corner I saw Palmyre leaving her house and walking down the rue Royale. We must wait until morn——"

Again a footfall on the doorstep, and the door, which was standing ajar, was pushed slightly by the force of the masculine knock which followed.

"Allow me," said the voice of Honoré Grandissime, as Aurora bowed at the door. "I should have handed you this; good-day."

She received a missive. It was long, like an official document; it bore evidence of having been carried for some hours in a coat-pocket, and was folded in one of those old, troublesome ways in use before the days of envelopes. Aurora pulled it open.

"It is all figures; light a candle."

The candle was lighted by Clotilde and held over Aurora's shoulder; they saw a heading and footing more conspicuous than the rest of the writing.

The heading read:

"Aurora and Clotilde Nancanou, owners of Fausse Rivière Plantation, in account with Honoré Grandissime."

The footing read:

"Balance at credit, subject to order of Aurora and Clotilde Nancanou, $105,000.00."

The date followed:

"March 9, 1804."

and the signature:

"H. Grandissime."

A small piece of torn white paper slipped from the account to the floor. Clotilde's eye followed it, but Aurora, without acknowledgment of having seen it, covered it with her foot.

In the morning Aurora awoke first. She drew from under her pillow this slip of paper. She had not dared look at it until now. The writing on it had been roughly scratched down with a pencil. It read:

"Not for love of woman, but in the name of justice and the fear of God."

"And I was so cruel," she whispered.

Ah! Honoré Grandissime, she was kind to that little writing! She did not put it back under her pillow; she *kept it warm,* Honoré Grandissime, from that time forth.

44 Bad for Charlie Keene

On the same evening of which we have been telling, about the time that Aurora and Clotilde were dropping their last tear of joy over the document of restitution, a noticeable figure stood alone at the corner of the rue du Canal and the rue Chartres. He had reached there and paused, just as the brighter glare of the set sun was growing dim above the tops of the cypresses. After walking with some rapidity of step, he had stopped aimlessly, and laid his hand with an air of weariness upon a rotting China-tree that leaned over the ditch at the edge of the unpaved walk.

"Setting in cypress," he murmured. We need not concern ourselves as to his meaning.

One could think aloud there with impunity. In 1804, Canal street was the upper boundary of New Orleans. Beyond it, to southward, the open plain was dotted with country-houses, brick-kilns, clumps of live-oak and groves of pecan. At the hour mentioned the outlines of these objects were already darkening. At one or two points the sky was reflected from marshy ponds. Out to westward rose conspicuously the old house and willow-copse of Jean-Poquelin. Down the empty street or road, which stretched with arrow-like straightness toward the north-west, the draining-canal that gave it its name tapered away between occasional overhanging willows and beside broken ranks of rotting palisades, its foul, crawling waters blushing and gliding and purpling under the swiftly waning light, and ending suddenly in the black shadow of the swamp. The observer of this dismal prospect leaned heavily on his arm, and cast his glance out along the beautified corruption of the canal. His eye seemed quickened to detect the smallest repellant details of the scene; every cypress stump that stood in or overhung the slimy water; every ruined indigo-vat or blasted tree, every broken thing, every bleached bone of ox or horse—and they were many—for roods around. As his eye passed them slowly over and swept back again around the dreary view, he sighed heavily and said: "Dissolution," and then again—"Dissolution! order of the day——"

A secret overhearer might have followed, by these occasional exclamatory utterances, the course of a devouring trouble prowling up and down through his thoughts, as one's eye tracks the shark by the occasional cutting of his fin above the water.

He spoke again:

"It is in such moods as this that fools drown themselves."

His speech was French. He straightened up, smote the tree softly with his palm, and breathed a long, deep sigh—such a sigh, if the very truth be told, as belongs by right to a lover. And yet his mind did not dwell on love.

He turned and left the place; but the trouble that was plowing hither and thither through the deep of his meditations went with him. As he turned into the rue Chartres it showed itself thus:

"Right; it is but right"; he shook his head slowly—"it is but right."

In the rue Douane he spoke again:

"Ah! Frowenfeld"—and smiled unpleasantly, with his head down.

And as he made yet another turn, and took his meditative way down the city's front, along the blacksmith-shops in the street afterward called Old Levee, he resumed, in English, and with a distinctness that made a staggering sailor halt and look after him:

"There are but two steps to civilization, the first easy, the second difficult; to construct—to reconstruct—ah! there it is! the tearing down! The tear——"

He was still, but repeated the thought by a gesture of distress turned into a slow stroke of the forehead.

"Monsieur Honoré Grandissime," said a voice just ahead.

"*Eh bien?*"

At the mouth of an alley, in the dim light of the street lamp, stood the dark figure of Honoré Grandissime, f. m. c., holding up the loosely hanging form of a small man, the whole front of whose clothing was saturated with blood.

"Why, Charlie Keene! Let him down again, quickly—quickly; do not hold him so!"

"Hands off," came in a ghastly whisper from the shape.

"Oh, Chahlie, my boy——"

"Go and finish your courtship," whispered the doctor.

"Oh Charlie, I have just made it forever impossible!"

"Then help me back to my bed; I don't care to die in the street."

45 More Reparation

"That is all," said the fairer Honoré, outside Doctor Keene's sick-room about ten o'clock at night. He was speaking to the black son of Clemence, who had been serving as errand-boy for some hours. He spoke in a low tone just without the half-open door, folding again a paper which the lad had lately borne to the apothecary of the rue Royale, and had now brought back with Joseph's answer written under Honoré's inquiry.

"That is all," said the other Honoré, standing partly behind the first, as the eyes of his little menial turned upon him that deprecatory glance of inquiry so common to slave children. The lad went a little way down the corridor, curled up upon the floor against the wall, and was soon asleep. The fairer Honoré handed the darker the slip of paper; it was received and returned in silence; the question was:

"Can you state anything positive concerning the duel?"

And the reply:

"Positively there will be none. Sylvestre my sworn friend for life."

The half-brothers sat down under a dim hanging lamp in the corridor, and except that every now and then one or the other
266

stepped noiselessly to the door to look in upon the sleeping sick man, or in the opposite direction to moderate by a push with the foot the snoring of Clemence's "boy," they sat the whole night through in whispered counsel.

The one, at the request of the other, explained how he had come to be with the little doctor in such extremity.

It seems that Clemence, seeing and understanding the doctor's imprudence, had sallied out with the resolve to set some person on his track. We have said that she went in search of her master. Him she met, and though she could not really count him one of the doctor's friends, yet, rightly believing in his humanity, she told him the matter. He set off in what was for him a quick pace in search of the rash invalid, was misdirected by a too confident child and had given up the hope of finding him, when a faint sound of distress just at hand drew him into an alley, where, close down against a wall, with his face to the earth, lay Doctor Keene. The f. m. c. had just raised him and borne him out of the alley when Honoré came up.

"And you say that, when you would have inquired for him at Frowenfeld's, you saw Palmyre there, standing and talking with Frowenfeld? Tell me more exactly."

And the other, with that grave and gentle economy of words which made his speech so unique, recounted what we amplify:

Palmyre had needed no pleading to induce her to exonerate Joseph. The doctors were present at Frowenfeld's in more than usual number. There was unusualness, too, in their manner and their talk. They were not entirely free from the excitement of the day, and as they talked—with an air of superiority, of Creole inflammability, and with some contempt—concerning Camille Brahmin's and Charlie Mandarin's efforts to precipitate a war, they were yet visibly in a state of expectation. Frowenfeld, they softly said, had in his odd way been indiscreet among these inflammables at Maspero's just when he could least afford to be so, and there was no telling what they might take the notion to do to him before bedtime. All that over and above the independent, unexplained scandal of the early morning. So Joseph and his friends this evening, like Aurora and Clotilde in the morning, were, as we nowadays say of buyers and sellers, "apart," when suddenly and unannounced, Palmyre presented herself among them. When the f. m. c. saw her, she had already handed Joseph his hat and with much sober grace was apologizing for her slave's

267

mistake. All evidence of her being wounded was concealed. The extraordinary excitement of the morning had not hurt her, and she seemed in perfect health. The doctors sat or stood around and gave rapt attention to her patois, one or two translating it for Joseph, and he blushing to the hair, but standing erect and receiving it at second-hand with silent bows. The f. m. c. had gazed on her for a moment, and then forced himself away. He was among the few who had not heard the morning scandal, and he did not comprehend the evening scene. He now asked Honoré concerning it, and quietly showed great relief when it was explained.

Then Honoré, breaking a silence, called the attention of the f. m. c. to the fact that the latter had two tenants at No. 19 rue Bienville. Honoré became the narrator now and told all, finally stating that the die was cast—restitution made.

And then the darker Honoré made a proposition to the other, which, it is little to say, was startling. They discussed it for hours.

"So just a condition," said the merchant, raising his whisper so much that the rentier laid a hand in his elbow,—"such mere justice," he said, more softly, "ought to be an easy condition. God knows"—he lifted his glance reverently—"my very right to exist comes after yours. You are the elder."

The solemn man offered no disclaimer.

What could the proposition be which involved so grave an issue, and to which M. Grandissime's final answer was "I will do it"?

It was that Honoré f. m. c. should become a member of the mercantile house of H. Grandissime, enlisting in its capital all his wealth. And the one condition was that the new style should be *Grandissime Brothers.*

46 The Pique-en-Terre Loses One of Her Crew

Ask the average resident of New Orleans if his town is on an island, and he will tell you no. He will also wonder how any one could have got that notion,—so completely has Orleans Island, whose name at the beginning of the present century was in everybody's mouth, been forgotten. It was once a question of national policy, a point of difference between Republican and Federalist, whether the United States ought to buy this little strip of semi-submerged land, or whether it would not be more righteous to steal it. The Kentuckians kept the question at a red heat by threatening to become an empire by themselves if one course or the other was not taken; but when the First Consul offered to sell all Louisiana, our commissioners were quite robbed of breath. They had approached to ask a hair from the elephant's tail, and were offered the elephant.

For Orleans Island—island it certainly was until General Jackson closed Bayou Manchac—is a narrow, irregular, flat tract of forest, swamp, city, prairie and sea-marsh lying east and west, with the Mississippi, trending south-eastward, for its southern boundary, and for its northern, a parallel and contiguous chain of alternate lakes and bayous, opening into the river through Bayou Manchac, and into the Gulf through the passes of the Malheureuse Islands. On the narrowest part of it stands New

Orleans. Turning and looking back over the rear of the town, one may easily see from her steeples Lake Pontchartrain glistening away to the northern horizon, and in his fancy extend the picture to right and left till Pontchartrain is linked in the west by Pass Manchac to Lake Maurepas, and in the east by the Rigolets and Chef Menteur to Lake Borgne.

An oddity of the Mississippi Delta is the habit the little streams have of running away from the big ones. The river makes its own bed and its own banks, and continuing season after season, through ages of alternate overflow and subsidence, to elevate those banks, creates a ridge which thus becomes a natural elevated aqueduct. Other slightly elevated ridges mark the present or former courses of minor outlets, by which the waters of the Mississippi have found the sea. Between these ridges lie the cypress swamps, through whose profound shades the clear, dark, deep bayous creep noiselessly away into the tall grasses of the shaking prairies. The original New Orleans was built on the Mississippi ridge, with one of these forest-and-water-covered basins stretching back behind her to westward and northward, closed in by Metairie Ridge and Lake Pontchartrain. Local engineers preserve the tradition that the Bayou Sauvage once had its rise, so to speak, in Toulouse street. Though depleted by the city's present drainage system and most likely poisoned by it as well, its waters still move seaward in a course almost due easterly, and empty into Chef Menteur, one of the watery threads of a tangled skein of "passes" between the lakes and the open Gulf. Three-quarters of a century ago this Bayou Sauvage (or Gentilly —corruption of Chantilly) was a navigable stream of wild and sombre beauty.

On a certain morning in August, 1804, and consequently some five months after the events last mentioned, there emerged from the darkness of Bayou Sauvage into the prairie-bordered waters of Chef Menteur, while the morning star was still luminous in the sky above and in the water below, and only the practised eye could detect the first glimmer of day, a small, stanch, single-masted, broad and very light-draught boat, whose innocent character, primarily indicated in its coat of many colors,—the hull being yellow below the water line and white above, with tasteful stripings of blue and red,—was further accentuated by the peaceful name of *Pique-en-terre* (the Sandpiper).

She seemed, too, as she entered the Chef Menteur, as if she

would have liked to turn southward; but the wind did not permit this, and in a moment more the water was rippling after her swift rudder, as she glided away in the direction of Pointe Aux Herbes. But when she had left behind her the mouth of the passage, she changed her course and, leaving the Pointe on her left, bore down toward Petites Coquilles, obviously bent upon passing through the Rigolets.

We know not how to describe the joyousness of the effect when at length one leaves behind him the shadow and gloom of the swamp, and there bursts upon his sight the widespread, flower-decked, bird-haunted prairies of Lake Catharine. The inside and outside of a prison scarcely furnish a greater contrast; and on this fair August morning the contrast was at its strongest. The day broke across a glad expanse of cool and fragrant green, silver-laced with a net-work of crisp salt pools and passes, lakes, bayous and lagoons, that gave a good smell, the inspiring odor of inter-clasped sea and shore, and both beautified and perfumed the happy earth, laid bare to the rising sun. Waving marshes of wild oats, drooping like sated youth from too much pleasure; watery acres hid under crisp-growing greenth starred with pond-lilies and rippled by water-fowl; broad stretches of high grass, with thousands of ecstatic wings palpitating above them; hundreds of thousands of white and pink mallows clapping their hands in voiceless rapture, and that amazon queen of the wild flowers, the morning-glory, stretching her myriad lines, lifting up the trumpet and waving her colors, white, azure and pink, with lacings of spider's web, heavy with pearls and diamonds—the gifts of the summer night. The crew of the *Pique-en-terre* saw all these and felt them; for, whatever they may have been or failed to be, they were men whose heart-strings responded to the touches of nature. One alone of their company, and he the one who should have felt them most, showed insensibility, sighed laughingly and then laughed sighingly in the face of his fellows and of all this beauty, and profanely confessed that his heart's desire was to get back to his wife. He had been absent from her now for nine hours!

But the sun is getting high; Petites Coquilles has been passed and left astern, the eastern end of Las Conchas is on the after-larboard-quarter, the briny waters of Lake Borgne flash far and wide their dazzling white and blue, and, as the little boat issues from the deep channel of the Rigolets, the white-armed waves catch her and toss her like a merry babe. A triumph for the helmsman—he it is who sighs, at intervals of tiresome frequency, for his wife. He had, from the very starting-place in the upper waters of Bayou Sauvage, declared in favor of the Rigolets as—wind and tide considered—the most practicable of all the passes. Now that they were out, he forgot for a moment the self-amusing plaint of conjugal separation to flaunt his triumph. Would any one hereafter dispute with him on the subject of Louisiana sea-coast-navigation? He knew every pass and piece of water like A, B, C, and could tell, faster, much faster than he could repeat the multiplication table (upon which he was a little slow and doubtful), the amount of water in each at ebb tide—Pass Jean or Petit Pass, Unknown Pass, Petit Rigolet, Chef Menteur,——

Out on the far southern horizon, in the Gulf—the Gulf of Mexico—there appears a speck of white. It is known to those on board the *Pique-en-terre*, the moment it is descried, as the canvas of a large schooner. The opinion, first expressed by the youthful husband, who still reclines with the tiller held firmly under his arm, and then by another member of the company who sits on the centre-board-well, is unanimously adopted, that she is making for the Rigolets, will pass Petites Coquilles by eleven o'clock, and will tie up at the little port of St. Jean, on the bayou of the same name, before sundown, if the wind holds anywise as it is.

On the other hand, the master of the distant schooner shuts his glass, and says to the single passenger whom he has aboard that the little sail just visible toward the Rigolets is a sloop with a half-deck, well filled with men, in all probability a pleasure-party bound to the Chandeleurs on a fishing and gunning excursion, and passes into comments on the superior skill of landsmen over seamen in the handling of small sailing craft.

By and by the two vessels near each other. They approach within hailing distance, and are announcing each to each their identity, when the young man at the tiller jerks himself to a squatting posture, and, from under a broad-brimmed and slouched straw hat, cries to the schooner's one passenger:

"Hello, Challie Keene!"

And the passenger more quietly answers back:

"Hello, Raoul, is that you?"

M. Innerarity replied, with a profane parenthesis, that it was he.

"You kin hask Sylvestre!" he concluded.

The doctor's eye passed around a semicircle of some eight men, the most of whom were quite young, but one or two of whom were gray, sitting with their arms thrown out upon the wash-board, in the dark négligé of amateur fishermen and with that exultant look of expectant deviltry in their handsome faces which characterizes the Creole with his collar off.

The mettlesome little doctor felt the odds against him in the exchange of greetings.

"Ola, Dawctah!"

"Hé, Doctah, que-ce qui t'après fé?"

"Ho, ho, compère Noyo!"

"Comment va, Docta?"

A light peppering of profanity accompanied each salute.

The doctor put on defensively a smile of superiority to the juniors and of courtesy to the others, and responsively spoke their names:

" 'Polyte—Sylvestre—Achille—Emile—ah! Agamemnon."

The Doctor and Agamemnon raised their hats.

As Agamemnon was about to speak, a general expostulatory outcry drowned his voice; the *Pique-en-terre* was going about close abreast of the schooner, and angry questions and orders were flying at Raoul's head like a volley of eggs.

"Messieurs," said Raoul, partially rising but still stooping over the tiller, and taking his hat off his bright curls with mock courtesy, "I am going back to New Orleans. I would not give *that* for all the fish in the sea; I want to see my wife. I am going back to New Orleans to see my wife—and to congratulate the city upon your absence." Incredulity, expostulation, reproach, taunt, malediction—he smiled unmoved upon them all. "Messieurs, I *must* go and see my wife."

Amid redoubled outcries he gave the helm to Camille Brah-min, and fighting his way with his pretty feet against half-real efforts to throw him overboard, clambered forward to the mast, whence a moment later, with the help of the schooner-master's hand, he reached the deck of the larger vessel. The *Pique-en-terre* turned, and with a little flutter spread her smooth wing and skimmed away.

"Doctah Keene, look yeh!" M. Innerarity held up a hand whose third finger wore the conventional ring of the Creole bridegroom. "W'at you got to say to dat?"

The little doctor felt a faintness run through his veins, and a thrill of anger follow it. The poor man could not imagine a love affair that did not include Clotilde Nancanou.

"Whom have you married?"

"De pritties' gal in de citty."

The questioner controlled himself.

"M-hum," he responded, with a contraction of the eyes.

Raoul waited an instant for some kindlier comment, and finding the hope vain, suddenly assumed a look of delighted admiration.

"Hi, yi, yi! Doctah, 'ow you har lookingue fine."

The true look of the doctor was that he had not much longer to live. A smile of bitter humor passed over his face, and he looked for a near seat, saying:

"How's Frowenfeld?"

Raoul struck an ecstatic attitude and stretched forth his hand as if the doctor could not fail to grasp it. The invalid's heart sank like lead.

"Frowenfeld has got her," he thought.

"Well?" said he with a frown of impatience and restraint; and Raoul cried:

"I sole my pig-shoe!"

The doctor could not help but laugh.

"Shades of the masters!"

"No; 'Louizyanna rif-using to hantre de h-Union.'"

The doctor stood corrected.

The two walked across the deck, following the shadow of the swinging sail. The doctor lay down in a low-swung hammock, and Raoul sat upon the deck *à la Turque*.

"Come, come, Raoul, tell me, what is the news?"

"News? Oh, I donno. You 'eard concernin' the dool?"

"You don't mean to say——"

"Yesseh!"

"Agricola and Sylvestre?"

"W'at de dev'! No! Burr an' 'Ammiltong; in Noo-Juzzylas-June. Collonnel Burr, 'e——"

"Oh, fudge! yes. How is Frowenfeld?"

"'E's well. Guess 'ow much I sole my pig-shoe."

"Well, how much?"

"Two 'ondred fifty." He laid himself out at length, his elbow on the deck, his head in his hand. "I believe I'm sorry I sole 'er."

"I don't wonder. How's Honoré? Tell me what has happened. Remember, I've been away five months."

"No; I am verrie glad dat I sole 'er. What? Ha! I should think so! If it have not had been fo' dat I would not be married to-day.

274

You think I would get married on dat sal'rie w'at Proffis-or Frowenfel' was payin' me? Twenty-five dolla' de mont'? Docta Keene, no gen'leman h-ought to git married if 'e 'ave not anny'ow fifty dolla' de mont'! If I wasn' a h-artiz I wouldn' git married; I gie you my word!"

"Yes," said the little doctor, "you are right. Now tell me the news."

"Well, dat Cong-ress gone an' mak'——"

"Raoul, stop. I know that Congress has divided the province into two territories; I know you Creoles think all your liberties are lost; I know the people are in a great stew because they are not allowed to elect their own officers and legislatures, and that in Opelousas and Attakapas they are as wild as their cattle about it——"

"We 'ad two big mitting' about it," interrupted Raoul; "my bro'r-in-law speak at both of them!"

"Who?"

"Chahlie Mandarin."

"Glad to hear it," said Doctor Keene,—which was the truth. "Besides that, I know Laussat has gone to Martinique; that the Américains have a newspaper, and that cotton is two bits a pound. Now what I want to know is, how are my friends? What has Honoré done? What has Frowenfeld done? And Palmyre,—and Agricole? They hustled me away from here as if I had been caught trying to cut my throat. Tell me everything."

And Raoul sank the artist and bridegroom in the historian, and told him.

47 The News

"My cousin Honoré,—well, you kin jus' say 'e bitray' is 'ole fam'ly."

"How so?" asked Doctor Keene, with a handkerchief over his face to shield his eyes from the sun.

"Well,—ce't'nly 'e did! Di'n' 'e gave dat money to Aurora De Grapion?—one 'undred five t'ousan' dolla'? Jis' as if to say, 'Yeh's de money my h-uncle stole from you' 'usban'.' Hah! w'en I will swear on a stack of Bible' as 'igh as yo' head, dat Agricole win dat 'abitation fair!—If I see it? No, sir; I don't 'ave to see it! I'll swear to it! Hah!"

"And have she and her daughter actually got the money?"

"She — an' — heh — daughtah — ac — shilly — got-'at-money-sir! W'at? Dey livin' in de rue Royale in mag-*niffy*cen' style on top de drug-sto' of Proffis-or Frowenfel'."

"But how, over Frowenfeld's, when Frowenfeld's is a one-story——"

"My dear frien'! Proffis-or Frowenfel' is *moove!* You rickleck dat big new t'ree-story buildin' w'at jus' finished in de rue Royale, a lill mo' farther up town from his old shop? Well, we open dare *a big sto'!* An' listen! You think Honoré di'n' bitrayed 'is family? Madame Nancanou an' heh daughtah livin' upstair' an' rissy-ving de finess soci'ty in de Province!—an' *me?*—down-stair' meckin' pill'! You call dat justice?"

276

But Doctor Keene, without waiting for this question, had asked one:

"Does Frowenfeld board with them?"

"Psh-sh-sh! Board! Dey woon board de Marquis of Casa-Calvo! I don't b'lieve dey would board Honoré Grandissime! All de king' an' queen' in de worl' couldn' board dare! No, sir!—'Owever, you know, I think dey are splendid ladies. Me an' my wife, we know them well. An' Honoré—I think my cousin Honoré's a splendid gen'leman, too." After a moment's pause he resumed, with a happy sigh, "Well, I don' care, I'm married. A man w'at's married, 'e don' care. But I di'n' think Honoré could ever do lak dat odder t'ing."

"Do he and Joe Frowenfeld visit there?"

"Doctah Keene," demanded Raoul, ignoring the question, "I hask you now, plain, don' you find dat mighty disgressful to do dat way, lak Honoré?"

"What way?"

"W'at? You dunno? You don' yeh 'ow 'e gone partner' wid a nigga?"

"What do you mean?"

Doctor Keene drew the handkerchief off his face and half lifted his feeble head.

"Yesseh! 'e gone partner' wid dat quadroon w'at call 'imself Honoré Grandissime, seh!"

The doctor dropped his head again and laid the handkerchief back on his face.

"What do the family say to that?"

"But w'at *can* dey say? It save dem from ruin! At de sem time, me, I think it is a disgress. Not dat he h-use de money, but it is dat name w'at 'e give de h-establishmen'—Grandissime Frères! H-only for 'is money we would 'av catch' dat quadroon gen'leman an' put some tar and fedder. Grandissime Frères! Agricole don' spik to my cousin Honoré no mo'. But I think dass wrong. W'at you t'ink, Doctor?"

That evening, at candle-light, Raoul got the right arm of his slender, laughing wife about his neck; but Doctor Keene tarried all night in suburb St. Jean. He hardly felt the moral courage to face the results of the last five months. Let us understand them better ourselves.

48 An Indignant Family and a Smashed Shop

It was indeed a fierce storm that had passed over the head of Honoré Grandissime. Taken up and carried by it, as it seemed to him, without volition, he had felt himself thrown here and there, wrenched, torn, gasping for moral breath, speaking the right word as if in delirium, doing the right deed as if by helpless instinct, and seeing himself in every case, at every turn, tricked by circumstance out of every vestige of merit. So it seemed to him. The long contemplated restitution was accomplished. On the morning when Aurora and Clotilde had expected to be turned shelterless into the open air, they had called upon him in his private office and presented the account of which he had put them in possession the evening before. He had honored it on the spot. To the two ladies who felt their own hearts stirred almost to tears of gratitude, he was—as he sat before them calm, unmoved, handling keen-edged facts with the easy rapidity of one accustomed to use them, smiling courteously and collectedly, parrying their expressions of appreciation—to them, we say, at least to one of them, he was "the prince of gentlemen." But, at the same time, there was within him, unseen, a surge of emotions, leaping, lashing, whirling, yet ever hurrying onward along the hidden, rugged bed of his honest intention.

The other restitution, which even twenty-four hours earlier

might have seemed a pure self-sacrifice, became a self-rescue. The f. m. c. was the elder brother. A remark of Honoré made the night they watched in the corridor by Doctor Keene's door, about the younger's "right to exist," was but the echo of a conversation they had once had together in Europe. There they had practised a familiarity of intercourse which Louisiana would not have endured, and once, when speaking upon the subject of their common fatherhood, the f. m. c., prone to melancholy speech, had said:

"You are the lawful son of Numa Grandissime; I had no right to be born."

But Honoré quickly answered:

"By the laws of men, it may be; but by the law of God's justice, you are the lawful son, and it is I who should not have been born."

But, returned to Louisiana, accepting with the amiable, old-fashioned philosophy of conservatism, the sins of the community, he had forgotten the unchampioned rights of his passive half-brother. Contact with Frowenfeld had robbed him of his pleasant mental drowsiness, and the oft-encountered apparition of the dark sharer of his name had become a slow-stepping, silent embodiment of reproach. The turn of events had brought him face to face with the problem of restitution, and he had solved it. But where had he come out? He had come out the beneficiary of this restitution, extricated from bankruptcy by an agreement which gave the f. m. c. only a public recognition of kinship which had always been his due. Bitter cup of humiliation!

Such was the stress within. Then there was the storm without. The Grandissimes were in a high state of excitement. The news had reached them all that Honoré had met the question of titles by selling one of their largest estates. It was received with wincing frowns, indrawn breath, and lifted feet, but without protest, and presently with a smile of returning confidence.

"Honoré knew; Honoré was informed; they had all authorized Honoré; and Honoré, though he might have his odd ways and notions, picked up during that unfortunate stay abroad, might safely be trusted to stand by the interests of his people."

After the first shock, some of them even raised a laugh:

"Ha, ha, ha! Honoré would show those Yankees!"

They went to his counting-room and elsewhere, in search of him, to smite their hands into the hands of their far-seeing young champion. But, as we have seen, they did not find him; none dreamed of looking for him in an enemy's camp (19 Bienville) or on the lonely suburban commons, talking to himself in the ghostly twilight; and the next morning, while Aurora and Clotilde were seated before him in his private office, looking first at the face and then at the back of two mighty drafts of equal amount on Philadelphia, the cry of treason flew forth to these astounded Grandissimes, followed by the word that the sacred fire was gone out in the Grandissime temple (counting-room), that Delilahs in duplicate were carrying off the holy treasures, and that the uncircumcised and unclean—even an f. m. c.—was about to be inducted into the Grandissime priesthood.

Aurora and Clotilde were still there, when the various members of the family began to arrive and display their outlines in impatient shadow-play upon the glass door of the private office; now one, and now another, dallied with the door-knob and by and by obtruded their lifted hats and urgent, anxious faces half into the apartment; but Honoré would only glance toward them, and with a smile equally courteous, authoritative and fleeting, say:

"Good-morning, Camille" (or Charlie—or Agamemnon, as the case might be), "I will see you later; let me trouble you to close the door."

To add yet another strain, the two ladies, like frightened, rescued children, would cling to their deliverer. They wished him to become the custodian and investor of their wealth. Ah, woman! who is a tempter like thee? But Honoré said no, and showed them the danger of such a course.

"Suppose I should die suddenly. You might have trouble with my executors."

The two beauties assented pensively; but in Aurora's bosom a great throb secretly responded that as for her, in that case, she should have no use for money—in a nunnery.

"Would not Monsieur at least consent to be their financial adviser?"

He hemmed, commenced a sentence twice, and finally said:

"You will need an agent; some one to take full charge of your affairs; some person on whose sagacity and integrity you can place the fullest dependence."

"Who, for instance?" asked Aurora.

"I should say, without hesitation, Professor Frowenfeld, the apothecary. You know his trouble of yesterday is quite cleared up. You had not heard? Yes. He is not what we call an enterprising man, but—so much the better. Take him all in all, I would choose him above all others; if you——"

Aurora interrupted him. There was an ill-concealed wildness in her eye and a slight tremor in her voice, as she spoke, which she had not expected to betray. The quick, though quiet, eye of Honoré Grandissime saw it, and it thrilled him through.

" 'Sieur Grandissime, I take the risk; I wish you to take care of my money."

"But, Maman," said Clotilde, turning with a timid look to her mother, "if Monsieur Grandissime would rather not——"

Aurora, feeling alarmed at what she had said, rose up. Clotilde and Honoré did the same, and he said:

"With Professor Frowenfeld in charge of your affairs, I shall feel them not entirely removed from my care also. We are very good friends."

Clotilde looked at her mother. The three exchanged glances. The ladies signified their assent and turned to go, but M. Grandissime stopped them.

"By your leave, I will send for him. If you will be seated again——"

They thanked him and resumed their seats; he excused himself, and passed into the counting-room and sent a messenger for the apothecary.

M. Grandissime's meeting with his kinsmen was a stormy one. Aurora and Clotilde heard the strife begin, increase, subside, rise again and decrease. They heard men stride heavily to and fro, they heard hands smite together, palms fall upon tables and fists upon desks, heard half-understood statement and unintelligible counter-statement and derisive laughter; and, in the midst of all, like the voice of a man who rules himself, the clear-noted, unimpassioned speech of Honoré, sounding so loftily beautiful in the ear of Aurora that when Clotilde looked at her, sitting motionless with her rapt eyes lifted up, those eyes came down to her own with a sparkle of enthusiasm and she softly said:

"It sounds like St. Gabriel!" and then blushed.

Clotilde answered with a happy, meaning look, which intensified the blush, and then leaning affectionately forward and holding the maman's eyes with her own, she said:

"You have my consent."

"Saucy!" said Aurora. "Wait till I get my own!"

Some of his kinsmen Honoré pacified; some he silenced. He invited all to withdraw their lands and moneys from his charge, and some accepted the invitation. They spurned his parting advice to sell, and the policy they then adopted, and never afterward modified, was that "all or nothing" attitude which, as years rolled by, bled them to penury in those famous cupping-leeching-and-bleeding establishments, the courts of Louisiana. You may see their grandchildren, to-day, anywhere within the angle of the old rues Esplanade and Rampart, holding up their heads in unspeakable poverty, their nobility kept green by unflinching self-respect, and their poetic and pathetic pride revelling in ancestral, perennial rebellion against common sense.

"That is Agricola," whispered Aurora, with lifted head and eyes dilated and askance, as one deep-chested voice roared above all others.

Agricola stormed.

"Uncle," Aurora by and by heard Honoré say, "shall I leave my own counting-room?"

At that moment Joseph Frowenfeld entered, pausing with one hand on the outer rail. No one noticed him but Honoré, who was watching for him, and who, by a silent motion, directed him into the private office.

"H-whe shake its dust from our feet!" said Agricola, gathering some young retainers by a sweep of his glance and going out down the stair in the arched way, unmoved by the fragrance of warm bread. On the banquette he harangued his followers.

He said that in such times as these every lover of liberty should go armed; that the age of trickery had come; that by trickery Louisianians had been sold, like cattle, to a nation of parvenues, to be dragged before juries for asserting the human right of free trade or ridding the earth of sneaks in the pay of the government; that laws, so-called, had been forged into thumb-screws, and a Congress which had bound itself to give them all the rights of American citizens—sorry boon!—was preparing to slip their birthright acres from under their feet, and leave them hanging, a bait to the vultures of the Américain immigration. Yes; the age of trickery! Its apostles, he said, were even then at work among their fellow-citizens, warping, distorting, blasting, corrupting, poisoning the noble, unsuspecting, confiding Creole mind. For months the devilish work had been allowed, by a patient, peace-loving people to go on. But shall it go on forever? (Cries of "No!" "No!") The smell of white blood comes on the south breeze. Dessalines and Christophe have recommenced their hellish work. Virginia, too, trembles for the safety of her fair mothers and daughters. We know not what is being plotted in the cane-brakes of Louisiana. But we know that in the face of these things the prelates of trickery are sitting in Washington allowing throats to go unthrottled that talked tenderly about the "negro slave"; we know worse: we know that mixed blood has asked for equal rights from a son of the Louisiana noblesse, and that those sacred rights have been treacherously, pusillanimously surrendered into its possession. Why did we not rise yesterday, when the public heart was stirred? The forbearance of this people would be absurd if it were not saintly. But the time has come when Louisiana must protect herself! If there is one here who will not strike for his lands, his rights and the purity of his race, let him speak! (Cries of "We will rise now!" "Give us a leader!" "Lead the way!")

"Kinsmen, friends," continued Agricola, "meet me at nightfall before the house of this too-long-spared mulatto. Come armed. Bring a few feet of stout rope. By morning the gentlemen of color will know their places better than they do to-day; h-whe shall understand each other! H-whe shall set the negrophiles to meditating."

He waved them away.

With a huzza the accumulated crowd moved off. Chance carried them up the rue Royale; they sang a song; they came to Frowenfeld's. It was an Américain establishment; that was against it. It was a gossiping place of Américain evening loungers; that was against it. It was a sorcerer's den—(we are on an ascending scale); its proprietor had refused employment to some there present, had refused credit to others, was an impudent condemner of the most approved Creole sins, had been beaten over the head only the day before; all these were against it. But, worse still, the building was owned by the f. m. c., and unluckiest of all, Raoul stood in the door and some of his kinsmen in the crowd stopped to have a word with him. The crowd stopped. A nameless fellow in the throng—he was still singing—said: "Here's the place," and dropped two bricks through the glass of the show-window. Raoul, with a cry of retaliative rage, drew and lifted a pistol; but a kinsman jerked it from him and three others quickly pinioned him and bore him off struggling, pleased to get him away unhurt. In ten minutes, Frowenfeld's was a broken-windowed, open-doored house, full of unrecognizable rubbish that had escaped the torch only through a chance rumor that the Governor's police were coming, and the consequent stampede of the mob.

Joseph was sitting in M. Grandissime's private office, in council with him and the ladies, and Aurora was just saying:

"Well, anny'ow, 'Sieur Frowenfel', ad laz you consen'!" and gathering her veil from her lap, when Raoul burst in, all sweat and rage.

"'Sieur Frowenfel', we ruin'! Ow pharmacie knock all in pieces! My pig-shoe is los'!"

He dropped into a chair and burst into tears.

Shall we never learn to withhold our tears until we are sure of our trouble? Raoul little knew the joy in store for him. 'Polyte, it transpired the next day, had rushed in after the first volley of missiles, and while others were gleefully making off with jars of asafœtida and decanters of distilled water, lifted in his arms and bore away unharmed "Louisiana" firmly refusing to the last to enter the Union. It may not be premature to add that about four weeks later Honoré Grandissime, upon Raoul's announcement that he was "betrothed," purchased this painting and presented it to a club of *natural connoisseurs*.

49 Over the New Store

The accident of the ladies Nancanou making their new home
over Frowenfeld's drug-store, occurred in the following rather
amusing way. It chanced that the building was about completed
at the time that the apothecary's stock in trade was destroyed;
Frowenfeld leased the lower floor. Honoré Grandissime f. m. c.
was the owner. He being concealed from his enemies, Joseph
treated with that person's inadequately remunerated employé.
In those days, as still in the old French Quarter, it was not uncommon for persons, even of wealth, to make their homes over
stores, and buildings were constructed with a view to their parti-
tion in this way. Hence, in Chartres and Decatur streets, to-day—
and in the cross-streets between, so many store-buildings with
balconies, dormer windows, and sometimes even belvederes. This
new building caught the eye and fancy of Aurora and Clotilde.
The apartments for the store were entirely isolated. Through a
large *porte-cochère,* opening upon the banquette immediately
beside and abreast of the store-front, one entered a high, covered
carriage-way with a tesselated pavement and green plastered
walls, and reached,—just where this way (corridor, the Creoles
always called it) opened into a sunny court surrounded with
narrow parterres,—a broad stairway leading to a hall over the
"corridor" and to the drawing-rooms over the store. They liked

285

it! Aurora would find out at once what sort of an establishment was likely to be opened below, and if that proved unexceptionable she would lease the upper part without more ado.

Next day she said:

"Clotilde, thou beautiful, I have signed the lease!"

"Then the store below is to be occupied by a—what?"

"Guess!"

"Ah!"

"Guess a pharmacien!"

Clotilde's lips parted, she was going to smile, when her thought changed and she blushed offendedly.

"Not——"

" 'Sieur Frowenf——ah, ha, ha, ha!—*ha, ha, ha!*"

Clotilde burst into tears.

Still they moved in—it was written in the bond; and so did the apothecary; and probably two sensible young lovers never before nor since behaved with such abject fear of each other—for a time. Later, and after much oft-repeated good advice given to each separately and to both together, Honoré Grandissime persuaded them that Clotilde could make excellent use of a portion of her means by re-enforcing Frowenfeld's very slender stock and well filling his rather empty-looking store, and so they signed regular articles of copartnership, blushing frightfully.

Frowenfeld became a visitor, Honoré not; once Honoré had seen the ladies' moneys satisfactorily invested, he kept aloof. It is pleasant here to remark that neither Aurora nor Clotilde made any waste of their sudden acquisitions; they furnished their rooms with much beauty at moderate cost, and their *salon* with artistic, not extravagant, elegance, and, for the sake of greater propriety, employed a decayed lady as housekeeper; but, being discreet in all other directions, they agreed upon one bold outlay —a volante.

Almost any afternoon you might have seen this vehicle on the Terre aux Bœuf, or Bayou, or Tchoupitoulas Road; and because of the brilliant beauty of its occupants it became known from all other volantes as the "meteor."

Frowenfeld's visits were not infrequent; he insisted on Clotilde's knowing just what was being done with her money. Without indulging ourselves in the pleasure of contemplating his continued mental unfolding, we may say that his growth became more rapid in this season of universal expansion; love had

286

entered into his still compacted soul like a cupid into a rose, and was crowding it wide open. However, as yet, it had not made him brave. Aurora used to slip out of the drawing-room, and in some secluded nook of the hall throw up her clasped hands and go through all the motions of screaming merriment.

"The little fool!"—it was of her own daughter she whispered this complimentary remark—"the little fool is afraid of the fish!"

"You!" she said to Clotilde, one evening after Joseph had gone, "you call yourself a Creole girl!"

But she expected too much. Nothing so terrorizes a blushing girl as a blushing man. And then—though they did sometimes digress—Clotilde and her partner met to "talk business" in a purely literal sense.

Aurora, after a time, had taken her money into her own keeping.

"You mighd gid robb' ag'in, you know, 'Sieur Frowenfel'," she said.

But when he mentioned Clotilde's fortune as subject to the same contingency, Aurora replied:

"Ah! bud Clotilde mighd gid robb'!"

But for all the exuberance of Aurora's spirits, there was a cloud in her sky. Indeed, we know it is only when clouds are in the sky that we get the rosiest tints; and so it was with Aurora. One night, when she had heard the wicket in the *porte-cochère* shut behind three evening callers, one of whom she had rejected a week before, another of whom she expected to dispose of similarly, and the last of whom was Joseph Frowenfeld, she began such a merry raillery at Clotilde and such a hilarious ridicule of the "Professor" that Clotilde would have wept again had not Aurora, all at once, in the midst of a laugh, dropped her face in her hands and run from the room in tears. It is one of the penalties we pay for being joyous, that nobody thinks us capable of care or the victim of trouble until, in some moment of extraordinary expansion, our bubble of gayety bursts. Aurora had been crying of nights. Even that same night, Clotilde awoke, opened her eyes and beheld her mother risen from the pillow and sitting upright in the bed beside her; the moon, shining brightly through the bars, revealed with distinctness her head slightly drooped, her face again in her hands and the dark folds of her hair falling about her shoulders, half-concealing the richly embroidered bosom of her snowy gown, and coiling in continuous abundance about her waist and on the slight summer covering of the bed. Before her on the sheet lay a white paper. Clotilde did not try to decipher the writing on it; she knew, at sight, the slip that had fallen from the statement of account on the evening of the ninth of March. Aurora withdrew her hands from her face—Clotilde shut her eyes; she heard Aurora put the paper in her bosom.

"Clotilde," she said, very softly.

"Maman," the daughter replied, opening her eyes, reached up her arms and drew the dear head down.

"Clotilde, once upon a time I woke this way, and, while you were asleep, left the bed and made a vow to Monsieur Danny. Oh! it was a sin! But I cannot do those things now; I have been frightened ever since. I shall never do so any more. I shall never commit another sin as long as I live!"

Their lips met fervently.

"My sweet sweet," whispered Clotilde, "you looked so beautiful sitting up with the moonlight all around you!"

"Clotilde, my beautiful daughter," said Aurora, pushing her bedmate from her and pretending to repress a smile, "I tell you now, because you don't know, and it is my duty as your mother to tell you—the meanest wickedness a woman can do in all this bad, bad world is to look ugly in bed!"

Clotilde answered nothing, and Aurora dropped her outstretched arms, turned away with an involuntary, tremulous sigh, and after two or three hours of patient wakefulness, fell asleep.

But at daybreak next morning, he that wrote the paper had not closed his eyes.

50 A Proposal of Marriage

There was always some flutter among Frowenfeld's employés
when he was asked for, and this time it was the more pronounced
because he was sought by a housemaid from the upper floor. It
was hard for these two or three young Ariels to keep their Creole
feet to the ground when it was presently revealed to their sharp
ears that the "proffis-or" was requested to come upstairs.

The new store was an extremely neat, bright, and well-ordered
establishment; yet to ascend into the drawing-rooms seemed to
the apothecary like going from the hold of one of those smart
old packet-ships of his day into the cabin. Aurora came forward,
with the slippers of a Cinderella twinkling at the edge of her
robe. It seemed unfit that the floor under them should not be
clouds.

"Proffis-or Frowenfel', good-day! Teg a cha'." She laughed. It
was the pure joy of existence. "You's well? You lookin' verrie
well! Halways bizzie? You fine dad agriz wid you' healt', 'Sieur
Frowenfel'? Yes? Ha, ha, ha!" She suddenly leaned toward him
across the arm of her chair, with an earnest face. " 'Sieur Frowenfel', Palmyre wand see you. You don' wan' come ad 'er 'ouse, eh?
—an' you don' wan' her to come ad yo' bureau. You know, 'Sieur
Frowenfel', she drez the hair of Clotilde an' mieself. So w'en she
tell me dad, I juz say, 'Palmyre, I will sen' for Proffis-or Frowenfel' to come yeh; but I don' thing 'e comin'.' You know, I din'
wan' you to 'ave dad troub'; but Clotilde—ha, ha, ha! Clotilde is

sudge a foolish—she nevva thing of dad troub' to you—she say she thing you was too kine-'arted to call dad troub'—ha, ha, ha! So anny'ow we sen' for you, eh!"

Frowenfeld said he was glad they had done so, whereupon Aurora rose lightly, saying:

"I go an' sen' her." She started away, but turned back to add: "You know, 'Sieur Frowenfel', she say she cann' truz nobody bud y'u." She ended with a low, melodious laugh, bending her joyous eyes upon the apothecary with her head dropped to one side in a way to move a heart of flint.

She turned and passed through a door, and by the same way Palmyre entered. The *philosophe* came forward noiselessly and with a subdued expression, different from any Frowenfeld had ever before seen. At the first sight of her a thrill of disrelish ran through him of which he was instantly ashamed; as she came nearer he met her with a deferential bow and the silent tender of a chair. She sat down, and, after a moment's pause, handed him a sealed letter.

He turned it over twice, recognized the handwriting, felt the disrelish return, and said:

"This is addressed to yourself."

She bowed.

"Do you know who wrote it?" he asked.

She bowed again.

"*Oui, Miché.*"

"You wish me to open it? I cannot read French."

She seemed to have some explanation to offer, but could not command the necessary English; however, with the aid of Frowenfeld's limited guessing powers, she made him understand that the bearer of the letter to her had brought word from the writer that it was written in English purposely that M. Frowenfeld—the only person he was willing should see it—might read it. Frowenfeld broke the seal and ran his eye over the writing, but remained silent.

The woman stirred, as if to say "Well?" But he hesitated.

"Palmyre," he suddenly said, with a slight, dissuasive smile, "it would be a profanation for me to read this."

She bowed to signify that she caught his meaning, then raised her elbows with an expression of dubiety, and said:

" 'E hask you——"

"Yes," murmured the apothecary. He shook his head as if to protest to himself, and read in a low but audible voice:

"Star of my soul, I approach to die. It is not for me possible to live without Palmyre. Long time have I so done, but now, cut off from to see thee, by imprisonment, as it may be called, love is starving to death. Oh, have pity on the faithful heart which, since ten years, change not, but forget heaven and earth for you. Now in the peril of the life, hidden away, that absence from the sight of you make his seclusion the more worse than death. Halas! I pine! Not other ten years of despair can I commence. Accept this love. If so I will live for you, but if to the contraire, I must die for you. Is there anything at all what I will not give or even do if Palmyre will be my wife? Ah, no, far otherwise, there is nothing!"

Frowenfeld looked over the top of the letter. Palmyre sat with her eyes cast down, slowly shaking her head. He returned his glance to the page, coloring somewhat with annoyance at being made a proposing medium.

"The English is very faulty here," he said, without looking up. "He mentions Bras-Coupé." Palmyre started and turned toward him; but he went on without lifting his eyes. "He speaks of your old pride and affection toward him as one who with your aid might have been a leader and deliverer of his people." Frowenfeld looked up. "Do you under——"

"*Allez, Miché,*" said she, leaning forward, her great eyes fixed on the apothecary and her face full of distress. "*Mo comprend bien.*"

"He asks you to let him be to you in the place of Bras-Coupé."

The eyes of the *philosophe*, probably for the first time since the death of the giant, lost their pride. They gazed upon Frowenfeld with almost piteousness; but she compressed her lips and again slowly shook her head.

"You see," said Frowenfeld, suddenly feeling a new interest, "he understands their wants. He knows their wrongs. He is acquainted with laws and men. He could speak for them. It would not be insurrection—it would be advocacy. He would give his time, his pen, his speech, his means to get them justice —to get them their rights."

She hushed the over-zealous advocate with a sad and bitter smile and essayed to speak, studied as if for English words, and, suddenly abandoning that attempt, said, with ill-concealed scorn and in the Creole patois:

"What is all that? What I want is vengeance!"

"I will finish reading," said Frowenfeld, quickly, not caring to understand the passionate speech.

"Ah, Palmyre! Palmyre! What you love and hope to love you because his heart keep itself free, he is loving another!"

"*Qui ci ça, Miché?*"
Frowenfeld was loth to repeat. She had understood, as her face showed; but she dared not believe. He made it shorter:
"He means that Honoré Grandissime loves another woman."
"'Tis a lie!" she exclaimed, a better command of English coming with the momentary loss of restraint.
The apothecary thought a moment and then decided to speak.
"I do not think so," he quietly said.
"'Ow you know dat?"
She, too, spoke quietly, but under a fearful strain. She had thrown herself forward, but, as she spoke, forced herself back into her seat.
"He told me so himself."
The tall figure of Palmyre rose slowly and silently from her chair, her eyes lifted up and her lips moving noiselessly. She seemed to have lost all knowledge of place or of human presence. She walked down the drawing-room quite to its curtained windows and there stopped, her face turned away and her hand laid with a visible tension on the back of a chair. She remained so long that Frowenfeld had begun to think of leaving her so, when she turned and came back. Her form was erect, her step firm and nerved, her lips set together and her hands dropped easily at her side; but when she came close up before the apothecary she was trembling. For a moment she seemed speechless, and then, while her eyes gleamed with passion, she said, in a cold, clear tone, and in her native patois:
"Very well; if I cannot love I can have my revenge." She took the letter from him and bowed her thanks, still adding, in the same tongue, "There is now no longer anything to prevent."
The apothecary understood the dark speech. She meant that, with no hope of Honoré's love, there was no restraining motive to withhold her from wreaking what vengeance she could upon Agricola. But he saw the folly of a debate.
"That is all I can do?" asked he.
"*Oui, merci, Miché*," she said; then she added, in perfect English, "but that is not all *I* can do," and then—laughed.
The apothecary had already turned to go, and the laugh was a low one; but it chilled his blood. He was glad to get back to his employments.

51 Business Changes

We have now recorded some of the events which characterized the five months during which Doctor Keene had been vainly seeking to recover his health in the West Indies.

"Is Mr. Frowenfeld in?" he asked, walking very slowly, and with a cane, into the new drug-store on the morning of his return to the city.

"If Professo' Frowenfel's in?" replied a young man in shirt-sleeves, speaking rapidly, slapping a paper package which he had just tied, and sliding it smartly down the counter. "No, seh."

A quick step behind the doctor caused him to turn; Raoul was just entering, with a bright look of business on his face, taking his coat off as he came.

"Docta Keene! *Teck* a chair. 'Ow you like de noo sto'? See? Fo' counters! T'ree clerk'! De whole interieure paint undre mie h-own direction! If dat is not a beautiful! eh? Look at dat sign."

He pointed to some lettering in harmonious colors near the ceiling at the farther end of the house. The doctor looked and read:

MANDARIN, AG'T, APOTHECARY

"Why not Frowenfeld?" he asked.
Raoul shrugged.

" 'Tis better dis way."

That was his explanation.

"Not the De Brahmin Mandarin who was Honoré's manager?"

"Yes. Honoré wasn' able to kip 'im no long-er. Honoré isn' so rich lak befo'."

"And Mandarin is really in charge here?"

"Oh, yes. Profess-or Frowenfel' all de time at de ole corner, w'ere 'e continue to keep 'is private room and h-use de ole shop fo' ware'ouse. 'E h-only come yeh w'en Mandarin cann' git 'long widout 'im."

"What does he do there? *He's* not rich."

Raoul bent down toward the doctor's chair and whispered the dark secret:

"Studyin'!"

Doctor Keene went out.

Everything seemed changed to the returned wanderer. Poor man! The changes were very slight save in their altered relation to him. To one broken in health, and still more to one with broken heart, old scenes fall upon the sight in broken rays. A sort of vague alienation seemed to the little doctor to come like a film over the long-familiar vistas of the town where he had once walked in the vigor and complacency of strength and distinction. This was not the same New Orleans. The people he met on the street were more or less familiar to his memory, but many that should have recognized him failed to do so, and others were made to notice him rather by his cough than by his face. Some did not know he had been away. It made him cross.

He had walked slowly down beyond the old Frowenfeld corner and had just crossed the street to avoid the dust of a building which was being torn down to make place for a new one, when he saw coming toward him, unconscious of his proximity, Joseph Frowenfeld.

"Doctor Keene!" said Frowenfeld, with almost the enthusiasm of Raoul.

The doctor was very much quieter.

"Hello, Joe."

They went back to the new drug-store, sat down in a pleasant little rear corner enclosed by a railing and curtains, and talked.

"And did the trip prove of no advantage to you?"

"You see. But never mind me; tell me about Honoré; how does that row with his family progress?"

"It still continues; the most of his people hold ideas of justice and prerogative that run parallel with family and party lines, lines of caste, of custom and the like; they have imparted their bad feeling against him to the community at large; very easy to do just now, for the election for President of the States comes on in the fall, and though we in Louisiana have little or nothing to do with it; the people are feverish."

"The country's chill day," said Doctor Keene; "dumb chill, hot fever."

"The excitement is intense," said Frowenfeld. "It seems we are not to be granted suffrage yet; but the Creoles have a way of casting votes in their mind. For example, they have voted Honoré Grandissime a traitor; they have voted me an encumbrance; I hear one of them casting that vote now."

Some one near the front of the store was talking excitedly with Raoul:

"An'—an'—an' w'at are the consequence? The consequence are that we smash his shop for him an' 'e 'ave to make a noo-start with a Creole partner's money an' put 'is sto' in charge of Creole'! If I know he is yo' frien'? Yesseh! Valuable citizen? An' w'at we care for valuable citizen? Let him be valuable if he want; it keep' him from gettin' the neck broke; but—he mus'-tek-kyeh—'ow—he—talk'! He-mus'-tek-kyeh 'ow he stir the 'ot blood of Louisyanna!"

"He is perfectly right," said the little doctor, in his husky undertone; "neither you nor Honoré is a bit sound, and I shouldn't wonder if they would hang you both, yet; and as for that darkey who has had the impudence to try to make a commercial white gentleman of himself—it may not be I that ought to say it, but —he will get his deserts—sure!"

"There are a great many Americans that think as you do," said Frowenfeld, quietly.

"But," said the little doctor, "what did that fellow mean by your Creole partner? Mandarin is in charge of your store, but he is not your partner, is he? Have you one?"

"A silent one," said the apothecary.

"So silent as to be none of my business?"

"No."

"Well, who is it, then?"

"It is Mademoiselle Nancanou."

"Your partner in business?"

Yes."

"Well, Joseph Frowenfeld,——"

The insinuation conveyed in the doctor's manner was very trying, but Joseph merely reddened.

"Purely business, I suppose," presently said the doctor, with a ghastly ironical smile. "Does the arrangem—" his utterance failed him—"does it end there?"

"It ends there."

"And you don't see that it ought either not to have begun, or else ought not to have ended there?"

Frowenfeld blushed angrily. The doctor asked:

"And who takes care of Aurora's money?"

"Herself."

"Exclusively?"

They both smiled more good-naturedly.

"Exclusively."

"She's a coon"; and the little doctor rose up and crawled away, ostensibly to see another friend, but really to drag himself into his bed-chamber and lock himself in. The next day—the yellow fever was bad again—he resumed the practice of his profession.

" 'Twill be a sort of decent suicide without the element of pusillanimity," he thought to himself.

52 Love Lies A-Bleeding

When Honoré Grandissime heard that Doctor Keene had returned to the city in a very feeble state of health, he rose at
once from the desk where he was sitting and went to see him;
but it was on that morning when the doctor was sitting and
talking with Joseph, and Honoré found his chamber door
locked. Doctor Keene called twice, within the following two
days, upon Honoré at his counting-room; but on both occasions
Honoré's chair was empty. So it was several days before they
met. But one hot morning in the latter part of August,—the
August days were hotter before the cypress forest was cut down
between the city and the lake than they are now,—as Doctor
Keene stood in the middle of his room breathing distressedly
after a sad fit of coughing, and looking toward one of his windows whose closed sash he longed to see opened, Honoré
knocked at the door.

"Well, come in!" said the fretful invalid. "Why, Honoré,—
well, it serves you right for stopping to knock. Sit down."

Each took a hasty, scrutinizing glance at the other; and, after
a pause, Doctor Keene said:

"Honoré, you are pretty badly stove."

M. Grandissime smiled.

"Do you think so, Doctor? I will be more complimentary to
you; you might look more sick."

"Oh, I have resumed my trade," replied Doctor Keene.

"So I have heard; but Charlie, that is all in favor of the people who want a skillful and advanced physician and do not mind killing him; I should advise you not to do it."

"You mean" (the incorrigible little doctor smiled cynically) "if I should ask your advice. I am going to get well, Honoré."

His visitor shrugged.

"So much the better. I do confess I am tempted to make use of you in your official capacity, right now. Do you feel strong enough to go with me in your gig a little way?"

"A professional call?"

"Yes, and a difficult case; also a confidential one."

"Ah! confidential!" said the little man, in his painful, husky irony. "You want to get me into the sort of scrape I got our 'professor' into, eh?"

"Possibly a worse one," replied the amiable Creole.

"And I must be mum, eh?"

"I would prefer."

"Shall I need any instruments? No?"—with a shade of disappointment on his face.

He pulled a bell-rope and ordered his gig to the street door.

"How are affairs about town?" he asked, as he made some slight preparation for the street.

"Excitement continues. Just as I came along, a private difficulty between a Creole and an Américain drew instantly half the street together to take sides strictly according to belongings and without asking a question. My-de'-seh, we are having, as Frowenfeld says, a war of human acids and alkalies."

They descended and drove away. At the first corner the lad who drove turned, by Honoré's direction, toward the rue Dauphine, entered it, passed down it to the rue Dumaine, turned into this toward the river again and entered the rue Condé. The route was circuitous. They stopped at the carriage-door of a large brick house. The wicket was opened by Clemence. They alighted without driving in.

"Hey, old witch," said the doctor, with mock severity; "not hung yet?"

The houses of any pretension to comfortable spaciousness in the closely built parts of the town were all of the one, general, Spanish-American plan. Honoré led the doctor through the cool, high, tesselated carriage-hall, on one side of which were the

298

drawing-rooms, closed and darkened. They turned at the bottom, ascended a broad, iron-railed staircase to the floor above, and halted before the open half of a glazed double door with a clumsy iron latch. It was the entrance to two spacious chambers, which were thrown into one by folded doors.

The doctor made a low, indrawn whistle and raised his eyebrows—the rooms were so sumptuously furnished; immovable largeness and heaviness, lofty sobriety, abundance of finely wrought brass mounting, motionless richness of upholstery, much silent twinkle of pendulous crystal, a soft semi-obscurity—such were the characteristics. The long windows of the farther apartment could be seen to open over the street, and the air from behind, coming in over a green mass of fig-trees that stood in the paved court below, moved through the rooms, making them cool and cavernous.

"You don't call this a hiding-place, do you—in his own bed-chamber?" the doctor whispered.

"It is necessary, now, only to keep out of sight," softly answered Honoré. "Agricole and some others ransacked this house one night last March—the day I announced the new firm; but of course, then, he was not here."

They entered, and the figure of Honoré Grandissime, f. m. c., came into view in the centre of the farther room, reclining in an attitude of extreme languor on a low couch, whither he had come from the high bed near by, as the impression of his form among its pillows showed. He turned upon the two visitors his slow, melancholy eyes, and, without an attempt to rise or speak, indicated, by a feeble motion of the hand, an invitation to be seated.

"Good-morning," said Doctor Keene, selecting a light chair and drawing it close to the side of the couch.

The patient before him was emaciated. The limp and bloodless hand, which had not responded to the doctor's friendly pressure but sank idly back upon the edge of the couch, was cool and moist, and its nails slightly blue.

"Lie still," said the doctor, reassuringly, as the rentier began to lift the one knee and slippered foot which was drawn up on the couch and the hand which hung out of sight across a large, linen-covered cushion.

By pleasant talk that seemed all chat, the physician soon acquainted himself with the case before him. It was a very plain one. By and by he rubbed his face and red curls and suddenly said:

"You will not take my prescription."

The f. m. c. did not say yes or no.

"Still,"—the doctor turned sidewise in his chair, as was his wont, and, as he spoke, allowed the corners of his mouth to take that little satirical downward pull which his friends disliked,— "I'll do my duty I'll give Honoré the details as to diet; no physic; but my prescription to you is, Get up and get out. Never mind the risk of rough handling; they can but kill you, and you will die anyhow if you stay here." He rose. "I'll send you a chalybeate tonic; or—I will leave it at Frowenfeld's to-morrow morning, and you can call there and get it. It will give you an object for going out."

The two visitors presently said adieu and retired together. Reaching the bottom of the stairs in the carriage "corridor," they turned in a direction opposite to the entrance and took chairs in a cool nook of the paved court, at a small table where the hospitality of Clemence had placed glasses of lemonade.

"No," said the doctor, as they sat down, "there is, as yet, no incurable organic derangement; a little heart trouble easily removed; still your—your patient——"

"My half-brother," said Honoré.

"Your patient," said Doctor Keene, "is an emphatic 'yes' to the question the girls sometimes ask us doctors—'Does love ever kill?' It will kill him *soon*, if you do not get him to rouse up. There is absolutely nothing the matter with him but his unrequited love."

"Fortunately, the most of us," said Honoré, with something of the doctor's smile, "do not love hard enough to be killed by it."

"Very few." The doctor paused, and his blue eyes, distended in reverie, gazed upon the glass which he was slowly turning around with his attenuated fingers as it stood on the board, while he added: "However, one *may* love as hopelessly and harder than that man upstairs, and yet not die."

"There is comfort in that—to those who must live," said Honoré, with gentle gravity.

"Yes," said the other, still toying with his glass.

He slowly lifted his glance, and the eyes of the two men met and remained steadfastly fixed each upon each.

"You've got it bad," said Doctor Keene, mechanically.

"And you?" retorted the Creole.

"It isn't going to kill me."

"It has not killed me. And," added M. Grandissime, as they passed through the carriage-way toward the street, "while I keep in mind the numberless other sorrows of life, the burials of wives and sons and daughters, the agonies and desolations, I shall never die of love, my-de'-seh, for very shame's sake."

This was much sentiment to risk within Doctor Keene's reach; but he took no advantage of it.

"Honoré," said he, as they joined hands on the banquette beside the doctor's gig, to say good-day, "if you think there's a chance for you, why stickle upon such fine-drawn points as I reckon you are mating? Why sir, as I understand it, this is the only weak spot your action has shown; you have taken an inoculation of Quixotic conscience from our transcendental apothecary and perpetrated a lot of heroic behavior that would have done honor to four-and-twenty Brutuses; and now that you have a chance to do something easy and human, you shiver and shrink at the 'looks o' the thing.' Why, what do you care——"

"Hush!" said Honoré; "do you suppose I have not temptation enough already?"

He began to move away.

"Honoré," said the doctor, following him a step, "I couldn't have made a mistake—it's the little Monk,—it's Aurora, isn't it?"

Honoré nodded, then faced his friend more directly, with a sudden new thought.

"But, Doctor, why not take your own advice? I know not how you are prevented; you have as good a right as Frowenfeld."

"It wouldn't be honest," said the doctor; "it wouldn't be the straight up and down manly thing."

"Why not?"

The doctor stepped into his gig——

"Not till I feel all right *here*." (In his chest.)

301

53 Frowenfeld
at the Grandissime Mansion

One afternoon—it seems to have been some time in June, and consequently earlier than Doctor Keene's return—the Grandissimes were set all a-tremble with vexation by the discovery that another of their number had, to use Agricola's expression, "gone over to the enemy,"—a phrase first applied by him to Honoré.

"What do you intend to convey by that term?" Frowenfeld had asked on that earlier occasion.

"Gone over to the enemy means, my son, gone over to the enemy!" replied Agricola. "It implies affiliation with Américains in matters of business and of government! It implies the exchange of social amenities with a race of upstarts! It implies a craven consent to submit the sacredest prejudices of our fathers to the new-fangled measuring-rods of pert, imported theories upon moral and political progress! It implies a listening to, and reasoning with, the condemners of some of our most time-honored and respectable practices! Reasoning with? N-a-hay! but Honoré has positively sat down and eaten with them! What?—and h-walked out into the stre-heet with them, arm in arm! It implies in his case an act—two separate and distinct acts—so base that —that—I simply do not understand them! H-you know, Professor Frowenfeld, what he has done! You know how ignominiously he has surrendered the key of a moral position which for the honor of the Grandissime-Fusilier name we have felt it necessary to hold against our hereditary enemies! And—you—know——" here Agricola actually dropped all artificiality and spoke from the depths of his feelings, without figure—"h-h-he has joined himself in business h-with a man of negro blood! What can we do? What can we say? It is Honoré Grandissime. We can only say, 'Farewell! He is gone over to the enemy.'"

The new cause of exasperation was the defection of Raoul Innerarity. Raoul had, somewhat from a distance, contemplated such part as he could understand of Joseph Frowenfeld's character with ever-broadening admiration. We know how devoted he became to the interests and fame of "Frowenfeld's." It was in April he had married. Not to divide his generous heart he took rooms opposite the drug-store, resolved that "Frowenfeld's" should be not only the latest closed but the earliest opened of all the pharmacies in New Orleans.

This, it is true, was allowable. Not many weeks afterward his bride fell suddenly and seriously ill. The overflowing souls of Aurora and Clotilde could not be so near to trouble and not know it, and before Raoul was nearly enough recovered from the shock of this peril to remember that he was a Grandissime, these last two of the De Grapions had hastened across the street to the small, white-walled sick-room and filled it as full of universal human love as the cup of a magnolia is full of perfume. Madame Innerarity recovered. A warm affection was all she and her husband could pay such ministration in, and this they paid bountifully; the four became friends. The little madame found herself drawn most toward Clotilde; to her she opened her heart —and her wardrobe, and showed her all her beautiful new underclothing. Clotilde, Raoul found to be, for him, rather—what shall we say?—starry, starrily inaccessible; but Aurora was emphatically after his liking; he was delighted with Aurora. He told her in confidence that "Profess-or Frowenfel'" was the best man in the world; but she boldly said, taking pains to speak with a tear and a half of genuine gratitude,—"Egcep' Monsieur Honoré Grandissime," and he assented, at first with hesitation and then with ardor. The four formed a group of their own; and it is not certain that this was not the very first specimen ever produced in the Crescent City of that social variety of New Orleans life now distinguished as Uptown Creoles.

Almost the first thing acquired by Raoul in the camp of the

303

enemy was a certain Aurorean audacity; and on the afternoon to which we allude, having told Frowenfeld a rousing fib to the effect that the multitudinous inmates of the maternal Grandissime mansion had insisted on his bringing his esteemed employer to see them, he and his bride had the hardihood to present him on the front veranda.

The straightforward Frowenfeld was much pleased with his reception. It was not possible for such as he to guess the ire with which his presence was secretly regarded. New Orleans, let us say once more, was small, and the apothecary of the rue Royale locally famed; and what with curiosity and that innate politeness which it is the Creole's boast that he cannot mortify, the veranda, about the top of the great front stair, was well crowded with people of both sexes and all ages. It would be most pleasant to tarry once more in description of this gathering of nobility and beauty; to recount the points of Creole loveliness in midsummer dress; to tell in particular of one and another eye-kindling face, form, manner, wit; to define the subtle qualities of Creole air and sky and scene, or the yet more delicate graces that characterize the music of Creole voice and speech and the light of Creole eyes; to set forth the gracious, unaccentuated dignity of the matrons and the ravishing archness of their daughters. To Frowenfeld the experience seemed all unreal. Nor was this unreality removed by conversation on grave subjects; for few among either the maturer or the younger beauty could do aught but listen to his foreign tongue like unearthly strangers in the old fairy tales. They came, however, in the course of their talk to the subject of love and marriage. It is not certain that they entered deeper into the great question than a comparison of its attendant Anglo-American and Franco-American conventionalities; but sure it is that somehow—let those young souls divine the method who can—every unearthly stranger on that veranda contrived to understand Frowenfeld's English. Suddenly the conversation began to move over the ground of inter-marriage between hostile families. Then what eyes and ears! A certain suspicion had already found lodgement in the universal Grandissime breast, and every one knew in a moment that, to all intents and purposes, they were about to argue the case of Honoré and Aurora.

The conversation became discussion, Frowenfeld, Raoul and Raoul's little seraph against the whole host, chariots, horse and archery. Ah! such strokes as the apothecary dealt! And if Raoul and "Madame Raoul" played parts most closely resembling the blowing of horns and breaking of pitchers, still they bore themselves gallantly. The engagement was short; we need not say that nobody surrendered; nobody ever gives up the ship in parlor or veranda debate; and yet—as is generally the case in such affairs—truth and justice made some unacknowledged headway. If anybody on either side came out wounded—this to the credit of the Creoles as a people—the sufferer had the heroic good manners not to say so. But the results were more marked than this; indeed, in more than one or two candid young hearts and impressible minds the wrongs and rights of sovereign true love began there on the spot to be more generously conceded and allowed. "My-de'-seh," Honoré had once on a time said to Frowenfeld, meaning that to prevail in a conversational debate one should never follow up a faltering opponent, "you mus' *crack* the egg, not smash it!" And Joseph, on rising to take his leave, could the more amiably overlook the feebleness of the invitation to call again, since he rejoiced, for Honoré's sake, in the conviction that the egg was cracked.

Agricola, the Grandissimes told the apothecary, was ill in his room, and Madame de Grandissime, his sister—Honoré's mother—begged to be excused that she might keep him company. The Fusiliers were a very close order; or one might say they garrisoned the citadel.

But Joseph's rising to go was not immediately upon the close of the discussion; those courtly people would not let even an unwelcome guest go with the faintest feeling of disrelish for them. They were casting about in their minds for some momentary diversion with which to add a finishing touch to their guest's entertainment, when Clemence appeared in the front garden-walk and was quickly surrounded by bounding children, alternately begging and demanding a song. Many of even the younger adults remembered well when she had been "one of the hands on the place," and a passionate lover of the African dance. In the same instant half a dozen voices proposed that for Joseph's amusement Clemence should put her cakes off her head, come up on the veranda and show a few of her best steps.

"But who will sing?"

"Raoul!"

"Very well; and what shall it be?"

"'Madame Gaba.'"

No, Clemence objected.

"Well, well, stand back—something better than 'Madame Gaba.'"

Raoul began to sing and Clemence instantly to pace and turn, posture, bow, respond to the song, start, swing, straighten, stamp, wheel, lift her hand, stoop, twist, walk, whirl, tip-toe with crossed ankles, smite her palms, march, circle, leap—an endless improvisation of rhythmic motion to this modulated responsive chant:

RAOUL. *"Mo pas l'aimein ça."*
CLEMENCE. *"Miché Igenne, oap! oap! oap!"*
HE. *"Yé donné vingt cinq sous pou' manzé poulé."*
SHE. *"Miché Igenne, dit—dit—dit——"*
HE. *"Mo pas l'aimein ça!"*
SHE. *"Miché Igenne, oap! oap! oap!"*
HE. *"Mo pas l'aimein ça!"*
SHE. *"Miché Igenne, oap! oap! oap!"*

Frowenfeld was not so greatly amused as the ladies thought he should have been, and was told that this was not a fair indication of what he would see if there were ten dancers instead of one.

How much less was it an indication of what he would have seen in that mansion early the next morning, when there was found just outside of Agricola's bedroom door a fresh egg, not cracked, according to Honoré's maxim, but smashed, according to the lore of the voudous. Who could have got in in the night? And did the intruder get in by magic, by outside lock-picking, or by inside collusion? Later in the morning, the children playing in the basement found—it had evidently been accidentally dropped, since the true uses of its contents required them to be scattered in some person's path—a small cloth bag, containing a quantity of dogs' and cats' hair, cut fine and mixed with salt and pepper.

"Clemence?"

"Pooh! Clemence. No! But as sure as the sun turns around the world—Palmyre Philosophe!"

54 "Cauldron Bubble"

The excitement and alarm produced by the practical threat of voudou curses upon Agricola was one thing, Creole lethargy was quite another; and when, three mornings later, a full quartette of voudou charms was found in the four corners of Agricola's pillow, the great Grandissime family were ignorant of how they could have come there. Let us examine these terrible engines of mischief. In one corner was an acorn drilled through with two holes at right angles to each other, a small feather run through each hole; in the second a joint of cornstalk with a cavity scooped from the middle, the pith left intact at the ends, and the space filled with parings from that small callous spot near the knee of the horse, called the "nail"; in the third corner a bunch of parti-colored feathers; something equally meaningless in the fourth. No thread was used in any of them. All fastening was done with the gum of trees. It was no easy task for his kindred to prevent Agricola, beside himself with rage and fright, from going straight to Palmyre's house and shooting her down in open day.

"We shall have to watch our house by night," said a gentleman of the household, when they had at length restored the Citizen to a condition of mind which enabled them to hold him in a chair.

"Watch this house?" cried a chorus. "You don't suppose she comes near here, do you? She does it all from a distance. No, no; watch *her* house."

Did Agricola believe in the supernatural potency of these gimcracks? No, and yes. Not to be foolhardy, he quietly slipped down every day to the levee, had a slave-boy row him across the river in a skiff, landed, re-embarked, and in the middle of the stream surreptitiously cast a picayune over his shoulder into the river. Monsieur D'Embarras, the imp of death thus placated, must have been a sort of spiritual Cheap John.

Several more nights passed. The house of Palmyre, closely watched, revealed nothing. No one came out, no one went in, no light was seen. They should have watched it in broad daylight. At last, one midnight, 'Polyte Grandissime stepped cautiously up to one of the batten doors with an auger, and succeeded, without arousing any one, in boring a hole. He discovered a lighted candle standing in a glass of water.

"Nothing but a bedroom light," said one.

"Ah, bah!" whispered the other; "it is to make the spell work strong."

"We will not tell Agricola first; we had better tell Honoré," said Sylvestre.

"You forget," said 'Polyte, "that I no longer have any acquaintance with Monsieur Honoré Grandissime."

They told Agamemnon; and it would have gone hard with the *"milatraise"* but for the additional fact that suspicion had fastened upon another person; but now this person in turn had to be identified. It was decided not to report progress to old Agricola, but to await and seek further developments. Agricola, having lost all ability to sleep in the mansion, moved into a small cottage in a grove near the house. But the very next morning, he turned cold with horror to find on his door-step, a small black-coffined doll, with pins run through the heart, a burned-out candle at the head and another at the feet.

"You know it is Palmyre, do you?" asked Agamemnon, seizing the old man as he was going at a headlong pace through the garden gate. "What if I should tell you that, by watching the Congo dancing-ground at midnight to-night, you will see the real author of this mischief—eh?"

"And why to-night?"

"Because the moon rises at midnight."

There was firing that night in the deserted Congo dancing-grounds under the ruins of Fort St. Joseph, or, as we would say now, in Congo Square, from three pistols—Agricola's, 'Polyte's, and the weapon of an ill-defined, retreating figure answering the description of the person who had stabbed Agricola the preceding February. "And yet," said 'Polyte, "I would have sworn that it was Palmyre doing this work."

Through Raoul these events came to the ear of Frowenfeld. It was about the time that Raoul's fishing-party, after a few days' mishaps, had returned home. Palmyre, on several later dates, had craved further audiences and shown other letters from the hidden f. m. c. She had heard them calmly, and steadfastly preserved the one attitude of refusal. But it could not escape Frowenfeld's notice that she encouraged the sending of additional letters. He easily guessed the courier to be Clemence; and now, as he came to ponder these revelations of Raoul, he found that within twenty-four hours after every visit of Clemence to the house of Palmyre, Agricola suffered a visitation.

55 Caught

The fig-tree, in Louisiana, sometimes sheds its leaves while it is yet summer. In the rear of the Grandissime mansion, about two hundred yards north-west of it and fifty north-east of the cottage in which Agricola had made his new abode, on the edge of the grove of which we have spoken, stood one of these trees, whose leaves were beginning to lie thickly upon the ground beneath it. An ancient and luxuriant hedge of Cherokee rose started from this tree and stretched toward the north-west across the level country, until it merged into the green confusion of gardened homes in the vicinity of Bayou St. Jean, or, by night, into the common obscurity of a starlit perspective. When an unclouded moon shone upon it, it cast a shadow as black as velvet.

Under this fig-tree, some three hours later than that at which Honoré bade Joseph good-night, a man was stooping down and covering something with the broad, fallen leaves.

"The moon will rise about three o'clock," thought he. "That, the hour of universal slumber, will be, by all odds, the thing most likely to bring developments."

He was the same person who had spent the most of the day in a blacksmith shop in St. Louis street, superintending a piece of smithing. Now that he seemed to have got the thing well hid, he turned to the base of the tree and tried the security of

310

some attachment. Yes, it was firmly chained. He was not a robber; he was not an assassin; he was an officer of police; and what is more notable, seeing he was a Louisianian, he was not a soldier nor even an ex-soldier; and this although, under his clothing, he was encased from head to foot in a complete suit of mail. Of steel? No. Of brass? No. It was all one piece—*a white skin;* and on his head he wore an invisible helmet—the name of Grandissime. As he straightened up and withdrew into the grove, you would have recognized at once—by his thick-set, powerful frame, clothed seemingly in black, but really, as you might guess, in blue cottonade, by his black beard and the general look of a seafarer—a frequent visitor at the Grandissime mansion, a country member of that great family, one whom we saw at the *fête de grandpère.*

Capitain Jean-Baptiste Grandissime was a man of few words, no sentiments, short methods; materialistic, we might say; quietly ferocious; indifferent as to means, positive as to ends, quick of perception, sure in matters of saltpetre, a stranger at the custom-house, and altogether—*take him right*—very much of a gentleman. He had been, for a whole day, beset with the idea that the way to catch a voudou was—to catch him; and as he had caught numbers of them on both sides of the tropical and semitropical Atlantic, he decided to try his skill privately on the one who—his experience told him—was likely to visit Agricola's door-step to-night. All things being now prepared, he sat down at the root of a tree in the grove, where the shadow was very dark, and seemed quite comfortable. He did not strike at the mosquitoes; they appeared to understand that he did not wish to trifle. Neither did his thoughts or feelings trouble him; he sat and sharpened a small pen-knife on his boot.

His mind—his occasional transient meditation—was the more comfortable because he was one of those few who had coolly and unsentimentally allowed Honoré Grandissime to sell their lands. It continued to grow plainer every day that the grants with which theirs were classed—grants of old French or Spanish under-officials—were bad. Their sagacious cousin seemed to have struck the right standard, and while those titles which he still held on to remained unimpeached, those that he had parted with to purchasers—as, for instance, the grant held by this Capitain Jean-Baptiste Grandissime—could be bought back now for half what he had got for it. Certainly, as to that, the Capitain might well have that quietude of mind which enabled him to find occupation in perfecting the edge of his penknife and trimming his nails in the dark.

By and by he put up the little tool and sat looking out upon the prospect. The time of greatest probability had not come, but the voudou might choose not to wait for that; and so he kept a watch. There was a great stillness. The cocks had finished a round and were silent. No dog barked. A few tiny crickets made the quiet land seem the more deserted. Its beauties were not entirely overlooked—the innumerable host of stars above, the twinkle of myriad fire-flies on the dark earth below. Between a quarter and a half mile away, almost in a line with the Cherokee hedge, was a faint rise of ground, and on it a wide-spreading live-oak. There the keen, seaman's eye of the Capitain came to a stop, fixed upon a spot which he had not noticed before. He kept his eye on it, and waited for the stronger light of the moon.

Presently behind the grove at his back she rose; and almost the first beam that passed over the tops of the trees, and stretched across the plain, struck the object of his scrutiny. What was it? The ground, he knew; the tree, he knew; he knew there ought to be a white paling enclosure about the trunk of the tree; for there were buried—ah!—he came as near laughing at himself as ever he did in his life; the apothecary of the rue Royale had lately erected some marble head-stones there, and——

"Oh! my God!"

While Capitain Jean-Baptiste had been trying to guess what the tombstones were, a woman had been coming toward him in shadow of the hedge. She was not expecting to meet him; she did not know that he was there; she knew she had risks to run, but was ignorant of what they were; she did not know there was anything under the fig-tree which she so nearly and noiselessly approached. One moment her foot was lifted above the spot where the unknown object lay with wide-stretched jaws under the leaves, and the next, she uttered that cry of agony and consternation which interrupted the watcher's meditation. She was caught in a huge steel-trap.

Capitain Jean-Baptiste Grandissime remained perfectly still. She fell, a snarling, struggling, groaning heap, to the ground, wild with pain and fright, and began the hopeless effort to draw the jaws of the trap apart with her fingers.

"*Ah! bon Dieu, bon Dieu!* Quit a-*bi-i-i-tin'* me! Oh! Lawd 'a'

312

mussy! Ow-ow-ow! lemme go! Dey go'n' to kyetch an' hang me! Oh! an' I hain' done nuttin' 'gainst *nobody!* Ah! *bon Dieu! ein pov' vié négresse!* Oh! Jemimy! I cyan' gid dis yeh t'ing loose—oh! m-m-m-m! An' dey'll tra to mek out 't I voudou' Mich-Agricole! An' I didn' had nutt'n' do wid it! Oh Lawd, oh, *Lawd,* you'll be mighty good ef you lemme loose! I'm a po' nigga! Oh! dey hadn' ought to mek it so *pow'ful!*"

Hands, teeth, the free foot, the writhing body, every combination of available forces failed to spread the savage jaws, though she strove until hands and mouth were bleeding.

Suddenly she became silent; a thought of precaution came to her; she lifted from the earth a burden she had dropped there, struggled to a half-standing posture, and, with her foot still in the trap, was endeavoring to approach the end of the hedge near by, to thrust this burden under it, when she opened her throat in a speechless ecstasy of fright on feeling her arm grasped by her captor.

"O-o-o-h! Lawd! o-o-oh! Lawd!" she cried, in a frantic, husky whisper, going down upon her knees, *"Oh, Miché! pou l'amou' du bon Dieu! Pou l'amou' du bon Dieu ayez pitié d'ein pov' négresses! Pov' négresse, Miché,* w'at nevva done nutt'n' to nobody on'y jis sell *calas!* I iss comin' 'long an' step inteh dis-yeh bah-trap by acci*dent!* Ah! *Miché, Miché,* ple-e-ease be good! *Ah! mon Dieu!*—an' de Lawd'll reward you—'deed 'E will, *Miché!"*

"Qui ci ça?" asked the Capitain, sternly, stooping and grasping her burden, which she had been trying to conceal under herself.

"Oh, Miché, don' trouble dat! Please jes tek dis-yeh trap offen me—da's all! Oh, don't, mawstah, ple-e-ease don' spill all my wash'n t'ings! 'Taint nutt'n but my old dress roll' up into a ball. Oh, please—now, you see? nutt'n' but a po' nigga's dr—*oh! fo' de love o' God, Miché Jean-Baptiste, don' open dat ah box! Y'en a erin du tout la-dans, Miché Jean-Baptiste; du tout, du tout!* Oh, my God! *Miché,* on'y jis teck dis-yeh t'ing off'n my laig, ef yo' *please,* it's bit'n ma lak a *dawg!*—if you please, *Miché!* Oh! you git kill' if you open dat ah box, Mawse Jean-Baptiste! *Mo' parole d'honneur le plus sacré*—I'll kiss de cross! Oh, *sweet Miché Jean, laisse moi aller!* Nutt'n but some dutty close *la-dans."* She repeated this again and again, even after Captain Jean-Baptiste had disengaged a small black coffin from the old dress in which it was wrapped. "*Rien du tout, Miché;* nutt'n' but some wash'n' fo' one o' de boys."

He removed the lid and saw within, resting on the cushioned bottom, the image, in myrtle-wax, moulded and painted with some rude skill, of a negro's bloody arm cut off near the shoulder—a *bras-coupé*—with a dirk grasped in its hand.

The old woman lifted her eyes to heaven; her teeth chattered; she gasped twice before she could recover utterance. "Oh, *Miché* Jean Baptiste, I di'n' mek dat ah! *Mo té pas fé ça!* I swea' befo' God! Oh, no, no, no! 'Tain' nutt'n' nohow but a lill playtoy, *Miché*. Oh, sweet *Miché Jean,* you not gwan to kill me? I di'n' mek it! It was—ef you lemme go, I tell you who mek it! Sho's I live I tell you, *Miché Jean*—ef you lemme go! Sho's God's good to me—ef you lemme go! Oh, God A'mighty, *Miché Jean,* sho's God's good to me."

She was becoming incoherent.

Then Capitain Jean-Baptiste Grandissime for the first time spoke at length:

"Do you see this?" he spoke the French of the Atchafalaya. He put his long flint-lock pistol close to her face. "I shall take the trap off; you will walk three feet in front of me; if you make it four I blow your brains out; we shall go to Agricole. But right here, just now, before I count ten, you will tell me who sent you here; at the word ten, if I reach it, I pull the trigger. One—two—three——"

"Oh, *Miché,* she gwan to gib me to de devil wid *houdou* ef I tell you—Oh, good *Lawdy!*"

But he did not pause.

"Four—five—six—seven—eight——"

"Palmyre!" gasped the negress, and grovelled on the ground.

The trap was loosened from her bleeding leg, the burden placed in her arms, and they disappeared in the direction of the mansion.

A black shape, a boy, the lad who had carried the basil to Frowenfeld, rose up from where he had all this time lain, close against the hedge, and glided off down its black shadow to warn the *philosophe.*

When Clemence was searched, there was found on her person an old table-knife with its end ground to a point.

314

56 Blood for a Blow

It seems to be one of the self-punitive characteristics of tyranny, whether the tyrant be a man, a community, or a caste, to have a pusillanimous fear of its victim. It was not when Clemence lay in irons, it is barely now, that our South is casting off a certain apprehensive tremor, generally latent, but at the slightest provocation active, and now and then violent, concerning her "blacks." This fear, like others similar elsewhere in the world, has always been met by the same one antidote—terrific cruelty to the tyrant's victim. So we shall presently see the Grandissime ladies, deeming themselves compassionate, urging their kinsmen to "give the poor wretch a sound whipping and let her go." Ah! what atrocities are we unconsciously perpetrating North and South now, in the name of mercy or defence, which the advancing light of progressive thought will presently show out in their enormity?

Agricola slept late. He had gone to his room the evening before much incensed at the presumption of some younger Grandissimes who had brought up the subject, and spoken in defence of, their cousin Honoré. He had retired, however, not to rest, but to construct an engine of offensive warfare which would revenge him a hundred-fold upon the miserable school of imported thought which had sent its revolting influences to the very Grandissime hearth-stone; he wrote a *"Phillipique Gé-nérale contre la Conduite du Gouvernement de la Louisiane,"* and a short but vigorous chapter in English on the "Insanity of educating the Masses." This accomplished, he had gone to bed in a condition of peaceful elation, eager for the next day to come that he might take these mighty productions to Joseph Frowenfeld, and make him a present of them for insertion in his book of tables.

Jean-Baptiste felt no need of his advice, that he should rouse him; and, for a long time before the old man awoke, his younger kinsmen were stirring about unwontedly, going and coming through the hall of the mansion, along its verandas and up and down its outer flight of stairs. Gates were opening and shutting, errands were being carried by negro boys on bareback horses, Charlie Mandarin of St. Bernard parish and an Armand Fusilier from Faubourg Ste. Marie had on some account come—as they told the ladies—"to take breakfast"; and the ladies, not yet informed, amusedly wondering at all this trampling and stage whispering, were up a trifle early. In those days Creole society was a ship, in which the fair sex were all passengers and the ruder sex the crew. The ladies of the Grandissime mansion this morning asked passengers' questions, got sailors' answers, retorted wittily and more or less satirically, and laughed often, feeling their constrained insignificance. However, in a house so full of bright-eyed children, with mothers and sisters of all ages as their confederates, the secret was soon out, and before Agricola had left his little cottage in the grove the topic of all tongues was the abysmal treachery and *ingratitude* of negro slaves. The whole tribe of Grandissime believed, this morning, in the doctrine of total depravity—of the negro.

And right in the face of this belief, the ladies put forth the generously intentioned prayer for mercy. They were answered that they little knew what frightful perils they were thus inviting upon themselves.

The male Grandissimes were not surprised at this exhibition of weak clemency in their lovely women; they were proud of it; it showed the magnanimity that was natural to the universal Grandissime heart, when not restrained and repressed by the stern necessities of the hour. But Agricola disappointed them. Why should he weaken and hesitate, and suggest delays and middle courses, and stammer over their proposed measures as

316

"extreme"? In very truth, it seemed as though that drivelling, woman-beaten Deutsch apotheke—ha! ha! ha!—in the rue Royale had bewitched Agricola as well as Honoré. The fact was, Agricola had never got over the interview which had saved Sylvestre his life.

"Here, Agricole," his kinsmen at length said, "you see you are too old for this sort of thing; besides, .. would be bad taste for you, who might be presumed to harbor feelings of revenge, to have a voice in this council." And then they added to one another: "We will wait until 'Polyte reports whether or not they have caught Palmyre; much will depend on that."

Agricola, thus ruled out, did a thing he did not fully understand; he rolled up the "Philippique Générale" and the "Insanity of Educating the Masses," and, with these in one hand and his staff in the other, set out for Frowenfeld's, not merely smarting but trembling under the humiliation of having been sent, for the first time in his life, to the rear as a non-combatant.

He found the apothecary among his clerks, preparing with his own hands the "chalybeate tonic" for which the f. m. c. was expected to call. Raoul Innerarity stood at his elbow, looking on with an amiable air of having been superseded for the moment by his master.

"Ha-ah! Professor Frowenfeld!"

The old man flourished his scroll.

Frowenfeld said good-morning, and they shook hands across the counter; but the old man's grasp was so tremulous that the apothecary looked at him again.

"Does my hand tremble, Joseph? It is not strange; I have had much to excite me this morning."

"W'at's de mattah?" demanded Raoul, quickly.

"My life—which I admit, Professor Frowenfeld, is of little value compared with such a one as yours—has been—if not attempted, at least threatened."

"How?" cried Raoul.

"H-really, Professor, we must agree that a trifle like that ought not to make old Agricola Fusilier nervous. But I find it painful, sir, very painful. I can lift up this right hand, Joseph, and swear I never gave a slave—man or woman—a blow in my life but according to my notion of justice. And now to find my life attempted by former slaves of my own household, and taunted with the righteous hamstringing of a dangerous runaway? But they have apprehended the miscreants; one is actually in hand, and justice will take its course; trust the Grandissimes for that—though, really, Joseph, I assure you, I counselled leniency."

"Do you say they have caught her?" Frowenfeld's question was sudden and excited; but the next moment he had controlled himself.

"H-h-my son, I did not say it was a 'her'!"

"Was it not Clemence? Have they caught her?"

"H-yes——"

The apothecary turned to Raoul.

"Go tell Honoré Grandissime."

"But, Professor Frowenfeld——," began Agricola.

Frowenfeld turned to repeat his instruction, but Raoul was already leaving the store.

Agricola straightened up angrily.

"Pro-hofessor Frowenfeld, by what right do you interfere?"

"No matter," said the apothecary, turning half-way and pouring the tonic into a vial.

"Sir," thundered the old lion, "h-I demand of you to answer! How dare you insinuate that my kinsmen may deal otherwise than justly?"

"Will they treat her exactly as if she were white, and had threatened the life of a slave?" asked Frowenfeld from behind the desk at the end of the counter.

The old man concentrated all the indignation of his nature in the reply.

"No-ho, sir!"

As he spoke, a shadow approaching from the door caused him to turn. The tall, dark, finely clad form of the f. m. c., in its old soft-stepping dignity and its sad emaciation, came silently toward the spot where he stood.

Frowenfeld saw this, and hurried forward inside the counter with the preparation in his hand.

"Professor Frowenfeld," said Agricola, pointing with his ugly staff, "I demand of you, as the keeper of a white man's pharmacy, to turn that negro out."

"Citizen Fusilier!" explained the apothecary; "Mister Grandis——"

He felt as though no price would be too dear at that moment to pay for the presence of the other Honoré. He had to go clear to the end of the counter and come down the outside again to

318

reach the two men. They did not wait for him. Agricola turned upon the f. m. c.

"Take off your hat!"

A sudden activity seized every one connected with the establishment as the quadroon let his thin right hand slowly into his bosom, and answered in French, in his soft, low voice:

"I wear my hat on my head."

Frowenfeld was hurrying toward them; others stepped forward, and from two or three there came half-uttered exclamations of protest; but unfortunately nothing had been done or said to provoke any one to rush upon them, when Agricola suddenly advanced a step and struck the f. m. c. on the head with his staff. Then the general outcry and forward rush came too late; the two crashed together and fell, Agricola above, the f. m. c. below, and a long knife lifted up from underneath and sinking to its hilt, once—twice—thrice,—in the old man's back.

The two men rose, one in the arms of his friends, the other upon his own feet. While every one's attention was directed toward the wounded man, his antagonist restored his dagger to its sheath, took up his hat and walked away unmolested. When Frowenfeld, with Agricola still in his arms, looked around for the quadroon, he was gone.

Doctor Keene, sent for instantly, was soon at Agricola's side.

"Take him upstairs; he can't be moved any further."

Frowenfeld turned and began to instruct some one to run upstairs and ask permission, but the little doctor stopped him.

"Joe, for shame! you don't know those women better than that? Take the old man right up!"

57 Voudou Cured

"Honoré," said Agricola, faintly, "where is Honoré!"

"He has been sent for," said Doctor Keene and the two ladies in a breath.

Raoul, bearing the word concerning Clemence, and the later messenger summoning him to Agricola's bedside, reached Honoré within a minute of each other. His instructions were quickly given, for Raoul to take his horse and ride down to the family mansion, to break gently to his mother the news of Agricola's disaster, and to say to his kinsmen with imperative emphasis, not to touch the *marchande des calas* till he should come. Then he hurried to the rue Royale.

But when Raoul arrived at the mansion he saw at a glance that the news had outrun him. The family carriage was already coming round the bottom of the front stairs for three Mesdames Grandissime and Madame Martinez. The children on all sides had dropped their play, and stood about, hushed and staring. The servants moved with quiet rapidity. In the hall he was stopped by two beautiful girls.

"Raoul! Oh, Raoul, how is he now? Oh! Raoul, if you could only stop them! They have taken old Clemence down into the swamp—as soon as they heard about Agricole—Oh, Raoul, surely that would be cruel! She nursed me—and me—when we were babies!"

"Where is Agamemnon?"

320

"Gone to the city."

"What did he say about it?"

"He said they were doing wrong, that he did not approve their action, and that they would get themselves into trouble: that he washed his hands of it."

"Ah-h-h!" exclaimed Raoul, "wash his hands! Oh, yes, wash his hands! Suppose we all wash our hands? But where is Valentine? Where is Charlie Mandarin?"

"Ah! Valentine is gone with Agamemnon, saying the same thing, and Charlie Mandarin is down in the swamp the worst of all of them!"

"But why did you let Agamemnon and Valentine go off that way, you?"

"Ah! listen to Raoul! What can a woman do?"

"What can a woman—Well, even if I was a woman, I would do something!"

He hurried from the house, leaped into the saddle and galloped across the fields toward the forest.

Some rods within the edge of the swamp, which, at this season, was quite dry in many places, on a spot where the fallen dead bodies of trees overlay one another and a dense growth of willows and vines and dwarf palmetto shut out the light of the open fields, the younger and some of the harsher senior members of the Grandissime family were sitting or standing about, in an irregular circle whose centre was a big and singularly misshapen water-willow. At the base of this tree sat Clemence, motionless and silent, a wan, sickly color in her face, and that vacant look in her large, white-balled, brown-veined eyes, with which hope-forsaken cowardice waits for death. Somewhat apart from the rest, on an old cypress stump, half-stood, half-sat, in whispered consultation, Jean-Baptiste Grandissime and Charlie Mandarin.

"*Eh bien*, old woman," said Mandarin, turning, without rising, and speaking sharply in the negro French, "have you any reason to give why you should not be hung to that limb over your head?"

She lifted her eyes slowly to his, and made a feeble gesture of deprecation.

"*Mo te pas fé cette bras*, Mawse Challie—I di'n't mek dat ahm; no 'ndeed I di'n', Mawse Challie. I ain' wuth hangin', gen'lemen; you'd oughteh jis' gimme fawty an' lemme go. I—I—I—I di'n' 'ten' no hawm to Maws-Agricole; I wa'n't gwan to hu't nobody in God's worl'; 'ndeed I wasn'. I done tote dat old case-knife fo' twenty year'—*mo po'te ça dipi vingt ans.* I'm a po' ole *marchande des calas; mo courri* 'mongs' de sojer boys to sell my cakes, you know, and da's de onyest reason why I cyah dat ah ole fool knife." She seemed to take some hope from the silence with which they heard her. Her eye brightened and her voice took a tone of excitement. "You'd oughteh tek me and put me in calaboose, an' let de law tek 'is co'se. You's all nice gen'lemen—werry nice gen'lemen, an' you sorter owes it to yo'sev's fo' to not do no sich nasty wuck as hangin' a po' ole nigga wench; 'deed you does. 'Tain' no use to hang me; you gwan to kyeth Palmyre yit; *li courri dans marais;* she is in de swamp yeh, sum'ers; but as concernin' me, you'd oughteh jis gimme fawty an' lemme go. You musn' b'lieve all dis-yeh nonsense 'bout insurrectionin'; all fool-nigga talk. W'at we want to be insurrectionin' faw? We de happies' people in de God's worl'!" She gave a start, and cast a furtive glance of alarm behind her. "Yes, we is; you jis' oughteh gimme fawty an' lemme go! Please, gen'lemen! God'll be good to you, you nice, sweet gen'lemen!"

Charlie Mandarin made a sign to one who stood at her back, who responded by dropping a rawhide noose over her head. She bounded up with a cry of terror; it may be that she had all along hoped that all was make-believe. She caught the noose wildly with both hands and tried to lift it over her head.

"Ah! no, mawsteh, you cyan' do dat! It's ag'in de law! I's 'bleeged to have my trial, yit. Oh, no, no! Oh, good God, no! Even if I is a nigga! You cyan' jis' murdeh me hyeh in de woods! *Mo dis la zize!* I tell de judge on you! You ain' got no mo' biznis to do me so 'an if I was a white 'oman! You dassent tek a white 'oman out'n de Pa'sh Pris'n an' do 'er so! Oh, sweet mawsteh, fo' de love o' God! Oh, Mawse Challie, *pou' l'amou du bon Dieu n'fé pas ça!* Oh, Mawse 'Polyte, is you gwan to let 'em kill ole Clemence? Oh, fo' de mussy o' Jesus Christ, Mawse 'Polyte, leas' of all, *you!* You dassent help to kill me, Mawse 'Polyte! You knows why! Oh God, Mawse 'Polyte, you knows why! Leas' of all you, Mawse 'Polyte! Oh, God 'a' mussy on my wicked ole soul! I aint fitt'n to die! Oh, gen'lemen, I kyan' look God in de face! *Oh, Michés, ayez pitié de moin!* Oh, God A'mighty ha' mussy on my soul! Oh, gen'lemen, dough yo' kinfolks kyvaeh up yo' tricks now, dey'll dwap f'um undeh you some day! *Solé levé là, li couché là!* Yo' t'un will come! Oh, God A'mighty! de God o' de po' nigga wench! Look down, oh God, look down an' stop dis-
322

yeh foolishness! Oh, God, fo' de love o' Jesus! *Oh, Michés, y'en a ein zizement!* Oh, yes, deh's a judgmen' day! Den it wont be a bit o' use to you to be white! Oh, oh, oh, oh, oh, oh, fo', fo', fo', de, de, *love o' God! Oh!*"

They drew her up.

Raoul was not far off. He heard the woman's last cry, and came threshing through the bushes on foot. He saw Sylvestre, unconscious of any approach, spring forward, jerk away the hands that had drawn the thong over the branch, let the strangling woman down and loosen the noose. Her eyes, starting out with horror, turned to him; she fell on her knees and clasped her hands. The tears were rolling down Sylvestre's face.

"My friends, we must not do this! You *shall* not do it!"

He hurled away, with twice his natural strength, one who put out a hand.

"No, sirs!" cried Raoul, "you shall not do it! I come from Honoré! Touch her who dares!"

He drew a weapon.

"Monsieur Innerarity," said 'Polyte, "*who is* Monsieur Honoré Grandissime? There are two of the name, you know,—partners —brothers. Which of—but it makes no difference; before either of them sees this assassin she is going to be a lump of nothing!"

The next word astonished every one. It was Charlie Mandarin who spoke.

"Let her go!"

"Let her go!" said Jean-Baptiste Grandissime; "give her a run for life. Old woman rise up. We propose to let you go. Can you run? Never mind, we shall see. Achille, put her upon her feet. Now, old woman, run!"

She walked rapidly, but with unsteady feet, toward the fields.

"Run! If you don't run I will shoot you this minute!"

She ran.

"Faster!"

She ran faster.

"Run!"

"Run!"

"Run, Clemence! Ha, ha, ha!" It was so funny to see her scuttling and tripping and stumbling. "*Courri! courri, Clemence! c'est pou' to vie!* ha, ha, ha——"

A pistol-shot rang out close behind Raoul's ear; it was never told who fired it. The negress leaped into the air and fell at full length to the ground, stone dead.

58 Dying Words

Drivers of vehicles in the rue Royale turned aside before two slight barriers spanning the way, one at the corner below, the other at that above, the house where the aged high-priest of a doomed civilization lay bleeding to death. The floor of the store below, the pavement of the corridor where stood the idle volante, were covered with straw, and servants came and went by the beckoning of the hand.

"This way," whispered a guide of the four ladies from the Grandissime mansion. As Honoré's mother turned the angle half-way up the muffled stair, she saw at the landing above, standing as if about to part, yet in grave council, a man and woman, the fairest—she noted it even in this moment of extreme distress—she had ever looked upon. He had already set one foot down upon the stair, but at sight of the ascending group drew back and said:

"It is my mother"; then turned to his mother and took her hand; they had been for months estranged, but now they silently kissed.

"He is sleeping," said Honoré. "Maman, Madame Nancanou."

The ladies bowed—the one looking very large and splendid, the other very sweet and small. There was a single instant of silence, and Aurora burst into tears.

324

For a moment Madame Grandissime assumed a frown that was almost a reminder of her brother's, and then the very pride of the Fusiliers broke down. She uttered an inaudible exclamation, drew the weeper firmly into her bosom, and with streaming eyes and choking voice, but yet with majesty, whispered, laying her hand on Aurora's head:

"Never mind, my child; never mind; never mind."

And Honoré's sister, when she was presently introduced, kissed Aurora and murmured:

"The good God bless thee! It is He who has brought us together."

"Who is with him just now?" whispered the two other ladies, while Honoré and his mother stood a moment aside in hurried consultation.

"My daughter," said Aurora, "and——"

"Agamemnon," suggested Madame Martinez.

"I believe so," said Aurora.

Valentine appeared from the direction of the sick-room and beckoned to Honoré. Doctor Keene did the same and continued to advance.

"Awake?" asked Honoré.

"Yes."

"Alas! my brother!" said Madame Grandissime, and started forward, followed by the other women.

"Wait," said Honoré, and they paused. "Charlie," he said, as the little doctor persistently pushed by him at the head of the stair.

"Oh, there's no chance, Honoré, you'd as well all go in there."

They gathered into the room and about the bed. Madame Grandissime bent over it.

"Ah! sister," said the dying man, "is that you? I had the sweetest dream just now—just for a minute." He sighed. "I feel very weak. Where is Charlie Keene?"

He had spoken in French; he repeated his question in English. He thought he saw the doctor.

"Charlie, if I must meet the worst I hope you will tell me so; I am fully prepared. Ah! excuse—I thought it was——

"My eyes seem dim this evening. *Est-ce-vous*, Honoré? Ah, Honoré, you went over to the enemy, did you?—Well,—the Fusilier blood would al—ways—do as it pleased. Here's your old uncle's hand, Honoré. I forgive you, Honoré—my noble-hearted, foolish—boy." He spoke feebly, and with great nervousness. "Water."

It was given him by Aurora. He looked in her face; they could not be sure whether he recognized her or not. He sank back, closed his eyes, and said, more softly and dreamily, as if to himself, "I forgive everybody. A man must die—I forgive—even the enemies—of Louisiana."

He lay still a few moments, and then revived excitedly. "Honoré! tell Professor Frowenfeld to take care of that *Philippique Générale.* 'Tis a grand thing, Honoré, on a grand theme! I wrote it myself in one evening. Your Yankee Government is a failure, Honoré, a drivelling failure. It may live a year or two, not longer. Truth will triumph. The old Louisiana will rise again. She will get back her trampled rights. When she does, remem——" His voice failed, but he held up one finger firmly by way of accentuation.

There was a stir among the kindred. Surely this was a turn for the better. The doctor ought to be brought back. A little while ago he was not nearly so strong. "Ask Honoré if the doctor should not come." But Honoré shook his head. The old man began again.

"Honoré! Where is Honoré? Stand by me, here, Honoré; and sister?—on this other side. My eyes are very poor to-day. Why do I perspire so? Give me a drink. You see—I am better now; I have ceased—to throw up blood. Nay, let me talk." He sighed, closed his eyes, and opened them again suddenly. "Oh, Honoré, you and the Yankees—you and—all—going wrong—education—masses—weaken—caste—indiscr—quarrels settl'—by affidav'—Oh! Honoré."

"If he would only forget," said one, in an agonized whisper, "that *philippique générale!*"

Aurora whispered earnestly and tearfully to Madame Grandissime. Surely they were not going to let him go thus! A priest could at least do no harm. But when the proposition was made to him by his sister, he said:

"No;—no priest. You have my will, Honoré,—in your iron box. Professor Frowenfeld,"—he changed his speech to English, —"I have written you an article on" his words died on his lips.

"Joseph, son, I do not see you. Beware, my son, of the doctrine of equal rights—a bottomless iniquity. Master and man—arch and pier—arch above—pier below." He tried to suit the gesture to the words, but both hands and feet were growing uncontrollably restless.

"Society, Professor,"—he addressed himself to a weeping girl, —"society has pyramids to build which make menials a necessity, and Nature furnishes the menials all in dark uniform. She—I cannot tell you—you will find—all in the *Philippique Générale.* Ah! Honoré, is it——"

He suddenly ceased.

"I have lost my glasses."

Beads of sweat stood out upon his face. He grew frightfully pale. There was a general dismayed haste, and they gave him a stimulant.

"Brother," said the sister, tenderly.

He did not notice her.

"Agamemnon! Go and tell Jean-Baptiste——" his eyes drooped and flashed again wildly.

"I am here, Agricole," said the voice of Jean-Baptiste, close beside the bed.

"I told you to let—that negress——"

"Yes, we have let her go. We have let all of them go."

"All of them," echoed the dying man, feebly, with wandering eyes. Suddenly he brightened again and tossed his arms. "Why, there you were wrong, Jean-Baptiste; the community must be protected." His voice sank to a murmur. "He would not take off—you must remem—" He was silent. "You must remem—those people are—are not—white people." He ceased a moment. "Where am I going?" He began evidently to look or try to look, for some person; but they could not divine his wish until, with piteous feebleness, he called:

"Aurore De Grapion!"

So he had known her all the time.

Honoré's mother had dropped on her knees beside the bed, dragging Aurora down with her. They rose together.

The old man groped distressfully with one hand. She laid her own in it.

"Honoré!"

"What could he want?" wondered the tearful family. He was feeling about with the other hand. "Hon—Honoré"—his weak clutch could scarcely close upon his nephew's hand.

"Put them—put—put them——"

What could it mean? The four hands clasped.

"Ah!" said one, with fresh tears, "he is trying to speak and cannot."

But he did.

"Aurore De Gra—I pledge'—pledge'—pledged—this union—to your fa—father—twenty—years—ago."

The family looked at each other in dejected amazement. They had never known it.

"He is going," said Agamemnon; and indeed it seemed as though he was gone; but he rallied.

"Agamemnon! Valentine! Honoré! patriots! protect the race! Beware of the"—that sentence escaped him. He seemed to fancy himself haranguing a crowd; made another struggle for intelligence, tried once, twice, to speak, and the third time succeeded:

"Louis—Louisian—a—for—ever!" and lay still.

They put those two words on his tomb.

59 Where Some Creole Money Goes

And yet the family committee that ordered the inscription, the mason who cut it in the marble—himself a sort of half-Grandissime, half-nobody—and even the fair women who each eve of All Saints came, attended by flower-laden slave girls, to lay coronals upon the old man's tomb, felt, feebly at first, and more and more distinctly as years went by, that Forever was a trifle long for one to confine one's patriotic affection to a small fraction of a great country.

"And you say your family decline to accept the assistance of the police in their endeavors to bring the killer of your uncle to justice?" asked some *Américain* or other of 'Polyte Grandissime.

"Sir, mie fam'lie do not want to fetch him to justice!—neither Palmyre! We are goin' to fetch the justice to them; and, sir, when we cannot do that, sir, by our selves, sir—no, sir! no police!"

So Clemence was the only victim of the family wrath; for the other two were never taken; and it helps our good feeling for the Grandissimes to know that in later times, under the gentler influences of a higher civilization, their old Spanish-colonial ferocity was gradually absorbed by the growth of better traits. To-day almost all the savagery that can justly be charged against

Louisiana must—strange to say—be laid at the door of the *Américain*. The Creole character has been diluted and sweetened.

One morning early in September, some two weeks after the death of Agricola, the same brig which something less than a year before had brought the Frowenfelds to New Orleans, crossed, outward bound, the sharp line dividing the sometimes tawny waters of Mobile Bay from the deep blue Gulf, and bent her way toward Europe.

She had two passengers; a tall, dark, wasted yet handsome man of thirty-seven or thirty-eight years of age, and a woman seemingly some three years younger, of beautiful though severe countenance; "very elegant-looking people and evidently rich," so the brig-master described them,—"had much the look of some of the Mississippi River 'Lower Coast' aristocracy." Their appearance was the more interesting for a look of mental distress evident on the face of each. Brother and sister, they called themselves; but, if so, she was the most severely reserved and distant sister the master of the vessel had ever seen.

They landed, if the account comes down to us right, at Bordeaux. The captain, a fellow of the peeping sort, found pastime in keeping them in sight after they had passed out of his care ashore. They went to different hotels!

The vessel was detained some weeks in this harbor, and her master continued to enjoy himself in the way in which he had begun. He saw his late passengers meet often, in a certain quiet path under the trees of the Quinconce. Their conversations were low; in the patois they used they could have afforded to speak louder; their faces were always grave and almost always troubled. The interviews seemed to give neither of them any pleasure. The monsieur grew thinner than ever, and sadly feeble.

"He wants to charter her," the seaman concluded, "but she doesn't like his rates."

One day, the last that he saw them together, they seemed to be, each in a way different from the other, under a great strain. He was haggard, woe-begone, nervous; she high-strung, resolute, —with "eyes that shone like lamps," as said the observer.

"She's a-sendin' him 'way to lew-ard," thought he. Finally the Monsieur handed her—or rather placed upon the seat near which she stood, what she would not receive—a folded and sealed document, seized her hand, kissed it, and hurried away. She

330

sank down upon the seat, weak and pale, and rose to go, leaving the document behind. The mariner picked it up; it was directed to *M. Honoré Grandissime, Nouvelle Orleans, États Unis, Amérique.* She turned suddenly, as if remembering, or possibly reconsidering, and received it from him.

"It looked like a last will and testament," the seaman used to say, in telling the story.

The next morning, being at the water's edge and seeing a number of persons gathering about something not far away, he sauntered down toward it to see how small a thing was required to draw a crowd of these Frenchmen. It was the drowned body of the f. m. c.

Did the brig-master never see the woman again? He always waited for this question to be asked him, in order to state the more impressively that he did. His brig became a regular Bordeaux packet, and he saw the Madame twice or thrice, apparently living at great ease, but solitarily, in the rue ——. He was free to relate that he tried to scrape acquaintance with her, but failed ignominiously.

The rents of No. 19 rue Bienville and of numerous other places, including the new drug-store in the rue Royale, were collected regularly by H. Grandissime, successor to Grandissime Frères. Rumor said, and tradition repeats, that neither for the advancement of a friendless people, nor even for the repair of the properties' wear and tear, did one dollar of it ever remain in New Orleans; but that once a year Honoré, "as instructed," remitted to Madame—say Madame Inconnue—of Bordeaux, the equivalent, in francs, of fifty thousand dollars. It is averred he did this without interruption for twenty years. "Let us see: fifty times twenty—one million dollars. But that is only a *part* of the *pecuniary* loss which this sort of thing costs Louisiana."

But we have wandered.

60 "All Right"

The sun is once more setting upon the Place d'Armes. Once more the shadows of cathedral and town-hall lie athwart the pleasant grounds where again the city's fashion and beauty sit about in the sedate Spanish way, or stand or slowly move in and out among the old willows and along the white walks. Children are again playing on the sward; some, you may observe, are in black, for Agricola. You see, too, a more peaceful river, a nearer-seeming and greener opposite shore, and many other evidences of the drowsy summer's unwillingness to leave the embrace of this seductive land; the dreamy quietude of birds; the spreading, folding, re-expanding and slow pulsating of the all-prevailing fan (how like the unfolding of an angel's wing is ofttimes the broadening of that little instrument!); the oftdrawn handkerchief; the pale, cool colors of summer costume; the swallow, circling and twittering overhead or darting across the sight; the languid movement of foot and hand; the reeking flanks and foaming bits of horses; the ear-piercing note of the cicada; the dancing butterfly; the dog, dropping upon the grass and looking up to his master with roping jaw and lolling tongue; the air sweetened with the merchandise of the flower *marchandes*.

On the levee road, bridles and saddles, whips, gigs, and carriages,—what a merry coming and going! We look, perforce,

332

toward the old bench where, six months ago, sat Joseph Frowenfeld. There is somebody there—a small, thin, weary-looking man, who leans his bared head slightly back against the tree, his thin fingers knit together in his lap, and his *chapeau-bras* pressed under his arm. You note his extreme neatness of dress, the bright, unhealthy restlessness of his eye, and—as a beam from the sun strikes them—the fineness of his short red curls. It is Doctor Keene.

He lifts his head and looks forward. Honoré and Frowenfeld are walking arm-in-arm under the furthermost row of willows. Honoré is speaking. How gracefully, in correspondence with his words, his free arm or hand—sometimes his head or even his lithe form—moves in quiet gesture, while the grave, receptive apothecary takes into his meditative mind, as into a large, cool cistern, the valued rain-fall of his friend's communications. They are near enough for the little doctor easily to call them; but he is silent. The unhappy feel so far away from the happy. Yet—"Take care!" comes suddenly to his lips, and is almost spoken; for the two, about to cross toward the Place d'Armes at the very spot where Aurora had once made her narrow escape, draw suddenly back, while the black driver of a volante reins up the horse he bestrides, and the animal himself swerves and stops.

The two friends, though startled apart, hasten with lifted hats to the side of the volante, profoundly convinced that one at least, of its two occupants, is heartily sorry that they were not rolled in the dust. Ah, ah! with what a wicked, ill-stifled merriment those two ethereal women bent forward in the faintly perfumed clouds of their ravishing summer-evening garb, to express their equivocal mortification and regret.

"Oh! I'm so sawry, oh! Almoze runned o——ah, ha, ha, ha!"

Aurora could keep the laugh back no longer.

"An' righd yeh befo' haivry *boddie!* Ah, ha, ha! 'Sieur Grandissime, 'tis *me-e-e* w'ad know 'ow dad is bad, ha, ha, ha! Oh! I assu' you, gen'lemen, id is hawful!"

And so on.

By and by Honoré seemed urging them to do something, the thought of which made them laugh, yet was entertained as not entirely absurd. It may have been that to which they presently seemed to consent; they alighted from the volante, dismissed it, and walked each at a partner's side down the grassy avenue of the levee. It was as Clotilde with one hand swept her light robes into perfect adjustment for the walk, and turned to take the first step with Frowenfeld, that she raised her eyes for the merest instant to his, and there passed between them an exchange of glance which made the heart of the little doctor suddenly burn like a ball of fire.

"Now we're all right," he murmured bitterly to himself, as, without having seen him, she took the arm of the apothecary, and they moved away.

Yes, if his irony was meant for this pair, he divined correctly. Their hearts had found utterance across the lips, and the future stood waiting for them on the threshold of a new existence, to usher them into a perpetual copartnership in all its joys and sorrows, its disappointments, its imperishable hopes, its aims, its conflicts, its rewards; and the true—the great—the everlasting God of love was with them. Yes, it had been "all right," now, for nearly twenty-four hours—an age of bliss. And now, as they walked beneath the willows where so many lovers had walked before them, they had whole histories to tell of the tremors, the dismays, the misconstructions and longings through which their hearts had come to this bliss; how at such a time, thus and so; and after such and such a meeting, so and so; no part of which was heard by alien ears, except a fragment of Clotilde's speech caught by a small boy in unintentioned ambush.

"——Evva sinze de firze nighd w'en I big-in to nurze you wid de fivver."

She was telling him, with that new, sweet boldness so wonderful to a lately accepted lover, how long she had loved him.

Later on they parted at the *porte-cochère*. Honoré and Aurora had got there before them, and were passing on up the stairs. Clotilde, catching, a moment before, a glimpse of her face, had seen that there was something wrong; weather-wise as to its indications she perceived an impending shower of tears. A faint shade of anxiety rested an instant on her own face. Frowenfeld could not go in. They paused a little within the obscurity of the corridor, and just to reassure themselves that everything *was* "all right," they——

God be praised for love's young dream.

The slippered feet of the happy girl, as she slowly mounted the stair alone, overburdened with the weight of her blissful reverie, made no sound. As she turned its mid-angle she remembered Aurora. She could guess pretty well the source of her trouble:

334

Honoré was trying to treat that hand-clasping at the bedside of Agricola as a binding compact; "which, of course, was not fair." She supposed they would have gone into the front drawing-room; she would go into the back. But she miscalculated; as she silently entered the door she saw Aurora standing a little way beyond her, close before Honoré, her eyes cast down, and the trembling fan hanging from her two hands like a broken pinion. He seemed to be reiterating, in a tender undertone, some question intended to bring her to a decision. She lifted up her eyes toward his with a mute, frightened glance.

The intruder, with an involuntary murmur of apology, drew back; but, as she turned, she was suddenly and unspeakably saddened to see Aurora drop her glance, and, with a solemn slowness whose momentous significance was not to be mistaken, silently shake her head.

"Alas!" cried the tender heart of Clotilde. "Alas! M. Grandissime!"

61 "No!"

If M. Grandissime had believed that he was prepared for the supreme bitterness of that moment, he had sadly erred. He could not speak. He extended his hand in a dumb farewell, when, all unsanctioned by his will, the voice of despair escaped him in a low groan. At the same moment, a tinkling sound drew near, and the room, which had grown dark with the fall of night, began to brighten with the softly widening light of an evening lamp, as a servant approached to place it in the front drawing-room.

Aurora gave her hand and withdrew it. In the act the two somewhat changed position, and the rays of the lamp, as the maid passed the door, falling upon Aurora's face, betrayed the again upturned eyes.

" 'Sieur Grandissime——"

They fell.

The lover paused.

"You thing I'm crool."

She was the statue of meekness.

"Hope has been cruel to me," replied M. Grandissime, "not you; that I cannot say. Adieu."

He was turning.

" 'Sieur Grandissime——"

She seemed to tremble.

336

He stood still.

" 'Sieur Grandissime,"—her voice was very tender,—"wad you' horry?"

There was a great silence.

" 'Sieur Grandissime, you know—teg a chair."

He hesitated a moment and then both sat down. The servant repassed the door; yet when Aurora broke the silence, she spoke in English—having such hazardous things to say. It would conceal possible stammerings.

" 'Sieur Grandissime—you know dad riz'n I——"

She slightly opened her fan, looking down upon it, and was still.

"I have no right to ask the reason," said M. Grandissime. "It is yours—not mine."

Her head went lower.

"Well, you know,"—she drooped it meditatively to one side, with her eyes on the floor,—" 'tis bick-ause—'tis bick-ause I thing in a few days I'm goin' to die."

M. Grandissime said never a word. He was not alarmed.

She looked up suddenly and took a quick breath, as if to resume, but her eyes fell before his, and she said, in a tone of half-soliloquy:

"I 'ave so mudge troub' wit dad hawt."

She lifted one little hand feebly to the cardiac region, and sighed softly, with a dying languor.

M. Grandissime gave no response. A vehicle rumbled by in the street below, and passed away. At the bottom of the room, where a gilded Mars was driving into battle, a soft note told the half-hour. The lady spoke again.

"Id mague"—she sighed once more—"so strange,—sometime' I thing I'm git'n' crezzy."

Still he to whom these fearful disclosures were being made remained as silent and motionless as an Indian captive, and, after another pause, with its painful accompaniment of small sounds, the fair speaker resumed with more energy, as befitting the approach to an incredible climax:

"Some day', 'Sieur Grandissime,—id mague me fo'gid my hage! I thing I'm young!"

She lifted her eyes with the evident determination to meet his own squarely, but it was too much; they fell as before; yet she went on speaking:

"An' w'en someboddie git'n' ti'ed livin' wid 'imsev an' big'n' to fill ole, an' wan' someboddie to teg de care of 'im an' wan' me to gid marri'd wid 'im—I thing 'e's in love to me." Her fingers kept up a little shuffling with the fan. "I thing I'm crezzy. I thing I muz be go'n' to die torecklie." She looked up to the ceiling with large eyes, and then again at the fan in her lap, which continued its spreading and shutting. "An' daz de riz'n, 'Sieur Grandissime." She waited until it was certain he was about to answer, and then interrupted him nervously: "You know 'Sieur Grandissime, id woon be righd! Id woon be de juztiz to *you!* An' you de bez man I evva know in my life, 'Sieur Grandissime!" Her hands shook. "A man w'at nevva wan' to gid marri'd wid noboddie in 'is life, and now trine to gid marri'd juz only to rip-ose de soul of 'is oncl'——"

M. Grandissime uttered an exclamation of protest, and she ceased.

"I asked you," continued he, with low-toned emphasis, "for the single and only reason that I want you for my wife."

"Yez," she quickly replied; "daz all. Daz wad I thing. An' I thing daz de rad weh to say, 'Sieur Grandissime. Bick-ause, you know, you an' me is too hole to talg aboud dad *lovin'*, you know. An' you godd dad grade *rizpeg* fo' me, an' me I godd dad 'ighez rispeg fo' you; bud——" she clutched the fan and her face sank lower still—"bud——" she swallowed—shook her head—"bud ——" She bit her lip; she could not go on.

"Aurora," said her lover, bending forward and taking one of her hands. "I *do* love you with all my soul."

She made a poor attempt to withdraw her hand, abandoned the effort, and looked up savagely through a pair of overflowing eyes, demanding:

"*Mais,* fo' w'y you di'n' wan' to sesso?"

M. Grandissime smiled argumentatively.

"I have said so a hundred times, in every way but in words." She lifted her head proudly, and bowed like a queen.

"*Mais,* you see, 'Sieur Grandissime, you bin meg one mizteg."

"Bud 'tis corrected in time," exclaimed he, with suppressed but eager joyousness.

"'Sieur Grandissime," she said with a tremendous solemnity, "I'm verrie sawrie, *mais*—you spogue too lade."

"No, no!" he cried, "the correction comes in time. Say that, lady; say that!"

His ardent gaze beat hers once more down; but she shook her head. He ignored the motion.

"And you will correct your answer; ah! say that, too!" he insisted, covering the captive hand with both his own, and leaning forward from his seat.

"*Mais*, 'Sieur Grandissime, you know, dad is so verrie unegspeg'."

"Oh! unexpected!"

"*Mais*, I was thing all dad time id was Clotilde wad you——"

She turned her face away and buried her mouth in her handkerchief.

"Ah!" he cried, "mock me no more, Aurore Nancanou!"

He rose erect and held the hand firmly which she strove to draw away:

"Say the word, sweet lady; say the word!"

She turned upon him suddenly, rose to her feet, was speechless an instant while her eyes flashed into his, and crying out:

"No!" burst into tears, laughed through them, and let him clasp her to his bosom.